The Journey Home

Eileen Susan Eckert

Other Titles by
Eileen Susan Eckert

Rebel Hearts
Harmonee
Legacy
Triple Play
Boiling Point
Cold War - Warm Hearts
Shadow Dancing
Hidden Fires
Shades of Courage

Printing: 2019
ISBN: 9781097333271

Thanks to my friends and support group members who've made invaluable contributions to this story. You know who you are.

Contact me through my website:
www.eileensusaneckert.com

PART ONE
Daniel

CHAPTER ONE

Mama is crying. Again.

The darkness of his tiny bedroom seems to make the crying louder. Like that echo when he walks through the tunnel near the park. Why does Mama cry so much? Does her tummy hurt all the time like his?

He looks over at his little sister, snuggled close to him, sound asleep. He's glad she doesn't hear Mama. It would make her cry, too. Maybe he should make sure Mama is all right. But what if Papa is with her? No, he hasn't seen Papa for a couple of days. When he is here, Mama and Papa yell at each other all the time and sometimes he hits her. Even though he is five-years-old he knows that for sure.

He rubs his sweaty hands down his jammies, the ones with dogs and cats on them. He puts his feet on the cold wood floor and sneaks to the door. Opening it, he slides into the dark hall and stands in front of his parents' bedroom. Mama is crying louder. He feels his heart beat faster. Can't wait any longer. Have to help Mama. He turns the doorknob and slips into the room. The light from Mama's little lamp makes shadows that look like ghosts flying around. Now he really is scared.

Mama is sitting on the bed, blowing her nose into a hanky. Mama is very brave. She isn't afraid to cry. Guess it's like Papa says, only girls and sissy boys cry. When she sees him she wipes her eyes. "What are you doing out of bed?"

"I don't like it when you cry."

He feels sad when she starts crying again. Then he sniffs and she smiles. "I'm all right, sweetie, just sad. Is your sister awake?"

"No."

She waves him over to her. "Come here."

When he gets closer she lifts him onto her lap. "I'm sorry I woke you." She kisses his cheek and hugs him like she can't let go. "You're my dearest boy."

"Why are you crying, Mama?"

"I was hoping Papa would find work so I could buy some groceries. I wanted to make you and your sister a roast chicken with lots of mashed potatoes and carrots and an apple pie for dessert. But Papa called. He hasn't found any work yet." She wipes her eyes again. "We'll have to make do with cereal and eggs and toast a little longer."

"It's okay, Mama. We love eggs and cereal. Really." He pleads with her to believe him. He doesn't want her to feel bad anymore.

"You're so brave," Mama says. "Let's get you back to bed before your sister wakes up. You have school tomorrow."

"I don't want to go to school. I want to go to work so you can have money for chicken."

She smiles. "Absolutely not. You will go to school until you're finished with college, get a good job and make lots of money. Until then, it's me and your Papa's job to worry about food and money."

She puts him on the floor and pushes herself off the bed. Back in the other bedroom, she tucks him in, careful not to wake his sister. Mama kisses him goodnight and closes the door.

In the dark, he stares up at the cracked ceiling. He gets angrier and angrier thinking about how Papa makes his Mama cry. He remembers all those times when they would yell at each other. And Papa would hit her. And he and his sister would hide in their bedroom so scared until he heard the front door slam and knew Papa had gone. Tears wet his cheeks. He grabs the sheet and curls it into his fisted hands. He hates Papa. He can't wait until he's bigger. Then he'll show him.

Daniel Logan kicked the sheet off his sweaty body and slung his arm across his forehead. It'd been a long time since those memories had plagued his dreams. Refusing to get hooked on them, he'd pushed them far away into the deepest recesses of his mind.

What had triggered them?

He glanced at the digital clock on his nightstand. Four a.m. An hour before he usually got up, but he didn't feel like lounging in bed. Needing to drown the past, he headed for the bathroom, turned on the shower and stood under the cascading water. As it heated to a scalding degree, he felt the ghosts drain away, yet he was left disquieted, his muscles still tense, his nerves edgy. He cursed under his breath, not wanting any distractions.

Work was his salvation. Yet a fog seemed to have taken over. He hadn't been able to drag himself through the soul-sucking boredom that was his shadowy companion the last few months. His driving need to take over someone's hard-earned business, screw them out of a fair price and watch their egos and pride shrivel in the dust at his feet, no longer filled the hole he'd been working compulsively to fill for nearly twenty years. He was bored. Restless. Takeovers no longer a challenge.

By the time he stepped out of the shower, his life-saving ability to repress unwanted thoughts and feelings returned. He didn't have time to wallow in self-pity, doubt or whatever else was going on with him. He had a business to run.

He dressed in a sharp Armani suit, slugged down a cup of steaming coffee, grabbed his briefcase and left his penthouse apartment.

*   *   *

"You better have a damn good reason for bothering me. In case you forgot, the Simco buyout is tomorrow." The light scent of aftershave drifted in with the opening of his midtown Manhattan office door signaling Logan that his assistant Brad Richmond waited.

Logan ignored the man standing in front of his glass-topped chrome desk, his concentration drawn like a magnet to the computer screen. He should've had the papers ready a week ago, but he'd been wallowing in that maze of boredom. So now he raced toward the Simco finish line like a frantic nag.

Brad put a file on his boss's desk. "Just got an Offer to Sell from Tyler Trading."

"Tyler can wait."

"Thought you'd be interested in seeing what's next. Might get those juices flowing again."

Logan gritted his teeth, punching the keyboard, eyes drilling the screen. Damn the man. It was uncanny how well Brad could sense Logan's moods. Do or say whatever to get his boss back on track. One of the reasons Logan had kept the younger man around the last seven years. Another...he just plain liked Brad. And there were damn few people in the world that he could pin that label on.

Curiosity got the better of him. Still working feverishly on his computer, Logan tossed Brad a concession. "Okay. What's the skinny on Tyler?"

"Tyler Trading is a one hundred-year-old designer and manufacturer of men and women's clothing. Owner Paul Fisher is heavily in debt. Gambling. He needs to sell so he can settle his accounts with the bookie before his estranged wife gets her hands on the cash through a divorce settlement. I think he'll take any offer as long as his debts are covered and he can shelter what's left offshore. Doesn't give a shit if his wife's left with nothing." Brad scolded. "A real bastard."

Logan snickered. "She's not my problem." He looked up into Brad's thick glasses, the first thing anyone noticed about the thirty-one-year-old. They gave him a boyish, bookish look that denied the man's brilliant mind and maturity, not to mention his keen instincts regarding others. His slight, medium built frame added to the effect. Logan had hired him right out of grad school and never regretted that decision.

Like a drug addict needing a stronger fix to jump-start his competitive edge, Logan decided to trust his assistant's instincts. He tapped his fingers on the top of his desk, staring out the windows that overlook the Hudson River and New Jersey.

"Set up a meeting with Fisher for day after tomorrow."

Brad smiled. "Will do, boss."

*   *   *

Paul Fisher slammed back his neat whiskey, waving to the bartender for another. He'd stopped counting. Didn't matter. There was no place he needed to be. In fact, he found the dimly lit bar with the slow-moving ceiling fans stirring the stale smell of booze and body odor relaxing. And the morbid mumbling of his fellow bar-huggers comforting. For damn sure more relaxing than the stinking one-room apartment he'd been renting since Julia the Bitch had kicked him out of their four-thousand square foot condo in Battery Park City. He gulped another shot that burned his throat and warmed him down to his toes.

Staring into the mirror behind the bar, he noticed his wicked sneering smile and the spark of delight that lit his eyes. Something besides whiskey warmed his insides. His plan would not only rid himself of the massive gambling debt that guillotined over his head but handily screw Julia the Bitch once and for all. And he didn't mean with his dick.

He hadn't heard from Daniel Logan since his attorney had mailed him the Offer to Sell. Why hadn't Logan called to set up an appointment? Fisher had lowered his price enough to whet the greedy bastard's appetite, and he needed to seal the deal before Julia the Bitch found out. Should he call Logan again? He didn't want to sound too desperate. Didn't want to take less than his original asking price. Ah, hell. He couldn't think.

Fisher blinked, shaking his head attempting to focus his manic thoughts. Maybe it was time to leave while he had some control over his body. It wouldn't be long before the barkeep refused to continue fueling his unrelenting thirst. Shit. He pulled out cash, tossed it on the scarred wooden bar and stumbled toward the door.

The cold New York night smacked his face but did little to perk him up. Nothing but his name on the bill of sale of Tyler Trading and a check in his pocket could rejuvenate his damaged ego. He would deny the thrill-seeking pull of gambling. He'd never again fall victim to the family curse that had plagued his father and grandfather. No more. He'd come away with enough dough to start over. Another city. Another business. And best of all, no more wife.

He waved down a cab and headed to the dump he temporarily called home.

CHAPTER TWO

Julia Tyler's eyes widened. Her mouth opened into an oval, words failing her. She couldn't believe the mind-boggling information leaping off the legal papers she held. After reading the Offer to Sell a third time, she stared up at her attorney who sat in a high-backed chair behind his antique oak desk in his midtown Manhattan office.

"How did you get a copy of this?" she asked.

George Boyle grinned, his eyes lined with age. "It was inadvertently addressed to you c/o my office. When Paul's attorney finds out, I'll bet some poor secretary will pay the price." He lost the grin. "However, by now I'm sure Paul's gotten his copy, minus the truth about the mix-up, most likely. I'd say you've got a day or two before he finds out you're aware of the Offer."

Julia sat back in the thick leather armchair stunned, resting the papers on her lap. Thoughts bounced around in her brain. She couldn't believe Paul was naïve enough to think he could get away with selling her family's company. While he'd never had the same business acumen as she, she'd always respected what he brought to the job. His ability to get up close and personal with everyone he met, fostering harmonious relationships with their customers and suppliers. At least until last year when his gambling had sidelined the business. Still staring at the papers in her hands, she struggled to wrap her mind around his betrayal.

Brain still reeling, Julia put her sense of vulnerability aside. The anger rising to the surface stiffened her. She shot Boyle a narrow glare. "What options do I have?"

"Depends on how dirty you want to play."

"Short of sending a hitman after Paul, as dirty as I can be within the law."

He smiled. "I'm glad you said that." He reached into the file drawer of his desk and pulled out a thick folder. "Guessing your response to this contract, I took the liberty of reviewing your father's will. I wanted the certainty of the facts before I made any suggestions. How much time do you have right now?"

Pushing an errant strand of long blond hair behind her ears, she adorned a corporate shark persona. "As much as I need to thwart the bastard from selling my company out from under my nose."

*   *   *

The following morning, Paul Fisher strolled into the conference room on the tenth floor of the Logan building, his attorney Howard Silver beside him. When he'd gotten the call from Logan's assistant to meet this morning, he'd breathed a sigh of relief. At last the drama dominating his life for the past six months was ending. Despite the recent alcohol excesses, this morning his mind was clear. He was ready to take on the vast corporate conglomerate that was Logan Enterprises.

A young, shapely woman ushered the two men to their seats at the long glass table. She smiled. "Can I offer you any refreshments?"

Fisher gave her lithe body the once-over, wondering if Logan had had a piece of her. He snickered to himself. What was the sense of having good-looking women working

for you if you didn't take advantage of all the skills they had?
Fisher certainly had at Tyler.

"Coffee for both of us," he said, hoping she noticed
the come-on look he flashed.

"Of course," she said. She left the room, returning a
few minutes later juggling a sterling silver tray with China
cups and saucers of steaming coffee, a bowl of sugar cubes
and a pitcher of cream. She placed them on the table, directing
them to help themselves. "Mr. Logan will be right in."

When they were alone, Fisher added several cubes to
his cup, surveying the room. Minimalist but expensive. "Nice
digs," he said.

Placing his briefcase on the table, Silver reached over
and took his coffee black. "The mergers and acquisitions
business must be thriving."

"It's called winners and losers, Howard." Fisher
sipped the dark roast blend. "And today we're on the winning
side of the equation." He salivated when he visualized Julia
the Bitch's expression when he handed her a copy of the sale.
For years he'd called himself an astute businessman, as smart,
if not more so, than his wife. However last year, he'd made a
colossal blunder on one account that cost the company
millions and the tenuous hold he had on his self-assurance
crumbled. He was a stupid, weak failure. His father's favorite
mantra had screamed in his head. And so the balance of power
in his marriage shifted, leaving him searching frantically for
his balls. Desperate to retain control over his life, he'd turned
to gambling, his latent addiction.

The door swung open and Daniel Logan entered,
outfitted in a dark striped, $3,000 Italian suit. With thick
brown hair streaked gray on the sides and intense brown eyes,
Fisher judged him to be fortyish. Logan approached the table,
sank his long body in a chair across from them, placing a
folder on top. He took a drink from the black mug he held.

No introduction. No handshake. No friendly greeting to put the meeting on a congenial plain. Fisher twisted toward the door expecting an attorney would've accompanied Logan, but then remembered Logan was an attorney.

"I'm Paul Fisher and this is my attorney, Howard Silver." He felt unnerved, as though his soul had been lanced by Logan's piercing stare.

Logan nodded to them. "Let's get directly to the matter. I have another meeting later this morning."

Fisher bristled at the man's arrogant attitude as though this meeting was only a pesky fly on Logan's calendar to be swept thoughtlessly away. But he quelled his anger, not needing any negative emotions getting in the way of the business at hand.

"Of course. I assume you've read the contract and are satisfied with our terms of the sale." Fisher spoke in his most professional voice.

Logan drank from his mug. "Honestly, I've been tied up with another matter recently and have only skimmed the papers you sent me. I called this meeting to get a sense of you. I like to know exactly whom I'm dealing with."

Disappointment and anger raged through Fisher. The fuck! Who did he think he was, anyway? Just because he had enough money to buy Tyler ten times over, didn't mean he could treat him like he was a piece of dog shit under his shoe. But he stowed his anger and spoke with an oily smile.

"Perfectly understandable. What do you need to know to assist you to make a quick decision? I'm under some pressure from my Board of Directors to settle this." In truth, the Board wasn't a problem. They were a bunch of old geezers who looked forward to their portion of the settlement cash to augment their retirement. It was Julia the Bitch he was worried about. If she found out what he was up to before the deal was signed and the Tyler keys and check handed over....

Logan pulled two pieces of paper out of the folder and slid one to each of them. "Since I'm rushed for time today, I've written down the questions and concerns I need clarified before I make my decision. The sooner you get this done, the sooner a decision can be made." He stood. "Again, I have to rush off. Hope to hear from you within the week."

Fisher stared dumbfounded at the door as it closed behind Logan. He shifted his gaze to Howard. "What an ego-maniacal son of a bitch. If this is the way he does all his business, it's a wonder he has any money at all." He drained the last of his coffee, his fear and rage nearly choking him. "I need a stiff drink. Let's get the hell out of here."

*   *   *

Logan strolled directly into Brad's office. "Get me a deep background check on Paul Fisher and Tyler Trading."

Brad looked up from his computer. "How'd the meeting go?"

Logan shoved his hands in his pants' pockets. He stared at the wall behind Brad, as though replaying the meeting through a video feed. "Off. Something's not right. The man or the offer. But red flags are waving."

"Those red flags have served you and the company well in the past," Brad said. "I'll get right on it."

CHAPTER THREE

Behind her desk at Tyler Trading, Julia read the document her attorney George Boyle had prepared. After hours of discussion in his office, she felt confident they'd come up with an offer Paul couldn't refuse. She smirked, an iconic scene from *The Godfather* flashed before her. She would confront Paul, ridding herself once and for all of him and his betrayals. His philandering and lousy work ethics had slowly eroded her love and respect for him over the five years of marriage. Given her philosophy that people can change, along with her wish that they could rekindle the spark they'd shared in the early years of their marriage, she might've stuck it out longer. But she was grateful his current deviousness had pushed her to divorce. And once she'd faced the final confrontation with him this morning, an enormous weight would lift off her shoulders.

Julia raised her head at the knock on her office door. Seeing her assistant Faith Higgins through the glass, she waved her in. Faith had been Julia's father, Whitby Tyler's, secretary while he'd held the reins of Tyler Trading until cancer took his life. The woman's hair had turned silvery gray years ago and was cut in a stylish short bob, making her appear younger than her mid-fifties. As a child Julia had spent more time in the Shop learning the business with her father and Faith than she had with her mother. With their guidance, Julia had come to love being in the warehouse. She'd soaked in the smell of clean new cloth, the sound of the sewing machines made by competent seamstresses, the low hum of voices of hundreds of employees throughout the old brick structure. Still did. Faith assumed the role of second mother and held a warm place in Julia's heart.

Julia's eyes swept over several silver-framed pictures on her desk. Her parent's wedding photo. She and her father standing in front of their building. Faith and her father and other managers at a Christmas party in the Tyler brownstone. Her father, a year before cancer had stolen him from her. Julia wondered how she would've gotten through those last months of her father's illness and death if it hadn't been for Faith. Since then, Julia and Paul had divided the work between them. She handled the day-to-day operation. He was responsible for marketing and sales. Faith's assistance made the transition flawless. Until now, that is, and the coup Paul planned to take it all.

Julia brushed aside the heartwarming memories of her father, closed the file she'd been reading, slid it across the desk and nodded for Faith to be seated. "Take a look at this," she told Faith. Julia trusted the woman with her life and wanted her input before seeing Paul.

Faith took time to read and assimilate the information, the expression on her face shifting from surprise to anger and finally a sly grin. She looked at Julia, handing the papers back and smiled. "Your father would be very proud of what you're about to do."

Julia wasn't surprised that Faith's first comment involved Julia's father. She had often suspected Faith had been in love with him.

"I should have listened to Dad a long time ago. He warned me not to get involved with Paul Fisher. Said he had a weak character and wasn't strong enough to be my partner."

Julia sighed. "But I had to prove my independence by marrying him anyway."

"They say we learn from our mistakes." Pointing to the file, Faith added, a slight smile on her lips. "It's obvious you've learned quite a bit."

"The private investigator I hired when I decided to divorce Paul was worth every penny." She wrinkled her brow. Playing dirty wasn't her usual style, but Paul had forced her hand and she wasn't one to back down from a fight.

Faith looked puzzled. "What I can't understand is, what made Paul think he owned this company? Your father never would've given him this idea."

Julia sighed. "I'm afraid I'm partly to blame. I let him have too much control, hoping to empower him. And any shady lawyer could interpret the essence of the corporate structure in Paul's favor. My mistake is obvious now. I overestimated his business acumen and underestimated his greed."

"When are you going to drop this bomb?"

"Shortly. I checked Paul's schedule this morning. He has a meeting set for later in the day with Daniel Logan. Time my dear husband and I settled this matter."

"Is there anything you need me to do?"

"I'm good." Julia stood and walked to the door, Faith at her heels. "Have security standby to escort Mr. Fisher from the building the minute I'm finished with him."

"It'll be my pleasure."

* * *

Paul was shuffling into his suit jacket when Julia walked into his office. "Going somewhere?" she asked.

Surprise registered on his face. He stared at her, recovered and said in a sharp voice, "Got a meeting."

"Daniel Logan can wait."

Paul's face turned a ghostly shade of white. "How did you..."

"Water under the bridge. You interested in saving your drowning ass before it's too late?"

"What the hell're you talking about?"

"Have a seat." Julia dropped into the chair in front of his desk, crossing her legs. Deep lines furrowed Paul's brow. After standing still for a long moment while tension built in him, he sat, his back rigid as though preparing himself for the worst.

Julia jumped right in. "First, you will stop dragging your feet and sign these divorce papers." She pushed a file onto the desk. "Second, you will sign the affidavit written by my attorney denying any claim you think you have or had to ownership of Tyler Trading, stipulating that I am the sole owner per my father's will." Another file left her hands for the desk. "Third, you will vacate these premises as soon as this meeting is over and forget you and I ever met."

It took a while before Fisher spoke. If Julia weren't so furious she would have laughed when his expression shifted from shock, to dead-in-the-water, then fury.

He spoke through gritted teeth, his jaw muscles pulsing. "And if I don't sign?"

Grateful for her private investigator's thorough work, she smiled at Paul, anxious to watch him squirm when confronted with the truth. Slowly, she slid another file across the desk.

"This one outlines a list of your outstanding gambling debts and the names of the bookies you owe, a certified copy of a recent audit of your financials showing a large amount of money you've been systematically siphoning from the company over the past year." Her cheeks burned with anger with the next announcement. "The last page contains the names of several young women, both in the company and outside, who have alleged sexual harassment charges against you." The one rape accusation she'd turn over to the police.

"What the hell is all this? An attempt to cheat me out of the money we've already agreed to in the final divorce papers? A coup to celebrate the end of our marriage?" Rage reddened his face. He tossed the files at her.

Sensing he was about to explode, Julia tamped down her anger, but her voice was rock-hard.

"This is no ploy, Paul. It's straightforward. When I found out you went behind my back to sell off the company I decided I'd had enough. I've put up with your bullshit for the last time." Her eyes drilled his. "I've subtracted the amount of money you embezzled from the company from the originally agreed-upon sum of the divorce settlement. Do with the balance as you wish. Pay off your bookies, take a long vacation, leave the country. I don't give a shit." She threw the papers back at him. "Now sign the damn docs."

His eyes held hers for a long moment as if measuring her resolve. Then he slumped back in his seat, shoulders dropping, wiped a hand across his face and stared at the papers. When he looked up at her, she sucked in a sharp breath. She'd never seen him so beaten, as though his soul had jettisoned his body and floated into the dark holes of space. A living corpse. Julia suffered a twinge of guilt. Maybe if she'd been a better wife, not a sharp businesswoman.... She shook those thoughts away. Paul's fall from grace wasn't her responsibility. The blame rested solely on his shoulders.

"I assume you were going to drop these bombs at our divorce settlement conference."

"Until I found out what you were planning. Too bad you never took the time to really know me. I still find it hard to believe you were clueless enough to think I wouldn't find out and shut you down as fast as I could." She glared at him. "Guess you underestimated Julia the Bitch after all."

He grimaced at the label he'd been pinning on her. "What are you going to do about the rape allegation?"

"You'll have to wait and see, won't you?"

"Fuck you." His eyes stabbed her with red-hot hate.

Ignoring his outburst, she pulled a pen out of her jacket pocket and tossed it on the desk. Wordlessly, he signed every page then dropped the pen. She glanced at each one making sure everything was perfect. Gathering the papers she stood. "Good-bye, Paul. Can't say it's been nice knowing you."

Julia stepped out of Paul's office, motioning security to assist him in leaving the building.

CHAPTER FOUR

Expecting to find Paul Fisher and his attorney sitting at his conference table, Logan was surprised to see an attractive woman in a crisp navy business suit. He raised his eyebrows as he took the seat across from her. Early thirties with long, blond hair. But what caught and held his attention was her startling green eyes that shown like sunlight dancing off flecks of jade.

"I'm Daniel Logan." He tilted his head. "And you're in the wrong office."

She raked those eyes over him, returning his thorough inspection of her. "Not if you're expecting to meet with the owner of Tyler Trading."

Logan's brow furrowed. He silently cursed Brad for not completing the in-depth background check on Tyler Trading and Paul Fisher. Although the company looked like a substantial investment, he had concerns about Fisher. Hated going into a meeting with one hand tied behind his back. And staring at the woman sitting ramrod straight in front of him, her eyes locked on his, he had a sneaking suspicion he'd need both hands and all his intellect to best her.

He nodded. "You have my attention."

"Please accept my apology. My ex-husband wasted your time. He put you in the center of a power struggle which is now resolved."

"A power struggle?"

She sat back in her chair. "Have you ever been married, Mr. Logan?"

"Never felt the need."

"You're a lucky man. I've found that often entanglements born of marriage can become cutthroat, especially for people in our position with a lot to lose."

"What are you saying, Mrs. Fisher?"

She grimaced. "It's Ms. Tyler and I came here today to advise you that Paul Fisher misrepresented himself when he proposed the sale of Tyler Trading. We discussed this issue recently and he clearly sees the error of his ways. He will no longer be bothering you."

Logan wondered if the man's balls had survived that conversation. "My first glance of the Offer to Sell tweaked my interest. The market is glutted with so many high-tech companies that I feel it's only a matter of time before the bubble bursts. I've been looking for a company with a solid long-standing history of integrity and a large market share to add to my portfolio and your company, if indeed you are the legal owner, may fit the bill."

Julia's eyes flashed with green fire. "I assure you I am the owner of Tyler Trading and as such I'm here to tell you that I am not interested in selling my company to you or anyone else."

Logan's chest tightened. He sat back in his chair and drummed his fingers on the desk, his gaze locked on hers. Rejection was a rare and ugly pill for him to swallow and it grated on his nerves. He sighed, bringing his anger under control.

"I see what you mean by your marital power struggle. I'm confused as to whom I should be dealing with, the husband who wants to sell, or the wife who doesn't."

She took a deep breath. "I've already explained that the issues between my *ex-husband* and I have been settled, but I see you need clarification." She drew out several documents and slid them across the desk. She folded her arms under her breasts and held his stare for a long while before he began reading.

The more he read, the angrier he got, not at the woman in front of him, but at the sheer audacity and disingenuous actions of Paul Fisher. The man was a scoundrel of enormous proportions, the kind of snake Logan met all too frequently. Yet he was always surprised when another showed up. He was briefly comforted with the knowledge that once again his instincts about the man had been crystal.

He finally looked up from the papers into her stony eyes. "I'll concede you're the legal owner. However, that doesn't change my interest in purchasing your company."

"As I said, my company isn't for sale. It's been in my family for over a hundred years and I have every intention of keeping it that way for another hundred." She slid her purse strap onto her shoulder and moved to stand. "I'll leave you to your business. Sorry for the inconvenience."

Before she stood, he reached out and grabbed her hand, holding her in her seat. "This isn't over, Ms. Tyler. If you've done your research, you'd know I don't give up until I get what I want."

She yanked her hand away, laughed and headed for the door, waving a dismissive hand over her shoulder. "Good luck with that, Mr. Logan."

*   *   *

Logan stormed into Brad's office, slamming the door behind him. Brad's attention shifted from his phone conversation when he saw his boss. "I'll get back with you, Stu," he said into the phone.

Logan threw the Tyler papers on his assistant's desk. "I just got fucked over by Julia Tyler. Apparently not only did that Fisher bastard not have the right to sell the company, but Ms. Tyler refuses to sell," he snarled. "Why didn't I know all this before going into that meeting?"

Brad grabbed the papers and gave them a quick read. He shook his head and looked up at Logan. "That was Stu Walenski on the phone. He's completed his check on Tyler and is in the process of sending it to your phone."

"An hour too late." Logan put his hands in his pockets and paced the office, stopping in front of the window that overlooked the Hudson. He was more pissed at himself than anyone, since he never took a meeting inadequately prepared. He chalked it up to the malaise hanging over him. But, dammit, that was over. He was back in his captain of industry persona, excited at the challenge stubborn Julia Tyler had unknowingly thrown at him. A bone to a starving dog. And he'd grab it with all his teeth, devouring it and anyone who got in his way.

He turned and advanced toward the door. "I expect to hear your suggestions on the best way to pursue the buyout. Keep in mind Julia Logan won't be easy to convince." He slammed the door behind him, excitement blowing away the gloom of the past few months. His mind clicked like the sound of train wheels on steel tracks. Scenes of Julia Tyler whimping away from the conference table check in hand after she agreed to sell. Shoulders bent, those glorious eyes now dulled by submission, flashing again and again. At the end of the proverbial day, he would have Tyler Trading lock stock and barrel and the hell with Julia Tyler.

As he reached his office, something tickled at the back of his neck, something undefined. Dangerous. Some emotion he'd cast deep into his psyche long ago for reasons he couldn't recall.

What the hell was that all about?

He shook his head, strolled to his desk and forced himself to concentrate on another project. But JuliaTyler's compelling face and the challenge she represented kept cutting into his thoughts.

And stirring up unwanted pictures of his worthless father.

He went to the credenza and poured himself a shot of Maker's Mark, downing it in one gulp. After slugging down another, his limit, he reminded himself, he thought about Julia Tyler. She'd be a smart, tough opponent to defeat, the strongest faced in a long time. But defeat her he would. No matter what it took. It wasn't beneath him to use his strong masculine presence to seduce her if it came down to that. The move had been useful in the past, with female executives or wives of business owners he pursued. Recalling Julia's gorgeous face and those startling eyes...the idea of seducing her wouldn't be too unpleasant.

Grabbing his phone, he called for his car while he shuffled into a woolen knee-length coat and slipped phone and wallet into his pockets. In the elevator, he ignored the other tenants who stared mindlessly at the floor numbers that rolled like a ticking clock downward toward the lobby of the Manhattan skyscraper. Consuming Logan's thoughts were pictures of the ownership papers of Tyler Trading lying on top of his nightstand and Julia Tyler writhing naked beneath him in total surrender.

*   *   *

It wasn't until Julia stepped out of the Logan building and felt the sunshine on her face that she breathed a sigh of relief. The pleasure she'd imagined by confronting Daniel Logan with the truth about Tyler Trading and Paul's betrayal had been replaced by trepidation the moment Logan had walked into the conference room. His strong chiseled face and tall intimidating body gave him an intimidating presence. She'd immediately recognized him as a powerful, driven man who wouldn't take kindly to her news. Too bad. She'd straightened shoulders and proceeded with the meeting.

Now hailing a cab, Julia settled into the back seat, cocooned in the lingering scents of aftershave, perfume and middle eastern spices. She pulled out her phone and waited for Faith to answer.

"How'd the meeting go?"

Julia stared out the side window. "I believe Daniel Logan is now clear who owns and runs Tyler Trading and that we're not for sale. But I doubt we've heard the last from him. He's a ruthless businessman who's used to getting what he wants. I suspect we're in for a hostile takeover attempt." She paused. "Have our P.I. do a deep dive into Logan Enterprises and the man himself. I'll need all the ammunition I can muster when he comes sniffing around."

"Got it."

"Have you contacted the Board regarding the emergency meeting I called for this afternoon?"

"Yes. At first the members were angry at being dragged away from whatever they were working on. But curiosity got the better of them. They'll all be here."

"Good. See you in a bit."

Clicking off, Julia continued watching the streets of Manhattan roll by. Her taxi darted in and out of rambling buses and trucks, yellow taxis and the recent influx of dozens of inexperienced Uber drivers all jockeying for positions on the busy city streets. Impatient New Yorkers leaned heavily on car horns and jaywalkers yelled obscenities at vehicles that nearly ran them over. Music to her ears. How she loved the city, with all its noise and smells and madness. She found the energy invigorating even on dreary days when she wanted to stay in bed and hide under the covers.

Fifteen minutes later the cab cruised down the old cobbled streets of the westside garment district. The dank smell of the Hudson drifted in through the poorly insulated window next to her. The hustle-bustle activity of men loading and unloading racks of colorful clothing that swung on hangars as well as the bolts of cloth of various hues piled high on wooden pallets. Invigorated, Julia let the stress of the meeting with Logan fade away. Instead she slipped into the familiar cloak of warmth and peace, of coming home when she approached the Tyler Trading warehouse. She found the lifelong memories of working beside her father and the efforts of their loyal employees comforting. The quality of the clothing and accessories they produced generated international acclaim which seemed to validate her very existence.

The cab pulled up in front of the warehouse. Julia paid the driver, exited the taxi and marched into the familiar sanctum. Making her way through the lobby and into an elevator, she stared at the advertisement above the door, ticked off the agenda items she'd planned for the impromptu Board meeting. It was time they found out what had happened in the last forty-eight hours and her plans for the future.

Her first stop after reaching her office was the private bathroom to freshen up. Task completed, she went to her desk where Faith stood waiting for instructions. "Did you get in touch with our P.I.?" Julia asked.

"He said he'll get right on it. Do you need anything else for the meeting?"

"No. I'm set." Julia adjusted her navy suit jacket and walked down the hall toward the conference room. Through the glass wall that faced the hallway, she noted with satisfaction that all ten members were seated around the large oval table. Their expressions ranged from annoyance, curiosity and outright anger. She got a kick out of visualizing how all their emotions would be validated before she was finished with her report. She took a deep breath and stepped into the meeting.

CHAPTER FIVE

Brad Richmond approached Logan's desk, handed him a thick folder and sat down. "Here's everything we found on Tyler Trading, Julia Tyler and Paul Fisher."

"About time," Logan grumbled. Instead of perusing the papers, he pushed back from his desk, crossed his hands behind his head and relaxed into his tall leather chair while he studied Brad. "Tell me. I'm anxious to hear your verbal assessment. Start with Fisher."

The younger man took a deep breath. "Fisher is the eldest of five. Father owned a small printing shop that barely met the family's survival needs. His high school grades were average to low. Majored in Business at City College, mostly B's and C's."

"How the hell did he hook up with a class act like Julia Tyler?"

"He spent several years working in small companies learning management skills. He compensated for his average intelligence with a driving need for wealth, societal respect and admiration. Apparently he could be very charismatic."

Logan snorted. "Not the man I met in the conference room."

"After a major investigation he'd conducted revealed several employees had been cooking the books, he'd earned a big promotion and the respect he'd always wanted. He began showing up at various social functions, mingling with the rich and famous of the business world."

Logan nodded. "Cue Julia Tyler."

"Exactly. Fisher smelled money and status as a member of the well-respected Tyler family. He chased Julia until she finally relented and they married. Much to Whitby Tyler's disappointment, we're told."

Logan mulled over the information. Maybe Julia Tyler wouldn't be that hard to manipulate after all. "What's he doing now?"

"Living in a run-down apartment in Chelsea. Do you want Stu to keep an eye on him?"

"No. Fisher no longer interests me." With more enthusiasm he said, "Move on to Tyler Trading."

"You already know most of the basic information. The company has been family-owned since Julia's grandfather Angus started Tyler Trading in the late 1890s. Within ten years 100 sweatshops were operating in Greenwich Village manufacturing ladies' shirtwaists. After a devastating fire in 1911 at the Triangle factory where over one hundred women and children died, most of these shabby businesses went bankrupt or closed their doors to avoid federal regulation. Tyler Trading remained open and followed the new laws regarding pay, work hours and child labor to the letter."

Logan nodded. "Disaster then reform. The litany of American greed and corruption vs. government regulation." He took a deep breath. "Continue."

"When the old man died, Julia's father, Whitby, took over. The company remained small but its reputation as an excellent enterprise grew. Over the years they've increased their product line to include clothing for men and more diversified apparel for women. They have an online presence, a catalog division and ship merchandise internationally. Whitby died three years ago and Julia and Fisher took over."

"I'm not surprised everything eventually fell apart," Logan said. "I don't know of a husband and wife team that has managed to keep their personal relationships afloat. Especially in venture capital. Too cutthroat. No room for divergent philosophies." He released a deep breath. "What about Julia?"

"She's thirty-five, an only child, but grew up differently than most privileged trust fund babies."

"How so?"

"She was raised to run the family business practically from the moment she was born. Spent every hour when she wasn't in school on the floors of the warehouse learning every facet of the business from the ground up. Even though being accepted into Harvard and Yale, she decided to stay local and went to Columbia, finally graduating magna cum laude with an MBA and CPA."

Logan pondered Brad's report and decided that with her life about education and the family business, he wondered how much time she'd had to develop social skills. Maybe that's why she fell so easily under Fisher's charismatic spell. Another weakness Logan hoped to exploit.

"What else?"

Brad's eyes seemed to sparkle like a spy about to reveal a secret that would shift the world on its axis. "Our P.I. Stu Wilensky managed to get someone close to Fisher recently and the bitter ex-husband let slip that Julia's planning to expand into children's clothes. To do this she needs a huge influx of cash."

Logan sat up in his chair. "So she's looking for investors."

"No. Tyler's going public."

A predatory smile twisted Logan's lips, a plan forming in his mind. "When?"

"The Initial Public Offer will be announced sometime next week."

Logan thought for a long moment, his fingers tapping the top of his desk. "As soon as it is, buy up as many of the shares as possible split between five of our holding companies. Make sure these transactions can't be traced back to Logan Enterprises." Logan's mouth salivated, assuming the persona of a big game hunter capturing and subduing the stubborn beast he'd been after.

"Let me know when everything's in place."

*   *   *

Julia sipped her white wine, forearms resting on the granite surface of the hotel ballroom's bar. Soft music from a six-piece orchestra drifted into her senses but she paid it little attention. Nor did the low hum of voices from the one-percenters standing around the room in small groups deep in conversation disturb her thoughts. She hated events like tonight, even though the beneficiary of the evening's proceeds was a local charity she admired. Much to Julia's relief, Paul had handled all this kind of schmoozing. But now that he was gone the job fell on her shoulders. Oh well. You win a little, you lose a little. In this case, she felt she'd gained a lot more by ridding herself of Paul's toxic presence. For a brief moment she wondered what he was doing with his time but swept that curiosity behind more pressing concerns.

In two days she would be announcing the opening of the IPO she'd been working on for months. When the Board had first heard the news of Paul's dismissal and of her goal to take Tyler Trading public, they'd balked. But as she methodically outlined the pros and cons with her powerpoint presentation, they saw that expanding the product line would increase revenues for the company as well as their own profits. Their appetites whetted.

A large hand on her shoulder turned her around to face James Navaro, an old friend from her days at Columbia. Julia was grateful for the mental shift. They laughed over some of their shared college antics as well as his stories about their mutual friends from school. When he asked her to dance she eagerly accepted.

*   *   *

The moment he spied Julia Tyler talking to the man at the bar, Logan pulled his gaze off the tall redhead who'd had his ear for what felt like an eternity. Julia was stunning in a bronze silk dress that made the gold highlights in her hair sparkle. No sooner had that thought crossed his mind than a self-satisfied grin played on his lips. So the woman was a little coquette after all. He looked forward to the conquest yet to come, taking a sip of his scotch, ignoring the redhead who was still filibustering. Logan watched Julia stroll toward the dance floor hand in hand with the man. When the guy swung her into his arms and they flowed along with the crowd, Logan felt his jaw tighten. A flash of anger ripped through him. Or was it jealousy? Yeah, that was it. He resented the man's arms around her, the way he held her close. Logan put the brakes on. He couldn't remember the last time he'd been jealous of another man's attention on a woman on his radar. The feeling didn't sit well with him, so he turned away from the dancing couple and took a deep breath. Soon enough he'd make his move and the woman and her company would be his.

His emotions in hand, he turned his attention back to the redhead who smiled gratefully at him. He needed to spend a few more minutes at the fundraiser before it would be acceptable for him to leave, after dropping a substantial contribution into the sterling silver bucket. Until then, he'd play the game, a wealthy businessman with a need to assuage his guilt for all the assets he'd accumulated over the years. In fact he felt no such guilt, only a deep satisfaction of how far he'd come since the days when his weak and pathetic father had failed to raise their family above the poverty level.

He drained his glass and reached for another from the tray of a passing waiter. Hopefully, once in bed, he could close his eyes without newsreels from the past flickering across his mind's eye.

CHAPTER SIX

Logan's concentration shifted from the file he'd been reading when Brad swept into the office without knocking. But when Logan heard the excitement in his assistant's voice, he dropped his glare.

"Have you heard the latest on Tyler?" Brad asked.

"No."

Brad grabbed the remote from Logan's desk, aimed it at the 60-inch flat-screen on the opposite wall, turning up the volume. The CNBC newscaster's voice came out loud and clear. "This morning the one-hundred-plus-year-old-family-owned Tyler Trading announced stock options of thirty percent shares to the public. There's been a feeding frenzy on Wall Street as investors grab shares. To protect its personal interests, the family has put a limit of 5% on any individual investor."

"Smart move," Logan said. "How many shares have we gotten so far?"

Brad muted the volume. "Four of our companies now own 5% each. At 20% we'll be the majority shareholders outside of the family."

Logan nodded, settling back into his chair. "Perfect. I'll give Ms. Tyler a few days to gloat over her venture before I make a move."

He *so* looked forward to that. Logan imagined a dimly lit five-star restaurant with Tyler sitting across from him, a confident, satisfied look in those green eyes. At first he'd play the vanquished loser, acknowledging her excellent business sense. He'd engage her in discussions about her new product line. Build up her impression of him as a congenial fellow businessman who no longer had designs on her company. Invite her out to the theatre. A few more dates. When he was confident he'd gained her trust he'd take her to bed. Then drop the bomb...his ownership of 20% of her company. Or perhaps he'd marry her and have access to the whole megillah. He felt his face glow with the sense of power he'd hold over her. Knew his eyes gleamed like an anxious predator waiting to pounce.

"Anything else, boss?"

Brad's question broke through Logan's musings. Shaking his head, he shed his fantasies and sat up. "What's happening with Dickson?"

And the conversation turned to other business.

*　　*　　*

Later that evening, Julia prepared to meet James Navaro for a casual dinner. He'd said he'd heard about the IPO and wanted to talk to her about it. She'd been surprised by his interest but agreed to the meeting. She was hustling into a pale green cotton top when her phone rang. She put the phone to her ear while wiggling into her designer jeans, surprise registering when she recognized the voice.

"Ms. Tyler. It's Daniel Logan. I wanted to call and congratulate you on the success of your IPO."

Julia's thoughts swirled, making a reply challenging. After a long pause she said, "Yes, well. Thanks." She grimaced at her childish response.

"I know it's last minute, but I was wondering if we could meet tonight to celebrate."

Now Julia *really* was nonplussed. But she corralled her confusion and recovered her equilibrium. "Sorry, but I'm busy this evening."

"Of course. No problem. How about I call again and give you more notice?"

Julia took a deep breath. Once the IPO had been announced she'd thought she'd never hear from him again. But here he was, asking for a simple get-together among fellow business owners. Did she really want to have anything to do with Daniel Logan?

"Thanks for your call, Mr. Logan, but I don't have time for casual meetings. Now, if you'll excuse me, I have to get ready for my appointment." She disconnected, a stab of guilt striking her conscience over her rudeness. Oh well. Better to remove a pimple before it festered.

But the conversation with Logan lay at the back of her mind all evening like a cobra waiting to strike. What was he up to? She had a hard time imagining his interest in her was anything other than business. And as far as she was concerned, they had no business dealings to discuss. Ergo... Goodbye Daniel Logan.

*   *   *

Paul Fisher slammed the *New York Times* down on the top of his rickety kitchen table, got up and pulled a beer from the fridge, downing half as soon as his hands wrapped around the cold can. A loud belch escaped his mouth. He walked into the living room and plopped down on the sofa. Julia the Bitch was at it again. An IPO. Expansion. And here he was struggling to find another job, any job that paid enough to get him into better digs. He'd even lost his ability to seduce women with his charms. He scanned the small apartment. Probably for the best. How the hell could he bring a woman up to a place like this?

He'd been hitting the streets, the employment sections of all the local papers shoved in his briefcase. Nothing. He wondered if his ex-wife was responsible for all the 'no's' he'd received the last few weeks. Admittedly that wasn't her style, yet hadn't she turned him over to the police with those ridiculous sexual harassment charges? Forcing himself on women! Really. He never had to beg for sex. Women always came onto him. Or at least they had. Lucky he had a good lawyer and none of the bitches had pressed charges.

Fisher pulled on his beer, closed his eyes and rested his head on the back of the sofa. He put the aluminum can against his cheek, needing to cool the hot anger crawling under his skin. When had his resentment of his ex-wife become the primary motivation of his life? Not the first years of his marriage. Those months had been happy. Julia was fun to be with and the sex was great. Learning the business kept his mind sharp and he'd looked forward to making a difference with Tyler Trading. It was that damn blunder he'd made with the Lopez account that slammed the door on his confidence and allowed the cesspool of self-doubt to take over, leading to his current situation.

He punched his fist into his other hand. Dammit! Maybe he should get out of town, live somewhere else. He'd checked the internet articles about the best places to live, where jobs were plentiful and real estate was cheap. Yeah. Maybe that was the answer. Dump New York City and start over. The thought tickled his nerves. But he needed cash to do that.

Renewed energy flowed through him as a plan formed. He rose, grabbed his wallet and left the apartment. The thought of a thick pink steak, garlic mashed potatoes and asparagus urged him toward his favorite bar. The place had a few tables in the quiet back room and served some of the best food in the city. What he needed was lots of food to stimulate his brain cells. One thing was now crystal clear.

Before he left Manhattan, he'd make Julia the Bitch pay for destroying his life.

*   *   *

Julia stood at the entrance to Faith's office and studied the woman who played the computer keyboard like a baby grand. After a moment Julia strolled toward the desk. Faith looked up. "Good morning. Thought I'd get a jump on the Newman account."

Julia shook her head in wonderment. "I can't believe you sweet-talked Harold into doubling his order. The old boy must've been off his meds that day."

Faith chuckled. "Nah, it was my matronly wiles that did him in."

"Faith Higgins the vamp. Who would've guessed."

The older woman changed the subject. "You need something?"

Julia relaxed into a chair. "I've been thinking about planning an Open House for our stockholders. Give them the grand tour of the facilities. Make them feel comfortable with their investment." Actually the idea had come to her after dinner with James. He'd expressed his concern about her taking TT public and the horror stories he'd heard that had ruined the companies.

"A great idea," Faith said, "especially since they haven't seen our new children's line. A tour of the design floor would be encouraging. Nothing like eyes-on to instill confidence."

Julia checked her watch. "How about we take an early lunch and hash out the details."

"Perfect. I need a change of scenery. My brain's turning to mush."

Julia stood. "I'll meet you in front of the elevators."

CHAPTER SEVEN

"Take a late supper," Logan told his driver, Max. "Pick me up in an hour." He left the Lincoln Town car, striding up to the wide entrance of Harmony House, an assisted living home north of Manhattan in Rockland County. He tensed as he approached the young blond receptionist. God, he hated coming here, often wondered why he did. Was it merely his compulsion to continually remind himself where he'd come from and why he'd accomplished as much as he had? Or was it only some unacknowledged need to forgive and forget? Damned if he knew and damned if he had the time or inclination to find out.

"Good evening, Mr. Logan." The young receptionist smiled up at him. "Nice to see you again."

Logan ignored her and signed the visitors' log. "Is Dr. Bartolo available?"

She checked the roster on her desk. "Doctor Bartolo is here. Let me call and see if he can meet with you." She dialed a number, spoke in a low voice and hung up. "He's in his office. You can go right in."

Logan nodded. After the receptionist buzzed him through the security door, he made his way down the hallway lined with pale yellow walls and pictures of past administrators. The faint antiseptic odor tickled his nostrils. Reaching Bartolo's office he knocked. After a quick, "Come in," he entered.

The medium-sized room, decorated in light blue and beige, boasted large windows that allowed daylight in as well as a serene view of the well-kept gardens, green and lush with bright colored flowers and shrubs.

Dr. Louis Bartolo stood, reaching out his hand when Logan approached. "Mr. Logan. A pleasure. Please. Have a seat."

Bartolo was in his sixties. With his round face, clear brown eyes and short round body, jolly Saint Nick flashed in Logan's mind whenever he saw him. He sat, folding his hands on his lap. "Any change I should know about?"

Bartolo shook his head. "Your father's condition remains the same. Physically he's as well as any recovering alcoholic and drug user could be. His depression hasn't lessened even after the electroconvulsive therapy he received last month. He continues to be lethargic, barely communicates with anyone, and remains in his room most of the time." The older man paused, then added. "I will say that after your visits he seems more present, responds when staff speaks to him, but unfortunately that only lasts a few hours."

Logan refused to acknowledge the guilt crawling up his spine, demanding attention. The bastard was lucky he came at all.

He rose, thanked Dr. Bartolo and walked down the hall to Andrew Logan's room. He opened the door, his eyes seeking his father. The man sat in a wheelchair staring out the window overlooking the green lawn. The room was spacious, containing a bed, dresser, lounge chair, bookcase and a large flat-screen TV mounted on one wall. The walls were painted light blue and the floor was covered with freshly scrubbed linoleum.

Logan closed the door behind him. He walked up to his father and stood beside him by the window. After a moment Andrew arched his withered face up to his son. Thick white hair still covered his nearly seventy-year-old head. His blue eyes were dull and expressionless, his gravelly voice a result of heavy chain-smoking. "'Bout time you showed up," he growled.

Logan sucked in a deep breath. Andrew Logan had never forgiven his son for bailing him out after he'd been picked up by the police for assaulting a tourist. Unfortunately, in his drunken state, Andrew had failed to notice the size and build of the tourist who had quickly subdued his attacker. The arresting officer had found a crumpled business card with Logan's name and phone number. The charges of public intoxication and attempted robbery were commuted to probation on the promise by Logan to get his father into rehab that night. After a few calls Logan found Harmony House. Upon admission, an in-depth examination suggested that Andrew's mental state demanded an extended, if not permanent stay, to ensure his safety. Ergo, his father's anger and hatred.

Logan sighed, all too familiar with Andrew's vitriolic nature. Nothing new. The old man had been like that from the moment Logan was old enough to grasp the abusive situation in his home. Yet here he was, paying a fortune for the ungrateful bastard's care. Masochist rang in his ears.

"Doc says you're doing fine."

Andrew sniffed. "I'd be a hell of a lot better if you'd get me out of here. Who the hell do you think you are, keeping me from making my own decisions. I was doing great till you interfered."

Logan snickered. "Only a crazy drunk would call living on the streets doing great. That's why the judge gave me power of attorney over your miserable life. So suck it up, old man. I doubt you'll be back on the street any time soon."

"Don't know why you care," Andrew grumbled.

"That makes two of us."

A cloud of heavy silence filled the room choking Logan. Body stiff, he struggled to push intense conflicting emotions from leaking out of the mental casket where he kept them. He checked his watch. Time to end his misery.

As the Lincoln snaked back to Manhattan, Logan texted his usual post-Andrew visit to his sister in Los Angeles. *Just saw Andrew. No change.* When he'd first informed her he'd institutionalized their father, she had asked for occasional updates from him. He often wondered why, but complied nonetheless. She had as much right to hate the old man as he did, having grown up a victim of Andrew's alcoholism and abuse. She never visited their father. Oh well. Everyone was entitled to tame their demons whatever way worked. Who was he to judge?

He sank back into the plush car seat, his usual migraine-following-visit headache making its appearance in the back of his skull. Time for a few shots of Bourbon.

CHAPTER EIGHT

Logan stood in front of Brad's desk. "I got calls from two of my CEO's this morning. Something about Tyler Trading having an Open House. Have you heard anything about this?"

Brad looked up from his computer. "Yeah. Read it in the Journal yesterday. Figured you knew about it."

Logan cursed to himself. He'd been unable to focus on work since he'd left Harmony House. Couldn't shake the oppressive cloud of...something...that hung over him. Nothing unusual after a visit with dear old Dad. But if the past was any indicator of the present, his malaise should've evaporated by now. Yet there it was, still holding him captive, like a prisoner wrapped in thick steel chains, unable to move. Shit! Maybe he was more like the old man than he thought.

That realization didn't help blow away his doldrums. "Refresh me."

Brad leaned back in his chair. "Ms. Tyler announced the company was hosting an invitation-only Open House for investors to tour Tyler's manufacturing facilities. A 'see how your money is working for you' concept." Brad raised his eyebrows. "A brilliant move. Not many CEO's want their investors sneaking around their businesses, at least not on this large a scale. The woman appears to enjoy shaking up the status quo."

The thought of Julia Tyler seemed to displace Logan's lethargy and regenerate the original challenge she represented. Why that woman had the power to do so, he had no idea, but she continued to intrigue him.

A provocative idea flashed in his mind. "Get me the list of our companies who bought the 20% of Tyler Trading."

"I already emailed it to you."

The fact that Logan hadn't looked at his emails in a couple of days reminded him of his recent state of mind. He shook his head in self-disgust. "Thanks." He whirled around and left Brad's office.

Having come to his next strategic move regarding Julia Tyler, Logan closed his office door behind him, reached for his cell and made a call.

"Tyler."

"Logan here." If Julia was surprised to hear from him he couldn't tell by her voice.

"Why are you calling? Thought we agreed we had nothing left to discuss."

Her soft melodious voice reminded him of honey drizzling down a slice of warm apple pie. The inference struck him hard in the gut. "We never got the chance to talk at the recent fundraiser so I decided to reach out, congratulate you on the Open House you're planning. Establish more congeniality between us."

"That's very magnanimous of you," she said sarcastically.

An unfamiliar smile teased his lips. Where it came from he had no idea. Maybe the image of himself patting the top of her head like a father humoring his child. Or was it her lilting voice that struck a deep chord in him. "How about drinks tonight. For old-time's sake?"

She laughed. "Not if you were the last wealthy man alive."

"Funny. I never expected you to walk away from a challenge."

"And what challenge is that?"

"Overcoming your fear of facing someone who once represented a threat to you." If nothing else, he knew that would get her to agree to meet with him. She'd jump at the dare he suggested. He could almost hear her teeth grinding, see steam wafting out her ears.

"Where and when?" she asked after a long pause.

"You know lower Manhattan better than I. Name the place."

"McGinty's on Eighth Avenue."

"Never heard of it." Logan said.

"It's a local landmark. Lots of history going back to prohibition days and old gangland rivalries."

Logan couldn't stop the chuckle. "Very appropriate. I'll meet you there. How's nine?"

"Fine." She hung up.

He clicked off the phone and stared out his office window. Damn, but that woman always caught him off guard. Off balance. Threatened the control he insisted on. But for some reason he didn't mind. She was a breath of fresh air from the fawning women he usually met.

Anticipating the meeting, he felt a new lightness fill him. Unsure what he expected to get out of the rendezvous, Logan shrugged, determined to catch up on work he'd carelessly neglected.

*　　*　　*

Julia had trouble concentrating on her laptop. She found it hard to believe she'd agreed to meet Daniel Logan for drinks. What had she been thinking? Damn him, anyway. Why had she gotten suckered into his dare? It wasn't like her. Julia shucked off the self-flagellation and sighed. Oh well. A casual meeting wouldn't hurt. And she'd find out in a few hours what he was up to.

Just then, her IT supervisor Eddie Donelson entered her office. In his mid-twenties, with short, thick brown hair and brown eyes, Eddie refused to dress like the brilliant geek he was. No jeans and t-shirts for him. Fitted gray dress slacks, a white cotton short-sleeved shirt and a black tie hung loosely on his medium, trim frame. Julia waved him forward and he sat in one of two chairs in front of her desk.

"Don't tell me you have the background on all two hundred of our biggest investors already?" She'd only asked for that information yesterday.

"Yes, ma'am," he said with a smile, handing her the file. "But it's only a precursory check. If anyone piques your interest, I'll go deep-diving on those folks."

"Perfect."

After Eddie left, Julia closed the design page she'd been viewing and scanned the list of invitees. The names of a few companies jumped out at her. Why do they seem so familiar?

She was five seconds from reaching for the phone and testing Faith's memory when she stopped. Why not leave the matter alone for now. She had a meeting to face tonight and didn't want anything to get in the way of psyching out Daniel Logan.

A glimmer of truth hit her. She hated to admit it, she felt inordinately attracted to him. On the surface she hated his proprietary attitude, his driven approach to business, as though he had nothing else in his life. Yet she sensed a lonely man lay deep beneath that tough-minded façade. The dichotomy intrigued her. She wanted to know who Daniel Logan really was.

*   *   *

When Julia arrived at McGinty's the place was still packed. Happy hour at the local bar lasted from five until closing. No music competed with the noisy chatter and loud laughter coming from suited executives and casually dressed garment workers entombed in the stale air. In her sleek jeans and white silk top, she shouldered her way through the mixed crowd spotting Logan seated at the bar, dressed as though he'd just come from a Board meeting.

"I see you found the place," she said as she reached him.

He looked up at her. "Apparently my driver is a regular customer of gritty lower Manhattan hangouts." He patted the barstool next to him. "I nearly got into a fistfight with two tipsy patrons who wanted that seat. Good thing you got here before I had to take on another drunk."

"How chivalrous of you." She slid onto the stool.

Instead of looking directly at her, he watched her through the mirror behind the display of uniquely shaped, colorful bottles of liquor. His eyes gave no hint of the thoughts behind them.

Logan waved the bartender over while he sipped his dark-colored drink, the ice cubes tinkling with the movement. "What's your poison?" he asked her.

She put her small pocketbook on the weathered bar and rested her folded hands on top. "Whatever you're having."

Her response must have surprised him, because he turned his head and looked directly at her.

"I took you for a white wine woman."

"Are you always in the habit of prejudging people?"

"That, and in-depth research into possible business associations, gives me the edge I like when making decisions." He ordered two more Maker's Mark. "Although, I admit my staff did a poor job of vetting your ex-husband."

"So they did." Julia found it difficult to read anything of significance into his character by the bland look he gave her. "Bet that doesn't happen often. You couldn't have amassed the enormous conglomerate you've built without a keen sense of people and their foibles."

Their drinks came, and she raised her glass toward his. "To a secession of hostilities and a peaceful future between our companies."

Several seconds passed before he met her glass with his, and this time she was sure she sensed a hidden agenda behind his dark eyes. A cold blast of air sweep over her. Rattled, she wondered just how committed he was to her toast. She straightened her spine, clicked his glass and sipped. The smooth liquid warmed her enough to recall her purpose for the meeting. To find out why he had insisted she meet him and to decipher the complex character that was Daniel Logan she had to play the game.

Once again his gaze studied her through the mirror. "I was hoping you'd invite me to your Open House."

"Why?"

"I've never been through your facility. Thought I'd check out the big fish I let get away."

His expression reflected only curiosity. Either he was a skilled actor or meant what he said. Julia was confident it was the former. A man in his position must possess the ability to speak out of both sides of his mouth.

"In that case, I'll make sure you get an invitation. Not that I want to rub your defeat into your face."

His unexpected laugh rippled through her like warm water at low tide. Julia felt her shoulders relax, the slight breath she hadn't realized she'd been holding slipped out. She didn't have time to analyze her strange response before he turned and held her gaze.

"Julia Tyler, you continue to shatter my preconceived notions about you."

Needing to avoid his intense stare, she took another sip of her bourbon. After gathering her wits, she returned to the game of one-upmanship they seemed to be playing. "And just what are those notions?"

"Do you really want to know?" He raised an eyebrow.

"Why not." She turned in her seat, looking directly at him, challenging him to complete honesty. "Apparently we're on a fact-finding mission to discover who each of us is, so share away."

Logan rested his arm on the old mahogany bar. "When your husband..."

"Ex-husband," Julia interrupted, bringing an amused quiver to Logan's lips. He tipped his head in acknowledgment.

"When your *ex*-husband brought his proposal to me I assumed your absence from the meeting signified you were the typical society wife who took little or no part in the running of the family business. I pictured a spoiled princess who spent her time shopping, lunching with the ladies, spending hours in salons, fitness centers and other feminine pursuits, while her less-than-capable husband ran the show."

"How flattering," she said.

"When I found you in my office I immediately saw my mistake, which by the way rarely happens. My next assumptions were that I faced a ruthless, ballbreaker businesswoman, who would do what it took to get what she wanted."

"Like a mirror to your own soul, I imagine."

This time he burst into laughter. "See what I mean? No flighty, empty-headed, weak-willed woman with low self-esteem whose ego needs to be propped up by focusing attention on her external attributes."

"You don't have a very high opinion of women, do you?"

"I haven't met many with the characteristics I need to change my opinion."

"And what might those be?"

He paused for a moment, his eyes boring into hers. "Highly intelligent, aware of her purpose in life and committed to it, integrity, a keen sense of humor, all with a natural grace and self-assurance that comes from within."

Logan's words stirred something deep inside her, shaking her composure. His expression left her wondering if he honestly saw who she was or was merely expressing an ideal. She lifted her chin, gathering her strength. "A lofty archetype."

"As I said, I've yet to meet such a woman. But I admit, your refreshing responses and obvious business smarts lead me to believe there's hope."

Julia sipped her drink, hoping the tangy liquid would calm her. "Well I wish you luck in your search."

"Never said I was searching. I have little need in my life for the personal restrictions a relationship with a woman demands. My work requires one hundred percent focus to the exclusion of everything else."

"Does that include family, or were you spawned from mud like other creatures?"

A dark cloud briefly floated over Logan's face before he spoke, his voice rough with undefined emotion. "I have no family."

For some reason Julia felt the need to press the issue. "Is that by fate or choice?"

Something flickered in his eyes like flashes of a camera moving from frame to frame of a scene. Logan let his shoulders drop slightly and assumed a more relaxed posture on the stool.

"My turn," he said. "What was it like for you growing up the only child?"

Julia decided to let slid the fact he refused to answer her question about his family. Apparently that was a sore point with him, one she'd take up at another time. She relaxed against the back of the barstool. "Sometimes lonely, wishful. But mostly I ate up all the attention I received from both my parents. And after my mother died when I was ten, my father's assistant Faith became my second mother. Between them I learned the business from the ground up and loved every minute of it."

"Then enter Paul Fisher."

"Which as you know turned out to be a disaster." She sighed. "But thankfully he's out of my hair once and for all."

Logan's brow furrowed. "I wouldn't be so sure."

"What do you mean? Has he bothered you again?"

"No, but I wouldn't trust him not to make another play for you or the company. The man has no soul."

Julia was shocked by the venom in his voice, a far cry from his lack of emotion she was familiar with. "Why do you say that?"

"I've dealt with many Paul Fishers of the world. They follow a very unsavory pattern. You thwart them and they retaliate, usually with drastic measures. I suggest you watch your back."

Julia scoffed at the idea that her cowardly ex-husband would try anything devious against her for revenge. Recalling how Paul had slinked off from their last meeting, a beaten man, she laughed off Logan's words. "You're wrong about Paul. He isn't smart or tough enough to do something like that."

He shrugged. "You've been warned."

Logan's assumption of trouble to come sent a shiver down Julia's spine. Realizing the meeting with Logan had strayed from her original purpose of checking out his motives, she decided to retreat. Hopefully she'd figure them out another time. Still, she'd learned quite a bit about the man himself. Arrogant. Secretive. Something dark lurked behind his inscrutable eyes. Yet she found no trace of an inflated ego there. Only self-confidence from an internal acceptance of who and what he was.

She drained her glass, grabbed her pocketbook and stood. "Thanks for the drinks. See you at the Open House."

"Count on it."

She nodded and hastened out of the bar.

*   *   *

Logan stared at her retreating figure, her husky voice reverberating in his ears. Tight jeans caressed swaying hips. Light brown hair streaked with shades of gold brushed her shoulders. Smart. Classy. Tough. Beautiful. The total package. He shifted in his seat. But she had a blind spot where her ex was concerned. Maybe relationships were her Achilles heel. Something he could exploit.

Or did he really want to?

That thought shook him. For some reason, the idea of besting Julia Tyler and taking over her company didn't have the same attraction it once had. But the possibility of seducing her to his bed, being inside her, had quadrupled in its appeal. Perhaps his monkey brain drove more of his motivation toward her than he'd initially thought.

Logan called for another drink, chugged it down as soon as the bartender placed it in front of him, tossed bills on the bar and walked outside into the cool evening air.

CHAPTER NINE

Julia strolled down the aisle of the main floor of the Shop greeting seamstresses along the way while they flawlessly sewed the garments that the design team had created. The women smiled back at her and continued stitching together the pieces of material that would eventually become blouses, skirts and dresses. The whine of the machines overshadowed the low voices of the more loquacious ladies. The light scent of lubricating oil and clean cotton, linen and silk tickled her nose, triggering memories of days gone by when she had prowled these same floors with her father. A wistful smile curved her lips. Good times.

She pulled her ringing phone out of her jean's pocket. "Tyler."

"It's Eddie. I found something interesting you should see regarding five of the companies who bought stock."

Julia sensed the urgency in his voice. "Meet me in my office." She clicked off and hurried toward the elevators.

Eddie was sitting in a chair when she arrived. Moving to her desk she sat behind it.

"What'd you have?"

The young man handed her a piece of paper. "Given the limit you set on how much stock any one company or individual can purchase, I took an in-depth look at all those who bought the most shares. At first nothing jumped out at me. Then something triggered my memories and I dug deeper at the five on that printout. See anything interesting?"

Julia squinted as she scanned the sheet. She recalled having déjà vu flashes the first time she'd seen most of the same names but had ignored them. Now red lights flashed as realization struck her. "Oh my God."

"My thoughts exactly. All five of these companies are linked to several shell companies out of the Caymans. It took a while to uncover the ownership layers, but there's no question in my mind that the companies belong to Logan Enterprises."

Julia sat back in her seat, shock reverberating through her. That son of a bitch. No wonder he'd been playing nice with her, finagling an invite to the Open House. The bastard wanted to toss this information in her face when it would do the most damage. Burst her bubble at the Open House. Julia gritted her teeth, her heart pounding as she imagined his handsome smug face when he dropped his bomb, dark eyes gleaming like a predator who'd just dined on his prey. Well that was never going to happen. Her ill-fated marriage to Paul Fisher had been the last victim role she was willing to take on. It was time to shrug off her complacency where Daniel Logan was concerned and take charge of the game he was playing.

"Good work, Eddie. I'll take it from here." Julia gave him a grateful smile. "Let's keep this between us. I don't want the Board to freak out. Some of the older guys might go into cardiac arrest."

Eddie grinned. "No problem. Let me know if there's anything else I can do."

She nodded and the techie left.

Still in shock, Julia stared at the picture of her father and herself that sat on her desk. It was taken in front of Tyler Trading not long after her mother's death. Whitby's arm was wrapped protectively around Julia's shoulders as they stared up at the old brick structure. Whitby had reminded her of the strength and determination she'd inherited from her ancestors who had built Tyler Trading. There was nothing in the world that could take those ingrained character traits away from her. She had loved her mother and missed her terribly, but she would survive and grow even stronger. Julia had never loved her father more than at that moment.

And she wouldn't let him down now.

She took in a deep breath, letting the oxygen spread through her body, bringing new energy. She grabbed the phone and made a decisive call.

*   *   *

"Logan." He'd been about to leave the office for the night and but knew better than to ignore a call. Often important news awaited him at the end of the line, news that couldn't wait until the following day.

"It's Julia Tyler."

Again the woman had taken him by surprise. After they'd parted the other evening, Logan was sure the next time he'd see his adversary would be at the Open House. He kept his voice calm when he spoke. "Ah, Ms. Tyler. Wonders will never cease where you're concerned."

"I like to keep it interesting."

"You're doing a splendid job."

"Glad you noticed."

Did he hear an edge to her voice? "What can I do for you?"

"I've been thinking about your comments regarding my ex-husband. I'd like to pick your brain about them."

Logan wrinkled his brow. What was she up to? "Any time, any place."

"How about dinner tomorrow evening?"

He paused. "Sounds like a plan."

"Good. Meet me at *Excuse My French* on Orchard Street. Say, eight."

"Will do. I'm looking forward to it."

Logan sensed a hard vibe beneath Julia's courteous words.

"So am I." She hung up.

Logan stared at the empty wall opposite his desk. No pictures of family or friends. No ego plaques with celebs or politicians. Nothing except stark white paint. He blinked as though wishing to change the scene. But the barren wall stared back at him. He shook away thoughts and feelings he didn't have time to investigate. Why did Julia Tyler *really* initiate a dinner meeting? He doubted it was personal. She'd never shown any interest in him other than as a ruthless rival hell-bent on taking over her company. Had something changed for her? His curiosity was definitely piqued.

*   *   *

The trendy but casual environment of the restaurant surprised Logan. He'd expected someplace chic, quiet, more indicative of the classy woman he saw in Julia Tyler. But instead the bistro buzzed with lively chatter. Patrons sat in booths that lined three walls and tables that were spread out in the center of the room. The French décor was modern, not provincial. Customers apparently not interested in a complete dining experience stood at the bar two-deep behind men and women who sat on padded wooden stools. And the scent of freshly cooked and spiced meat and vegetables permeated the air. Logan's watering mouth reminded him he'd skipped lunch.

He scanned the room and eventually spied Julia waving him over to one of the booths. Distance, noise and dim lights might have precluded another man from reacting so strongly to the woman, but Logan felt his breath catch, his heart race. He wanted to resent his infatuation with her but instead decided to ignore it.

He strolled over to Julia and slid into the soft brown leather booth, stretching his long legs out as far as possible. Noticing the shot of bourbon that awaited him, he nodded appreciatively at her and held it out. She reached for hers and their glasses touched.

"To a pleasant and informative evening," she said.

They emptied their glasses. Logan relaxed back into the booth while he watched Julia's face for any sign of what was to come, but she gave no hint of her true purpose for the invite.

"I'm glad you were able to adjust your schedule and meet with me." She gave him a friendly smile as though wanting to disarm him. He chuckled to himself. The little minx was good at this game. A worthy opponent.

"I took the liberty of ordering dinner for you. I hope you don't mind."

"Not at all." Logan gazed around the room, his eyes settling back on hers. "Interesting place. I've never been here before."

"I doubt you frequent many restaurants south of 42nd Street. I picture you in posh upscale establishments."

He shrugged. "Truth is, I rarely eat out. If I have lunch at all, I order in. As far as dinner...I'm a good cook when the mood strikes me."

That comment seemed to surprise Julia. "Really? Guess you're not the only person guilty of pre-judging. We'll both have to censure our thoughts."

Logan nodded. "I'll make a valiant effort to do so."

Julia sat back when a waiter placed appetizers in front of them. She picked up a small pronged fork and stabbed grilled escargot dripping in garlic sauce.

"I regret that we got off on the wrong foot," she said after swallowing the delicacy. "Now that Paul Fisher is out of the picture, there's no need for us to be enemies."

"I agree." He sampled one of the tiny morsels on his plate and had to admit he'd never tasted anything as succulent. His gurgling stomach demanded another piece.

"Tell me," she said, "why did you feel the need to warn me about my ex?"

"I wanted to show you I'm not the bastard you may think I am, that I have your best interest at heart." Logan's dormant conscience suddenly woke like a bear out of hibernation poking his gut. But he pushed the pesky beast aside.

"I find your comments confusing since you admitted you haven't been in a serious relationship. And have no interest in one."

"All true, but I also mentioned that I have excellent instincts about people. I didn't want to see that scumbag hurt you further."

"Why is that?"

God, she was making this difficult. It was almost as though she knew what he was up to and wanted to force the truth out of him.

When he took a moment before answering, she continued. "I'll answer my own question. You want me to focus my attention on my ex so I won't see you coming when you swoop in to take over my company."

Logan put his hand over his heart. "You wound me deeply, Ms. Tyler. I can assure you I have no illicit designs on your company. I surrendered to your will on that matter the moment you left my office."

Julia pursed her lips as though wanting to hide a smile. "With all this goodwill floating around, I think first names are in order."

"Agreed."

"Then I repeat, Daniel. Why do you feel the need to protect me from my ex?" She broke off a section of a sourdough biscuit and laved it with unsalted butter.

Logan's breath caught. Was that what he was doing? What a strange concept. He was confident he'd never felt a need like that before. Well, maybe when he was a child and had watched his father's angry tirades against his mother. When he would take his sister's hand and pull her into their room and hid in the closet, his arm around her tiny shoulders, pulling her close. But never as an adult. He believed that if adults couldn't protect themselves, it wasn't his job to do so.

He studied Julia's face, curiosity penetrating her steady gaze. He took a few moments to settle his thoughts. For some reason he felt compelled to give her at least a modicum of truth, if for no other reason to assuage his nagging conscience.

"Honestly, I don't know."

Julia's eyes widened enough for Logan to assume he had surprised her with his words. The waitress came with their main courses and she fastidiously examined the grilled bluefish, garlic mashed potatoes and asparagus on her plate.

Logan took a forkful of fish, watching her closely, anxious for her next comments. Her full breasts rose. She remained silent.

"Julia. Regardless of what you may think of me, I wouldn't like to see as worthy an opponent as yourself taken down by a soulless bastard like Paul Fisher." He flinched when he saw her hackles rise at the idea. "Not that I don't believe you could handle it. I'd just don't think you deserve to be put into that position again." The sincerity of his words surprised him and seemed to calm her.

"I think we're going around in circles here." She took another deep breath as if coming to an important decision. "I still believe that you pose more of a threat to my company than my ex-husband does."

"I thought that was a dead issue. What's changed your mind?"

She took a sip of water, her eyes glared into his. "My techie and I found some inconsistencies in several companies who purchased large portions of our stock. While at this time I have no direct evidence, everything points to Logan Enterprises being behind the grabs."

Logan felt a chill run through him. How the hell had they found out? He could hardly wait to call Brad and ream his ass. While he hated being bested, he felt his shoulders drop a speck as though a gentle wind had brushed over him, washing away the pretense, as though the gloves were off. He signaled to the waiter to bring another round of drinks, staring at her while he waited, her green eyes refusing to leave his. When the bourbon arrived he downed the shot. Well, so be it. Game over. Time for a gust of fresh air between them.

"I decided if I couldn't buy Tyler Trading outright, I'd settle for being a significant shareholder."

Julia sat back in her seat, still watching him apparently mildly curious. "Interesting," she finally said. "I don't know whether to be worried or flattered."

Logan shifted in his seat, feeling out of his depth, afloat with feelings that rose from deep inside. His limited experience with being honest with a woman left him feeling vulnerable. He was drawn to Julia, wanted her respect, not her fear. For some reason this was very important to him.

The waiter came and removed their plates, brushed crumbs from the table and asked about dessert. Julia gave the man a polite refusal as did Logan. "Coffee will be fine." Logan sat back in his seat. "The dynamics between us have changed. I no longer want to pursue a business relationship with you. The thought of having you as a friend is more intriguing."

"You expect me to drop my defenses and suddenly become your buddy?"

"I don't expect anything, Julia. I'm only offering you a white flag. You do with it as you wish."

She softened as she eyed him thoughtfully. "I see."

"And in that regard, I have tickets for *Hamilton* Saturday night and if you haven't already seen it, I'd love to take you to dinner and then the show."

Those green eyes roamed over his face as though looking for some hidden agenda behind his invitation. Apparently not finding any she said, "Sounds like an excellent way to shift gears."

Logan smiled. "Is that a yes?"

She chuckled. "It is."

CHAPTER TEN

"The magic's gone."

From the glass observation deck, Paul Fisher gazed out over the floor of the New York Stock Exchange, hands in his pockets, suddenly filled with a deep sense of loss. He'd stood in that exact spot before many times, courting potential investors, mesmerized by the scene below on the trading floor. Frantic brokers weaving in and out of the crowd yelling buy/sell orders, arms waving, transaction tickets clutched desperately in their hands. The overwhelming noise might've intimidated a weaker man, but Paul had always found the electric atmosphere of men and women vying for the best price totally stimulating. Like when he'd place a bet and every nerve in his body stood at attention waiting for the results of the gamble. After all, wasn't playing the stock market a high risk on any given day no matter what the analysts said?

But now, electronic stock orders made coming to the floor of the exchange superfluous and the number of brokers had decreased substantially over the past few years. The energy was diluted. The fight for dominance among brokers paled in comparison to the past. Paul sensed melancholia he hadn't felt in a long time.

A firm hand rapped him on his arm, pulling his attention off the scene below.

"I got us a spot in the back. Let's go."

Paul turned and dutifully followed Art Catalongo to a grained leather booth which afforded them privacy. Paul had known the broker of the small firm with a dubious reputation that handled investment funds of extremely wealthy clients. Requesting a meeting with the man reminded Paul just how desperate he was and he resented Julia the Bitch even more for putting him in the position of having to deal directly with a man of Catalongo's ilk.

On the way they passed other booths, mostly men apparently engaged in whispered negotiations, possibly similar to the one Paul was about to have with Catalongo.

Sliding into their seats, the broker signaled the waiter and ordered two scotches. "I was surprised to hear from you. It's been a while." The expression in his cold dark eyes was blank.

Paul shrugged. "Yeah, well, I've had a change of circumstances and it's taken a while for me to plan my next move." He watched as the waiter brought their drinks.

Catalongo raised his. "To the future. May it bring us both greater wealth and prosperity."

Paul took his glass and nodded his head. They slugged down the liquor, both empty glasses striking the table in unison. "So what can I do you for, my friend."

Paul winced at the ambiguous expression that was typical Catalongo. "I have an offer to extend to you. Guaranteed to meet the requirements of that future you just mentioned."

Emboldened by the greedy gleam in Catalongo's eyes, Paul continued. "I understand you got a piece of the IPO my ex-wife recently offered."

"Quite a few pieces, in fact," Catalongo said. "I'm already making a nice profit."

"How'd you like to make a lot more?"

Catalongo eyed him suspiciously. "Get to the point."

Paul folded his hands on the table. He leaned in, giving Catalongo a sly smile. "It's short and sweet. Anonymous tips to the media suggest Tyler Trading is having serious financial trouble. You start the stampede and sell. The bad news continues and I short the stock. When it hits bottom, I cash in. Suddenly the news is positive about Tyler's position and you start the buying frenzy."

Catalongo stared at Paul for a long moment. Paul could almost see the wheels turning in the man's mind.

"It's risky. The Feds are watching the market closely these days."

"Fuck the Feds," Paul said. "There's no way they can figure out what we've done. It'll look like the analysts and the media got it all wrong again." Paul sat back. "Even if the analysts suggest manipulation, there's no way to prove it."

"This reeks of revenge against your ex-wife. Those situations don't usually turn out too good." Catalongo folded his arms across his chest.

"Call it what you will. I got screwed in the divorce and need a large influx of capital to start over."

Catalongo sat straight. "I'll pass this on to my guys. See what they think. I'll get back with you in a coupla days one way or the other."

*   *   *

Julia sat uncomfortably on the plush leather seat of Logan's Lincoln. Whatever had possessed her to agree to the "date" with him? Just because the dinner the other night had gone better than she'd expected didn't mean she could trust him any more than she had. Sure, he'd seemed sincere in the sudden shift of his focus on her. She definitely sensed a softening in his attitude, slight as it was. His dark eyes hadn't seemed to pierce hers as sharply. The tone of his voice no longer held the suggestion of power and manipulation. Logan appeared genuinely interested in a secession of the veiled hostilities that had characterized their relationship from the beginning. And she'd felt a strong pull to meet him halfway, to discover another side of the complicated man she sensed Daniel Logan was.

Now as she sat across from him, Julia realized she had no idea how to act around him. The solid ground beneath her had suddenly morphed into quicksand threatening to suck her down into some unknown abyss. And the more she thought about her vulnerability, the angrier she became at her own foolishness in putting herself in such a precarious position.

Julia shifted her gaze from his strong handsome presence and stared out the side window, the sharp colors and bright lights from stores and pedestrians melted into each other forming a tableau Jackson Pollack would've been proud of.

"You look lovely night," Logan said.

Julia recalled the stress she'd put herself through when trying to decide what to wear, finally settling on mint green silk slacks and a cream-colored blouse. Definitely nothing she'd wear on the Shop floor or at a Board meeting. The outfit seemed ambiguous enough to stave off any suggestive vibes.

A slight smile touched her lips and she nodded, giving him a positive appraisal of his causal black slacks and pale blue linen shirt. "And you certainly dress down nicely."

Logan chuckled. "Touche. Sounds like we're on the road to creating the beginning of a new relationship."

Julia frowned and shifted uncomfortably in her seat. "I'll be honest with you, Daniel. I'm not sure how to be with all this. It seems so awkward. Unnatural."

"That's because we got off on the wrong foot. It's difficult to easily switch from adversary to friend. There are major trust issues involved and those may take time to build."

His warm, genuine smile surprised her. Disarmed some of her concerns. "How do you suggest we do that?"

"For a start, by being truthful with each other," he said, "and in that regard I want you to know that I'll be as honest with you as possible."

"And what does 'as possible' mean?"

Darkness blew over his face and quickly disappeared. "There are some areas in my personal life I find difficult to talk about. I'm not sure if I'll ever be able to open up with a woman to the degree I'd feel comfortable enough to explain."

Julia was touched by his sincerity. Remembering his slick diversion off the topic of his family recently, she was now certain family was a hot button for him. "That admission is honest enough for me for the present. Thank you." She let out a deep breath and sat back in her seat, letting herself relax for the first time since Logan had proposed a change in their relationship. Maybe they could pull this off after all.

CHAPTER ELEVEN

"Why Daniel Logan, I do believe I see a glint of fear in your gorgeous brown eyes." Julia laughed as she slid into the back seat of his Lincoln. His driver closed the door behind her, returned to the front seat and drove off into midtown traffic. Their two evenings at dinner, the theatre and conversations regarding general business activities hadn't helped to loosen up the tight control Logan maintained over his emotions. Julia came to the conclusion it was up to her to take command of the situation if she had any hope of reaching the man inside. Ergo...today's trip to the Bronx Zoo.

Even the casual shrug of his shoulder couldn't hide the uncomfortable look on Logan's face. "You do realize I've never been to a zoo before." His near-growl closely resembled several of the zoo's inhabitants.

"My point exactly." Julia smiled. "I've made it my mission to introduce you to new experiences, ones you should've had as a child."

He eyed her suspiciously. "One of my many judgments about you never included being the kind of woman who had to change a man."

"You don't need to change, Daniel. I just thought you might enjoy spending time in a new environment." Julia sighed and looked out the window. "The first time my parents took me to the zoo I zoomed from one enclosure to another, fascinated by each animal I saw. My parents had read the usual bedtime stories to me which often included animal tales, but to see them in person made me aware of the difference between what is real and what isn't. After that visit, when they read to me, I was able to bring the stories to life. The characters seemed bigger and stronger, the colors more vibrant." She turned and gave him a shy smile. "I love the zoo."

Logan's face seemed to relax. He smiled at her. "Then I'm pleased to escort you to the zoo, my lady." He leaned over and brushed his lips across hers in a gentle kiss.

He pulled back and Julia wasn't sure which of them was more surprised by his actions. She cleared her throat. Then rewarded him with a smile that lit up her entire face. "We'll check out the sea lions first. Their antics are always good for a few laughs."

As the day at the zoo progressed, Julia watched Logan continue to relax, their conversations light and unforced, flowing smoothly from one topic to another. Her growing attraction to him niggled at the corner of her mind but she pushed her concerns aside and enjoyed his company. Once, as they strolled from one enclosure to another, she reached out and held his hand and a jolt of warmth spread through her.

He looked down at her. "I think I've had my fill of the zoo experience for now. How about something to eat?"

"You must've heard my stomach growling. There's a small café near my brownstone. The fare is light and the atmosphere casual."

"Lead on." Logan said, his expression stoic.

He called his driver to meet them at the zoo entrance. Contentment filled Julia as they strolled toward it. They were silent, neither apparently needing to fill the time with chatter. Occasionally Logan gave her hand a light squeeze. By the time they reached the entrance, the car was waiting for them. They slid into the back seat and took off.

"Where to?" Max asked.

"Broadway and 80th Street," Julia told him.

While the car snaked through rush hour traffic, Julia noticed Logan staring out the side window. Mentally exhausted from the emotional rollercoaster she'd ridden all afternoon, she rested her head against the soft leather, closed her eyes, her mind swimming in unanswered questions. She wished she had the gift of second sight and could read his thoughts, understand what he'd been feeling all day. She must have been crazy to even suggest taking a man like Daniel Logan to the Bronx Zoo. He'd probably lost all respect for her and her silly emotional explanation of why she enjoyed the zoo. Yet he seemed to have weathered the trip without any critical meltdowns. But what was he thinking now? Was he sorry he'd gone along with her? Would he want to see her again?

That thought nearly brought tears to her eyes. Stupid girl. She was thirty-five years old and a victim of teenage angst. She sighed. Oh well. What's done was done. She was still committed to her mission to save Daniel Logan from himself, no matter how self-righteous that sounded.

Julia's thoughts were interrupted when the car stopped at the corner of Broadway and 80th. Logan exited and reached out to help her, calling to the driver Max. "Come back in an hour and a half." The driver nodded and the car pulled away.

They walked down Broadway and stopped in front of Zabar's, a landmark Manhattan deli and catering restaurant. She looked up at him. "Inside or out?"

Logan peered through the window. He seemed to compare the obviously noisy crowded interior with the relative calm of the few guests enjoying the late afternoon sun at the outside tables.

"Outside."

"Good choice," she said.

After settling at a table in the corner and ordering iced tea, Julia locked eyes with him. "Thanks for going along with me today. I hope it wasn't too boring for you." She shrugged. "Not everyone has the same fascination for zoos as I do."

A server in jeans, black tee and white apron took their orders. Logan waited for her to leave before responding. "I wasn't bored. A person would have to be a total robot not to be moved by watching the various critters play, sleep or stroll around their pens." He clicked his glass to hers. "Thank *you* for the opportunity."

Julia's worries were put to rest with his words. "I admit I'm conflicted with opposing views whenever I think about what the animals had to go through to get to the zoo. I hate the idea of them being hunted, caged and shipped from their natural environments to wind up being gawked at by curious humans."

Logan shrugged. "For some of them, that trip might've been a lifesaver. What with progress encroaching on so many open spaces around the world, food sources for the animals have been drastically reduced over the years, not to mention the number of endangered species continues to grow."

"You're right." Julia sat up straighter. "It is what it is." She shifted their conversation. "Are you still planning to come to my Open House?"

"Definitely." He smiled. "I want to see what my money bought."

"You'll be impressed. Our designers have been hard at work on the new line of children's clothes. Machines have been retooled and fabrics are arriving daily. I expect production to begin shortly, just before the Open House."

His eyes held hers with a sincerity that tingled her nerves. "I wouldn't expect anything else from you."

Julia felt her face flush. "I'll take that as a compliment."

"You should."

The server brought their entrees and Julia dug in, suddenly realizing how hungry spending the day in the fresh air had made her and glad for a change of subject.

After dinner, she locked her arm through his as they took advantage of the warm night air and strolled around the corner to her brownstone on 61st Street, Max and the Lincoln following at a slow pace. At her front door Logan slid his hands up and down her bare arms. "When can I see you again?"

Ignoring her racing heart, Julia smiled. "How's Monday afternoon? It shouldn't be too crowded."

Logan raised an eyebrow, his lips curving in a little smile. "What's that devious mind of yours up to now?"

Her eyes held the challenge of her next words. "Do you trust me?"

"Is it safe?"

She laughed. "Probably."

"Not very convincing."

She gave him a light punch on the arm. "Oh, come on, big fella. You can't possibly be afraid of little ole' me?"

Logan grunted. "Said the tic to the deer." Then he smiled. "Okay, let's have it."

Julia grinned. "Leave your driver at home. We'll take an alternative means of transportation."

He frowned.

"Don't worry. I promise to get you home safe and sound."

"Well, since you put it that way..." He bent and brought his lips to hers. This time the kiss was deeper and longer.

Julia fell into the softness of his mouth, wrapping her arms around his neck. His arms encircled her body, pulling her closer. After a long moment, they parted, each breathing a little harder.

"Until Monday," he said. Then kissed the edge of her nose, turned and headed for his car.

Julia watched him pull away, her arms locked under her breasts, heart pounding, nerves rattling. My God. What had she unleashed with her hairbrained scheme to draw out the hidden Daniel Logan?

*   *   *

Bad idea, Logan thought. The steamy spray of the shower only helped intensify the heat of those final moments on Julia's steps. What had he been thinking, kissing her like that? He scoffed. Obviously, he hadn't been. The attraction he'd felt for her had only increased during their excursion through the Bronx Zoo, leaving him no alternative but to act on it, a victim of his long-suppressed emotions.

It amazed him how much he'd enjoyed not only her company but also the animals in their not-so-natural environments. Julia had been right about the sea lions. Their aquatic play darting in out of the water chasing each other had brought an unfamiliar smile to his face. The same had happened when he'd watched the monkeys swinging in the trees, but this time a little jealousy popped up at the freedom from responsibility and censure they had. Something he'd never experienced.

His smile had faded, his emotions taking a sharp downward curve, when he'd stared into the elephant enclosure. He could relate to these mammoth, magnificent beasts caged in so small a place, their innate need to roam freely being thwarted behind waist-high cement walls. The rapid beating of Logan's heart at the thought had scared the shit out of him. But watching Julia's enjoyment of the animals, listening to her stories of past visits to the zoo and the feel of her hand in his, had calmed him once again. Thus, his impulsive need to kiss her.

Dammit. He wanted her more than any other woman he'd ever met.

He turned off the water, grabbed a thick towel and dried off. As he slid into bed, he wondered what plans she had for them on Monday. A part of him looked forward with unfamiliar anticipation of her company, no to mention what he might discover about himself. Those internal mysteries produced dark fears that gave him chills even another hot shower couldn't lessen.

CHAPTER TWELVE

Walking toward Julia's brownstone in the waning afternoon light, her arm tucked beneath his, Logan silently recalled the events of the day, including his surprise when he'd realized where they were going and how they were going to get there.

Coney Island.

It was the last place on earth he would've expected beautiful, classy Julia Tyler to take him. Maybe years ago it was considered a great place to spend a fun day with the family, but no more. The Russian mob had taken over the Brighton Beach section of Brooklyn in which Coney Island rested and it was no longer the safest place for a family outing.

And then there was the alternate mode of transportation his gorgeous guide had alluded to. Logan could barely remember the last time he'd ridden on the New York City subway system. Truthfully, that was a lie. He did remember. It had been more than thirty years ago, the hot summer sun blasting down on him. His mother had been nagging her husband to act like a real father and spend the day with them at Coney Island. In a rare mood of compliance, Andrew had shuffled everyone onto the subway from their crappy apartment in Astoria, Queens to the seashore.

Logan remembered feeling excited about a trip to the amusement park he'd often heard his friends at school exult. But not trusting his father to stay sane and sober, he'd approached the excursion with mounting apprehension. And true to form, it hadn't taken the old man long to find a place to buy beer, slug down a few quick ones and become mean and surly. When Logan's sister, then five, had refused to go on the Ferris wheel, Andrew had slapped her face, grabbed her arm ruthlessly and yanked her down on the rocking seat beside him. Logan could still see her brown eyes wide with fright before he and his mother took the car behind them and the wheel jerk to a start. He heard his sister's sobs above the swish of hot air that brushed his sweaty face along with Andrew's mean laugh. His hatred for his father had been cemented that day.

"You're very quiet," Julia said, looking up at him as they strolled, her brow furrowed. "Are you sorry you agreed to come today?"

Logan looked down at her, taking in a sharp breath. So beautiful. So alive. So open. Unlike himself who currently rode emotional waves similar to the physical upheavals that had assaulted his body on the rides. Waves that left him feeling out of control, shaky. His stomach clenched.

"No."

She took a moment, apparently uncomfortable with his silence, then sighed. "Well, I had a great time, and you braved the unknown like a soldier."

If only Logan could tell her of the conflicting, unfamiliar emotions the day had brought him. He'd wanted to scream in fear, his hands gripping the safety bar of the Cyclone roller coaster. As it raced up and down and around the narrow tracks he'd flinched, afraid it would fly off the rails into the blue sky and smash down to the ground below. But he'd remained silent. On the Parachute Jump, his body had jerked convulsively, flooding with fear when their car hit the top of the ride. But on the slow quiet drift down several hundred feet his nerves had calmed. He let himself absorb the sense of letting go that was so foreign to him. And finally the view from the top of the Ferris wheel, the silver spires of Manhattan piercing the sky, had left him awed. But Logan had been unable to share these feelings with Julia, who'd sat beside him, smiling and enjoying every moment.

As they walked back to the subway after hours at the park, he no longer felt the physical turmoil and fear the rides had triggered. What he was left with was the profound sense of helplessness and emotional vulnerability that entrapped him. And since he could never share this with Julia, he toughened, gave her a weak smile and held her hand tightly, like an anchor in a rough sea.

No sooner had they reached her brownstone, than Logan's phone rang. Angered by the interruption, he was about to ignore it, when he noticed the name of the caller. He cursed under his breath and gave Julia a rueful shake of his head. "Sorry. I have to take this."

"No problem."

Logan put the phone to his ear. "Mr. Logan, this is Doctor Bartolo. I'm afraid I have bad news. Your father has taken a turn to the worst. I doubt he'll live through the night."

Logan's first reaction was anger, with "just like the old bastard to pick tonight to die" screaming in his head. Tonight, when he'd wanted to spend more time with Julia, hoping the day would end with her in bed in his arms. Resentment at his father's untimely march toward death followed closely. With that thought an unexpected jolt of sadness shook him. Unsettled him. Then he remembered the doctor at the other end of the line.

"I'll be there as soon as I can," he said stiffly and hung up. Without a glance at the woman beside him, he called Max to bring the car and pick him up at Eighth and

79th. Stuffing his phone in his pocket, he looked down at Julia. The look of concern in her eyes left him speechless for a moment. He pushed himself back behind his emotional barriers.

"I'm sorry. An emergency has come up. I have to go."

She put her hand on his arm. "Of course. Anything I can do?"

He wanted to smile at her kindness but was afraid the emotions he held at bay would flood the gates so he remained sullen. "Not necessary. My driver will be here shortly." He took a deep breath. "Sorry to end the day like this." He wanted to tell her how much the day had meant to him but couldn't find the words. So he pulled her into his arms and kissed her. Gently, yet with the passion he'd withheld from the nameless women who constituted his sterile sex life. Her arms went around him. After a long while, he pulled away.

She spoke quietly. "Thanks for being such a good sport today. I had a lot of fun. I'm glad I'm getting to know you better, Daniel Logan. You're a good man." Her hands on his cheeks, she kissed him again, then turned, put her key in the front door and entered her home.

*   *   *

Julia stared out the front window, watching Logan stride purposefully down the street until he disappeared into the back seat of the car. She sighed deeply, shaking her head. He *had* been a good sport today. Julia knew he'd been touched by the new experiences, but if only she could read his mind, see into his soul, know exactly what he felt, what had been going on with him throughout the day. At first he'd been skeptical, eying the different rides with curiosity, approaching them with caution. But after a while he seemed to settle down and enjoy himself. Well, maybe not really enjoy, but certainly accept each new experience. Although he never said a word, just went along, as though tasting every new morsel of food, chewing on it, and letting it slide harmless down his throat. Funny thing, his acceptance only made her own day better. She loved being with him. No more the cold, calculating businessman, he seemed more approachable, more attractive. Vulnerable. And she found herself falling for him, wanting more.

Wanting to invite him in for a drink and who knows what may have followed, she was very disappointed when he'd gotten that phone call. Something about it had changed him into the stoic man he'd been when they'd first met. Sent him back behind the gates that imprisoned the part of him she had just begun to see. When his arms drew her close and his mouth captured hers, she sensed a desperation in him she'd never seen before. She'd wanted time to figure it out, but then his phone had rung.

Julia turned away from the window and headed for a hot shower and bed. It had been a long day and she was tired, mentally and physically. Perhaps the next time they met she'd be able to reach him further.

*   *   *

Logan stood at the side of his father's bed, staring at the pale shrunken face. Andrew Logan's withered body was covered with white cotton sheets. Life-sustaining nutrition and fluids dripped slowly into thin veins. The old man's heartbeat bleeped erratically on the monitor. Looking at his father, it was hard for Logan to imagine the loud, angry man Andrew had been. Arrogance had left the man's ashen face. There were no closed fists to threaten anyone. No booming voice that had sent Logan and his sister into hiding under the bed or in the closet. Logan stared at the soon-to-be-corpse and he felt nothing.

The alarm from the monitor startled Logan out of his thoughts and brought nurses and Dr. Bartolo into the room. Logan stepped away from the bed, watching as they attempted to revive Andrew. After a few minutes, the doctor shook his head and called for the time of death. Logan stared at the clock on the wall, burning the imprint of its hands into his mind. Then he stepped outside the room and leaned against the wall. Farewell, old man. Can't say it's been good to know you. But the relief he'd always imagined would come with his father's death escaped Logan.

Doctor Bartolo joined him in the corridor and they walked to Bartolo's office to handle the paperwork. By the time Logan was finished, he stepped out of Harmony House for the last time, reached the Lincoln, slid into the back seat, and stared out the window as the car drove down the long driveway onto the street. A cold numbness seemed to encase him, his mind as empty as his heart.

*   *   *

Two hours later, Logan stood at Julia's door, his eyes boring into the thick antique wood. After driving around in circles for a while he'd given into the screaming need he had to see her, feel her, suck up the healing warmth he knew he'd find in her arms. Taking a deep breath, he rang the bell.

After a few long minutes, Julia opened the door. The foyer was muted in darkness lighted only by the gleam of street lamps that crept through the front windows of the brownstone, shrouding them in an eerie ghostly glow. Yet Logan could see the outline of her full breasts, small waist and long legs thinly veiled beneath a cotton robe. Her shoulder-length hair was mussed, her eyes wide with surprise.

"Daniel? What's wrong?"

He couldn't speak. Just stared at her. With a worried look on her face, she took his hand and drew him into her home, closing the door behind him. He nearly jumped from the spark of heat he felt at her touch, like a shaft of hope at the end of a cold winter night. When they reached the living room she turned and stood in front of him, still holding his hand. He shook his head.

"I shouldn't have come here." His deep gravelly voice hammered the block of ice inside him like a chisel, chipping it away.

Julia must have sensed his dark mood. She gave him a gentle smile that nearly undid him. "It's okay." She moved closer, her hands resting at his waist. "What do you need?"

Logan barely heard the low groan that passed his lips. He reached out and pulled her to him, a desperate beast needing to halt its slide into starvation. She turned her face up to his. He took her month, hard at first. When her arms encircled his neck, her fingers laced in his thick hair, he felt her surrender and pulled back, staring into her glistening hazel eyes. Seeing acceptance, his arms tightened around her and he held on, savoring the incredible moment of peace until stronger needs took over. His mouth came down on hers. He caressed her lips, her cheeks, her eyelids. She moaned. Breaking away, she silently took hold of his hand, walked him to the stairs and into the darkness down the hall.

*   *   *

It was still dark when Julia awoke. As she shook off the last remnants of sleep she smiled to herself, savoring the peace and contentment that filled her. She didn't mind the few aching muscles that protested the exertion they'd been put through. It had been a while. Smiling, she reached but Daniel wasn't there. Loss flooded her senses, leaving her with a scary emptiness. She blinked to become accustomed to the dark and scanned the room. She found him, his back to her, staring out the window, wearing only boxers. Respecting his silence, she got out of bed, went to him and put her arms around him, brushing her breasts against his muscled back. His hands rested on hers across his bare stomach. After a long moment he spoke softly.

"My father died tonight."

Julia sucked in a sharp breath. "I'm so sorry, Daniel."

"Don't be," he said in a quiet, dull voice. "He was a bastard who terrorized us for years. A weak, pathetic excuse for a human being. I'm only sorry he took this long to finally die. I could've saved a lot of money on nursing home bills."

Julia stiffened at his harsh words. "You hated him, yet you took care of him."

Logan snickered. "Yeah. Stupid, huh." She felt his hands press on hers.

"It's not uncommon for abused and neglected children to still love their parents no matter what." She kissed the rigid muscles on his back. "It only shows the kind of man you really are underneath that hard shell." She hugged him tighter, rubbing her cheek against his back. "Thank you for sharing that with me."

Julia felt him take a deep, shaky breath, then turn around. He cradled her face in his big hands, his eyes once again hard. "Don't get used to it. It's not something that comes easily to me."

She gave him a weak smile. "I know. I'll take whatever you want to give." She stood on her tiptoes and kissed him. As the heat between them rose, Logan picked her up and took her back to bed.

CHAPTER THIRTEEN

With his phone tucked under his chin, Logan fished through the pile of papers on his desk, half-listening to the strident voice of one of his CEO's who rambled on and on. Something about the rapid decline of a particular stock he'd recently invested in...at Logan's insistence, the man groused. Suddenly Logan zeroed in on the name of the company the man was ranting about.

"Did you say Tyler Trading?"

"Only three times? Haven't you been listening?"

Logan frowned. "Tell me again."

He heard a frustrated sigh at the other end of the phone. "My assistant came into my office and turned up the volume on the flatscreen. Apparently the S&P has sharply devaluated TT's stock, based on poor projections of future earnings of their new clothing line. The foreign markets are getting hit with massive sell orders."

Logan's mouth tightened. What the hell was going on? He knew for a fact that the new line hadn't even gone into production. At the Open House he'd witnessed the new designs first-hand, the tooling changes made to the various machines used to cut patterns and fabric as well as the skill of the employees who would painstakingly complete the finished pieces. What was the basis of S&P's new rating of TT's stock?

Logan was determined to find out. He hung up.

He pressed the intercom button on his phone. "Brad. Get in here. Fast."

Logan tossed his pen on the desk and sat back. Julia's beautiful face appeared before him, translucent with the glow of satisfaction he'd seen the other night, a night that had left him changed forever. Logan's jaw clenched. He'd get down to the bottom of this no matter what, even if he had to bribe those who'd dared to slander Julia and her company. While the role of knight in shining armor was entirely unfamiliar to him, at this moment it felt right. A twinge of guilt pinched his heart. He sucked up a deep breath. He hadn't been able to help his mother, but by God he'd protect Julia.

Brad Richmond rushed into Logan's office. "What's up, boss?" he said, his iPad clutched in his hand as though ready to do battle.

"I assume you've heard the latest on Tyler Trading's stock. I need to know what information S&P has and where it came from. And I need it yesterday."

"Got it. I'll call in some favors from my contacts I have at S&P. I should have something for you in a few hours."

"The sooner the better."

As Brad hurried out of the office, dread overwhelmed Daniel, like a fog rolling in. He expected to hear from Julia sometime during the day and he needed to be prepared to reassure her that all would be corrected.

He only hoped to God that he'd be able to fulfill that promise.

*   *   *

With her head stuck in the sports section of the *New York Times* morning edition, Julia relaxed on the highback stool at her kitchen counter sipping her coffee. The Yankees were on a hot streak. Maybe this year they'd make it to the World Series. Yet her interest over this possibility was diminished as memories of Daniel and the amazing night they'd shared shimmered like a silk veil in front of every activity she did. His face gripped in passion, the feel of his hands on her body, the utter ecstasy of him inside her. Even the launch of the new line couldn't hold her attention.

The loud ring of her cell phone blasted her back to reality. She reached for it, drinking down the last of her coffee.

"Turn on the TV," Faith's voice demanded.

"What..."

"Just turn it on."

Dread crept up Julia's spine. It wasn't like the unflappable Faith Higgins to sound so panicky. Julia grabbed the remote and clicked on the TV. Always preprogrammed to CNBC, the reporter's voice boomed through the kitchen with breaking news.

"CNBC has just learned that Standard & Poors has announced a significant change in its rating of Tyler Trading. The company's long-standing rate of A+ has been devalued to a negative C. We expect a run on the stock the moment the domestic markets open. We've already seen a sell-off from the markets across the pond. So far no word has been heard from either Tyler's spokesperson or S&P. Stand by for ongoing developments."

Julia nearly dropped the phone, her pulse racing. "What's going on? Why the sudden negative report? You filed all the necessary papers to S&P regarding the expansion, haven't you?"

"Of course," Faith said between ragged breaths. "I have no idea what happened."

Steel resolve replaced Julia's initial wave of fear. "We better find out fast before its too late to stem the sell-off." She looked at her watch. Seven-thirty. "We have two hours before the market opens. Call S&P. Find out the basis of their rating drop. I'll be in the office in twenty minutes."

She jammed the phone into the pocket of her jeans and stared at the ribbon of financial news that streamed across the bottom of the TV screen. Her heart missed a few beats when she saw the Tyler Trading symbol roll by. My God! What could have caused this sudden drop in confidence in her company? Where had S&P gotten their information? Who was responsible for the attack?

At once Julia grabbed the edge of the counter when a horrifying thought crossed her mind. Logan. Could he be behind this? He'd wanted to take over Tyler Trading from the first. His arrogant, hard-line approach to business had infused mistrust of him in Julia the moment she'd met him. Then the sudden shift of his personality, his so-called interest in her as a friend, his smooth pursuit of her that finalized in their remarkable night in bed. God damn him. The deceit. The manipulation. He'd used her apparent lack of good judgment of men against her. And God damn her for falling for it all.

She picked up her empty mug and threw it across the kitchen where it shattered into a million pieces against the stainless steel refrigerator. Refusing to sink into the deep hole of self-hatred that rose in her she shoved it aside, grabbed onto all the fury she could muster and focused it on Daniel Logan instead. This was on him, and she'd make him pay.

                    *   *   *

"You sonofabitch!"

Logan abruptly turned away from the window he'd been starting out to see Julia storm into his office. His expression hardened when he heard the fierce anger in her voice and saw the hatred in her eyes and then the ugly thought that he had betrayed her.

"You used me," she raged, "strung me along all this time with your sudden romantic interest. Softened me up so I wouldn't see what you were planning behind my back. Worst of all you waited until after I'd given myself to you to drop the hammer down on my company. What did you do...flood the business community with a bunch of bullshit stories about information you'd suddenly discovered that forced you to sell off? Or did you short the 20% your conglomerate owns so you could make a killing on the buy-back?"

Her chest heaved. Her eyes glared. The sudden picture of a bull snorting and pawing the ground ready to pounce would've made Logan smile if the situation wasn't so serious. He cleared his throat, his voice gruff.

"Paul Fisher," was all he said.

Julia's tirade stopped short, as though she'd been slapped. "What...what?"

"Sit down." He moved to his desk and pressed the intercom. "Brad. Bring me that file you're putting together." Logan sat on the edge of his desk, his arms folded across his chest. Julia remained standing, staring at him, eyes squinting, forehead lined. Silence hung heavy in the room. In a moment the office door swung open and Brad hurried in, a thick folder in his hand. He gave it to Logan.

"Thanks."

Brad left the office as quickly as he'd entered.

"I'm sorry about this, Julia. I triple checked Brad's work, made several calls to confirm what's in this file." He handed it to her. "I'm convinced it's accurate."

Still standing, Julia glared at him before she took the file and read through it. As though the breath had left her body, she slowly sank down into the chair in front of him and went over the file again. When she looked up at him, tears filled her eyes.

"I can't believe he'd do this to me," she whispered. "You're sure?"

Logan suppressed the need to pull her into his arms and comfort her.

"Yes."

Julia stared at the file on her lap. "You warned me about him, but I was too naïve to listen."

"Don't beat yourself up. And now isn't the time for that. We have to take steps to counteract Fisher's attack."

She pulled herself together, sat straighter, blinked away the tears, took a deep breath and looked him straight in the eye. "What do you suggest?"

"We have an appointment in an hour with the chairman of the SEC and the president of S&P."

She frowned. "We?"

"You're a fighter, Julia. I knew you'd want to face this thing head-on." He gave her a slight smile. "As evidenced by your visit here."

"You knew I'd accuse you."

"It was only logical. I would've reacted the same way."

The warmth in Julia's eyes nearly melted Logan's reserve. "I'm sorry, Daniel. Truly sorry."

He cleared his throat. "Save your pity for your ex-husband. After the law gets through with him, he won't be able to show his face anywhere in this country. That's if he's not in jail." Logan stood. "Let's go. We have a meeting to attend."

She took his outstretched hand and stood. Small and soft, it felt like silk in his. Mindless of anyone who might see them through the glass wall, he brought it to his lips and kissed the palm, then turned away quickly toward the door. He let her pass through, closing it behind him.

CHAPTER FOURTEEN

"Drop me at my office."

Concern furrowed Logan's brow at the empty flatness of Julia's voice. The disturbing possibility of the end of her company narrowly avoided, she stared out the Lincoln window, as though shell-shocked by the enormity of the morning events. Their meeting with the SEC and S&P had gone as he'd expected. With Julia beside him, Logan had explained to the heads of the two most influential financial institutions in the world the result of his recent investigation. He'd handed over copies of the documentation supporting his claim that Paul Fisher was behind a plot to ruin Tyler Trading. With the massive influence Logan Enterprises yielded, he had all but threatened the two chairmen to suspend trading on TT's stock until they could conclude their own investigation. So by the time Wall Street opened its proverbial doors promptly at 9:30 a.m., the ticker tape noted the suspension.

They rode through Chelsea and finally stopped on Eight Avenue and 26th street in front of Tyler Trading. Max called out, "We're here, Mr. Logan."

Logan looked out the window, then at Julia and spoke to Max. "Leave us for a moment. Get yourself a cup of coffee."

The man left them alone.

Logan turned in his seat to Julia, reaching for her hand that rested on her knee.

"It's over, Julia. Once trading resumes the European markets will rebound. Your company is safe."

She turned to face him. "What do you think will happen to Paul?"

Anger flushed Logan's face. "Probably less than he deserves. We can only hope that the new regulations the feds have in place will put him behind bars." He shook his head. "But I wouldn't hold my breath if I were you."

She looked away for a moment as though gathering her strength, her thoughts. "I have an enormous need to let him know we know what he did. To slap him dizzy."

Logan let out a chuckle. "I got it. But I wouldn't recommend it. I suggest you stay away from him. He's going to be furious that his scheme didn't work and he might take his revenge on you physically this time."

A sly grin slid over her face. "At least then I could put him away for assaulting me."

Logan was glad the trauma of the morning had apparently dissipated and she appeared to be her usual in-control self. He brushed his hand over her cheek. "And mess up that beautiful face? Then I'd have to kill him."

Julia grabbed his hand. "I don't know what I would've done, Daniel, if you hadn't..."

He stopped her with a kiss on her forehead. "I have every faith you would've figured out something. I only helped facilitate a speedy fix."

"Thank you," she whispered.

Logan wanted to tell her how much she'd come to mean to him, but the words jammed behind his clogged throat. He wished they were in his apartment so he could take her to bed again. With his arms holding her, his body inside hers, words weren't necessary.

Julia broke away and straightened. "I have a lot of work to do calming fears and building confidence."

Back to her old self. Good. "How about dinner tonight? I'll pick you up at eight."

"Sounds perfect. I'll be starved by then." She leaned over and planted a kiss on his lips.

Logan opened the door and stepped out, offering Julia his hand. She exited the car.

"Later," she said and hurried into the building.

*   *   *

The roar that hurricaned up Paul Fisher's throat and exited his mouth would've sent wild lions running. He sailed the remote across the room with an arm like a 100 mile-an-hour major league baseball pitcher. It slammed against the television screen, cracking it. Goddammit! How the hell had Julia the Bitch gotten TT stock suspended so fast? He'd missed out on selling it short. All that dough lost. And Art Catalongo...had he sneaked through a sell order? Fisher felt drops of sweat form on his forehead. If Catalongo hadn't, Fisher was in a world of hurt. He owed the ruthless broker for the cost of shorting TT. But now there'd be no cash to do so, at least not any time soon.

And Catalongo had the reputation of teaching those who stiffed him unspeakable lessons.

Heart pounding, Fisher jolted off the sofa and grabbed a beer from the fridge, sucking down half of it. Fear raced through him. He took several deep breaths to get his blood pressure under control.

What was he going to do?

*   *   *

Julia stared out her office window, thoughts of Paul and Daniel swirling around in her head. Paul and how their marriage had sucked away her confidence in herself as a woman. Daniel. He'd never doubted her. Always treated her as an equal with a good head on her shoulders and the courage to take on and successfully complete significant commitments. His confidence in her had filled the deep volcanic crater her relationship with Paul Fisher had caused. Daniel's strong commanding presence, his stability, his wry sense of humor...he was the partner she wanted to spend the rest of her life with.

Julia slumped back in her chair, her heart pounding with a sudden realization. She was in love with him.

They had come so far. First the anger, manipulation and mistrust that had initially been the basis of their relationship. Then his slow pursuit of her as a woman. Julia wondered what internal forces had compelled him to drop his guard and let her in to the extent he had. Now, months later, they were in entirely new emotional territory and while this thrilled her, she hoped it didn't scare him away. Worry lines pinched her forehead. A rush of fear swept through her. What if he decided he didn't want or need her? That she represented too great a distraction and it was safer to slide back behind those thick walls where he'd spent most of his life? The abandonment she'd experienced after her parents had died had devastated her. She wasn't sure she could handle going through something like that again.

Julia checked her watch. Seven. Just enough time to shower and dress. Nervous energy blew away the umbrella of mental and physical exhaustion she'd labored under all day. All thoughts of TT, the SEC and S&P instantly evaporated leaving her senses fully alive. Emboldened by her newly discovered feelings for Daniel, Julia decided it was time she took another proactive step in the transformation of Daniel Logan.

CHAPTER FIFTEEN

"Take me to your place."

Logan glanced down at Julia, raising an eyebrow. "Guess I'll have to add mind-reading to your list of skills," he said in a deep voice.

The intense look she gave him began a slow melt of the ice he kept around his heart, heating his body. His eyes penetrated hers when he spoke. "You heard what the lady said, Max."

"Yes, Sir."

Logan tore his gaze off her and watched the streets pass by as the Lincoln left the restaurant and crawled toward Fifth Avenue and East 58th. By the time they reached Logan's apartment the heat of sexual tension in the back seat could've melted an igloo. Taking Julia's hand, he led her into the lobby of his building. An elevator sped them to the penthouse. No sooner had Logan's foot slammed the door behind them than he pulled her roughly into his arms. Julia dropped her purse and wrapped her arms around his neck, pressing her whole body against his. Logan sucked in his breath seconds before locking his mouth against hers. When he felt her return the intense kiss, he picked her up and strode into his bedroom, wanting her in his bed where she belonged. Need urged him on. The more he gave of himself, the more she demanded. They continued their dance for what seemed hours, hands, mouths, probing, touching, until each surrendered. The explosion that followed rocked him, breaking apart his defenses, leaving him sated and vulnerable.

He rolled onto his back and drew her on top. The rapid beating of her heart against his reminded him how alive he felt.

Resting her head on his chest, Julia whispered so low he could barely hear. "I love you, Daniel."

He sucked in a deep breath.

Julia's gaze met his, her face flushed with pleasure. "You don't have to say anything. I just want you to know." She rested her head back against his chest.

Her eyelashes tickled him when she closed her eyes and snuggled in his tight grasp. Instinctively he planted a gentle kiss in her soft hair, inhaling the light scent of vanilla. She had given him the greatest gift a woman could give a man like him, the knowledge of her true feelings and the freedom to choose his response.

His jaw clenched, suddenly feeling trapped, wanting to run far away, pretend he didn't care for her, that he didn't need her. He'd prided himself on being courageous in the face of any of life's challenges, refusing to let himself get mired in doubt or fear. Now he saw what a lie his life had been. It was fear that had motivated his actions, not courage. And that hit him with the ferocity of a cannonball in his gut.

Logan drew in deep breaths. His thoughts embraced the woman who lay snuggled against him, her warm soft body covering his. He couldn't lose her. She was the light to his darkness, a chance to be the authentic human being he'd been before he'd buried the past, denied his family and became the cold, ruthless unfeeling person that dominated his adulthood. For his own sanity, it was time to man-up.

"You asked me once about my family and I changed the subject. I was ashamed to tell you."

"The night your father died you said he was a mean drunk. That's nothing for you to be ashamed of. You were just a child."

Logan sighed. "I was never able to protect my family from his abuse, his selfish neglect of our basic needs. The last time I saw the old man as a child was when I was seven and he never returned from one of his long binges." He paused as if needing to galvanize behind thick walls. "My mother got a divorce and we moved to L.A. Eventually she remarried. "I started getting into fights at school, cut classes, felt bad about giving my mother a hard time. But I couldn't seem to stop rebelling. After a while, seeing how much my behavior hurt my mother, the guilt became unbearable. I ran away when I was fourteen and have been on my own ever since."

His hand glided over soft skin caressing her back. "Wanting to get as far away as possible, I hitchhiked across the country back to New York. I lived on the streets for nearly two years, in and out of teen shelters where I was able to eventually get my GED. I became a talented thief." He kissed her shoulder. "One day I tried to piltch a wallet from a big guy in a business suit. For some reason he felt sorry for me and instead of turning me over to the authorities he gave me a job running errands."

Julia raised her head and looked at him. "Is your mother still alive?"

He closed his eyes briefly conjuring up a faded picture of his mother the last time he'd seen her, hanging wash, while he hid in the bushes outside their rundown house. Even at a distance, Logan could see the sadness in her face, the lethargy in her movements. Guilt struck again, realizing his absence probably had caused her more pain and worry.

Logan opened his eyes. "As far as I know she is. I believe my sister would've texted me if something had changed."

Curiosity filled Julia's eyes. "Your sister?"

"We text when something important happens." Sadness washed over him. "I haven't seen any of them in over twenty years."

"Any of them?"

Logan had gone as far down memory lane as could. He'd save the rest of the story for another time. So he remained silent, all the while staring at her, as though waiting for her condemnation. "Now you know the ugly truth about the man you're giving yourself to." He kissed her forehead. "I'm returning the favor you gifted me. If you want to get up and walk out that door and never see me again, I won't blame you."

She frowned. "Is that what you want?"

"This isn't about me, Julia. It's about your life from here on."

She stared at him as though she couldn't believe what he was saying. He could see her trying to make sense of everything, struggling to find the words to answer him. Suddenly, she raised up on her forearms and glared at him, giving him a light punch in the chest. "You are such an idiot."

Logan's mouth opened in shock, momentarily speechless. "What the hell, Julia, why'd you do that?"

"To snap you out of your stupidity."

His confusion turned quickly to anger. And to make matters worse, she began laughing at him.

"I'm sorry, Daniel, I just couldn't help it. Don't be insulted." She finally got her merriment under control. Her hands cradled his face and she kissed him. "You make beautiful passionate love to me, share intimately about your life for the first time and expect me to walk away? And all this after I show you, tell you, how much I love you? I thought you knew me better than that." She gave him a small scolding smile and kissed him again. "You're not getting rid of me that easily, Daniel Logan. I'll fight for you if I have to, but I much prefer spending our life together making love."

Logan released the breath he'd been holding. This woman who sprawled over him, loving him, declaring her commitment continued to surprise him. He would spend eternity thanking God her ex-husband had walked into his office months before, eventually bringing her into his life.

"Guess I'll have to make it legal then. With the Open House next week, we wouldn't want any hint of impropriety to color our reps."

Her beautiful face lit up, reminding him of pictures he'd seen of children staring in awe at a sparkling tree surrounded with presents on Christmas morning.

She laughed. "If that's a marriage proposal, you should definitely re-read Romeo and Juliet." She kissed him. "If it's not, well, too damn bad. You're stuck with me."

Before Logan could show her how very pleasant that would be, his phone rang. He was about to ignore it when his skin began to crawl, as though warning him something malevolent was coming.

"I have to take this."

Julia shifted and rested against his side, her arm across his chest.

He reached for the phone. "Danny? Mom's in trouble. She needs you."

PART TWO
Eve

CHAPTER ONE

Eve Mitchell had just made it into her Westwood apartment before the summer storm struck. Cursing, she recalled narrowly missing the drunken UCLA frat boys as they staggered across Wilshire Boulevard hurrying to get on campus before the rain began. She stared into the bathroom mirror. Bleary eyes cuffed with dark bags stared back at her. Pale cheeks. Swollen lips. Shaking her head she reached for the Advil and swallowed two extra-strength tablets, nearly gagging. She downed them with a glass of water, wondering if two pills would take the edge off her booze-induced splitting headache. It had been her usual long night of drink and sex. She blinked at her reflection trying to remember which bar and what partner she'd partied with. Did it really matter? After a while they all looked and felt the same. A deep sigh reached down into her soul. She turned away and went into her bedroom. Sleep and two days off from work would magically transform her back to the competent home care nurse that paid her bills.

Her phone buzzed before she hit the pillow. Shit! She answered it.

"Mitchell. Hate to cut your vacation short, but we need you."

Eve moaned into the pleading voice of the director of the Home Health Care program connected with Santa Monica Hospital. "You've got to be kidding."

Les Cohen laughed. "Just got assigned a new patient. Firefighter. Severely injured both legs jumping out of a helicopter two months ago. The only caveat the doctor insisted on before signing the stubborn guy out of the Hospital was that he hook up with us ASAP."

"Give it to Joyce," she grumbled, hardly recognizing her throaty voice.

"She's backlogged. Doc says we have to monitor the big guy's injuries as well as get him fully functioning without crutches. I'll text you his address. Tomorrow. Eight a.m. sharp." Before Eve could bitch and moan further, Cohen hung up.

Damn. She wasn't ready for another case. She'd just come off two weeks of 24/7 in-home care without a break and she needed some downtime to unwind and regenerate. The flash of lightning that sneaked through her bedroom shutters grabbed her attention. The clap of thunder that followed shook the apartment, temporarily blocking the incessant sound of rain pelting the windows. Great. Even the weather was against her.

After cursing her boss and the new patient, Eve tossed the phone on the floor and collapsed on the bed, hoping the booze that still ran through her bloodstream would prevent the nightmares from disturbing the sleep she craved.

*   *   *

Standing in the dark, miserable in his rain-soaked jeans and hooded sweatshirt, the man stared up at the second-story window until the bedroom light went out. His prey was finally in for the night. He was getting sick and tired of chasing her around Hollywood in and out of bars and seedy motels. It wouldn't be long before he decided to end both their miseries and make his move. He raced toward the car he'd parked two blocks away and slid into the front seat, shaking much of the rain off. Even in the warm summer air, he was chilled. Damn. He felt his patience dropping away like the rain from his clothes. Soon, very soon, she'd pay for what she'd done.

*   *   *

"Why'd you leava the Hospital?"

Vincent Ramone couldn't help the smile that curved his mouth at the sound of his mother's scolding voice over the phone. He was thirty-seven, but no matter how old he got, how many times she nagged, berated or yelled, he got a kick out of it. No sense getting pissed. He was her little boy now and forever. Must be some recessive mother gene, especially in Italian mamas.

He gulped down the rest of his protein shake. "I'm fine, Mom. Doc wouldn't't've let me out if I wasn't."

"You livin' by yourself?"

"I'm at my place in Venice."

"Why you no stay here? Who's agonna cook for you, cleana you house, washa you clothes?"

Four questions down, sixteen more to go. "I've been taking care of myself since I was eighteen, Mom. I'll be fine. Don't worry. As soon as I'm settled you can come and see for yourself." He sighed. Mothers. The doorbell chimed. Thank God. "I've gotta go, Mom. Promise I'll call soon. Love, you." He hung up.

Vin grabbed his crutches and hobbled to the door. "Who is it?"

A deep almost sultry female voice came through the door. "Home health care."

God. They didn't give him a minute's peace. All he wanted was to be left alone to heal and train on his own schedule. But he'd promised his doctor he'd be a "good patient" and he always kept his word. At least most of the time. He put on a happy face and opened the door.

And was pleasantly surprised at the gorgeous woman who stood there.

Glossy mink-colored hair pulled back in a ponytail accentuated the large light brown eyes. A creamy complexion and full lips. He was sure the blue scrubs didn't do justice to the full breasts, trim waist and hips that her clothing concealed.

"I'm Eve Mitchell." She gave his tall frame and the crutches under his arms a brief scan. "I assume you're Vincent Ramone. I've been assigned your case." The weak smile she gave him never reached her eyes. It was apparent she wasn't overjoyed to be working with him. He turned on the charm.

"That's me. Come on in." He shuffled sideways for her to enter and then shut the door. He glanced around the small living room. Jeans and shirts lay carelessly on the sofa. Firefighter's gear dotted the wood floor. "Sorry for the mess. My housekeeper quit when I was in the hospital."

"No problem. I have paperwork for you to fill out before we begin."

"Follow me." He led her into the tiny utility kitchen and gestured to the small pine table. The wide ceiling to floor patio doors allowed a view of the boat dock and canal off the deck. "Coffee, tea, water? Something stronger?"

She flinched at the thought of liquor."Nothing, thanks."

Sitting, she reached into her briefcase and withdrew a few sheets of paper, explaining what each was and where he was to sign. Offered him a pen. Very professional. Very uptight. He raised his eyebrows and calmly asked her, "Do you dislike all your patients or are your hemorrhoids bothering you today?"

Her eyes widened. Her mouth opened. It took a moment before she suppressed her surprise and her stoic expression returned.

Vin chuckled, glad to see he could knock her off her stride. He took the seat opposite her. A whiff of guilt blew over him upon seeing the fatigue that clouded her beautiful eyes. He decided to back off. Maybe she'd just had a bad night. He'd had a few of them himself, especially since his injury.

"Sorry," he said. Taking the proffered pen, he scanned and signed each page at the yellow arrows. "We can start tomorrow if that works for you. Better yet, why don't we forget the whole thing. Tell you the truth, I'm not too thrilled about having a babysitter."

"No can do. The only reason you were released from the hospital against medical advice was that you promised you'd work with Home Care in monitoring your recovery progress." She shrugged. "You're stuck with me."

"Okay, then. Let's start over." He reached for her hand. "Hi. I'm Vin. Nice to meet you."

She ignored his hand and the truce he offered. Instead, she gathered the papers and stuck them back in her briefcase, the clinical mask remaining in place. "I read your file. I was impressed with how quickly you've recovered given the extent of your injuries. And you seem to be getting around remarkably well on crutches." She held his gaze. "I'm surprised the doctor didn't demand you do PT in the Hospital gym."

"I've been working out and in training for one thing or another for the last fifteen years. Got a gym right here in the house with everything I need."

"Your needs now are more significant than basic fitness. You have practically two new legs. Your muscles need specific exercises to learn to cope with the rods and pins you've acquired. It's my job to help you with that."

"We'll see." Vin studied her face. Oh, well. He could deal with her attitude for a while. In fact, it wouldn't be too much of a burden to have her company. Besides being easy on the eyes, Eve Mitchell held a lot of secrets behind them. It'd be interesting to find out what made her tick. The only male in a sea of female siblings, Vin knew women pretty well. Found them fascinating. Thought-provoking. Maybe the challenge she presented would keep his mind off that jump from the helo into the raging fire below.

"Okay, Eve. I'm game if you are. So what's the plan for today?"

*   *   *

Eve sunk back into the leather seat of her Highlander, glad to be away from her new patient. She breathed a sigh of relief, cursing her boss at the same time. Vincent Ramone was just too damn good looking. Thought he was God's gift to women. She was sick to death of macho Italian men who believed the world owed them a living. What an asshole. But she had to acknowledge, only to herself of course, he had a fantastic body, tall, muscular. God knew how much bigger his already colossal ego would inflate if he could read her thoughts. And his endurance was amazing. She'd been with him for over two hours and he'd handled the strenuous workout she'd given him without complaint.

After viewing his home gym, she had to give him credit. He'd been right. The gym was as good as any Hospital's she'd ever been in. And with only a few minor changes from his usual routine that she'd insisted upon, he knew just how to work the equipment for maximum results. He'd readily accepted the little coaching she offered. In fact, he actually thanked her after realizing how beneficial her suggestions had been.

"Before I go I have to check your vitals and your injuries." She avoided looking at him while she sat and reached into her large black and white striped carryon.

Vin sat on the sofa in a tank top and loose jogging shorts, a rolled-up towel around his neck to absorb the drops of sweat that beaded down his face and chest. "Go for it," he said and rested his legs on the edge of the coffee table. Lounging back against the sofa, he guzzled down nearly an entire bottle of water.

Eve had a difficult time maintaining her usual stoic professional mask. Touching the warm skin on Vin's muscular bicep while wrapping the blood pressure strap around it made her feel very uncomfortable. Ditto when she clipped the pulse and heart rate monitor on his long index finger.

She cleared her throat and muttered, "BP and other vitals are normal." Not once did she look at him. Putting her instruments back into her carryon, she shifted her vision to the ugly, dark pink healing scars that ran down both his long legs from mid-thighs to ankles. Her chest rose and fell as she imagined the pain he must have suffered over the last several months. Was probably still experiencing. She felt his eyes on the back of her head as she leaned over to examine the wounds thoroughly.

"They're healing nicely. Do you need more pain meds?"

"Don't need them. Apparently I have a high tolerance for pain."

She finally looked at him and was surprised at the boyish smile that crinkled his eyes and mouth. Angry at the warm reaction that flooded her body, Eve abruptly stood.

"We're done for now. Continue with the routine you did today. I'll be back in two days for a follow-up." She grabbed her carryon.

Vin attempted to rise, but she stopped him. "No bother. I'll show myself out."

Eve put the key into her Toyota and headed for her apartment in Westwood, near the UCLA campus. She'd shower and sleep for a few hours, then head out for a light supper and more mind-numbing drinking. With any luck, she'd find some willing stud to take to bed and spend another shadowy night where childhood memories and loneliness couldn't find her. And maybe even wipe away her troubling reaction to Vincent Ramone.

*   *   *

"What do you mean, you won't sign off as my shrink?"

The following day, Vin hugged his crutches and stood in front of Dr. Rosemary Cross's desk, staring at her in shock. Her chuckle threatened to project his anger off the Richter scale.

"This isn't funny," he whined. "Before I could get out of the Hospital I had to agree to endure a stranger with a bad attitude invading my home taking my vitals and overseeing my PT. And now my Chief's insisting he won't let me back on the job until I see a shrink and work out my PTSD issues. How the hell does he know I have PTSD anyway?"

Rosie pushed her chair away from the desk, and folded her arms, shaking her head at the man across from her. "Sit before you fall down." She frowned. "Really, Vin, you know I can't treat family members. Why get yourself all in a dither over it?"

"A dither? Really, Rosie? Who says dither? You sound more and more like your blueblood limey husband every day." Maneuvering awkwardly with his crutches, Vin plopped down in a chair across from his eldest sister. "I don't have the time to sit and blab about my problems. Don't need to. What happened, happened. It's in the past. I'm dealing." He let out a gust of frustration. "I just have to get my legs working like they used to."

"Methinks thou doth protest too much, little brother. Makes me wonder what's going on in that thick skull of yours."

Vin scoffed. "You sound more and more like Mom every day. At least now she's obsessing on my health rather than the usual...'Finda gooda woman. Settle down. I wanna grandbabies'. I swear she takes it personally that I'm not married with a dozen rugrats hanging around."

Rosie shuffled some papers on her desk. "You're the only son, head of the family since Pop died. Mom feels you owe it to him to continue the Ramone name. Maybe it's time to stop playing superhero fireman and lady killer and step up." She paused. "So, other than wanting me to put my license at risk and sign off on some non-existent treatment plan, what other peeves can I help you with? I can recommend a good psychiatrist if you want."

Vin rubbed his right calf before resting his elbows on his knees and glared at his sister. "No thanks." This topic was getting old. Time for a change of subject. He slid into the carefree, bachelor role he preferred.

Rosie shook her head, ignoring his attempt to minimize the visit. "You know, Vin, you forget as a shrink I have uncanny abilities to read between the lines, so don't bullshit me."

With eyes wide he raised his hands and opened his palms. "See. Nothing up my sleeves. No hidden agenda. Just a brother calling on his sister."

Coming here had been a mistake. He knew Rosie wouldn't do anything unethical. Maybe he just needed to connect with someone he cared about. A temporary fix, he knew, anything to stop the nightmares. Nameless. Faceless.

Swarming colors of energy, hot and consuming. He always woke up in a bed of sweat, his heart pounding, his head ready to explode. Maybe the pros were right. He needed to get a handle on this PTSD thing before it got worse and kept him off the job.

He watched Rosie concentrating on her computer screen. He wanted her to wave her magic wand and disappear the anxiety that ran in his veins, but he knew unless he confided entirely in her, she'd be unable to help him. And for some reason he couldn't talk about the fire, the dreams, the crippling fear that raged in him. Not with anyone. Shame and guilt had too tight a grip on him.

Rosie looked up from her computer. "Why don't you come for dinner tonight? Brian bought some new high-tech gadget I know he'd love to show you." She chuckled. "I think he's frustrated with my lack of interest in technology and would love to geek-speak with you."

Vin shook off the melancholia that threatened to overwhelm him. "Sorry. Hot date. Maybe another time. Tell Bri to call me. We'll set something up." Arranging the crutches under his arms and stifling the grimace of pain that shot up from his legs, he stood, leaned over the desk and gave Rosie a soft kiss on her cheek. "Say hi for me. Love Ya."

Whistling, he hobbled out of her office.

CHAPTER TWO

A week later, Eve slid onto the wooden seat, placing her small purse on the scarred mahogany bar. Her third stop for the night. No music. Just the low murmur of conversation among the few remaining drinkers. The seedy Hollywood establishment boasted a score of regulars of which she might be considered one, although she tried not to frequent the same place more than once a week. It wouldn't do to get chummy with the patrons. She never knew who might show up on her patient roster. And it would be a problem if they recognized her as the sexy barfly they were always hitting on. As much as she sometimes hated her job, she needed it.

She signaled to the bartender and nodded when he approached. "The usual, Sal." And after a second, added. "And leave the bottle."

He smiled at her as he put a shot glass on the bar. "Rough day, huh?"

Eve grimaced. "You could say that."

Sal gave an understanding nod and reached behind for a bottle of Black Label and poured a double.

Her mind shifted to four-year-old Debbie Jones, the cerebral palsy patient she'd been working with for over six months, as she struggled with her tiny crutches. The child had fallen victim to pneumonia and died, leaving a spear in Eve's gut, threatening to eviscerate her heart. And so the pull to the numbing alcohol and mindless sex called. With a shaking hand she slugged down the scotch.

But it wasn't enough to stop her thoughts from straying to her new patient. Ramone was all she despised in a man...gorgeous, superhero body with a quick mind and tongue and playful personality. A great catch on the outside. Too bad he so closely resembled Tony Parma, her slick, cheating second ex-husband. And then there was the controlling first ex-husband. But since that relationship only lasted long enough for her to get away from her drama-filled fucked-up family, she barely remembered him.

She poured more amber liquor into her glass and gulped it down. A few more and she'd be ready to go home and hope for a few hours of empty sleep. She'd need it to face Ramone again.

Her cell phone buzzed. Cursing she grabbed it from her purse and looked at the time. Twelve-fifteen. Then caller ID. Shit. "Mom? It's late. Why're you up?"

A light laugh echoed in Eve's ear. "I don't want you to worry, but I thought I'd tell you before you came to the house in the morning and I wasn't there."

"What are you talking about? Where are you?"

"It's nothing, dear, really. I fell on the way to the bathroom and couldn't get up. Since your step-father is out of town and I didn't want to bother you, I called the EMT's and they brought me to the ER. My blasted hip went out again. They put it back but insisted I stay the night to make sure I was okay." Her mother sighed. "You sound so groggy. Oh dear, did I wake you up?"

Her sainted mother Mary. Thoughtful. Selfless. Hardworking. Her first thought always for her children. "What Hospital are you at? I'll be right there."

"No need. I'm fine. Really. The ER staff are taking good care of me. In fact, your friend, Annette is on duty tonight. She's been very helpful. I'll call Sloan after they release me in the morning."

"Don't bother your driver, Mom. Call me when you're ready and I'll pick you up. I mean it. I'll be really pissed if you don't."

"All right, Eve, if you insist."

Eve heard a yawn coming through the phone.

"I think the drugs are working on me. I'm suddenly feeling drained. I'll speak to you when I'm discharged. Go back to sleep. I love you, dear."

"Yeah," Eve said in a husky voice.

God damn it. Her mother's quiet strength and commitment to her family above her own wants and needs always produced a strong sense of guilt in Eve. And resentment. Why couldn't she have taken on her mother's decent human characteristics instead of the destructive ones that seemed to drive Eve?

A man strolled alongside her. "Can I buy you the next round?" he said in a deep husky voice that spoke of years of cigarettes and booze.

She turned and gave him the once over. Thirtyish. Medium height and build. Jeans and tee. Tats running up both arms. Rancid breath. More lines around the eyes and mouth than his years indicated. A life hard-lived. The perfect way to end a lousy day and a not-too-great tomorrow.

"Sure, why not?"

*   *   *

"Where do you want to rest?" With an arm through her mother's, Eve slowly walked Mary into the expansive living room of her Beverly Hills home.

"I'm starving. There's enough leftover pasta in the refrigerator for the both of us. Let's have an early lunch. It's been ages since we've shared a quiet meal together."

Eve wasn't in the mood for the not-too-subtle drilling about her personal life that she suffered through every time she and her mother had some alone time. She took in a deep breath, knowing full well she couldn't say no to her. Mary was the most stubborn woman Eve knew. On the outside she was affable and easy-going, but inside rested the heart of a lion, probably forged through all the health issues she'd suffered from early childhood. And then there were the scars from her first marriage.

Eve surrendered to the inevitable and assisted her mother to the ultra-modern granite and stainless steel kitchen. It didn't matter that Mary's wealthy husband could afford a cook. Since retiring from a supervisory position with the L.A. County Department of Children and Family Services two years before, Mary discovered gourmet cooking and loved to play around in the kitchen. Her words. Eve had to admit the large room would've felt sterile if not for the potted herbs and other scented plants and flowers that graced the room.

"Do you want a pillow to sit on?" she asked as Mary clumsily slid onto a wooden bar stool.

"No, this is fine. The pasta's on the second shelf. Just heat it in the microwave."

Eve followed the instructions and laid out place settings and brewed green tea. In minutes the warm scent of Italian spices wafted through the room and the microwave pinged.

Between forkfuls, Mary began the inquisition. "So. What've you been up to lately? How's that little girl you told me about? I'm sure she's making remarkable strides because of the wonderful care you give her."

Eve wished that was the case. "She died."

"Oh Eve, I'm so sorry. You must be devastated. Do you want to talk about it?" Mary took a sip of hot tea.

"No." That's all she needed. Mary poking around in Eve's head, finding out things Eve would die from if her mother knew.

Mary looked disappointed, but shifted a bit on the stool, changing the subject. "Any interesting new patients?"

Vin Ramone was another topic Eve didn't what to discuss. "Are you in pain? Do you want one of those pills the doctor gave you?"

"No. No pills. They make me groggy. I'm fine."

"So what did the doctor say about your hip? This is the third time it dislocated. What treatment plan did he recommend?"

Mary waved her hand in dismissal. "Oh, he said something about replacement surgery, but I don't think it's necessary. I just have to be more careful."

"Yeah," Eve retorted, "and maybe next time when you fall you'll hit your head and no one will find you for days." She ratcheted down her anger. "At least get one of those medical alert bracelets you've been putting off buying. It'll make me feel better when you're alone."

Mary finished the last of her pasta and tea and sighed. "I'll think about it."

Eve was surprised her mother had given even that small concession. Satisfied for the moment, she rose from the island and put the dishes in the dishwasher. "I have to get going. Where do you want to rest?"

"I can get to the first-floor guest bedroom myself. I'll stay there until I'm strong enough to manage the stairs. Run along now."

"Don't be stupid, Mom. I can see you're in pain. I'll help you to the bedroom. When's your husband coming home?"

"I spoke with him last night before I fell. He's sure he'll be home in a day or so."

"And I bet you didn't tell him about your hip."

"Of course I didn't. Why worry him? He has enough on his mind and will be home soon."

Eve shook her head in disgust. Always the saint. "Let's go." She went to her mother's side and offered her arm. Mary took it and rose carefully. They walked at a slow pace out of the kitchen. Eve settled her mother on the queen-sized bed in the guest room and handed her the TV remote.

"Do you need anything else?"

"No. I'll be fine." She smiled. "Thanks for picking me up. It was good spending a little time with you."

Toss some more guilt on me, why don't you. Eve bent and kissed Mary's cheek. "Call if you need anything."

"I will, dear."

Sure. And pigs can fly.

*   *   *

He'd followed his prey from her home to her mother's. The woman looked like hell. Not like the beauty he'd known before. Sure, it'd been a few years since he'd seen her. Five exactly. That's how long he'd been behind bars dreaming about the day he'd get his revenge on the bitch who'd ratted him to the cops and then had the nerve to divorce him while he was in the slammer. He chuckled behind the wheel of his beat-up 150. Guess boozing didn't help clear those dark circles under her eyes or the brighten the sheen of her hair he remembered. He'd loved to weave his hands through that dark mass, yanking her head back while he spread her legs and rammed into her. She'd had the nerve to push him away, forgotten her marriage vow to obey. Well, he'd show her. Divorce or no. No one betrays Anthony Louis Parma without suffering the consequences.

He punched the steering wheel, anger heating his face. Time he let her know her worst nightmare was in town. Put a little fear in her. He grabbed his cell phone and called the number he'd found in the phone book. It went to voice mail. Fuck! Oh well. A message would have to do for now.

"Hey, baby. Long time no see. I just got out and your name was on the top of my list of folks to see. Bet you know why. Call me. No sense dragging this out." He left his number and hung up.

A deep sigh of satisfaction left his body. There. It's begun. Anticipation whetted his mouth. He wondered how long she'd play this cat and mouse game before she caved in and called. In the meantime, he'd keep following her around. Call and harass her whenever he felt like it. Maybe even let her see him from a distance once in a while. Parma could almost taste her fear.

CHAPTER THREE

Vin watched Eve stuff the blood pressure and pulse monitor back into her carryon. "Everything looks good," she said.

"Of course I'm good. I told those doctors I didn't need someone checking up on me every day." Vin grunted and stood up adjusting the crutches under his arms. Then he smiled at her. "Sure I can't convince you to tell your boss I don't need services anymore?"

"Yup." Eve stood and led the way to the treadmill in his gym. "Hop up."

It was two weeks since his babysitter first made her appearance at his door and still those amber eyes rarely looked at him directly. She clenched her jaw when she massaged the muscles in his legs after a long workout. What was her problem anyway? Not getting enough sleep? Didn't like male patients? Maybe she was gay.

They were in the second half of his workout, his legs striding on the treadmill, when her phone rang. Vin couldn't help but notice the immediate change in her demeanor when she viewed the call screen. Her face turned ashen and fear clouded her eyes. Her shoulders slumped, then straightened. She licked her lips. Pushed a button on the phone and shoved it back into the pocket of her scrubs.

Vin slowed his pace. Pulled off his earphones. "Something wrong?"

"Don't slow down." Her voice was harsh. "Keep the same tempo."

Apparently she wasn't much on sharing. Oh well. He put the earbuds back in and resumed monitoring the weather channel, a firefighter's early warning necessity. It was the end of the hot season in the west and recent gusty winds had blown thick unhealthy smoke from a huge conflagration in British Columbia as far south as Idaho. Not to mention the nasty smoker in the Santa Monica mountains where he'd gotten injured. After a long dry winter and summer, the probability of more fires was imminent. And the already-poor air quality of L.A. would be tough on folks with respiratory problems. Damn. He needed to be at 100% so he could get back on the line.

From time-to-time he glanced over at Eve. She sat on a nearby bench, staring at her phone, worry lines etched the corners of her eyes. That call had definitely upset her usual stoic reserve. He wondered what could be so bad as to put a dent in her mask. And the more he saw her, the more he was confident a soft caring woman lay behind it. No one who trained to be a nurse could be all bad. He shook the thoughts away. Let her be. We all have our reasons for who we are and what we do, and hers were none of his business. He forced his attention back and pumped harder as he listened to the weatherman who spoke into his ears.

Half-hour later, bored and restless, Vin stopped the machine and dried the sweat from his face.

"Hey, Florence. You up for a change in scenery?"

Her head jerked up and she caught his gaze for the first time that morning. "Florence?"

A wide grin lit his face. "Yeah, you know. Florence Nightingale."

She smirked. "Cute."

"I thought so."

She sighed and handed him a bottle of water. "We have another hour to go. What'd you need?"

"A break." He took the water and drank half. "How about you accompany me on an outing."

Eve stared at him. "An outing?"

"Yeah. I need to go to my firehouse. See the guys and meet with the chief."

"You're not ready for a trip like that."

"And just how can I get ready if I stay in this house and never venture out into the real world? Come on, Eve. Just drop me off. I'll Uber back."

She wrinkled her forehead. "Go shower and change."

He smiled again. "Yes, Florence."

Eve's face wrinkled in annoyance. "And don't call me that again."

"Yes, ma'am." Vin gingerly stepped off the treadmill, grabbed the crutches she offered and hobbled into the adjoining bathroom.

He came out of the bedroom, showered, shaved and dressed, sans crutches, but limping using a cane. With more pressure on his nearly-bionic legs, the pain was greater, but he gritted his teeth and pushed through it. A bit unsteady, he drew upon as much strength as he could and approached his babysitter.

Eve stared at him. "And just what do you think you're doing without your crutches?"

His face muscles strained as he manufactured what he hoped was a sincere smile. "Surprise. I've been rehearsing in the apartment and am ready for the show. Gotta get back to work, honey. The fall fire season has begun."

Eve grimaced. "You seem to have a problem with my name, so I'll repeat. It's Eve. And I'd appreciate it if you'd refrain from calling me by any other. That includes Florence or honey." She stood. "And we're not leaving here until your crutches are under your arms. Am I making myself clear?"

He laughed. "Crystal. However, since there's no way my doctors will drag me back to the hospital after two weeks, you're still here because you've been very helpful. Which I fully appreciate. But I'm going to the firehouse whether you drive me or not. So what'd you say, *Eve,* friend or foe?"

*   *   *

Eve wanted to strangle him. The arrogant bastard. She should grab the opportunity to end this miserable assignment and run, not walk, out the door. She had enough stress in her life, especially since the voice mail message from Tony. What the hell was he up to? How had he gotten her phone number? If someone at the office had told him, she'd have the loose-tongued cretin fired for breaking confidentiality. Her anger boiled up.

Eve pushed all thought of her ex away and faced down the man standing on shaky legs in front of her. She really should leave him to fend for himself. Let him fall down and land back in the Hospital. That would serve him. But she couldn't deny the strength and conviction she saw in his face and heard in his voice. The man had guts. She'd give him that. And for a moment she felt sad because she'd never had the courage to spit at the crappy cards she'd been dealt. Instead she'd spent the last eighteen years wallowing in self-pity and guilt. She'd read somewhere that riding the guilt train will get you into a dark tunnel with no exit. She finally understood exactly what that meant. And Vin Ramone was a prime example of someone who'd taken that saying on face value and instead of getting sucked onto the train had manned-up and moved forward in his life.

She straightened her back against the overwhelming pain of facing her own weaknesses and choices. Determination rallied Eve's conscience. She wouldn't blame Vin Ramone for her failures.

Shaking her head, she picked up her tote bag. "Let's go."

*   *   *

Eve stayed in the car while Vin strolled toward the Santa Monica firehouse. She watched as several firemen who'd been outside tossing a football back and forth approached him. The men laughed and slapped Vin on his back, apparently happy to see him. A wave of jealousy hit her, remembering the perfunctory greetings she received from her colleagues whenever she entered her office. The fact that she had no close friends anytime, anywhere, who sincerely welcomed her presence hurt more than she would've thought. Her eyes burned with unshed tears. The raucous conversation from the firefighters as they walked into the building felt like spikes attacking her eardrums. Again she wanted to run away as fast as she could.

But instead she stayed where she was, parked at the curb eyeballing the gleaming red fire engines and a couple of white emergency ambulances, the expansive garage doors open to catch the warm salty breeze that wafted off the ocean. An impressive display of man and machine ready to respond at a moment's notice to protect their community and anywhere else they were needed.

A new thought struck her. As a home health care professional wasn't that precisely what she was committed to? Sure, she bitched and moaned about her job constantly, mostly to herself but sometimes to her boss, Les Cohen. Suddenly, painfully, she saw how split her personality was, the professional by day, the drunken slut by night. What the hell was wrong with her?

Both the realization and the question forced bile to rise. Gagging, she put a hand over her mouth to suppress the urge to vomit. Once she settled, her need to run away from the firehouse overwhelmed her. She grabbed onto the steering wheel and turned on the engine. Wheels gripped the concrete, speeding away as if pursued by demons.

Her first thought was to stop at the nearest bar she could find, but the idea of slugging down hard liquor in the morning only made her more nauseous. And her office was definitely out of the question. Cohen would wonder why she'd left her patient so early. Since she had no intention of explaining her motivation for letting Vin Ramone go off on his own, she put that whole scenario aside. Her mind frantically searched for a place of refuge, but none came to mind, only solidifying just how lost and alone she was.

As Eve turned onto California Street, a beautiful old stone structure came into view. She immediately recognized St. Monica's Catholic church where she'd spent many a morning as a young child dragged along by her mother to attend mass. A strange sense of peace filled her. Maybe within its quiet reflective walls she could put her inner demons to rest. She pulled into the nearest parking spot, left her car and slowly walked up the broad steps to the entrance of the stone church. Filled with both trepidation and slow-rising hope, she pushed open the heavy wooden doors and entered.

Warm dry air and the scent of wax from lighted votive candles immediately wrapped Eve in a comforting blanket. She stood in the back of the church for several long minutes breathing in the soothing atmosphere. Then she slowly made her way to the first row of pews, genuflected while making the sign of the cross and bent down onto the padded kneeler. Her eyes sought the six-foot crucifix on the far wall behind the altar upon which Jesus' mutilated body hung. Expecting to find condemnation in the knowing eyes that stared deeply into her very soul she cringed. But condemnation never came. Instead, love and acceptance seemed to stream outward surrounding her.

Eve vehemently shook her head, pulled her eyes away from the forgiveness and salvation the martyred man seemed to offer. No. She didn't deserve to be cleansed of her sins. There were too many. She'd hurt too many people, her family, her lovers. She'd lost her faith, rejected God's grace. And she'd allowed the darkness to take over. Her shoulders slumped. When had her slide from grace begun?

Memories long denied spewed out like a geyser reaching into the sky toward freedom. She was fourteen...the worst year of her life. Danny...they'd been so close all their lives. Warriors banned together against the onslaught of rage and neglect by their abusive father and stuck in the mire by their mother who'd taken too long to get them out of the awful situation. Even though he was only two years older than she, Danny had been her protector, the one person she could count on, talk to, who understand what she was feeling. Like that time in the schoolyard when the other kids were making fun of the old dress she was wearing, pushing her around, laughing at her. The moment Danny had seen this he'd stepped into the circle of bullies, punched two of the loudest antagonists, picked Eve up from the ground where she'd fallen and with his arm around her shoulders, walked her over to the corner of the yard and hugged her until she stopped crying.

Danny... her best friend. Her savior. Eve had been too young to realize how much he'd been suffering in their home, and the guilt when she'd realized this still pierced her gut like a dagger. He'd left her a letter begging her to forgive him, but he couldn't stay in the house any longer. He was a coward, he knew, leaving her to fend for herself, but he had to leave before he did something he'd regret. He would always love her. As soon as he got himself settled somewhere else, he'd come and get her and together they'd be happy and safe.

Eve had dropped the letter and ran to his room. The bed was still made up, the dresser drawers pulled out and empty. She couldn't breathe. She felt as empty as his bedroom. Hollow. Alone. Petrified. Abandoned just like with her father. She'd gone back to her room, flung herself on her bed and sobbed herself to sleep.

Now in the quiet of the church, Eve's body shook. She squeezed her eyes shut but tears streamed down anyway. Like a dying person, the proverbial years of her miserable empty life flicked through her mind. The alcohol and nameless men she'd hoped would fill the deep hollows of her soul.

Sensing someone beside her, the flashbacks stopped. Through swollen eyes she noticed a clean handkerchief being placed in her hand. Eve sucked in a shaky breath and turned to stare into the gentle brown eyes of an old priest.

"Thought you might need this." His voice was soft.

Eve continued staring at him, embarrassed, not sure what to do or say. But seeing the kindness in his lined face, she accepted the hanky and wiped her eyes.

"Thank you," she whispered.

He smiled, slid onto the pew and looked up at the crucifix. "I often find myself burdened with life's challenges. It's only when I kneel and give over my worries to Him, admit I can't do it all myself, that I feel my courage returning."

Eve took another calming breath and hiccupped. "You're lucky."

"Luck has nothing to do with it. It's only a matter of surrendering my stubborn ego and acknowledging my shortcomings."

Eve snickered. "If you mean failures, I have too many to name."

"I'm sure you're no different from the rest of us. We all feel hopeless from time to time."

She turned her eyes and scanned the church. Cool plaster walls that kept out the Southern California heat. High vaulted ceiling supported several antique lighting fixtures. Highly lacquered wooden pews and confessional boxes. The empty choir loft and massive organ at the back. Her eyes returned to the priest.

"My mother used to drag me here every Sunday and holiday as a child. She prayed her rosary every night. She's the strongest woman I know. Yet she suffered for years. God never answered her prayers."

"It's easy to judge a life by looking from the outside. But only God really knows what's in our hearts."

His kind expression triggered an angry response in Eve. "I don't know where God was those days, Father, but I was there and know what I saw."

He frowned. "You were a child, too young to understand the concept of faith."

With each word the old priest spoke, Eve found herself slowly coming out of the self-pity, self-flagellation fog she'd been under. "Well, I'm no longer a child, Father, and yet that mysterious concept still alludes me." Her protective walls returning in full force, she stood and handed the priest back his hanky. Bitterness couched her words. "Thanks for the sermon, Father, but I don't have time for more mental masturbation. But I tell you what. If I ever find the peace you say is out there for me, I'll buy you a drink." She slid past him and strolled out the church, feeling a lot stronger than she had when she'd arrived.

CHAPTER FOUR

Vin closed his front door with a bang. Eve had been right. His first excursion outside the house without crutches had almost proved too much. Pain kept shooting up his legs which had begun to weaken as the time past. He'd barely made it home.

A part of him had hoped Eve would've waited for him, but when he limped out of the firehouse and she wasn't there he really wasn't surprised. The woman was prickly if nothing else. He ordered an Uber and thankfully didn't have to wait long. Traffic wasn't bad that time of day so he was home in Venice in twenty minutes. Tired. Exhausted. But satisfied that his body had held up better than expected.

Standing in front of the open fridge, Vin grabbed a bottle of cold water and slugged down nearly half. He then searched for the leftover Kung Pao Chicken, put it in a bowl and nuked it. The spicy smell got his stomach juices going. He wolfed down an over-filled forkful when his phone rang.

"Yeah?" he said with his mouth full of the savory food.

"Is thata enna way to answer the phone? Didn't I teacha you better than that?"

Vin cringed. "Hi, Mom."

"How comea you no call me likea you said? It's been weeks since you beena home. Rosie said you visited her. You forgeta you mama's phone number? Where she lives?"

"Sorry, Mom. I've been busy. I have a nurse over here every day helping me with my exercises." Vin hated exaggerating but his mother was so relentless he had to give her an excuse she could feel good about. "Uh, why don't I come over in a couple of days. I'll make time."

"You stay. I bring lunch in two days. A nice pan of lasagna. You'll hava left-overs."

Vin wondered if he could get rid of Eve before his mother came. If Ida Ramone got a look at his gorgeous babysitter, she'd either toss her out or bring a priest the next day. Just thinking of it made Vin chuckle. He nearly choked on a forkful of Kung Pao.

"Ah, okay. Sounds good. Can't wait for some good ole home cooking."

After a few questions about his health, his mother added some long-winded updates regarding his sisters and their families and the call ended.

Vin shook his head and finished off the Kung Pao. He shouldn't be so hard on his mom. He loved her to death, but being the youngest child and the only son to boot, was a burden that had become heavier to carry since his father's death five years before. Ida hated the fact that he was in a dangerous profession. Her worry had obviously increased with his accident.

He tossed the empty container in the trash, put the bowl in the sink and limped into the living room. While he channel-surfed, his thoughts turned to Eve Mitchell. What was her deal? First she demanded he stay home and then she didn't wait outside the firehouse to find out how he'd done? The woman was a basketful of contradictions. He couldn't wait to pick her brain.

*　　*　　*

Les Cohen waved Eve into his office situated on the administrative floor of Santa Monica Hospital. She entered and sat in front of his desk, waiting nervously for him to pull his eyes off the computer and look at her. By the time she'd gotten home yesterday, she'd made up her mind. Working with Vin Ramone was too stressful. Brought up thoughts and feelings she didn't want to contemplate. Her "breakdown" the day before had proven that. So she spent hours last night going over how she would present her case to her boss without divulging her real feelings about deserting her patient. Something she'd never done.

When Cohen finally looked up, Eve handed him the paperwork on her last visit with Ramone, eliminating the fact that she'd dropped him off at the firehouse and left him there.

"How's Mr. Ramone?" Les was in his mid-fifties and his nearly white hair showed the effects of the thirty years he'd put into his career with Home Health Care. His natural empathy for their patients as well as the stress of hiring, training and sometimes firing staff showed on his lined face. Eve had to admit some of this stress came from worrying about her. For some reason, he'd taken on the role of her mentor. She had a suspicion he knew what she did after hours. At least the drinking. The man was a genius at reading people. Ergo his tough-love approach with her.

"Mr. Ramone no longer requires our services. He's now using a cane and going out of the house on his own."

Cohen frowned. "So soon?"

Eve cleared her throat. "He's a firefighter, strong and physically fit before the injury. He claims he never asked for our services from the beginning."

"Did he give you an attitude about that?"

"Not really. Appears to be a man who lets challenges roll off him."

"A handy trait." Cohen raised his eyebrows, piercing her gaze with knowing intensity. "Wish I could teach that to some of my employees."

Eve licked her lips and stared at him, lifting her chin, refusing to let his taunt get to her. They locked gazes for a long moment before he spoke.

"How did you leave it with him?"

Eve wasn't surprised by his question. Her boss had this thing about completion. "I wasn't sure how you wanted to handle it. If you feel he needs more services you can assign someone else. As far as I'm concerned, I'm finished with Mr. Ramone."

Cohen sat back in his chair watching her closely as though attempting to read some hidden agenda behind her words. Eve gave him only a blank stare. Finally he sat forward. "Okay. But I want you to go back there and tell him his case is closed. If he needs anything else, yada, yada. Then hand in the report on your final visit."

Eve was about to protest, but Cohen's hand waved her off. "Forget it. Just do it. And soon. I've got another assignment coming in for you."

"Fine," she said between gritted teeth. "Anything else?"

Cohen shook his head and shooed her out.

Eve closed the door behind her, a little harder than she'd have liked. Damn him. Why did she always feel like he was in her head, poking around, hoping to find out what made her tick? And even worse, how he could help her.

She grabbed her purse and stormed out of the office. By the time she reached her Highlander she decided she needed a break. She'd wait a couple of days before seeing Vin Ramone for his grand "completion" session. She'd check him out medically, assure him he was fine and that he didn't need any more services. Then she'd leave and close more than his front down behind her. Back to a new patient and her nightly routine which, while it filled a temporary void, really did nothing to change the direction her life was heading. And for some unknown reason that thought scared the shit out of her.

Anticipating the relief of dumping Vin Ramone, Eve decided she'd celebrate with a few drinks. Nothing much. Maybe even find a sucker to wile away the hours before she ditched him and made it home. She had all day tomorrow to recoup. Then she'd grit her teeth and visit Ramone for the last time.

*   *   *

Two days later, standing at Ramone's front door, Eve could smell the mouth-watering aroma of homecooked Italian food that wafted under the door. Garlic, basil, oregano assaulted her senses, reminding her how long it'd been since she'd had dinner at her mother's home. She hated going there. The vast amount of delicious dishes her mom cooked only reminded her of the meager amount of food she'd had as a child. That was, when food had been available at all. There were times they'd skipped a day or two between meals. Her stomach clenched at the thought.

So now standing at Ramone's door, she resented even further the final visit her boss had insisted on. Gritting her teeth, Eve rang the bell. In a few minutes the door swung open. To her surprise it wasn't her patient staring at her, but a short middle-aged woman with salt and pepper hair pulled back in a bun. It took Eve a moment to find her words.

"Um...is Vincent Ramone at home?" Eve silently hoped he was MIA so she could postpone the visit even longer.

"Thatsa my son." The woman turned and called out. "Vincent. You gotta visita." Then she turned back to Eve. "You the nurse?"

She eyed Eve up and down then smiled at her. Eve had a sneaky suspicion the woman had some kind of agenda hidden behind those wise brown eyes.

Vin came to the door. Upon seeing her, his first look of surprise quickly turned to curiosity, confusion. He looked at his watch. "Did our schedule change? You never come in the afternoon."

"Vincent. Wheresa you manners." Ida frowned and gave him a light punch on his chest then turned to smile again at Eve. "Come in. Come in. We havin' lunch." Ida took Eve's arm and gently pulled her into the living. "You likea lasagna? I made plenty. You try some."

Eve reluctantly followed the woman into the kitchen, her arm still ensnared in the older woman's small but tight grasp. "Really, I'm not hungry. I just have to speak to Mr. Ramone for a moment and then I'll leave you both to your lunch."

"Nonsense. You gotta eat. You too skinny. Beautiful, but too skinny. My husband Ralphy used to say, 'a man likesa his woman with a little meat on her bones.' She laughed "Isn't thata right, Vincent?"

Vin had seen and heard enough. He easily removed Ida's hand from Eve's arm. "Mom, I'm sure Ms. Mitchell has a full day of patients to see." He turned to Eve. "Sorry. My mother gets carried away sometimes. She forgets not everyone loves to eat as much as we do." He turned to his mother. "Why don't you dish out the lasagna? I'll speak with Eve for a few minutes and then join you." Before Ida could respond, Vin ushered Eve into the living room, closing the kitchen door behind them. He knew he'd never hear the last of this from his mother, but she had to learn the hard way that he wasn't interested in her matchmaking plans.

He motioned for Eve to sit on the sofa then dropped down into a cushioned chair across from her resting his cane on the floor. He gave her a contrite smile.

"Again, I'm sorry. My wonderful Italian mother has a tendency to get ideas fast and act upon them even faster."

He shrugged. "Only unmarried child and a son to boot. So what can I do for you? I expected to see you this morning."

Eve couldn't help but stare. He was dressed in loose-fitting jeans that hid his scarred legs. A short-sleeved red tee with some kind of firefighter logo on it screamed out from his broad chest. His hair was longer than she remembered. Or maybe she'd never really looked too hard at him, avoidance being the keyword around Vin Ramone. She sucked in her breath, even more confident than before that she was doing the right thing by releasing him from her care.

"My supervisor agrees with my reports that you are progressing nicely and no longer need our services." She tried to paste a sincere smile on her face but knew she failed miserably.

"Really?" Vin stared at her, his brow wrinkled. His intelligent eyes seemed to be scanning pictures of their past sessions as though looking for some reason other than the generic, "you no longer need us". She sensed he knew there was something deeper behind her statement, but apparently he couldn't latch onto what that was.

Eve cleared her throat and pulled paperwork out of her briefcase. "I have some termination papers for you to read and sign. If this isn't a good time, I can come back tomorrow." She had her fingers theoretically crossed behind her back hoping he'd take care of this now.

Vin glanced down at the papers and then back at her. "Why don't you leave them with me. I'd like to read them carefully before I sign."

She cringed. Damn him. "No problem." She left the papers on the coffee table and stood up. "Call me if you have any questions." She handed him a business card from her purse. "When they're ready for pickup I'll come by and get them."

This time he gave her a big smile. "Will do. Sure you don't want lasagna? I guarantee it's the best pasta you'll ever have."

Her mouth eked out a weak smile. "No thanks." She headed for the front door.

Once in her Highlander, Eve sat back against the seat and let out a frustrated breath. One more visit. Then she'd be free of Mr. Vincent Ramone. Now she only had to worry about what Tony the Ex was up to.

*   *   *

Vin ushered his mother to the waiting Uber with a good-bye-thanks-for-lunch kiss on her cheek. After she stretched her arms around his waist and gave him a big hug, she stepped into the van and waved as the car pulled away from his house.

He closed the front door, exhaling the breath he'd been holding. Those two women were going to drive him crazy. Thank God the comforting aroma of pasta lingered. His legs were tired and rather than hit the gym he decided to soak in the outdoor spa that held dominion on his small back porch overlooking the canal. Striping down to his shorts, he limped out on the deck and slowly eased himself into the hot therapeutic water. With his arms spread out on the edge of the ceramic tub, he rested his head back, closed his eyes and let his thoughts wander. He recalled the women he dated, scoring their marriage potential based on his level of emotional involvement with them. He had to admit he couldn't see himself falling in love with any of them.

He frowned when Eve Mitchell's face came front and center in his mind. Sure, she was gorgeous. Educated. Committed to helping people. And her almost surly attitude, rather than put him off, intrigued him. Compelled him to find out more about her. And whether it would lead to a long-term relationship he had no idea. But the process of finding out might be fun.

But now it appeared she'd had enough and was ending their sessions. If he wanted to pursue her it would have to be on a personal level, not a professional one. He grinned into the steamy air. All the better.

He ducked his head under the water and came up determined. He was a man who needed a project, a goal to reach, and since he couldn't get back to work for a while he'd make Eve Mitchell that project.

The cooler air wrapped around Vin's hot body as he lifted himself out of the tub. After toweling off, he reached for his cane and walked into the bedroom, showered and dressed in light-weight sweatpants and a tee. In the kitchen he grabbed a chilled bottle of water from the fridge and limped into the living room. Plopping down on the sofa, he took the TV remote in hand and was about to click on the set when he spied a matchbook on the floor. Curious, he reached down and picked it up. It read *Denny's Dive* on the cover. There was nothing else written on the outside. A full display of matches was inside.

He thought for a moment. Neither he nor his mother smoked so the matchbook must have fallen from Eve's briefcase when she pulled out the paperwork. Hmm...

He put the matchbook in his pocket for safekeeping, sensing that in the near future, he might use it as a possible means of tracking down his beautiful nurse once she dropped him.

*   *   *

Anthony Louis Parma grew more and more agitated watching the photos he'd recently taken flashed by on his laptop. Once again he appreciated the five years he'd spent in lockup, having used the time improving his computer skills. The parade of shots he'd synced together showed a clear pattern of his ex-wife's activities. She was currently working with one guy, some injured smoke-eater, then trolled Hollywood dive bars at night, often leaving with some poor bastard and finally getting home a few hours later. The fucking slut. The fact that her life had apparently gone downhill since he'd been away thrilled him to the bone. Maybe she felt guilty about turning him in to the cops after she'd discovered the ledger he kept outlining the scam he'd been running on seniors. Pretending to represent their grandkids who needed money to get out of trouble had proven very lucrative. He chuckled. Stupid old goats. They deserved to be conned. But in any case, Eve Mitchell Parma was going to pay for her betrayal.

He pulled his eyes off the screen long enough to scan the one-room studio he'd rented after leaving Wayside prison. Luckily he'd managed to hide away some of the dough he'd accumulated with his scam, but this place didn't suit him. He needed more money to get back on track. Maybe even out of town. Start over.

Then Parma remembered there was that one stop Eve had made to her mother's swanky home in Beverly Hills. Dollars signs sparkled in his mind like diamonds. He scanned his photos until the picture of the old lady's mini-mansion came into view. He smiled. Suddenly revenge looked even sweeter than it had before.

CHAPTER FIVE

The quiet, dank atmosphere of the Hollywood bar didn't register on Eve's senses. Instead she focused on absorbing enough booze to ensure a deep dreamless sleep when she finally made it home. She gulped down another shot of scotch and closed her eyes, savoring the hearty taste of premium alcohol. She planned on staying home in bed, alone, until Vin Ramone called for her to pick up his signed discharge papers. Les Cohen be damned. She'd told him before she needed a vacation but instead he'd assigned Ramone to her. And look how that had turned out.

Determining she'd reached her saturation point, she was about to pull bills out of her pocket and toss them on the bar when a spidery chill crawled up her back. A moment later she felt a thick body slid onto the seat beside her. Her defenses went on alert. Her stomach clenched as though waiting for an attack. Fight or flight choices raced through her mind, but she knew she couldn't run. So instead she stared through the mirror in front of her into the cold eyes of her ex-husband with all the courage she could muster.

"Fancy meetin' you here, darlin'." Tony Parma returned her stare through the mirror, a malicious gleam penetrating his black eyes.

Eve chose to ignore him, hoping he'd take the hint and leave. Fat chance.

"What? Nothing to say to your dear husband after five years? Tsk. Tsk. Now you've hurt my feelings."

"Ex-husband." She signaled the bartender for another drink, figuring she'd probably need a few more until the bastard was gone. "Get lost."

"I'll take whatever she's having," Tony said to the bartender and then to Eve, "You know, baby, you ain't lookin' so good these days. Maybe you been missin' me more than you want to admit."

"In your dreams." Eve continued staring at him through the mirror.

Tony grabbed the shot glass as soon as it arrived and emptied it in one gulp. "Funny you should mention dreams. Can't tell you how many nights I layed awake in the dark listening to my cellmate snore and the nightmare cries of other guys in the block. But no nightmares for me. No sir. My dreams were happy. Peaceful. Thinking about you and what I'd do to you when I got out was a real godsend. Guess I owe you some thanks after all." He cackled like the psychopath he was, playing with a captured mouse he was about to devour.

"Yeah, well don't bother. Can't say I ever thought about you at all."

He sneered and turned to face her. "You always was a lying bitch."

Eve casually sipped her scotch, refusing to let him see how threatened she felt. "What do you want, Tony?"

"Ah, the 64 million dollar question. Just wanted to give you a heads up. There's a note waiting for you at your place. Be sure to read it carefully. Give it lots of thought. Then call me." He put a ten on the bar, patted her arm, slid off the stool and strolled out whistling.

When she was sure he was gone, Eve hung her head, slumped her shoulders, closed her eyes and let out a deep breath. He left a note at her place? How did he know where she lived? And how had he found her at the bar? Remembering the two miserable years of verbal and sometimes physical abuse that had bookmarked their stormy marriage, she began to sweat. Sure, she'd gotten her revenge when she alerted the police about the con he was running, but now she wondered if the five years of freedom from him had been worth the trouble he apparently had in store for her. What did they say? Payback's a bitch?

After paying for her drinks she walked out of the bar on shaky legs. Whether that was because she was under the influence or afraid for her life she didn't know. Either way she'd find out soon enough.

*   *   *

By the time Eve got home her foggy, booze-soaked brain had cleared enough for the fear to rise and cause her steps to falter. She staggered into her apartment, a migraine raging. She was both surprised and thankful she'd gotten home without totaling her car as well as herself. As she closed the door, her foot slid on a large manila envelope knocking her off balance. She grabbed onto the small entry table to stop from falling, then reached down and picked up the envelope. Tossing her purse on the table she walked into the living room and dropped down on the sofa, continually staring at the envelope. Her heart pounded. She wanted to toss the menacing thing into the garbage and pretend she hadn't met Tony in the bar and he'd never threatened her. She knew she could do it. Hadn't most of her life been about running away from the truth, both literally and figuratively? She'd gotten good at it. But something told her that she could no longer run. Tony would find her wherever she went.

Trapped. Like that little hamster in the cage spinning on its treadmill. There was no getting off. Unless one jumped.

Maybe it was time to jump.

Fingers trembling, she opened the envelope. Several small photos fell out. She stared at each as fear crawled up from her belly to her neck. There was a picture of her outside her apartment. One of her and Ramone getting into her car. One watching Vin walk into the firehouse. One taken through the window of her mother's home showing her and Mary sitting in the kitchen. And several shots of Eve taken at night stumbling out of several dive bars hanging onto the arms of different lowlifes.

Eve dropped the photos onto the coffee table as though they burned her fingers. She sank back into the sofa. My God. The bastard had been stalking her. Were the pictures a sadistic reminder he had control over her and there was no escape? Or were they meant to be a real threat against people in her life? What the hell did he want from her?

Intent on finding answers, she sat up and searched inside the envelope. Maybe there was something...her fingers touched a small piece of paper. She pulled it out. Her heart sank. The phone number written in thick broad strokes needed no explanation. Her only choice was to decide when she'd make the call. She put her head in her hands and sobbed.

*   *   *

Early the next morning, Eve woked from a fitful sleep by the ringing of her cell phone. Half asleep, she dropped it on the floor. It took several more incessant rings before she was conscious enough to answer in a groggy voice.

"What?"

Les Cohen's disgustingly calm voice echoed in her ear. "Rise and shine Sleeping Beauty."

She groaned. "Bye, boss."

He laughed. "Before you drift back into dreamland, I wanted to let you know that Vin Ramone called. Said you could pick up the termination papers anytime this morning."

She rolled over on her back and rubbed her tired eyes. "I'm having my phone disconnected."

"Just get those papers here today. I have another client for you."

"In your dreams." She hung up, curled into a fetal position and drifted back to sleep. To hell with them both.

*   *   *

The hot shower might have brought Eve fully back into the present, but it didn't help soothe her anxiety. In front of the dressing mirror, she wiggled into tight jeans that hugged her hips and slim legs. The long-sleeved tee clung to her full breasts. The dark puffy circles under her light brown eyes told anyone who bothered to look that she was in trouble. Who should she confront first? Tony or Vin. She didn't look forward to either so she categorized her choices as good news/bad news. There was no question who headed the bad news list. So, being true to her avoidance personality, she put Tony Parma last. Getting Vin Ramone out of her life definitely seemed to warrant the good news label. And compared to the stress value her ex represented Ramone was a pesky mosquito to be swatted away.

She left the bathroom, pushing all thought of Tony Parma out of her mind, at least for the time being. She grabbed her keys and left the apartment. She'd stop at Starbucks for her morning shot of caffeine then head over to Ramone's. Hopefully he would be there and she could cross him off her to-do list once and for all.

*   *   *

This time a younger, very attractive woman answered his door. Her long dark blond hair was pulled back into a ponytail. Honey-colored eyes gave Eve a curious look. There was no denying the family resemblance to both Ramone and his mother. Probably his sister. Eve took a deep breath. Was she going to meet his entire family before she terminated his services?

"Hi. My name is Eve Mitchell. Is Mr. Ramone home?"

The woman smiled at her. "Sorry, he just left to run an errand. Can I help you?"

"He called my office to say he had some papers for me to pick up."

"Ah. You must be Vin's nurse." She stepped aside. "He'll be right back. Why don't you come in and wait." She ushered Eve into the house.

The woman reached out her hand. "I'm his sister, Rosemary. Rosie for short. Can I get you some coffee? Tea?"

"Nothing thanks."

"Have a seat. As I mentioned, Vin should be back any minute." Rosie smiled. "He was on his way out when I stopped by. Said he had to get to the cleaners before they closed. Some Asian holiday, I believe. You sure I can't get you anything?"

Eve mustered up a slight smile. "No, really. I'm fine."

Rosie pointed to the sofa. Eve sat and Rosie plopped down into the chair across from her. "Actually I'm glad I have a chance to thank you for all you've done for my brother these past few weeks." A worried shadow dusted her face. "We've been very concerned about his state of mind since the accident. I'm sure you've had a lot of experience with this sort of case...a strong healthy man who loves his very physical job suddenly told by the doctors he might never walk again." Sadness filled Rosie's eyes. "At first they wanted to amputate both legs. Of course, Vin carried on so much they where afraid he'd hurt himself by trying to get out of the bed." She sighed. "Anyway they finally agreed to try to put his legs back together." She paused. "But you probably know all this."

Eve stared at her, surprised. Nothing about any of that had been in his file. He'd always seemed so calm, easy-going. But it wasn't hard to imagine the rage that must have consumed him upon hearing the bad news from his doctors. Eve visualized the scene Rosie had described in the Hospital. Felt a sudden rush of fear for what might have happened if Vin had fallen out of bed as he thrashed around. She couldn't breathe for a moment then pushed the thoughts and feelings safely aside.

"I didn't know." She managed to say softly.

Just then the door opened and Vin entered carrying a plastic garment bag over his arm that held the cane, and a large bag of what smelled like Chinese food in the other hand. He stopped short when he spied Eve. She thought she saw his face light up. Then he smiled.

"If it isn't Nurse Cratchet. Good thing I bought plenty of food."

Rosie stared at him. "Vin. I can't believe you just called Ms. Mitchell Nurse Cratchet. Mom was right. You've lost your mind as well as your manners."

Eve wanted to laugh. His sister sounded just like their mother. Poor Vin, surrounded by so many caring but bossy women. "Don't worry. He's called me worse. Just a little game we like to play."

"Ah, shucks, Eve. You gave me away." He smiled. "Come on let's eat. Food's getting cold." Without waiting for a response, Vin tossed his clothes on the back of the sofa and limped into the kitchen.

Rosie watched him then shook her head. "Don't even try to object. My brother can be a spoiled little boy from time to time, but that's really his charm." She stood. "Join us." And followed Vin.

Eve was exasperated. Spoiled little boy. No kidding. A part of her wanted to tell him to go to hell and walk out the door. Another part felt drawn to him. Impossible. Must be the delicious aroma of hot Chinese food that clouded her mind. She shook her head and headed for the kitchen.

CHAPTER SIX

Rosie smiled and pointed to one of the padded wooden kitchen chairs. "Have a seat. I'll put on tea."

Again that trapped feeling tightened Eve's chest. She stood ramrod straight watching Rosie and Vin move about the small kitchen. He grabbed plates out of a cabinet. After putting green tea bags in the boiling water from a kettle, Rosie found utensils in a drawer. Vin was much taller than his sister but even with his cane and limp his movements were smooth and graceful. Eve felt her heart quicken as she stared at him. The moment he looked at her she jerked her attention to the table and sat quickly down, but not before she noticed a strange look in his eyes. No longer the look of a patient toward his nurse, but rather that of a friend. She swallowed. If only she could get through this damn lunch she'd never see him again. The thought helped her relax.

Vin sat down and heaped steamy shrimp in garlic sauce and vegetable fried rice onto his plate. "Don't be shy. Help yourself." He waved his fork toward her before stuffing a pink shrimp in his mouth.

Rosie poured hot tea into their mugs, sat down and started filling her plate. The aroma was too compelling for Eve to resist. She shook her head, sighed, and reached for the serving spoon.

Between forkfuls Rosie spoke. "So tell me about yourself, Eve. How did you get into nursing?"

Vin pointed his shrimp-laden fork at Eve. "You don't have to answer that. Rosie loves to pry but is short on sharing. I've been trying to find out for years why my sister decided to become a shrink."

"And I told you a million times how it was my only way to make a decent law-abiding citizen out of you."

"Come on. I wasn't that bad."

"What about the time you stole a stop sign in the dead of night? Or removed a picture of President Reagan from the high school hallway. And those stray cats and dogs you occasionally hid in your room until the smell was overwhelming." Rosie curled up her nose. "Not to mention the time you insisted on getting a mohawk." She let out a chuckle and looked at Eve. "Vin was already over six feet in high school. Can you imagine a big guy like that adding another four inches on the top of his head?"

Vin turned his attention to Eve. "See what I mean. Just normal teenage boy stuff. Being the oldest she always thought she had to lighten our parents' burden by taking on the job of fixing me."

"Kept you out of jail a few times, didn't I." Fried rice found her mouth.

Eve couldn't stop staring with wonder at the two of them. Was this what it was like to have a typical family where siblings teased each other through laughing eyes and harmless words? She couldn't wrap her mind around the concept, so foreign was it from her own childhood experience where alcohol and abuse dampened the family fun.

"Sounds wonderful," she whispered before she realized it had slipped out.

Eve noticed the conversation had stopped and Vin and Rosie were watching her. She felt her face get hot and wished she could drop down into a deep dark hole where faces and memories couldn't be found.

Rosie broke up the silence. "Sorry for all our teasing." She raised an eyebrow in apology. "It's so natural for us. We get carried away sometimes and forget anyone who didn't know us would probably think we're nuts."

Vin grinned at Eve. "See. Told you. The reason Rosie when to shrink school."

Eve was quick to regain her stoic composure. Straightening her back she gave them a weak smile. "No problem."

Rosie continued eating. Vin's gaze remained fixed on Eve, much to her discomfort. She wished she could burrow into his head and find out what he was thinking. She decided to take on some false bravado and answer Rosie's original question.

"Actually, my mother was a social worker in the helping profession. Guess I just felt it was a way of carrying on a family tradition." Yeah, right. It was either follow Mary or Eve's very dysfunctional father.

"What field is your father in?" Rosie asked.

"Drunk and disorderly." Eve's deadpan expression gave nothing away.

Silence reigned for a few moments.

"So. How about those RAMS?" Vin's mention of L.A.'s hot football team almost brought a sigh of relief to Eve, not to mention a slight curve to her mouth. It washed away the thickening air that seemed to have enveloped the kitchen. The fact that now she owed him wasn't going to make it any easier to walk away. That link would always be there.

Eve slipped on her professional mask. "I understand you signed the papers I left with you."

Rosie gave them a curious look. "What papers?"

"We're terminating home health care for your brother."

"Is that wise?" Eve frowned. "Doesn't he need more follow-up?"

"Ignore my sister. She still treats me like a scrawny kid instead of a Marine and a firefighter."

"Who jumped out of a plane into a raging fire like an insecure teen trying to prove how brave he was."

"Not my fault the wind changed."

Eve watched both of them intrigued as words volleyed back and forth. She was learning so much about Vin.

Rosie shrugged. "I'll give you that." She refilled their mugs with hot tea.

After finishing off two huge portions of shrimp and rice Vin set his plate aside.

Rosie turned her gaze to Eve's plate. "You've hardly eaten a thing. Not a fan of Chinese food?"

"It was very good. I'm just not hungry."

Vin reached into the bag and pulled out three fortune cookies. "This is the best part of a Chinese meal."

Rosie took hers and with a childish smile of anticipation, split it and removed the thin white strip of paper. *"With A happy disposition comes peace and joy."* She wrinkled her nose. "Corny." Then pursed her lips and feigned disappointment.

Vin read his. *"All possibilities await your choices."* He paused as if deciding what the saying could mean, then turned to Eve. "You're next."

Unnerved by his look and hating those stupid fortunes cookies, Eve reluctantly cracked open hers and read, *"Keep your heart open and love will find you."* She dropped the paper onto the table as if the words burned her fingers. "You're right, Rosie. Corny as hell." Enough was enough. She stood and looked at Vin. "I have another appointment," she lied. "Do you have the papers?"

"In the living room." He stared at her then stood and limped out of the kitchen.

Eve watched him and turned to Rosie. "Thanks for lunch. It was nice meeting you." She started to follow Vin but then turned and looked at Rosie. "Vin is lucky to have you." She left the kitchen.

Vin handed her the paperwork. Without reviewing them she stuffed them into her briefcase and walked toward the front door, Vin on her heels. As he grabbed the doorknob he said with a small smile, "I really appreciate all you did for me. I'd like to take you to lunch to thank you properly."

Her eyes drilling into the door, she refused to look at him. "Not necessary. Just doing my job. Stay healthy." She yanked his hand off the doorknob and flung open the door, feeling his intense stare on her back as she got into her SUV.

*   *   *

Vin strolled back into the kitchen and reclaimed his chair, watching his sister clean up the remains of lunch, putting plates and utensils in the dishwasher. When she was finished, she joined him at the table, folding her hands on the smooth wood top.

"Mom was right. Your nurse is a knockout. Must have been an interesting few weeks working with her." She seemed to watch for his reaction.

"Yeah, well don't get your hopes up. Ms. Eve Mitchell is a complicated woman with lots of secrets."

"I guessed that by some of her reactions. But then you never did like things easy. So I'll say no more."

Vin grunted. "That'll be the day."

"I gotta go. Brian said he'll be home early. We're planning a getaway to Santa Barbara for the weekend."

Rosie got up and ruffled his hair. "I'll let myself out." She bent and kissed his cheek. "Good luck."

Vin shook his head. Damn woman. Her instincts were too sharp, but that was why she was so good at her job. He couldn't deny Rosie her impressions, although he'd never admit that to her. Eve Mitchell definitely presented a challenge and now that he was no longer her patient he was free to take her on.

*   *   *

By the time Eve got home she was exhausted. She put her briefcase on the entry table and headed to the kitchen and her stash of scotch. Standing in front of the sink, she gulped down several shots. After the warm smooth liquid caressed her throat all the way to her belly the tightened muscles finally relaxed. The entire visit with Vin and his sister had been an emotional disaster. She'd been tossed up, down and around like a speeding rollercoaster, never reaching the end of the ride until her SUV tires had screeched away from his house.

She went into her bedroom and threw herself down on the bed, still unmade from the restless night before. Grabbing a pillow she hugged it to her chest as she curled into a fetal position. For a second she was transported back to her childhood remembering all the times she'd found similar comfort, but then it had been an old battered stuffed bear she'd clung to. When had her soft cuddly friend turned into a bottle of scotch?

Her head spun. She barely felt the tears roll down her cheeks as she fell into a turbulent sleep.

CHAPTER SEVEN

Eve sat at a corner table in an outdoor café sipping hot steaming latte loaded with caffeine and sugar. She watched men and women dressed in California business casual and tourists speaking several languages jam the crowded Westwood Village sidewalks. And then there were the usual groups of UCLA students in shorts and tees loaded down with backpacks on their way to and from campus. Everyone strolled carefree, cheerful, under the welcoming southern sun, blissfully unaware of the fear that raged inside Eve, tearing her body, her world apart.

She'd finally ratcheted up her nerve and made the ominous call to Tony. The moment she'd heard his slimy voice and heart-stabbing threat, she'd slammed the phone down and raced from her condo seeking solace from someone, someplace. It wasn't until she'd slumped down on the wrought-iron chair at the café that she had to face the fact there was no one to whom she could turn and no place she could find to be safe. She was alone. Lost. Desperate.

Tony's threat hadn't been physical. It had been financial. His voice was gruff and oily when he explained the situation as he saw it.

"You owe me, baby. I lost five-years' worth of income when you ratted me out and sent me to lockup. And then there was the pain and suffering angle."

Eve's anger rose. "Forget it. I didn't run that con. And you're lucky you only got five years. Whatever happened is on you."

Tony ignored her. "Since I'm on the short end of the third-strike rule I decided that hurting you wouldn't get me what I need. I'm looking to start over someplace else and to do this I need seed money. So," he paused, his voice dripping with menace, "I figure a nice round sum of $50,000 should cover everything."

Eve's heart dropped. Fifty thousand dollars. "You're crazy. I don't owe you anything."

"This isn't a negotiation, bitch. You come up with the cash or I'll call on your mom and let her know just what kind of woman her little girl turned out to be. Does 'drunken slut' sound familiar?"

The thought of her mother finding out about Eve's late-night activities caused her sweat glands to ring the bell at the top of the thermometer. She pictured Mary's look of fear and then revulsion on her face when Tony visited her. Eve couldn't let that happen. But where the hell was she going to get the money?

"I don't have that much."

"Tough shit. You've got a rich stepfather don't you? Talk to him. I'm sure he wouldn't want me bothering his dear little wife with all this."

"But..."

"Just make it happen." His voice hissed over the phone, stingy her ears, making her shudder. "And don't even think about going to the cops. If I find out you did, I'll take my chances with a third strike and make you an orphan. You got one week. Am I clear?"

Eve couldn't speak.

"You there, bitch?"

"Yes." She whispered.

"Thata girl." His hideous chuckle sent shivers down her back. "Happy hunting." He hung up.

Even now, hours later, Eve felt as though a cataclysmic eruption had Mt. Vesuviused her world, tossing her down into the belly of the beast. She'd never felt so hopeless. That bottle of sleeping pills on her nightstand looked more inviting than ever. So this was it. The culmination of all the lousy choices she'd made in the last ten years with no end in sight. Two bad marriages, booze and meaningless sex. Guess what goes around does come around.

Staring into space, oblivious to the crowds that strolled by, Eve sensed, rather than saw, a shadowy figure of a large man slid into the chair opposite her. At the sound of his deep voice, she faced the figure and blinked several times before recognizing Vin Ramone, his face awash with surprise and...was it concern?

"Hello? Earth to Eve."

His voice vibrated like an echo in her brain. Desperately trying to pull herself out of the deep quagmire, she stammered. "I...huh...what?"

"I called you several times. You seem out of it. Are you alright?"

"Ah...yeah...peachy." She ignored the worried look in his eyes, turned again and ogled the pedestrians.

"Hmm. Haven't heard that one for a while."

Ignoring him she started to rise but his hand shot out and grabbed her wrist.

"Sorry, Eve. Just trying to erase the dark cloud I see hovering around you."

If her eyes were daggers he'd be dead.

"Truthfully, you look like a sad, lost puppy."

The sincerity in his eyes caused Eve to suck in a sharp breath. She gritted her teeth and returned to her seat. Vin hadn't released her wrist, but loosened his grasp, his thumb brushing her skin. Her heart quickened. She needed a change of subject fast.

"What brings you to Westwood?"

"I gave a presentation on fire safety at one of the sorority houses." A small smile curved his mouth. "My chief figured I was good for something until I can get back to fighting fires so I'm talking about them instead."

"How soon before that will happen?" Keeping the focus on his career rather than herself, she nonchalantly extracted her wrist from his hold.

He lost his smile. "Soon I hope. I might not be able to jump out of planes anymore but I can still man a truck."

"Must be tough having to give up something you love."

"Yeah, well. Life sucks sometimes. But the options are either adjust or sink into a black hole that's nearly impossible to get out of."

Yanked back into her previous dark mood, Eve sighed. Ah, the story of her miserable life.

Vin squinted. "I'm guessing you know something about black holes." When she remained silent, he pressed on. "Feel like talking about it?"

She snickered. "You sound like your sister. Sure you don't have an honorary shrink license hanging on a wall somewhere?"

"Yikes. Touche. I figured now that we've ended our professional relationship we could move onto the next step."

"And just what would that be?"

"Friends."

"Why would you want to be friends with me?" Eve said.

Vin shrugged. "I appreciate all you did for me, and when I saw you just now you looked like you'd lost your best friend. Just wanted to offer my services."

The gigantic effort to push down the rays of light that drifted up from her soul caused Eve's throat to close. Truth was, unless he had an extra 50k hanging around, there was nothing he could do to help.

"No thanks." She drained her cooled latte. "I've gotta go. See you around."

"Running away? Something tells me you do a lot of that."

She felt her cheeks turn bright red with anger. "And what business of that is yours?"

"No one can have enough close friends."

"And you're volunteering? No thanks. Go back to your sorority chicks. I'm sure they're all dying to take advantage of any service you might offer."

Vin grinned and sat back against the chair, his hand over his heart. "Whoa. Low blow."

Eve was getting more and more pissed. This time she did stand and lance him with her eyes. "You can drop the Prince Charming or Knight in Shining Armour or any other role you want to play with me, Vin. You were my patient and I was your nurse. That's all. It's over. And I'm not interested in being your friend."

He held her gaze for a long moment. "I'm not the one playing a role here, Eve, and one of these days you're going to run out of the energy you need to keep up your tough 'I don't give a damn' attitude. Because from what I can see you're close to killing off that sensitive, caring woman you try so hard to cover up." He stood. "For some reason I care about you. And I'd like to be around to pick up the pieces when that happens."

Totally freaking out now, Eve tossed her empty mug at his chest and stormed away, knocking her chair out of the way.

*   *   *

Vin watched through the crowd until he could no longer see Eve's retreating back. He dropped down into his seat. Dammit, he was worried about her. When he spied her sitting at the café he'd been shocked at the expression on her face. The closest he'd ever come to seeing someone with a similar look was at that call the year before. He'd pulled a woman out of a roaring fire that had entirely destroyed her home and taken the life of her husband and daughter. To boot, he'd found out later they'd had no insurance. Total loss. Desolation. Despair. He often wondered what had happened to her.

His mind shifted again. Eve. His beautiful, haunted nurse. Pain waves rolled off her like a thundering tsunami. What was going on with her? He had to find out before she self-destructed. For he was sure she was headed that way.

CHAPTER EIGHT

Using the business card Eve had given him, Vin wound his way to Santa Monica Hospital's top floor. After much consideration, he decided to speak to her boss, Les Cohen. Maybe if Vin could convince the man of his concerns about Eve's state of mind, Cohen would be willing to bend the privacy rules. He shrugged when he opened the door marked HOME HEALTH CARE. It was worth a try.

Vin gave the receptionist his most compelling smile. Might've even limped more than usual, hoping to gain the sympathy vote. He knew from experience getting past women that guarded back offices from invasion was the key. "I don't have an appointment, but I'd like to speak with Mr. Cohen if he's available."

She smiled back, apparently taken in by the tall charming man who leaned heavily on his cane in front of her. "Your name, sir?"

"Vincent Ramone. I used to be a patient with HHC."

"If you take a seat over there," pointing a polished red fingernail to a row of metal chairs, "I'll see if Mr. Cohen has time to meet with you." She reached for the phone.

Vin nodded and limped to a chair. A few minutes later, a middle-aged man of medium height and weight with a mane of thick white hair approached him, hand outstretched.

"Les Cohen, Mr. Ramone. What can I do for you?"

Vin stood and shook the man's hand. "I'd like to speak to you for a moment regarding Eve Mitchell, the nurse you assigned to my case."

Gulleys spread across Cohen's forehead. After giving Vin a lengthy appraisal he nodded. "Why don't you follow me to my office?"

Once inside, Cohen closed the door and offered Vin a chair in front of a large metal desk.

"Eve turned in your termination papers to me yesterday. Is there a problem now?"

"No. Not with me." Vin gave Eve's boss a calm direct look. "I'll be truthful with you, Mr. Cohen. "Eve helped me tremendously getting used to managing with my new legs. I feel I owe her something. I'm concerned about her and want to help."

Cohen looked confused. "I don't understand."

Vin wasn't sure how to handle the conversation. He knew he had to tread lightly or alienate any chance of getting Cohen's help. After a short pause he pressed on.

"I'm going out on a limb here, Mr. Cohen, so I'll make it simple." Vin took a deep breath. "I think Eve's in trouble. When we initially started working together she was cool, professional and unflappable. I admit I was a bit of a pain in the ass but she just ignored my moods. The last week she was on edge, refused to have eye contact, her sentences short. Seemed preoccupied. Nervous. The few times I caught her looking at me I saw fear in her eyes before she turned away quickly. And now she decided I didn't need her assistance anymore." He paused. "I was wondering if you knew if she was alright, or if something had happened to her." Then he added, "I care about her."

Cohen stared at him, his frown deepening. Had Vin gone too far? Maybe honesty wasn't the best policy after all. He was suddenly embarrassed. Fear clung to the edge of his growing anxiety. Dammit, he'd blown his chance. What now?

                    *   *   *

Cohen sat back in his chair. Ramone's words had knocked the breath out of him. He took a few moments to consider them. Recalled the last two times he'd seen Eve. Rather than her usual prickly self, she had seemed shaken, unsure, angry. At the time Cohen hadn't paid any attention to her attitude change. He'd been in business mode and failed to take the time to notice and question her. He cursed himself. Some mentor he was. It took a near stranger to bring Eve's demeanor to his attention. Now he was worried.

He sat forward again. "I'm ashamed to say I wasn't aware until now that Eve was having problems. She's usually so tough on the outside it's easy to forget she has feelings like the rest of us." He sighed. "She's taking a few days off until her next assignment. "I'll give her a call. See if I can get her to open up."

"Sir, I was hoping you'd let me talk to her." He gave the man a quirky smile. "Seems like I always trigger an emotional response from her. Usually annoyance or anger. Maybe she'll let me in. I know it's against your privacy policy but I'm worried about her. I want to help."

Cohen used his excellent people skills honed by years of working with patients and staff to read Vin's face, his eyes. There was something there that assured him Vin Ramone was telling the truth. Maybe, just maybe, the man could get through to Eve. After all the years he'd worked with her, he'd never been able to pierce that thick shell she kept around her heart.

He tapped his fingers on his desk, watching Ramone. Eventually Cohen came to a decision, one he hoped he'd never regret. He turned to his computer and after punching in a few keys, grabbed a pen and wrote down an address and phone number.

"This goes against all my principles, but something tells me you'd be the one to finally get to Eve. God knows I haven't been very successful." He handed Ramone the slip of paper.

The young man looked down at it, then up at Cohen. "Thanks. I won't abuse the trust you've just handed me. You have my word."

Cohen stood. "If I hear you've taken advantage of Eve I'll come after you with all the resources I have. I care about her, too."

Vin stuck out his hand and nodded. Leaning on his cane, he limped out.

*   *   *

Even the constant ringing of the phone couldn't pull Eve out of her alcoholic stupor. Ignoring the screeching that seemed to pierce her skull she rolled over onto her side and pulled the pillow over her head. Colors swirled around in her mind's eye. She clung to the covers with tight fists to keep from falling off the bed. When she couldn't stand the noise any longer she reached for the phone on her nightstand, her shaking hand knocking over the empty bottle of scotch. She barely recognized her own gravelly voice. "Leave me alone, Tony. I'll get it for you. Just leave me alone." Hiccuping a begging sob, Eve flung the phone across the room and sank lower under the warmth of the covers, until sleep grabbed her, shutting everything off.

*   *   *

Vin knocked several times on the front door of Eve's Westwood condo. Putting his ear against the lightly stained wood door he didn't detect any sound, but he knew she was in there. She'd finally answered his calls, mumbling a short almost indecipherable sentence. He then heard the phone bang on the hardwood floors. Something was definitely wrong and he'd get into her apartment even if he had to break down the door.

"Eve. I know you're in there. It's Vin. Open the door." He paused. "Please." Not wanting to scare her off he tried to hide the concern he felt.

Several minutes passed. Slowly he heard the locks disengage. The door opened a few inches, held in place by a metal chain.

"What'd you want?" She spoke in a thick groggy voice.

"Les Cohen gave me your address. We're worried about you."

"Damn him," she muttered. "I'm fine. Just a cold. Now go away."

"Not until I see for myself you're okay."

"Why's my wellbeing so important to you? Your case is closed, remember. I don't want to see you again."

"Eve. Why don't we continue this conversation inside? You don't want your neighbors to know your business, do you?"

Silence. After a long pause the chain dropped off and the door opened. By the time Vin got into the room, Eve was already back in bed curled up under the comforter.

Vin quickly scanned the bedroom. Even though only tiny fingers of light crept in through the closed wooden shutters, he could see the room was a mess. Clothes were littered about on a chair, the floor, across the bed. An empty scotch bottle rested next to another alongside the bed. He saw no sign of cold medication on the nightstand.

Eve lay in the middle of the bed in a fetal position, hugging a pillow. He approached and sat down, wiping a long strand of soft hair away from her face.

She pulled away from his hand. "Don't touch me."

"Are you really sick? I can take you to Urgent Care."

"Just tired. You should leave."

Vin looked down at the empty bottles on the floor. "Tired, huh. Anyone ever tell you you were a lousy liar?"

"Just a few shrinks over the years. No one else's bothered to point that out." She kept her eyes shut as she mumbled into another pillow. "Not that I'm complaining. I get off on fooling everyone."

"Ah, yes. I can see how satisfied you are." He paused. "You know, Eve. I think you're beginning to realize you can no longer fool yourself. Whatever's been eating you up is starting to take over. A seething volcano waiting to erupt. You're about to hit bottom, if you haven't already."

Sweat peppered her forehead. Her face twisted as in a desperate attempt to stave off the emotional explosion waiting to happen. She gripped the pillow tighter against her chest.

"And you're what...my savior?"

"Firefighter here. Besides putting out fires, I rescue cats out of trees. Damsels in distress out of burning buildings. Can't help it. It's in my genes."

"I don't need you or anyone else to rescue me. So get lost."

Vin chuckled. "Sorry, kiddo. No can do."

Frustration seemed to be taking over Eve's emotions. "I want you to leave. NOW."

"I'm not going anywhere."

She started to tremble. Then pulled herself into a sitting position and began punching him in his chest. He absorbed her weak hits, letting her release some of the anger she'd been holding in for God knew how long. Her chest heaved. After a while her pummeling slowed. Her shoulders slumped. Sensing a hint of surrender, Vin wrapped his arms around her, holding her tightly.

"Let it go, baby," he whispered. "It's all right. I'm here. I'll keep you safe."

The dam burst and a flood of tears ran down her face. She shook with deep retching sobs, fisting her hands in his shirt as if letting go would send her careening down some bottomless pit. Vin was silent, letting her vent without interruption. Meanwhile, his hands moved gently up and down her back in a soothing motion.

She pulled her head away from his chest. "I'm going to be sick."

He drew her into his arms, stood on shaky legs and walked into the bathroom, ignoring his cane that lay on the bedroom floor. She knelt down on the ceramic tiles and emptied her stomach, while Vin held her hair away from her face and rubbed her back. He visualized more than food and alcohol spewing out. Hoped that some of the anger and pain she'd hidden away was also going into the toilet.

When her body relaxed, he flushed and reached for a facecloth, dampened it and handed it to her. She sat back on her heels.

He wished he had his healthy legs back so he could kneel behind her and hold her. But he couldn't. Not yet. So he pulled down the toilet seat, sat on it, and lifted her onto his lap. Rather than fight him, she sank into his arms, wrapped hers around his waist, her rapid heartbeat slowing. She hiccupped sobs away.

It seemed like hours passed before she gained the ability to speak coherently.

"You're a fool. You should've walked away the minute you signed the termination papers."

"No one ever accused me of being smart. Just steadfast and determined."

She pushed away, stood and walked out of the bathroom. For the first time he realized she wore only a lacy white bra and matching thong that rode up between her shapely buttocks and wrapped around hips that swayed when she walked. He shook all sexual thoughts out of his head and followed her into the small kitchen, leaning against the doorway for support, legs throbbing, arms folded across his chest. She seemed unconscious about her near nakedness which was all right with him since he enjoyed watching her move.

Eve rummaged through several cabinets before slamming her hands on the counter. "Shit."

"Out of booze?" He asked.

"Fuck you."

"Maybe another time. Right now I want you to tell me who Tony is."

What he could see of her profile turned white. She hung her head down, her hands resting on the counter as if holding herself up. She seemed to be breathing heavier again.

"Tony who?" She whispered.

"When you finally answered my numerous calls, you said, and I quote, 'Leave me alone, Tony. I'll get it for you. Just leave me alone.'"

"None of your business."

"Steadfast and determined. Remember? I'm making it my business."

"Who asked you?"

Vin hobbled to her, put his hands on her shoulders and turned her to face him. "We've already established that you don't want me here, I'm not very smart, you wished I'd left you alone and you want to fuck me. So enough bullshit. Who's Tony? And what's he got on you that makes you numb out on booze and hide under the covers?"

After staring at him for a long while, she pulled away, strolled into the living room and sat on the sofa, wrapping a thick paisley throw around her body. Her mask of defiance slipped away and Vin saw a vulnerability in her haunted eyes and beautiful face he'd never seen before. He joined her in the living room, and sat back in a chair waiting for her to speak.

"Tony Parma. My ex-husband." She looked up at him to check out his reaction. He remained quiet and patient, so she continued.

"He just got out of prison and wants some money from me so he can get out of town and start over."

Vin frowned. "That's it? A loan. He wants a loan and that turned you into a Sylvia Plath wannabe?"

She snickered. "More like blackmail."

"Blackmail?"

"Yeah. Seems the bastard's a wee bit angry that I put the cops on him and sent him away."

"Why blackmail? Sounds more like revenge. What's he got on you?"

She stared at the wall across from him and slowly shook her head. "Let's just say I've made some bad choices in my life and he's rubbing my face into them. Leave it at that."

Eve stared at him and finally shook her head, closed her eyes and sank farther back into the sofa. "You won't let it go, will you?"

Vin remained stoic. It was up to her now. Time to take that first step toward the healing he knew she had to do. He mentally crossed his fingers.

CHAPTER NINE

Swirling in the blackness behind her eyelids, Eve felt her heart pounding. Drums foreshadowing a cataclysmic disaster. The end of the world. At least the world as she knew it. She saw herself standing on the edge of a precipice staring down into the raging red fires of the earth's core. Pulling her forward. Offering an end to it all. Fear sent smoldering lasers of light piercing every part of her body. She sucked in a gulp of air to calm the rising panic.

After a few seconds her rational mind took over. She blinked several times and the horrible scene disappeared. When her eyes focused her gaze fell on the man sitting across from her. Vincent Ramone. The embodiment of strength, courage and reason, all of which had never played a part in her life. He now appeared as someone she could trust. Someone who'd never betray her, use her. In short...hurt her. Maybe there was a way to avoid the hell she'd imagined earlier. Maybe the end that was coming could also be the beginning of a more honest, satisfying, nurturing life. She debated the possibility of believing in such a transformation for only a moment before she admitted she had no choice if she wanted to really live.

Still wrapped in the throw, she rose from the sofa and went to the hall table, pulled open the drawer and removed a large manila envelope. Walking back to Vin she handed it to him and regained her seat on the sofa, tucking her feet under her. "They say a picture is worth a thousand words."

He looked at her, raised his eyebrows and then opened the envelope. His expression didn't change until he saw the ones of her in her drunken state with her nightly lovers. At that his eyes got hard. Lips pulled tight. Jaw clenched. Eve nearly flinched waiting to feel the blows from his accusing words.

"Fucking bastard." He growled, staring at the pictures.

She bit her bottom lip still waiting but nothing came.

"Your ex took these?"

She nodded, like a kid caught combing the dog's hair with her mother's toothbrush.

"And this is your mother?"

Again she nodded.

"And if you don't meet his terms she gets a special delivery package under her door." He shook his head. "How much does he want?"

Relief suddenly slackened her tense body. He wasn't judging her. He was angry with Tony. Tears burned behind her eyelids. She hugged herself to keep from sinking into the sofa.

"Fifty K." She whispered.

"Fucking bastard," he repeated. He put the pictures back in the envelope, tossed them on the coffee table and rose.

The silence in the room sucked out the oxygen, constricting her breathing. Vin paced, hands in his pockets, face a hard mask of concentration. Finally he stopped and sat beside her.

"We can't let him win. We have to come up with a plan."

She shook her head quickly. "There's no 'we' here. I have to. This isn't your problem. I'll figure something out."

"When I said I wasn't leaving, I meant it. We'll do this together."

"No. It's my mess to clean up. I haven't led a very virtuous life and you don't need this crap in yours."

"I don't care why you made the choices you did. We all make mistakes." He took her hands in his. "There was some truth to what my sister Rosie said the other day about why I made that jump. I thought I was bulletproof. Nothing would ever slow me down. I was aiming for a Lieutenant spot. Wanted to impress the big boys. And look where that mistake got me." He squeezed her hands. "We'll work on a plan and get this asshole out of your life once and for all."

Eve didn't realize the hidden tears now ran down her cheeks. She suddenly had an understanding of the words the priest had told her recently. Maybe God really was out there, waiting for her to accept the grace he offered. Maybe He was working through the man sitting in front of her, holding her hands, his dark eyes filled with purpose and resolve. All she had to do was surrender her stubbornness, her need to protect herself, to push people away. But she was afraid to let go of what had protected her for so long. Yet if there was the slightest chance...She had to test him the only way she knew.

Eve leaned over and kissed him, moving her lips seductively across his, licking them, wanting access to his mouth. She heard his heart quicken. He opened and their tongues danced. He tasted like gentle spring air full of promise. She moved closer and cradled his face. His hands moved to her waist and he held her lightly.

It wasn't long before Eve's passion erupted and she wanted more. Her lips moved to his cheeks, his neck, his throat and back to his mouth. She wrapped her arms around his neck and clung to him hoping to stop the freefalling emotions that threatened to consume her.

Suddenly Vin's hands left her waist and grabbed hold of her arms, pulling them away from his neck. He pushed her back and stared at her through eyes that mirrored her own desires.

Dazed, surprised, she frowned. "What...what's wrong? Why'd you stop?"

"You don't want to do this."

"Of course I do." Eve moved closer to gain his lips again, but he shook his head.

"You don't have to seduce me, Eve. I want you, but not now, not like this. When we do make love, and believe me we will, you'll be in a bed and it will be love, not just sex for sex sake. I won't use you that way."

Myriad emotions swam through Eve. The need to complete what she'd started. Frustration at the thwarted attempt to get release from all the tension that riddled her. Disappointment. Embarrassment. Gut-wrenching shame. What a fool she'd made of herself. Then slowly her faithful friend and protector, anger, took over and rage flushed her face a deep red. No man had ever refused her before. Who did he think he was, anyway?

She pulled her hand back to slap him, but he was quicker and grabbed her wrist. Seething she pushed away and marched to the door, the throw dropping on the floor, leaving her standing there nearly naked. "You've worn out your welcome. Get out and don't come back." She pulled on the knob and the door swung open.

Vin stood and stared at her as though he could see into her very soul. His calm demeanor infuriated her even more.

"I mean it. GET OUT!"

"I'll be back when I have a plan. In the meantime, I suggest you don't speak to your ex. Let him worry for a change." He went to the door, bent and kissed her softly on her lips. "Remember. You're not alone anymore."

*   *   *

Eve slammed the door so hard behind Vin, she was surprised it didn't come loose from its hinges. She didn't care if he could hear the pounding of her fists on the door as Hulky rage consumed her. Broke skin on her knuckles. Not until the red drops that dripped from her raw joints shocked her out of the haze of violence did she slowly slip back into reality. With a heaving chest she stormed into the kitchen and ran cold water over her still-clenched fists. Shutting off the water, she turned and slid down to the floor, leaned back exhausted against the cabinets. She closed her eyes and finally her pulse slowed. Tension seeped out of her body. Taking humongous breaths of air, she finally settled.

Vin's strong handsome face filled her mind. He now represented more of a problem to her than Tony. She'd wanted to test him. And Goddammit, he'd passed with flying colors. What was she going to do about him?

*   *   *

Tony Parma watched Eve's lover leave her condo and get into his truck. He put the camera with the long-distance lens on the seat and stared at her front door. This was the first time he'd seen the same man with her at her condo. He must be someone special. Tony needed to find out more about the guy and how much of a problem he might be. He needed that money and would stop at nothing to get it. Three strikes be damned.

*   *   *

When Vin entered his small house on the Venice canal, he went directly into the kitchen, pulled a cold bottle of water from the fridge and nearly downed the whole thing. Some of his firefighter pals who were vets would call what had just happened in Eve's condo a FUBAR...fucked up beyond all recognition. Except he recalled every moment, every word, every feeling that had attacked his senses. Eve, drunk, depressed, huddling in her bed. Eve, sobbing like a helpless child in his arms. Her revelation of the shit she was in. Her attempt to seduce him. And finally her uncontrolled anger.

Damn, but he'd grown more and more connected to her in each moment, his need to protect her rising to the surface like Atlantis from the sea. Unbelievable. Overwhelming. Now he clearly saw where the past months had led him. Down the path toward love and commitment. He knew his mother and sisters would jump for joy if they knew. Ah, how the mighty had fallen, they'd chuckle. And they'd be right. But some things had to be worked out before that happily ever after scene could be attained, one of which was to have Eve on board with the whole Magilla. And at the moment he was stymied about how to proceed.

CHAPTER TEN

The dim lights of the church along with the heavy scent of burning candles soothed Eve's broken spirit the moment she entered St. Monica's. The tumultuous events of recent days had left her empty inside and she'd come to the sanctuary desperate to find the peace and healing she needed. Making her way to the front pew she knelt, clasped her hands in front of her and stared up at the Savior on the cross. She took a deep breath, her eyes laser-beaming onto the crucifix willing a lightning bolt to pierce her soul with renewed life, for if it didn't, all hope was lost.

At that moment Vin Ramone's face materialized in her mind, blocking her view of the cross. At first she was annoyed and willed the image away, but when that didn't happen she stopped resisting. Suddenly a vision-like picture appeared of two circles. The one on the left, shimmering in pale yellow, showed the nurturing family in which Vin had been raised. Mother, father, several girls, one boy. Then appeared a dark circle next to the yellow. Eve cringed when she recognized her own dysfunctional childhood. Mother, father, brother. Night and day. Light and dark. Two worlds that were diametrically opposed. Separate. Melancholia blanketed her soul. She blinked a few times to disappear the frightening comparison.

But as suddenly as the circles had appeared, she swept them away, refusing to give in to hopelessness, replaced by another possibility, one where the two worlds converged into one complete entity, like a valuable coin with different pictures on both sides.

Eve flounched back into the seat, staring once again at the altar and the cross behind it. What did it all mean? Metaphysics had never been her thing. Life experiences had been harsh enough to keep her focused on surviving the real world, never mind conjuring up an alternate universe. But something nagged at her, compelled her to find answers. Did Vin Ramone represent a way for her to heal her wounds? Was there some good in her after all? Did she have enough courage to change?

She closed her eyes. A tiny flame rose inside warming her, bringing the possibility of hope back into her cold spirit. The longer she sat ruminating over what had happened the more peaceful she felt. Something was definitely cooking in her and it felt right. She had no idea how it would apply to her life, but she was committed to finding out. And letting it happen.

*   *   *

Two days later, Eve wasn't surprised to open her front door to find Vin standing there, a big smile on his face lighting his eyes. With raised hands, he proffered a bag of something that smelled like it had just come from the oven along with the scent of rich hot coffee.

"Good morning," he said.

Eve's first instinct to slam the door in his cheerful face was instantly replaced with a sigh of resignation and a shake of her head. After all, he did look rather cute standing there. Silently she stepped back and allowed him entrance. As he walked a bit stiffly toward the kitchen, she realized he was sans cane. She hugged her thick terry bathrobe closer and followed him. He put his offerings on the table and searched cabinets for two mugs. She walked up behind him, eased him aside, and found them. When she turned and faced him he put his arms on her shoulders, bent and kissed her lightly. With her hands holding the mugs she could only stand there in shock. He let her go and sat on a chair, stretching his long legs.

"Dig in before everything gets cold." He waved her to the table.

Recovering from his kiss, she said, "Maybe I've already had breakfast."

"No one can refuse French pastry no matter how full they are." He took a big bite of a cheese croissant, closed his eyes and seemed to savor the taste.

She was glad his eyes were closed because it was difficult to hide her smile. "Anyone ever tell you that little-boy charm didn't work?"

He looked at her. "Never."

Rolling her eyes, she sat, reached for a warm pastry and sampled it. Vin was right. It definitely hit the spot.

"You know, Ramone, you have to stop popping in like this. What if I had company?"

"If it were a female, I'd offer her a pastry. If it were a male, I'd toss his ass out the door and then sit down and enjoy my breakfast."

"You're impossible."

Vin's face lost that boyish edge. "No, what's impossible is how're we going to come up with the $50K for dear old Tony. Any ideas yet? You tell me yours and I'll tell you mine." He drank his coffee.

His play on the old hookup line took some of the drama out of the question. Eve sat back in her chair, appetite gone. "Not only do I not have that kind of money, but I have no equity I could use to get a bank loan." She paused. "So, apart from robbing a bank myself, the only option I see is asking my stepfather and I refuse to do that." She crossed her arms under her breasts.

Vin took the last bite of his croissant. "So we have to go to the cops."

Eve vehemently shook her head. "No way. I know Tony. He'll be good to his word and show my mother those pictures and there's no way I'll let that happen." She gritted her teeth.

"I have a few buddies on the LAPD. They'll make sure he never gets to your mother."

"Are you serious? Apparently he's constantly watching me. He probably saw you come here this morning. He'll know."

"Then while he's watching you, I'll go to my guys and we'll work out a sting that will catch him. Cops do this kind of thing all the time. They know what they're doing."

Eve stood and paced the small kitchen, tightening the robe's belt around herself. "I can't take the chance. I can't let my mother see those pictures."

Vin watched her for a long moment before he spoke. "I'm sure she'd understand and forgive you. She loves you, doesn't she?"

Propelled by fear and shame, she whirled around to face him. "You don't understand. This wasn't one little mistake. One foolish night on the town. This is what my life has been like for the past ten years. I'm an alcoholic and I pick up men in bars for mind-numbing sex in cheap motels." Her chest was heaving. "Can you imagine the sorrow and guilt my mother would feel if she ever found that out her daughter is a reincarnation of Doctor Jekyll and Mr. Hyde? I can't do that to her."

Vin gripped her shoulders. "Listen, Eve. I don't know what your childhood was like, what hurt you so bad you've had to self-medicate to survive, but that's not who you are. It's just a way you've chosen to live and you can choose another path anytime you want. You're young, strong and you care about people or you wouldn't be in the helping profession. Stop denying that part of yourself."

His voice rose as he spoke, his face getting more and more determined, color flaming his cheeks. When he stopped talking he pulled her into his arms and kissed her. Hard this time. Demanding. Invading her mouth. Like she had to believe him. Like her life depended on it. And maybe it did.

Rather than fight him, she put her arms around his neck and pulled him as close as she could, needing his warmth, the strength of his convictions. She surrendered to the feel of his lips as they touched her eyelids, her cheeks. His tongue caressed her ears and slide down her neck sending hot sparks down to her toes. His hands moved down her arms and up under her robe seeking soft skin under her breasts. And when his lips returned to hers and his hands lifted her breasts and played with her nipples she cried out.

He stopped and pulled back. "Did I hurt you?" His slanted eyes looked worried.

"No," she whispered. "Don't stop."

He teased her mouth again and continued his seduction of not only her body but her soul.

Eve felt as though some foreign entity had taken over. She lost all sense of herself. Feelings swirled around in her mushy brain. She was so weak she could barely stand. The only thing she was aware of was Vin's mouth on hers, his hands on her body, his strength holding her up. He was the cross on which she hung. She shivered.

"You cold, baby?" He pulled her closer, wrapping his body around her, sharing his warmth.

"Take me to bed, Vin. Please. I need you."

Through her foggy brain she thought she heard a smile in his voice. "I thought you'd never ask." He swept her into his arms, still kissing her, and strode into the bedroom.

*   *   *

Eve lay cuddled tight against Vin's hard body behind her. With his arm resting on her thigh and the other under her shoulders against her breast she felt like a vulnerable baby, safe, protected, surrounded by his warmth and strength. The feeling was foreign, yet very welcome. Maybe some primal instinct deep in her DNA had awakened sometime during their lovemaking. No matter. All she wanted to do was lie there and continue to absorb the wondrous halo of peace in which she floated.

Vin's shallow breathing told her he was asleep. And this too was a wonder. Never before had she allowed a man other than her two deadbeat ex-husbands into her home, never mind her bed. Wasn't that what those cheap by-the-hour motel rooms were for? Slam, bam, thank you ma'am and don't let the door hit your ass on the way out? Even more mindblowing was the fact that she was brave enough not to crawl back inside the impenetrable cement cage she'd built around her heart. Instead it now seemed to be nestled inside a thin shell that could be easily cracked from time to time with no permanent damage to her psyche.

As she moved closer to him, his breath whispered across her neck. "You still here?"

Instead of resentment she almost smiled. "My house."

"Oh. Yeah." He kissed her nape and drew her even closer. "Anyone ever tell you what an amazing lover you are?"

"Actually...not so much."

"Well, whoever they were, they were fools." More soft lips on her neck and cheek.

She turned to face him and angled for his mouth. After a long lazy moment, she pulled back and stared into his dark eyes. "What's going on here, Vin? I'm ashamed to admit this is all new to me. I bow to your vast relationship experience."

"Trust me, baby. This is new to me, too."

"I find that hard to believe."

He kissed her nose. "Cross my heart. Being with you is like the difference between iced tea and hot chocolate."

"That doesn't really help me understand."

"Don't overthink this. Take it for what it's worth to you. Either 'here's your hat, what's your hurry' or 'wow, round two, my place or yours'. Simple."

Eve pulled away, drew a sheet protectively over her breasts and sat up against the headboard, cushioned by soft pillows. "How can you be so cavalier when you don't know a thing about me?"

Vin shifted himself next to her, unconcerned that the sheet slipped down to his waist. "I've been lucky to come from a big, loving, albeit sometimes crazy-making family, with my ego fairly intact." He grinned sheepishly. "Although I'm sure Rosie would have a few words to say about that." He reached for her hand and moved his thumb along her wrist. "My guess is you can't say the same thing about your humble beginnings. I know you carry a lot of sadness and anger from secrets that cut you deep. I'll never judge you for what you've done to survive. I only want to be there to protect you from getting hurt in the future."

Her eyes burned from hidden tears. "Right now I see no happy end to the path I put myself on years ago. There's nothing you can do to help."

He brought her hand to his lips. "I'm only asking for a chance. Don't give up on yourself. On me." He kissed her again. "I'm meeting with some of my buddies at the station tomorrow. Two of them have brothers in law enforcement. We're going to figure out the best way to handle Mister Slimeball."

Great. Just what she needed. The L.A. County Fire Department knowing what a fuckup she was. "You can't tell anyone about this. Please, Vin. I'll never survive the shame if your friends find out about me."

He drew her into his arms. "Don't worry. They'll get a vanilla version of the story. Believe me, we've all faced situations on the job where women have been victimized by abusive, unscrupulous men."

Overcome by the sincerity in his voice and the safety she felt in his arms, Eve relaxed. Maybe it was time to trust. Time to open her dark heart and let in the sunshine.

"Vin?"

"Yeah?" He nuzzled her neck.

"Someday I'll tell you everything. I promise."

"Whenever you're ready. I'm not going anywhere."

She snuggled closer, her arm around his neck and kissed him with trembling lips. Surrendering, she mentally crossed her fingers and dove into the pool not knowing where the bottom would be or what she would find on her way down.

CHAPTER ELEVEN

Vin sat at the lunch table at his firehouse on Santa Monica Boulevard studying his buddies. Larry, married with three kids. Dave, single, who loved the ladies. Steve, hardened by a recent, ugly divorce. And Guy, still looking for Ms. Right. Vin had known them for nearly eight years and they shared an unbreakable bond. They were family and had each other's backs.

The hearty aroma of hot beef stew still permeated the lunchroom, reminding Vin he'd vacuumed down the stew like a starving man facing his last meal. Probably all that energy he'd spent with Eve the night before. But, man, it'd been worth it. She was incredible. So loving. Trusting. She'd given him a gift and he was humbled by her generosity.

"What's put that sappy look on your face, Vin?" Dave said. "Don't tell me the mighty Vincent Ramone has finally met his match? Does she have a sister?"

"If she did, you'd be the last man I'd recommend."

They volleyed back and forth, playfully mocking each other's positions regarding women. Finally Larry broke up the banter.

"Something's going on with you, brother. What is it?"

Vin got serious. "A friend of mine is having trouble with a nasty piece of work ex-husband out on parole. Mean son of a bitch. Threatening blackmail and bodily harm. I need some guidance on how to stop him before he escalates and makes good on his threats."

"Your friend?"

"Yeah."

The guys let Vin's lack of explanation go by without further comment. He felt their eyes lasering into his soul. Finally Steve, whose brother was an LAPD Lieutenant, spoke.

"Parole, huh. There're two ways to deal with scum like him. Get him to violate his parole or have the cops open an investigation with the intent to push a trial. In either case, the bastard gets put away for a long time."

Vin shook his head. "No case, no trial. Nothing public. So how do I get enough on him to violate him back to lockup?"

*   *   *

Eve couldn't believe how good she felt. Light. Free, as though a humongous weight had been lifted off her shoulders. Inspired by her new-found energy, she hustled around her condo, tossing away empty liquor bottles, dried up pizza in messy boxes, scrubbed her bedroom rug where remnants of spilled booze had left ugly stains near her bed. Doing three loads of dirty clothes that had accumulated on the floor of her closet. When she stopped to take a breath, she sniffed the air. The stale smell of booze had morphed into light pine and the fresh scent of laundry detergent. She'd never felt so satisfied. Except of course after the night she'd spent with Vin. That miracle needed no explanation.

Feeling hunger pains she checked the frig and pantry. Nothing much. She grabbed her purse, locked the front door and headed for the underground garage. She'd gotten about ten yards from her Highlander when she heard heavy footsteps behind her. And then a nauseatingly familiar smell. She turned and faced Tony Parma.

"What the fuck..." she said.

A lascivious grin creased his leather-grained face. "Surprised? You should've figured I'd come looking when I didn't hear from you." He scanned the garage and apparently finding it empty of witnesses, he pushed her against the nearest wall, his strong hands grabbing her shoulders in a brutal crush. Her head banged against concrete. Stars appeared in her eyes. Bees buzzed in her ears.

"You said I had a week. It isn't up yet." She spoke through clenched teeth.

"Guess I got impatient. Five years in the slammer will do that to a guy." He went all Hulk on her, his face contorted in rage, holding her fast against the wall. "So where's the money?" He hissed.

"I'm working on it."

"Something tells me you ain't gonna come up with it. Guess I'll have to take my pleasure while I wait." His thick, calloused hand grabbed her breast, squeezing it hard. She winced as he pinched her nipple through her tee, unable to cry out when he silenced her with his mouth. Eve gagged as he shoved his tongue in, his foul breath reeking of booze and cigarettes. Parma's hand pressed the back of her head holding her against his mouth leaving her only one way to escape. With all her strength she kneed him in the groin. He yelped, pulled back, grabbed his crotch and bent over. Eve took advantage of his plight, pushing him hard. Wiggling away from his writhing bulk, she turned and raced toward her car, beeped the door unlocked and jumped in. Shaking fingers fumbled with her keys, but she finally got the car started and rabbited out of the garage. Heart pounding, she raced down Wilshire Boulevard with no particular destination in mind, save to put miles and miles between herself and her ex-husband.

When she finally got her screaming emotions under control, Eve pulled into the parking lot of one of her

Hollywood barroom haunts and stared at the door for a long time. Thoughts raced through her mind. What to do? Where to go? What was Tony's next move? Suddenly her mother's face flashed in front of her. And she knew what she had to do.

The Highlander spun gravel as she sped out of the lot and headed toward Beverly Hills.

Eve's mind was churning as she drove. Her mother would be surprised to say the least when she barged in without notice but she had no choice. She had to protect her. Just how she was going to do that remained a challenge. She knew Tony was bastard enough to follow up on his threat to hurt her mother. Maybe Eve should call Vin. But no. This was her problem and she had to handle it. Didn't she owe her mother for the miserable way she'd practically ignored her for the last ten years? Yet for someone who needed to be in control to survive, the thought of her mother knowing about her only daughter's degenerate after-dark activities petrified her.

As Eve pulled up to her mother's front door, she gritted her teeth, digging deep for whatever ounce of courage might remain inside her. Her only hope was that she could limit the damage the next few minutes would do to her shaky relationship with her mother.

Eve had trouble with the key, but finally the door opened. Her low-heeled boots clicked on the tile floor as she made her way into the kitchen. Her mother stood at the stove stirring a large pot of something that smelled like beef in rich brown gravy. Mary turned when she heard the sound, surprise written on her face. Next a big smile.

"Eve, dear. Just in time for dinner."

Eve took in the picture of the happy housewife greeting her family home. Right out of June Cleaver. But instead of resentment, this time Eve felt sad. If only they shared even a spec of that fantasy....

She approached her mother and put a soft kiss on her cheek, something so unusual Mary's eyes opened wide. "I'm not really hungry, Mom. I...I need to talk to you."

Mary blinked a few times, confused. "Of course. Let me turn off the pot. Would you like some tea or coffee or soda?"

Eve stepped back and sat at the granite-topped island. "No thanks."

Mary joined her, folding her hands on the island, her brow lowered in concern. "Are you alright? Is something wrong?"

"Is your husband home?" Scanning the room Eve's eyes landed again on her mother.

"He's in Europe on business."

A slight sigh of relief passed Eve's lips. Now came the hard part. Where to begin?

"I, uh, I'm worried about you being home alone so much."

Mary scoffed. "I've been alone many times when your stepfather travels. Don't worry. I'm fine." She studied her daughter's face. "We may not have been close over the years, but I know you, Eve, and you look like the world is about to end."

"No, Mom, you really don't know me."

"Then let me in." Mary's eyes filled. "There's nothing you can say that would make me love you less."

Eve rose and paced around the kitchen, hugging herself, wishing she could poof into another reality like the vampires she read about in those crazy romance books. But no. She was stuck in this realm and she'd better man-up fast.

She turned and faced her mother. "I'm in trouble, Mom. Someone is blackmailing me and threatening to hurt you if I don't come up with the money." There. She'd said it. Now all she had to do was face the fallout.

Mary's face turned ashen but she held her daughter's gaze steadily. "Who's blackmailing you?"

Eve took a deep breath. "My ex-husband."

"Do you mean Jerry? Why would he do that?"

Eve shook her head. "Not Jerry." It was after she'd divorced her first husband that Eve had begun her downfall with drinking and promiscuity. She'd turned away from her mother, ashamed of her behavior and the love and support Mary might have offered. "I, uh, got married again to a loser named Tony Parma. It only lasted a couple years. When I found out he was running scams on seniors, I turned him in to the cops and he went to prison. He's out now looking for revenge." There. That hadn't been too hard. Once she'd gotten started the rest slid out like a baby from the womb.

"I don't understand why he'd want to hurt me?"

"I know it's hard for someone like you to believe there are people in the world who like to cause pain. But trust me, this guy's an asshole. I want you to get some kind of protection."

Eve saw a defensive shield rise up her mother's face.

"What do you mean people like me?" Mary asked.

Eve swallowed. "You're a good person, Mom. You see the half-full glass in everyone. But that's not me. I've known a lot of assholes in my life and Tony Parma is the worst."

When Mary seemed to deflate, Eve's guilt meter went off the chart. Without thinking, she reached out and put her hand on top of Mary's. "Don't you dare blame yourself for the choices I've made. They're mine to deal with. The only reason I'm telling you this now is that I don't want you hurt in the process of my cleaning up this shit. I wanted you to know what's going on so that you can protect yourself. A bodyguard or something." She wanted to crawl into a hole and disappear. Her stomach twisted in knots. Her mouth dry. She licked her lips. Man, she needed a drink.

Mary straightened her back and bore her eyes into Eve's. "How much does he want?"

"More than I have. But my friend Vin is working out a plan. I just want you safe until Tony's locked up for good. Why don't you move into a hotel room. In the meantime...."

Mary stood, her small five-three frame growing taller by the second. "I won't be threatened by some lowlife. Never again will I let a man treat me like a doormat." She stood even taller. "You do what you have to and make this go away but I won't run scared anymore."

Eve was shocked by the strength and vehemence that couched her mother's words. Pictures of their earlier life with her drunken abusive father reminded Eve just how far her mother had come since then. The warmth of pride filled her. Yet the woman was still in danger. Fear grew again. She had to talk to Vin right away.

Eve rose, tears threatening, and stared at her mother. "I understand. I'll check with Vin and keep you informed. I'm...I'm sorry, Mom. I haven't been a very good daughter and now..."

Mary came around the island and embraced her. Eve felt wet tears on her mother's cheeks. "I've known for years you've been unhappy," Mary said, "and I'm sorry for the childhood your father and I put you through. I hope you can forgive me."

As difficult as it was to feel her mother's arms around her, hear her words, Eve managed to gingerly put her hands on Mary's back.

"We'll get through, this Eve. Don't worry. The only thing that matters is we love each other."

Eve pulled away, unable to look her mother in the eye. She cleared her throat. "I'll call you. Be careful," she said in an emotionally charged hoarse voice, then turned and left the house before her burning eyes released gallons of tears.

CHAPTER TWELVE

After texting Vin Eve waited for him outside her office. As soon as she slid into his RAM, he leaned over, a big smile on his face, and kissed her, surprising the heck out of her. This having a boyfriend/lover thing was going to take getting used to.

"Hungry?" he asked.

"Famished."

"Good. I thought we'd have dinner at the firehouse. Dave's cooking tonight and he makes a mean chicken *enchilada*. And his rice and beans are the best you'll find in any Mexican restaurant in town."

The thought of meeting Vin's buddies sent blood rushing into migraine territory. She'd either slept with a man or married him. Never had male friends. And she had a premonition that any girlfriend of Vin's would be included in the firefighter family. She let loose a deep sigh.

Vin gave her a quick grin before putting all his attention on the road. "Don't worry. The guys'll love you. And they're all open books. What you see is what you get."

"If you say so."

He patted her knee. "How'd your day go?"

"Could've been better."

He must've heard the tension in her voice. "What happened."

The side window got Eve's attention again. "Tony surprised me in my apartment garage this morning demanding the money. Told him we still had time on the week he'd promised me, but that only made him madder."

"Did he hurt you?" Vin's jaw clenched.

"Pushed me around. No biggie. But he did threaten my mother if I didn't come up with the money."

"Shit."

She looked at him. "I'm worried about her, Vin. My stepfather travels a lot with his work. I, uh, went over there to talk to her."

"That must have been rough. How much did you tell her."

"Most of it. I felt like a heel. I've pushed her away for so long she didn't even know about Tony. I begged her to hire a bodyguard but she refused." A small smile settled over Eve's face. "Something you have to know about my mother. Her first marriage was a nightmare she lived in for a long time. When she finally made a break, she got divorced, went to college and earned a Ph.d. She's determined never to let a man run her life again."

A large brick building loomed ahead. Vin slowed the truck and parked in front of the fire station. Turning off the engine he shifted in his seat and faced her. "Sounds like a tough lady." He reached over and brushed her cheek with his hand. "Guess that's where you get your courage."

Eve shook her head. "Not even close."

He leaned over and kissed her mouth. "One of these days you'll finally see the woman inside you that I see." He pulled her into his arms and kissed her again. "And don't worry about your Mom. The guys and I have come up with a plan. It's a beaut. It's only a matter of days before Mr. Tony Parma is back behind bars. We want you to hear it. That's one of the reasons for this meet and greet. Come on." He took her hand. "I can smell the jalapenos from here."

*   *   *

Lounging into the seat of his beat-up Ford, Tony stretched out his cramped legs. He'd been parked outside Eve's mother's house for an hour waiting for dark to get down to business. Fucking Eve! She'd never come up with the money, no matter the amount. She was such a bitch. Thought she could best him. Well, wouldn't she be surprised when she got the news. And by then he'd be far away. He'd managed to score some cash and new ID recently. It wasn't a windfall, but it was enough to get started somewhere else. He couldn't wait to get out of California and start up a new scam. Solo. If he needed a woman, he'd pick up one in a bar. No more long-term bitches to deal with. He'd keep it simple.

He looked at his watch and then at the darkening sky. Just a little longer....

*   *   *

"That's the plan." Fireman Steve pushed back from the table and glanced around at his buddies, his eyes finally landing on Eve. "The minute your man Vin here told us you were in trouble, I spoke with my brother Dennie. He's an LAPD Lieutenant. He said he'd have his men check out your ex and put a tail on him."

After introductions had been made, the six of them settled down to enjoy Dave's Mexican feast. Even her nerves couldn't suppress her appetite for the delicious food. While they chowed down, the guys regaled her with funny stories about some of the weird scenes they'd been called to handle.

Now that dinner and dessert had been consumed, Eve looked at all the men around the table. Vin had been right. She could trust his buddies to have her back. When her eyes landed on Vin, she blinked to keep the tears at bay.

"I don't know what to say." Her voice trembled. "I feel like 'thanks' isn't enough. To know my mother's safe...It means a lot."

Greg spoke up. "No need to thank us. It's what we do. Especially since you're Vin's girl. Family." He smiled and saluted her.

Conversation was interrupted by a blaring fire alarm and a voice blasting through a loudspeaker. "Engine 42, Squad 3, Ambu 59. Respond to a situ at 726 Morningside, Beverly Hills."

Eve immediately rose out of her chair. "That's my mother's address. Oh God. Vin. He got to her."

*   *   *

Vin and Eve jumped into his truck and followed behind the speeding hook and ladder whose deafening siren forced traffic out of its way. While his eyes were glued on the rear of the red engine, he occasionally glanced at Eve. She stared out the front window, her face flushed, her hands twisting in her lap. He could only imagine what was going through her mind. Damn Tony Parma for bringing this shit to her. Vin prayed they got to Eve's mother before Tony did.

When they finally arrived, the house in Beverly Hills was fully engaged in red and gold flames licking high into the sky. Inside his truck, Vin felt the heat wafting off the burning structure sucking up breathable air. His heart lurched when Eve leaped out before the vehicle came to a full stop.

"Eve! Wait!" Vin shouted, racing behind her. When he reached her, he grabbed her arm but she managed to wriggle free. It took a few moments for the firefighters who were hauling hoses and hooking them up to the nearest hydrant to notice the woman and man run past them.

"Stop!" Several of the smoke eaters yelled. One grabbed Vin's arm. "You can't go in without gear."

Vin recognized his friend Dave and shouted back. "I have to. Eve just ran in. She's frantic. Her mother may be in there."

"I'll find them. You stay back."

His heart pounding, Vin nodded. He had to trust his brothers to bring both Eve and her mother to safety.

Dave slapped him on the back and rushed into the burning house, followed by Steve who clutched the thick hose.

Vin's chest rose and fell, as he stood by helplessly, hugging himself. He damned his weak legs that left him hamstrung. He'd been unable to stop Eve before she entered the unstable structure. All he could do was wait and pray his buddies would get there in time.

*   *   *

The moment Eve raced into the house, she felt she'd entered another world. Thick gray smoke sliced her vision to nearly zero and heavy hot air choked her. Her hand flew to her mouth. She blinked away tears. She ran through the foyer oblivious to the red-gold flames that raged near her. "Mom! Mom! Where are you?" No response. Could her mother hear her above the roar of the fire? Eve raced toward the kitchen. "Mom!" Nothing. Raging fear drove her. Where was Mary? Was she even in the house? Or had Tony taken her before setting the fire? There was no doubt Tony was behind this. His evil, revengeful fingerprints were all over it.

She continued searching the first floor, unable to stop trembling. This was her fault. The punishment due for her depraved lifestyle. For cutting out people who cared for her. For not giving a shit about anyone other than her own pathetic needs. She deserved to die in this fire, not her mother. Oh, God, where was Mary?

After finding the first floor absent of anyone, Eve started up the stairs, coughing through the increasingly heavy smoke, unaware of the heat that threatened to burn through the soles of her shoes. Somewhere in the back of her mind she thought she heard a voice call her. She ignored it. Midway up the stairs her foot cracked one of the blackened steps. She stumbled. Her hands flared out for something to grab. Failed. She fell onto the burning stairs. A scream of searing pain left her mouth.

Her last thoughts were of Vin's smiling face and her conviction he would be better off without her. She remembered feeling a slight smile crack her lips before everything when black.

CHAPTER THIRTEEN

The wail of a siren and a swaying motion dragged Eve reluctantly out of the comforting darkness. Bright lights pierced her eyes as she struggled to open them. Something was over her mouth and she attempted to push it away, but a large warm hand stopped her.

"Leave it, Baby. You need help breathing," a male voice explained.

Eve felt the dull pain that corseted her. She turned her head and gazed at the man who sat with his elbows on his knees, leaning over to speak with her.

"Vin? What...what happened?" She rasped. "Why do I hurt so much?"

His dark eyes held hers. "Don't try to talk. You inhaled a lot of smoke and your throat and lungs have been affected. You have some light burns on your left hand but nothing significant."

When she tried to take a deep breath she grimaced. He was right. Her throat felt like sandpaper and her chest like a hundred-pound brick weighed on it. Anxiety rushed through her and she moved restlessly on the gurney trying to catch her breath.

Vin put his hand on her cheek. "It's okay. You're doing great. Try to relax. It'll be easier to breathe."

Fear. Fire. Pain. Tears ran down her face as she relived the drama. "My mom. I couldn't find her." She grabbed his hand. "Is she alright?"

"She wasn't in the house. We were lucky the guys found you and got you out before the staircase collapsed and you tumbled into the flames. You'll be okay. Just need time to heal." Vin spoke to the EMT tech on the other side of the gurney. "Can you give her anything for the pain?"

The woman checked Eve's vitals, and nodding, reached for a syringe and plunged a clear liquid to the IV which hung alongside the gurney.

"Where's my mother?" Eve croaked.

"As soon as you're settled in the Hospital I'll make some calls. Don't worry. I'll find her."

As the drugs began to cloud her thoughts she became agitated. "Tony set the fire." She had to take several breaths before she spoke again. "He has her. You have to find her."

"I will. I promise."

Vin's reassuring words didn't lessen her fears.

"But you have to take care of yourself," he said. "Let me worry about your mother. I promise I'll have some news soon. Now close your eyes and sleep. We'll talk when you wake up."

Eve couldn't fight the drugs any longer. She drifted off into a realm where pain and fear ceased to exist.

*   *   *

As soon as Vin was sure Eve was settled in her Hospital bed and getting whatever treatment she needed, he bee-lined into the hall and grabbed his cell phone. Steve answered on the second ring.

"I'm still at the scene cleaning up but I did call my brother at the LAPD. He said his guys lost the bastard for a while. When the cops went to the house to check on the mother, it was already in flames. But our guys assured me the woman wasn't in the house." After a brief pause, Steve spoke. "Sorry, bro."

"Don't be. You did your best. Does your brother have any idea what to do next?"

"They put an APB out on Parma as a person of interest in the fire and possible kidnapping. Our inspectors have already determined it was arson. They're accumulating the evidence now. Hopefully they'll find something that can link the fire to Parma."

"We can only hope." Vin sighed. "Thanks, Steve. Keep me updated."

"Will do." The firefighter clicked off.

Where was Eve's mother? Vin stared at the light green wall opposite him wondering how he was going to tell Eve her mother was still missing.

*   *   *

Eve sat at the counter in Vin's house sipping cool herbal tea. While it soothed her throat, it did little to ease the tension that charged through her. It had been three days since the fire and still no word about her mother. Where was she? Was she with Tony? Had he hurt her? Why hadn't he contacted her about ransom or whatever his game was? Dammit. She was going crazy.

Her thoughts turned to Vin. Thank God for him. Her rock. Her salvation. He never asked anything for himself. Just gave her all the comfort and love he had. Love. She never thought she'd find someone who'd love her unconditionally. He never asked about her background. Just accepted her the way she was. And she knew if he weren't in her life now she'd have found herself back on Hollywood Boulevard chasing the numbing effects of booze and any warm body she could find.

She put her face in her hands. She didn't deserve him. He was too good for her. She was a worthless alcoholic slut. Just like Tony had said. She belonged on Hollywood Boulevard. Her heart pumped wildly, her mind plagued with childhood memories. Her mother's screams. Hiding under the bed and in the closet. Danny's little arm around her shoulders protecting her. The loss of the fantasy family she'd always longed for. Pain spiked in her head. Her ragged breath hurt her scorched lungs and throat. Needing a release, she threw the mug against the far wall, spraying hot liquid everywhere.

Eve couldn't stay any longer. She had to get out. Racing toward the front door, Vin opened it. She crashed into him.

"Eve. What's wrong?" His arms tightened around her.

"Let me go," she cried out, struggling to get free. "I have to leave."

Instead of releasing her, Vin's arms tightened. "Not like this. Not until you tell me what's wrong."

"I need...I need...." She stammered, bitter tears running down her cheeks. She looked up at him.

"What, Baby? What do you need? Talk to me." His eyes, full of worry, pleaded with her.

Wild, animal instincts seemed to take over. She locked onto his mouth. Hard. Demanding. At first she felt him pull away, but then, as if realizing what she needed, his mouth claimed hers, matching her same fierce hunger. With one hand on the back of her neck, the other on her bottom, he held her close. His strength seemed to kindle the fire that burned hotter in her. He pushed her back against the door, made fast work of half of their clothes and suckled her breast while he drove inside her. They came together a moment later.

Panting, Eve slouched, her head resting against his heaving chest. His hand caressed her cheek. She felt tears burst forth and she trembled as years of pent-up emotion spilled out like cascading falls. Grabbing onto his shirt for support, she let the deluge flow, unable, unwilling to stop it. His arms held her tight. He kissed the top of her head.

"It's okay, Baby. Let it out. Let it all out." Eve felt his quiet breath on her cheek.

It seemed like they stood there locked together for a hundred years before her sobbing slowed and she settled.

Straightening their clothes, Vin led the way to the sofa, Eve still locked in his arms. He sat and pulled her onto his lap.

"I'm sorry." She struggled to talk but her throat hurt worse than ever. "I shouldn't have attacked you." She spoke into his shirt, ashamed for him to see her face.

"Happy camper here." She heard a spark of humor in his voice. "You can use me like that anytime you want."

"Pig." She gave him a light rap on his chest. Snuggled closer.

He chuckled. "Life with you is going to be interesting. I doubt you have a boring bone in your body."

"Right now I'm boneless." Suddenly realizing what he'd said, she pushed away and stared at him. "Life with me?"

"Yeah. Why not?"

She shook her head. "Too many reasons to count."

"Only if you say so. Me, I'm ready to jump on the rollercoaster." He kissed her lightly. "How about it? You up for the ride of your life?"

"I'll be lucky if I can bury the past enough to stay out of my way. And I can't even think about the future. My God, Vin. Where's my mother? Where's Tony? The blackmail..."

Before he could answer, his phone rang. Checking the readout, his expression turned grim. "It's Steve." Vin put the call on speaker and click on.

"Hey, Vin. News. The cops found Parma's truck lying at the bottom of a ravine off a remote section of the San Bernadino mountains. Apparently it crashed through the guardrail and careened down the steep hillside. His neck broke when the vehicle slammed into a tree."

Eve sucked in her breath. Good. Bastard deserved to die. Then she panicked. "What about my mother? Is she alive?"

The deadly silence that hung over the phone for a minute sent fear ripping through her. "She wasn't in or around the truck. Must've been thrown out. The cops and first responders did a thorough search but didn't find her. We're calling all the Hospitals in the area. I should have news soon. Just wanted to give you an update."

Eve was numb. Where was Mary? And what condition would she be in when they found her?

"Thanks, Steve. Keep in touch," Vin said.

Eve paced the living room, arms akimbo. "Will this nightmare ever end?"

"They'll find her, Eve. At least we know she's alive and not badly injured or she wouldn't have been able to walk away." He went to her and put his arms around her. "How about a hot shower. You'll feel better."

Eve looked up at him. Vin. His strength. So grounded. They were definitely ying and yang. Maybe they could make a go of it. God, she loved him.

Another thought slipped into her mind. "Why don't you run the water. I'll be right there." She smiled at him.

"Your wish is my command, madam." He kissed her. "Always." He walked down the hall to the bathroom.

She took a deep breath and let it out slowly, needing to reach out. She found her cell phone on the table and punched in a number. A deep male voice answered.

"Hey, it's me. Mom's in trouble. She needs you."

PART THREE
Gabriel

CHAPTER ONE

Sixteen-year-old Gabriel Carter crept alongside the seedy shops that circled the mall, careful to remain in the gray shadows of the warm summer night. He'd been watching the front of the Spin and Dry Laundry until the middle-aged matron locked the door after her. Slinking around the back, he'd seen the last man exit the building a couple of hours later. It was now midnight-quiet. No one shopping or stopping except for a few cars in front of the bar on the far corner. Time to make his move.

He slinked toward the back door. This wouldn't be his first B&E, but he was sure even if the cops spied him they'd let him go with a warning. Afterall, why should they care if he ripped off a bunch of sleazy bookies? Probably give him a high-five. A concerned citizen helping law enforcement do their job. He deserved a medal, for God's sake. And he needed the money. No more nickel and dime jobs. He had to get away from home before he went stark raving mad.

Using the lock-opening kit he'd bought online, he put a small pick-like thing into the lock, jiggling it until he heard the mechanisms click. Turning the knob he stepped into the dark room. Anxiety flashed through him as memories flickered in his mind.

The deep sense of anger he'd always felt had reached the boiling point when he was about twelve. The need to escape the constant nagging and pressure from his parents to behave, study hard, go to church... blah, blah, blah...he was sick and tired of having to be the good son. But fighting in the school hallway, cutting those boring classes, climbing out his bedroom window at night to sit alone in the garage were no longer good enough. Needing to let off steam, he'd turned to Howie Simkowitz.

He'd begun running numbers for the local bookie. Howie had gotten a kick out of the boy's interest and used him often, paying him a few bucks each time Gabe returned to the room at the back of the laundry with the day's receipts in hand. The more money he accumulated, the more he wanted. Now a few years later with the large take from this job, he planned to grab the go-bag he'd hidden in the garage and get the hell out of Dodge. Free at last.

Having been in the betting parlor many times, he had no trouble finding his way in the dark. The room was large, with TV monitors lining one wall where every sporting event scheduled each day was shown. Jackasses full of hope and a sure thing placed bets and went home poorer than when they'd arrived. He knew he should feel sorry for those suckers, but hell, they had choices just like everyone else. It wasn't Gabe's fault if fools gave into the need to score the big one and make up for all the losses.

He inched over to the tall safe in Howie's office. Kneeling in front of the black box, he punched in the combination he'd watched Howie use. The lock clicked and Gabe opened the safe. His mouth watered when he spied the stacks of money wrapped according to denomination. After stuffing as many as could fit into his canvas backpack, Gabe retraced his steps out the back door, locking it behind him. Chuckling, he wished he could see the expression on Howie's face when he discovered his stash was gone.

He made his way to the beat-up truck he'd stolen earlier in the evening. While he only had his Learner's Permit, he figured if he drove slow, didn't do anything to attract attention, he'd get far away from L.A. before daybreak. Once he was out of the city, he'd sleep for a while before deciding where to go. Maybe Mexico. His Spanish was decent. Or Canada and not have to deal with a different language at all. Maybe he'd road-trip it across the country and find a good place to hang for a while. Anywhere. The choice was his. The road was open.

He'd just put his hand on the front door of the truck, when bright headlights flashed, blinding him. Blocking his eyes with a bent arm, heart racing, ears pounding, he heard a loud deep voice call out.

"Gotcha this time, punk."

Shit! Gabe's head jerked back and forth looking for an escape route, but realized that he was no match for the two armed cops that faced him. Fear closed his throat. Deep down dread filled him. Made him weak.

"Drop the backpack and get down on your knees. Hands behind your back."

"Listen, guys. Maybe we can work something out. You don't have to go all Magnum on me. Let's talk..."

"Shut the fuck up and get down."

As his eyes got accustomed to the bright light, he saw the vicious expressions on the Five-Ohs in front of him and knew they meant business. Still shots of his parents, school and his self-enforced refuge in the garage flashed Kodak moments in his mind. Hot pulsing rage took over. Fueled him.

No more.

Refusing to feel the walls pressing in on him, Gabe lashed out. He threw his backpack at the cop standing the closest, then charged the other one knocking him down. But before he could stop the guy from getting an aim on him, Gabe felt the cold butt of the man's Glock on the side of his head. He staggered. Stars swirled in his vision. Reality crashed in on him. That beautiful picture of freedom he'd imagined was replaced by deep darkness as he floated to the floor.

*   *   *

Alone in the dark in the corner of the large holding cell that reeked of vomit and piss, Gabe sat on the floor against the cold cinderblock wall arms hugging his knees. Most of the other poor suckers were either sleeping off the haze of whatever drink or drug they'd used to dull their pain or whispering to anyone who'd listen. Gabe wasn't afraid of them. Tall, muscular, looking years older than sixteen, no one ever dared mess with him. So he sat huddled, a bloody bandage on his head, sunk in the familiar, almost comforting loneliness that had always been with him, eyes laser-locked on the opposite wall.

*   *   *

The following morning the Juvenile Court judge frowned at the teen standing hands cuffed behind the defendant's table in the courtroom. "I'm sorry to see you here again, son. I had hoped you'd have learned from your past appearances before me that I meant what I said about second and third chances."

The white-haired jurist stared down at a file on his desk, then looked up at the young man. "I've spoken with your social worker, probation officer, attorney, and both your parents. While they are willing to give you another chance, I am not." The judge cleared his throat. "Gabriel

Carter, I sentence you to two years in detention at Sylmar Juvenile Hall, to be released on your eighteenth birthday." He sighed. "I hope you'll make good use of the time to learn to control your temper, respect authority and accumulate the skills necessary for you to live a productive law-abiding adult life." He banged a gavel. "Next case."

The long-awaited hot rage raced up Gabe's spine. Now he had a face he could stamp his anger on. Another asshole who lorded over him. He fought back the urge to spit at the judge, who sat there above everyone else like a king on his throne. Black robes aside, Gabe was reminded of his puny little be-speckled math teacher, Mr. Burns, who thought he had all the answers just because he knew advanced Trig. Ha. Gabe had taught himself advanced Calc and Newtonian physics before the little man had started teaching at the high school several years before.

Gabe stuffed down his boiling rage. The time would come for retribution, but not now.

The Sheriff's deputy put his hand on Gabe's arm and walked him out of the courtroom. Before the door closed behind him, Gabe glanced at his parents who sat in the visitor section. The tears on his mother's face and the sadness in his father's eyes, only made him angrier. He yanked away from the deputy but the man's grip got tighter.

"Easy, son. Don't make this harder."

"I'm not your son, so fuck off."

The deputy just shook his head and led the way down the hall to another cell. "You'll be transferred to the Hall in a couple hours. Until then you wait here."

Gabe stepped into the small room. The clang of the cell door seemed a fitting end to one part of his life. But he knew as sure as shit that whatever the future held it would be on his terms and no one else's.

*   *   *

Gabe was reminded about the juvenile court judge's words advising him to learn his lesson when he stood once again inside a courtroom. It hadn't taken him long to get into trouble once he'd been released from the Hall. The two years he'd spent there had only been a continuation of the crushing weight of adult supervision that had gotten him into the Hall in the first place. At least he'd been smart enough to bury his temper. He'd only engaged in fights that others had started. Self-defense stuff. He had to laugh about that, visualizing a gold crown signifying sainthood atop his thick dark hair.

School had been even more worthless, the teachers gearing coursework at an elementary level to accommodate his fellow delinquents with "dumb as dirt" engraved on their foreheads.

The only thing of value Gabe had taken out of the last two years had been his new-found interest in all things computer. He'd taught himself basic programming, became highly efficient surfing the internet, including the Dark Web, where he'd learned valuable hacking skills he knew would pay off in the future. But he'd have to put those skills on hold for a while.

After he kissed the Hall good-bye, Gabe admitted to himself he'd gone crazy...drinking, fighting and getting into trouble with the fast-food managers he'd convinced to hire him. Damn, he could still smell the greasy odor of fried foods. So now he stood in front of a judge again, unfortunately this time as an adult looking at serious lockup time.

"I see," Mr. Carter, "you've had a very colorful history. Apparently two years in juvie hadn't shone that 'come to Jesus' light on you." The dark-haired jurist pushed his glasses onto the edge of his nose and seared Gabe with piercing eyes. "But I'm feeling generous this morning and have a choice to offer you."

Gabe gave his court-appointed suit a scowl for apparently failing to get his juvenile records sealed, then stared defiantly at the judge.

"Two years in Wayside correctional facility or two years in the Army." The judge took a deep breath. "Chocolate or vanilla. Choose." He waited for the young man's response.

Gabe's heart skipped a beat. He couldn't believe his good luck. For once he was given a chance, albeit limited, to pick his own destiny. And the choice was clear. An eight-by-eight cell or fresh air and new adventures. He answered before the judge changed his mind.

"Army."

The judge nodded. "Good choice. Your attorney will give you the necessary papers to sign." The man frowned. "But take heed, son. The military life is no picnic and if you continue on the road you've been on, you'll find yourself in front of a military court. And Leavenworth is no Juvenile Hall or Wayside correctional." He banged the gavel. "Next case."

Before being ushered out of the courtroom, Gabe glanced over at his parents who sat a few rows back. He hadn't seen them since his last court appearance, had refused any contact with them, still blaming them for the way his life had turned out. He refused to acknowledge the whispery hints of shame and guilt that tended to niggle at the back of his mind from time to time. Like now, when tears ran down his mother's cheeks and a sad and worried expression lined his father's face. Maybe someday...

But not now. Instead he followed the deputy out of the courtroom, eyes straight ahead, focusing on new adventures that awaited him in the army.

CHAPTER TWO

Gabe slinked back in the padded booth, cracked his knuckles and took a break from deep diving. He glanced around Sunland's internet café which had become his home away from home since getting out of the Army a year before. The room smelled of hot spiced coffee and freshly baked goods. The only sound came from the clicking of computer keys and an occasional murmur of "fuck me" or "ah-ha." Heaven, compared to the two years of hell he'd left behind in the hot dry sand dunes of Afghanistan. That juvie judge had been right...the military had been an education, one he was glad to be done with. So what if he'd gotten a dishonorable discharge for putting three of those asshole privates in the Hospital when he found them raping an Afghan girl. His conscience was clear. Never planned on a career in the Army anyway.

Scanning the small store, he recognized many of the geeks who slouched behind their laptops thriving on sugar and caffeine. Teens. Twenty-somethings. Even an older dude with gray hair and a greasy beard. Probably a die-hard leftover from the sixties. Mostly males with a few females sprinkled in for eye-candy.

Stretching, he got up and ambled over to the counter. Ordered a large black coffee. The barista looked at Gabe as though he sported two heads then rolled his eyes and turned to fill the order. A light hint of gingerbread filled Gabe's senses, reminding him of his mom and Christmas and his old life, but he torpedoed those memories. He turned and faced a pretty young girl whose head barely reached his shoulders. Short blond curly hair. The greenest eyes he'd ever seen. And when she smiled at him the room seemed to lite up.

"Not a big risk-taker, huh?" She inclined her head at his black coffee when the barista put the paper cup in front of him.

Unable to hold her stare, he pulled bills out of his pocket and paid the cashier.

"I've been dying to meet you," she said. "I'm Belle." She reached out her hand, but he ignored it. She shrugged, paid her tab, grabbed her latte and followed him to his booth. Gabe slid in and Belle slid across from him.

He gave her his best pissed off glare. "Don't you have something to do little girl or do you always come onto strangers in internet cafes?"

Instead of being insulted she laughed. "Actually, this is a first. I rarely come out of my fem cave, but your skills intrigued me. So I tracked you down and here I am. I watched you cruise. Noticed how intense you are, those big wide shoulders hunched, eyebrows deep in thought." She grinned. "Besides, I may be short but my brain is beyond the pale."

"Huh. Bragg much, do you?'

"It's not bragging when it's true."

He squinted, giving her a more thorough appraisal. There was something about her that was intriguing, but he had no desire to get involved with anyone, friendly or otherwise. Besides, what the hell did she mean, she tracked him down? He'd never seen her before. Who was she? Who was she working for? Gabe got a little worried thinking about any number of government agencies that might be after him. He'd better play it cool. He turned away and sipped his coffee.

"Sorry to end this stimulating conversation, but I have to get back to work." He waved his hand to shoo her off and opened his laptop. "Bye-bye now."

Instead of leaving, Belle put her elbows on the table and rested her head in her hands. "I like your eyes. Dark pools. Mysterious." She frowned as if trying to figure it out. "No, it's the Intelligence. Self-confidence. No nonsense. A man of mystery." She nodded, pleased as if she'd come to some kind of understanding.

Gabe sighed. "What can I say to get rid of you?"

She wiggled her nose as she thought. "How about 'I'll show you mine if you show me yours'?"

"What?"

"You're crib. What's your place like? Then I'll take you to mine. You can decide which one you'd rather work out of."

"You're nuts."

"Probably. But one can only do so much in an unsecured environment like this. And I'm guessing you don't have a more private place to do what you have to. So I'm offering you a look-see at mine. It's the perfect base for us raiders. Safe. Secure. Private. You'd be free to stay there or come and go as you please. Up to you." She smiled. "And since I've got enough money to last a lifetime, I won't charge you rent."

He stared at her, eyes open wide. "You always in the habit of offering your home to strangers?"

"Nope. Another first. Never had the inclination before. But like I said...I've been watching you for a few weeks. Decided it was time to make your acquaintance." She shrugged. "Unlike you I'm not opposed to taking a risk. What'da you say?"

"I say you're certifiable. Should be locked up."

"Been there. Done that." Belle grinned.

Behind her smiling clear green eyes Gabe saw a grain of truth. An invisible string seemed to snake out from her and wrap around him. A connection. Something he hadn't felt in a very long time, if ever. Another lost soul. It pulled him up short.

"Come on. Take a chance. I promise you won't regret it."

He continued staring at her. *She* was the mystery. Young. Lived alone. Plenty of money. He needed answers.

"How old are you?"

"Sixteen."

Ah. Jail bait. That solved one of his concerns. No way he'd have to worry about getting sexually involved.

"How come you live alone?"

"I'm an orphan."

"No family?"

"That's what orphan means, genius."

"How come the state hasn't picked you up?"

She sighed as though bored to death with his questions. "They haven't found a home that could hold me. Anything else? I'm not asking you to marry me, for God's sake. Just looking for a partner."

Gabe raised his eyebrows. "Partner?"

"Yeah. Like I said I have piles of money, but it gets boring after a while. I'm up for a change." She leaned forward. "Done with the twenty questions?"

"One more. How'd a kid like you accumulate so much money?"

"Let's just say I have unique skills, but none I'm willing to explain in a public café." Belle finished her latte. "So what will it be, dude? Chocolate or vanilla?"

What the hell was it with all the ice cream favor metaphors, recalling that judge he'd appeared before. He squinted at her. "How do you know you can trust me? It's pretty stupid of a pixie like you to brag to a stranger about living alone and having lots of money. What could stop me from Jack the Rippering you and taking all your money?"

She laughed. "First, trust me when I say many have tried but none have succeeded. And second, my money's not accessible to anyone but me."

Gabe's mind was spinning. He was sick of menial jobs working like a slave for crumbs. But without college and with a bad military record he was dog shit to reputable employers. Right now his future looked like an empty black sky. Lots of same ole, same ole. And it was only a matter of time before the feds found him. Maybe the kid was right. He needed to suck new air into his universe.

She watched him, sipping her latte, waiting patiently. He imagined her in his head reading all his thoughts and cheering him on to make the right decision. He took a deep breath and closed his laptop. What the hell.

"Lead the way."

*   *   *

Surprise couldn't adequately describe Gabe's shock as he followed Belle out the back of the café to a sparkling new black and gold Ducati Scrambler that sat in the alleyway. He was still gaping when she pulled two helmets out of the storage box under the seat and handed one to him.

"This is yours?"

"She's a beaut isn't she? The latest model. Runs smoother, quieter. Got a good trade-in on my old one."

"I thought you said you were sixteen."

She gave him an impish smile. "Not according to my ID." She straddled the bike, her short legs barely reaching the peddles. He wondered where the hell such a small girl got the strength to handle such a powerful machine.

She laughed at his frown. "Don't worry. This isn't my first bike. Been riding for a couple of years. Hop on."

He cursed at his hesitation, shrugged and slung his long legs over the bike, snuggling behind her. No sooner had his arms wrapped around her slim waist than the powerful engine revved up. Gabe's body tightened. They pulled out of the alley and raced down Sunland Boulevard. Made a sharp right onto Oro Valley Avenue. By the time they turned north on Big Tujunga Canyon Road, Gabe had relaxed, reassured by Belle's driving ability. He settled down and enjoyed the exhilarating sense of freedom. The roar of the bike as it snaked along the empty road through the barren countryside framed by rocky hills. The soft whisper of breeze as they sped through the desolate canyons. He wished he could throw away his helmet and feel the cool summer air on his face. A crazy need to stretch his arms in the air and scream out the joy that consumed him. His heart pounded. He became one with Belle as she drove skillfully along the twisting, turning road, rolling from side-to-side with her, like they were one figure urging the machine forward. It was the most exhilarating feeling Gabe had ever had.

He couldn't tell how many miles had passed before Belle slowed the bike and made a turn onto a dirt road that cut a path through one of the hills. After a few minutes he spied what looked like an abandoned cabin in a clearing ahead. Maybe forty-by-twenty feet of old weathered brown boards. A small porch in front. She slowed to a stop. He instinctively stretched out his legs to support the bike from tipping to the side, but Belle already had the kickstand out and jumped to the ground. She turned to him, pulled off her helmet and grinned.

"Pretty cool, huh?"

It took a moment for Gabe to come down from the high he'd been on. He took a deep breath. "The ride or the cabin?"

When she smiled her jade green eyes twinkled. "Both actually. Come on." She turned and skipped up the two ratty steps to the front door, used a key to open it and entered. Gabe shook his head and followed. Then stopped short after Belle closed and locked the door behind him.

While the outside reeked of neglect and decay, the inside was pure new-age. Walls of light pine facia logs. Gleaming pine floorboards. Beamed ceiling. Two windows on the front wall, one large on the left side, each letting in whatever sunlight managed to sneak in through the thick vegetation of the surrounding woods. A sofa, a stuffed chair and end tables were sprinkled around the room. But most impressive was the bank of two-foot computer monitors that glowed dull blue. Printers, scanners and file cabinets sat begging to be put to good use. At the other end was a counter with a tiny workable kitchen area behind it. A door that Gabe assumed led to the bedroom and bathroom was on the left.

He stared, open-mouthed. Who the hell was this kid?

He strolled over to the middle computer and touched a key. The whimsical caricature of a little girl about ten in long curly blond pigtails flashed across the screen. The kid jumped up and down hitting a bright orange balloon into the air and back again as she ran across a sandy beach, the clear blue ocean and bright yellow sun in the background. She had on white shorts and a blue cotton shirt.

Gabe didn't know why, but something compelled him to strike a key of the computer on the left-hand side. Instantly the monitor came to life. This time the screensaver showed a faceless man dressed in a long dark coat running toward the girl, hands reaching out, against the background of a stormy night with streaks of lightning breaking through the gray sky. Curiosity forced Gabe to move to the computer on the far side. This screen was pitch black with blood red flames reaching into the sky in demonic rage.

Taking a step back, Gabe tennis-matched in fascination left to right and back again taking in the threatening scene that rolled across the three computers on a continuous loop. Mesmerized. Unable to break away. Suddenly all three monitors went blank. He turned and saw Belle standing by the kitchen counter, cell phone in hand.

"Wouldn't want you to get cross-eyed." No expression. Low even voice. She put the phone down and buried her head in the open refrigerator. "Herbal tea? Orange Juice? Water? Sorry, no beer." She glanced at him, waiting for a response. When he just stared at her, she shrugged and pulled out a plastic pitcher half-filled with tea. Two glasses appeared on the countertop. She plopped down on a high stool.

"I've seen something like that before." Gabe finally found his words. "How'd you copy it?"

"Who said I did?"

He stared at her confused. Then a light turned on. "Are you telling me you put this on the Web?"

"Bingo."

Gabe could only shift his vision between the screensavers and the girl trying to understand what his eyes and ears were telling him. Finally his eyes landed on hers. This was her online screen tag. This little bit of a girl with blond curly hair and green eyes who looked more like a young Shirley Temple than an average sixteen-year-old. He couldn't believe his own conclusions.

"Hi. I'm Prima," she said.

This time when she stuck out her hand, he took it.

CHAPTER THREE

Gabe shifted on the counter stool and drank his glass of tea nearly draining the whole thing. He'd heard rumors about the legend known as Prima. She was on every agency and corporations' most wanted list after infiltrating their networks, reallocating money, corrupting files and destroying evidence. Everyone in the business knew about Prima. But no one knew who she really was or where she lived. A genius. A ghost. And now he sat across from her, a million questions going through his mind.

"Of all the hackers in the world, why am I here?" Gabe said.

She sipped her tea. "Six months ago I noticed your work. I was impressed. Nothing outrageous. Brilliantly simple. Smooth. Small takes. Nothing to wave red flags. Always government. At first I thought you were military so I followed your trail."

"And..."

"I found out everything about you."

Instead of being pissed at her invasion, he felt his chest inflate, along with his ego. "Again, why am I here?"

She shrugged and pushed a lock of curls away from her face. "I told you. I'm bored. I figured if we partnered up you could expand your horizons. Discover a new road, you know, the one less traveled."

Gabe frowned. "Like what?"

"You ever hear of Robin Hood?"

He snickered. "Stupid question."

"Maybe not. If I'm reading your goals right, you seem to have a hard-on for all groups with government or military connections and have been sticking pins in them like little voodoo dolls. Pocketing small change, but mostly just messing up their systems causing havoc. Very juvenile. I can introduce you to a new way of doing business that's much more satisfying than creating rebellious tantrums with your fingertips."

Now Gabe's anger threatened to boil over. His mouth thinned. His eyes flashed. A man's ego could take just so much. His thoughts were interrupted by her raised hand.

"Now hold on, slick," she laughed. "No insult intended. Just telling you the way I see it. And if you give me a chance I'll explain."

Slowly Gabe got his temper under control. He breathed deep. Pushed his empty tea glass away. "Got anything stronger?"

"Sorry, pal. This is a non-alcoholic house." Belle grinned. "Underage here."

This time it was Gabe who laughed. "You're kidding, right?"

Prima shook her head. "Nope. Drugs kill brain cells and I like mind sharp and focused."

They stared at each other. It was Gabe who spoke first. "What do I call you?"

"For now 'Belle' will do."

"Okay. Fine. Belle. Maybe I don't want to expand. Maybe I'm content with my meager-by-your-standards way of working. What happens if I walk out that door? You going to find a hitman on the Dark Web and send him after me now that I know who you are and where you live?"

She stared at him with soul-piercing eyes. "I wasn't inflating your ego when I said I thought you were special. Unique. I did my research. I'm betting you have more integrity in your little finger than most people have in their entire being. Besides, you're too smart to be so stupid. So, no. No hitman. Not necessary. I trust you. You can leave anytime you want. No fuss. No foul. Just regret on my part. But I've survived worse and lived to tell about it."

Gabe saw a wisp of deep sadness fill her eyes, then flash away. Something grabbed him like before. He lounged against the back of the stool, stretching his long legs.

"Partners, huh?"

She grinned. "Yeah."

Slowly Gabe nodded.

*   *   *

Back in his cheap motel room, Gabe lay down on the lumpy bed hands under his head staring at the old ceiling fan which slowly pushed the stale air around. He recalled every word of the conversation he and Belle or Prima or whatever her name was had shared, including every feeling he'd struggled to get a grip on since meeting her. Came up with the same conclusion. As impossible as it seemed, for once in his chaotic life the fates had smiled down on him. The heady taste of freedom and self-determination that had powered through him on the wild ride on the Ducati had returned. He let himself wallow in it. Hang on to it like fingertips gripping the edge of a twenty-storied building, afraid if he let go he'd crash and burn.

As reality weaved its way back, Gabe's stomach twisted with anxiety. Dammit. It wasn't like him to jump headlong into something without doing deep-diving research. Had she so mesmerized him he'd forgotten to follow the simple rules of survival which had kept him out of serious trouble? He couldn't even blame his lack of good sense on some stupid irresistible sexual impulse. They hadn't entered into the equation. No, Belle was no honeytrap. But what was her story? Maybe little by little he'd discover pieces of the puzzle that formed the Ghost. The thought of working with his new partner took on a whole new interest.

He fell into a restless sleep, with bright swirling colors filling the place where darkness had thrived.

*   *   *

Belle was six when her worldview shifted.

That's when she learned her father had been right. "Don't let anyone know how smart you are...it's safer to play dumb" had been the mantra he'd drummed into her from infancy.

Stretched out on her sofa, Belle stared at the crumpled photo of a young man and woman and blinked back tears. No. She wouldn't cry. Crying was for cowards and weaklings. She brushed her thumb over the picture and thought about Jeannie and Roy and the joy and wonder that lit their faces. Her freewheeling life-loving parents. They'd blossomed after escaping from the cold, regimented environment of the think-tank their folks had basically sold them into as children. They'd built a solitary life in a cabin deep in the forests of Northern California where Belle had eventually been born and raised. She'd been homeschooled by her mother on liberal arts subjects which included five languages and her father on math, science and computers. But by the time Belle was six, her parents decided she needed to develop the social skills she'd need to survive in the outside world once her parents were no longer there to protect her. So they enrolled her in a local public elementary school.

Belle remembered being shy the first week at school. She didn't know how to be with people other than her parents. Desperately wanted to fit in with the kids, she watched them play in the schoolyard. Listened to how they chatted with each other and interacted with teachers.

And concluded her classmates weren't very smart.

So when asked to do assignments, Belle was the first to finish the classwork perfectly. It was her hand that shot up to answer questions posed by the teachers. It didn't take long for her to realize that everything she did raised her teacher's eyebrows and made her classmates give her mean looks. No one played with her. She felt more and more isolated. The meaning of her father's words finally made sense. It was safer to be a dull copper penny than a shiny silver dollar.

Belle shoved the photo back in her wallet. She cleared the counter of drinks and the remaining Junior Mints and M&M peanuts she and Gabe had pigged out on while they'd chatted. At her computer, she keyed in *Raiders of the New World,* the access to the Dark Web site where the most skilled hackers could chat and network under deep cover. Hum. Nothing new or interesting. After all this time they were still lamenting over the arrest of the Dark Web and Silk Road creator known as Dread Pirate Roberts. Boring.

She closed the site and opened her own private IP address where she could read her emails, discover who'd been poking around her privacy walls seeking entrance and then track them. Ah. There's one poor fool. She inserted her favorite worm into his files along with a picture of a raised middle finger and threw him an invisible kiss. So much for nosy assholes who thought they were smarter than she.

Belle smiled when she saw Gabe's ID sniffing around looking for background info on Prima the Ghost. She couldn't blame the paranoid stud. After all he'd only known her for a day and trust took time to build. She sighed.

Construction would begin tomorrow. In the meantime she had to make her small home ready for its new inhabitant.

* * *

The following morning Gabe woke early, stuffed his meager belongings into his backpack, slung it over his shoulders and headed to the parking lot, where Belle and her flying Ducati waited. Without any greetings, he grabbed the helmet she offered and straddled behind her. The fast and furious ride through the hillsides didn't hold as much interest to him as the day before. Funny, how easily memories could fade when replaced by the excitement of new horizons. And that morning Gabe's mind was clear, sharp, waiting hungrily to absorb the new possibilities that teaming up with Prima, the mysterious Ghost, presented. He was bone-deep thrilled.

They stopped at Mickey D's for take-out breakfast and lunch and continued through the hills to his new home. Well, not really new. The outside still looked like a hundred-year-old run-down shack, but it was what awaited him inside that revved his engine. Once in, Belle showed him where to stow his stuff. He followed her to the counter. They sat and she spoke between bites of her bacon and cheese egg McSandwich.

"What I'm going to suggest will send your already-always internal dialogue into freak-out mode. But don't fret. You'll see the wisdom."

Gabe washed down a huge mouthful of his breakfast burrito with several slugs of Coke.

"Do you always preface your upcoming statements with get-out-of-jail-free cards?"

"It saves time and energy. And I hate confrontation." She sipped her Coke. "To continue...You've been used to concentrating on government/military groups for the sole purpose of snagging a few bucks and stickin' it to the Man.

Like I said yesterday. Little juvenal fits of revenge." She wiped her mouth with a clean napkin. "How would you like to tweak that hidden part of your soul you've managed to bury and see what pops up."

"What the hell are you talking about?"

"You wanted to know how I've managed to accumulate all the money I have and still have a cheery outlook on life."

Gabe scowled. "I don't give a shit about your outlook on life. I'm only interested in how to steal bigger without getting caught."

"Liar." She smiled, crumbled the food wrapper and tossed it in the trash at the end of the counter. "All right. I surrender. I'll leave your soul to your own devices."

"Damn straight. Now get on with the money part or I'll grab that get-out-of-jail card and hoof it down the mountain back to civilization faster than a *Game of Thrones* dragon."

"Fine. Go. I don't need you. But you, Sir Surly, definitely need me."

Gabe imagined smoke steaming out of his nostrils, a bull snorting and pawing the ground with sharp hooves. After staring at her with daggers he finally managed to get his anger under control, sheathing the horns. A few deep breaths helped. Clear of the billowing rage, a new thought came to mind.

"You know just what to say to piss me off. And you do it on purpose. Why?"

Belle shrugged. "You need to be reminded once in a while where that rage has gotten you."

Gabe took a long honest look at his life, maybe for the first time. He'd abandoned his family, spent two years locked up in juvie and another two fighting for who-knew-what in another kind of prison. All because of his need to solve problems with his fists instead of using his clever mind. The kid was right. But he'd be damned if he'd let her know.

"So what's next?"

She got up from the counter and strolled toward her computers, pulling a metal folding chair next to hers and patted it. "Sit. Your education is about to begin."

CHAPTER FOUR

Gabe loved the sound his sneakers made as he pounded dirt. Tough, strong, powerful, in sync with the heavy rock beat that screamed in his ears. Arms pumping, chest heaving, heart racing, he was one with the forest that surrounded him. In the zone. Even the crisp autumn air that kissed his skin as he ran seemed to welcome him.

"Fuck!" The single word slipped out between his teeth as he tripped and fell, scraping his knees on the hard unforgiving trail. He pulled himself up and kicked the offending branch that had snaked its way across the path partially hidden beneath fallen leaves. As he came down from the exhilarating high he'd been on, he shook his head in disgust. Just like life...it gave a little then took it all away. He brushed himself off and started toward home at a slow trot.

He shut off the iPod and let his thoughts wander over the last year and a half. After the initial sparing with Belle, they'd settled into a surprisingly comfortable daily rhythm. Work at the computer. Work on the cabin and grounds. Back at the computer after dinner. Quiet time by the fireplace before bed. Together they'd built a small addition to the cabin allowing him to abandon his sleeping bag on the floor in the living room for a bed. Privacy. Finally. Their next project had been to cut hiking/jogging trails through the woods.

He'd been amazed how strong his little partner was. She hefted boards, pounded nails with heavy hammers and could shovel dirt with the best of them, proving to be more than just a cute kid with globe-sized brains. The longer he was with her, the more he admired and respected her.

As far as his hacking education...that had been mind-boggling. When she first explained how she made money and kept her soul squeaky clean, her words, light bulbs had gone off. Why hadn't he ever thought about stealing then diverting dirty money from criminals like drug cartels, pharmaceutical companies engaged in deceptive research, counterfeiters and financial swindlers? Probably too hung up in malwaring and worming through government databases. He smiled to himself as he neared the cabin. If Belle had been active during the sub-prime mortgage debacle and the Bernie Madoff scandal, hundreds of thousands of people would have been spared a lot of grief and loss.

And the best part...after taking a meager ten percent of the 'withdrawal' for his and Belle's personal off-shore accounts, the rest was donated anonymously to their favorite non-profit charities.

And this was where Gabe's education about swarming came into play.

Being a loner, he'd done his hacking on his own timetable, content with the satisfaction screwing with the authorities gave him. Swarming opened up a whole new level of participation and thus rewards. Over the years Belle had accumulated a group of highly-skilled, moral hackers who wanted to make a difference. Once she depleted the crooks' bank accounts, she sent an equal amount of the leftover money to each of her hacker buddies, who then duplicated her action...steal, take a share and divert to non-profits. And so forth through many levels. The trickle-down theory of economics was no longer just a theory. It became a pyramid scheme that benefited non-profit organizations. The amount to each player was small enough so no flags caught the attention of the IRS or government techno whizzes. And she gave Gabe the job of policing the participants to make sure they were sticking to the rules; a small percent to themselves, the rest to charity.

He had to hand it to the kid. It was perfect. For some reason he didn't want to explore too deeply he slept better at night. But, yeah, he had to admit, she'd been right...helping was definitely more satisfying than hurting.

He stood in front of the cabin, sucked in a few deep breaths, slowed his pulse and wiped sweat off his face with the towel around his neck, clearing his mind. Belle had let it slip that today was her eighteenth birthday and Gabe decided they should celebrate.

He stepped into the main room. She was at the computer doing God-knew-what. "Hey, Tink," he said. "Shut that thing off and spruce up. I'm taking you out for your BD."

She turned, annoyed at being interrupted. "What?"

"You said today was your birthday. Eighteenth, I believe. That's something to celebrate. So get ready. Us two hermits are going out on the town today."

"Huh," she grunted. "I don't think so. Not my style."

"Sprucing up or celebrating?"

"Both." She turned back to the computer.

The tension he felt build in her took him by surprise. He watched her clicking away, her face tight, shoulders rounded, concentration beaming off her. This was not the easy-going kid he'd known for the past two years.

"I wanted to take you to Universal Studios to celebrate."

"Not interested."

"You ever been there?"

"Go away. I'm trying to work."

But Gabe decided to push. Find out what was going on with her. "I went once when I was a kid. Had a lot of stupid fun. I thought we could use some of that. Get out of here for a change. Commune with the masses."

"Drop it, Gabe."

"Don't you ever get sick of hanging out alone up here, just the two of us?"

"Nope. I enjoy my privacy."

Gabe shrugged, walked to the fridge and took out the orange juice. Slugged a few gulps. "You know, you're legal now. You don't have to worry about the cops or social services picking you up and dumping you into the system again. You're free to join the real world whenever you want."

Still Mozarting on her keyboard she mumbled, "Don't want."

He leaned against the counter. "You don't have to be afraid of the world, Belle. I wouldn't let anything happen to you."

With that she stopped and turned around, stabbing him with angry eyes. "I don't need you to protect me. I've done a good job for the past four years taking care of myself." She took a deep breath and let out some of the steam she'd been holding. "Sounds like you're the one getting restless with our partnership. Maybe you should leave and do all the communing you want. I won't hold you back."

Gabe couldn't believe what he was seeing and hearing. What the hell had gotten her so riled up? He pounded her with questions. "Why does going out in public scare you? Why did you run away years ago and hide in these hills? And who did you run away from? Where's your family?"

Belle glared at him. "You like questions...answer me this. Why are you so interested in my past all of a sudden?

You used to be satisfied with who I am now. What's changed?"

Gabe put the juice bottle on the table and walked to her. Her eyes were clear, penetrating, challenging. He frowned. "I don't know." He reached out to touch her cheek but she slapped his hand. He backed away. "I think of you as a brilliant tough kid. Nothing gets to you. But now I see another part of Prima the Ghost and I'm fascinated. I want to get to know that part of you. To understand."

She laughed with a nervous trill. "Ah, I see. You're tired of feeling like my brother. Now that I'm no longer jail bait you want more from me." She moved closer, put her hands on his chest and move them up toward his neck. Gabe was shocked and embarrassed by his body's reaction to her touch. She was actually trying to seduce him. He grabbed her wrists and pulled them to her sides.

"Cut it out. You're deflecting. Why can't you open up with me? You know you can trust me. I want to help."

Rage colored her face, her body so tense he thought she might jump and claw him. She jerked away, ran into her room and slammed the door.

Gabe's breath came in short gulps. What the hell had just happened? One minute she was at the computer and the next she was tripping into Jekyll and Hyde land. Fuck. He'd hit some nerve, but damn if he knew which one and why. He rubbed his face and sat on the sofa. Now what.

*   *   *

When your brain was a dizzy mass of swirling cells...chop wood.

So here he was, bare-chested, muscles straining, sweat dripping, mindlessly physical, heavy metal again screaming through his earbuds. If he kept this up much longer he'd have enough wood to build another house. He'd stopped trying to figure Belle out two hours ago when he pictured his head cannoning off his shoulders. So now he simply heaved and swung. Heaved and swung. Cool breeze caressing his hot body. Two-foot logs flying off the tree stump left and right. Davy Crocket Carter. Frontierman. He chuckled.

He felt the air stir when she approached, mumbling. He rested the ax in the stump, pulled off his headset and turned to Belle. She handed him a cold glass of orange juice. He nodded in thanks and slugged down the whole thing, wiping his mouth with the back of his hand.

She stared at the scratched and calloused hand. "You better wash those cuts before they get infected."

His eyes followed hers. "Soon as I'm done."

Belle gazed at the piles of split logs on the ground and grinned. "I'd say we've got enough firewood for ten winters. You hungry?"

Gabe felt like a little boy whose mama had caught him doing something stupid. He raised his eyebrows and shrugged. "I could eat."

She turned and headed up the front steps. "Got chili on the stove and cornbread in the oven. Wash up."

Gabe's eyes followed her into the house, her hips in tight short shorts swaying. He breathed deep. Then took a moment to pile the logs neatly near the side of the house before going inside and hitting the shower.

Belle sat at the kitchen counter with two bowls of hot spicy chili and warm cornbread set out. Gabe plopped down on the other barstool. Salivating over the chili, he dug in. The silence that filled the house seemed to him like a period at the end of a long heavy sentence. The air now clear, clean, waiting for something to take shape in it.

They were nearly finished with their supper when Belle spoke softly into her chili. "I don't like being pushed and shoved around. Strangers touching me. Crowding me.

Had too much of that as a kid. So I rabbited to the forest to feel safe."

Gabe looked at her. "When you were fourteen?"

She nodded, still mesmerized by her chili.

"And before that you weren't safe?"

She shook her head so slightly. He had to blink a few times to be certain he'd seen it.

"Your parents didn't protect you?"

"They died when I was three."

"That when you went into foster care?"

Again with a barely visible nod.

Chills crawled up Gabe's spine. He'd heard stories from his Juviemates about the abuse they'd suffered in foster homes. The idea of someone hurting Belle like that filled him with rage. He wanted to pummel someone. Or maybe lay waste to more trees.

She finally stared at him through steely eyes. "I've been content for four years now. I'm not willing to face the outside world ever again. If being here no longer works for you, I'll understand if you leave." She grabbed her iced tea, took a few gulps, then returned to her chili.

Gabe stopped eating and watched her for a long moment. So small. So tough. So vulnerable. For the first time he saw himself in her. Exchange small for big and there he was, hiding, afraid to face his past. Joining with her had seemed like a great adventure. Now it felt like same ole' same ole', been there, done that. Hurting. Running. Guess if he didn't make changes on the inside, he'd continue dragging his body around like a zombie facing an endless winter.

Hell no!

He wasn't much of a deep-thinking kind of guy. Had no interest in digging around in his or anyone else's brain looking for answers. But instinct told him relationships were built on trust. Just how he'd go about doing that he had no idea. But somehow he'd figure out how. Feeling hopeful, excited about a new future. Gabe smiled.

"Sorry, kiddo," he said, "you can't get rid of me that easy." He stood, took his empty bowl to the sink and headed outdoors, whistling.

CHAPTER FIVE

Rook to Knight four.

Gabe keyed in the chess move, sat back and waited for his opponent to respond. He stretched out his long legs and took another drink of black coffee, letting his eyes scan the same internet café where he'd met Belle. He breathed deep. The soft sound of clicking keyboards, whispered voices and the aroma of fresh sweet coffee and baked goods felt familiar as did his restlessness. A restlessness that had grown more insistent since the birthday fiasco with Belle a year before.

Not that he was unhappy with their arrangement. To the contrary. He was getting more involved with the game he played on the Dark Web...bilking crooks out of their dirty money and siphoning it off to the other players. Thinking of all the charities they were helping was very gratifying.

Then there was Belle. She was excited that he'd offered to work with her in her garden, her favorite project besides Dark Webbing. And after supper they played old board games like *Clue* and *Risk* that Gabe had found in the local thrift shop. She especially loved *Trivial Pursuit* which got her competitive juices going, putting a sparkle in her green eyes. Unfortunately for Gabe, the more time he spent with her the more uncomfortable he was around her.

Ergo, his erotic dreams had begun. Belle, nude, laying in his arms, stirring his body, waking him in a hot sweat with the need for release. Even cold showers hadn't dampened his wanting her. And so, his occasional trips to the café and whatever hook-ups he could find.

The door opened and a tall, curvy brunette walked in and headed for the counter. Jeans and tee hugged her body like a second skin. Light brown eyes and a pert nose highlighted her oval face. A definite looker. He'd been with Ginger a couple of times. They'd spent a few hours together in a seedy motel down the block and then went their separate ways. Little conversation. No commitment. Perfect. Now, looking at her Gabe sighed, having to admit to himself that all the hook-ups in the world didn't really help.

He was in deep shit.

His computer pinged, bringing his attention back to the game. He thoughtlessly made a move and then cursed himself when his opponent responded and signaled 'Checkmate.' Gabe conceded, thanked the guy for the game and signed off. He rose, grabbed his laptop and strolled into the men's room, hoping Ginger didn't see him, hadn't planned on staying and would be gone with a takeout order.

He waited for ten long minutes before venturing into the main room. No sign of Ginger. The gods were with him. After getting a half dozen pastries to go, Gabe fled the café, got in his truck and headed home.

And halted in shock when he opened the front door.

Belle sat in the middle of the floor, legs budda-style, a large golden curly-haired dog playfully tugging at a rope she held. When it jumped up at her and licked her face Belle shrieked in laughter, hugged the furry beast and continued playing tug-of-war with the mutt. When she heard the door close, she looked up and spied Gabe. He didn't believe eyes could sparkle any more than hers did at that moment.

"Say hello to Cleo," she said, a broad smile on her face.

Gabe just stared. Then he found his words. "Where did it come from?"

"Not it. She, and man, did I have a struggle getting her here on my Ducati."

Just picturing the scene of Belle speeding through the hills with the dog in her lap gave him a tension headache. And almost a smile.

"It's a wonder you and the mutt didn't wind up down one of those ravines."

Belle looked insulted. "Cleo is not a mutt. She's a pedigreed Labradoodle." The dog gave her another exuberant lick on her cheek. Belle laughed.

"What the hell is a Labradoodle?"

"It's a relatively new breed between a Labrador Retriever and a Standard Poodle that was created to work as service dogs. Since they're amazingly smart and don't shed, poodles make a perfect match with a Lab as guide dogs for the blind and other service organizations."

Gabe frowned. "How old is this dog?"

"Cleo is only four-months-old. She'll be a lot bigger when she's full grown."

Gabe sat down on a nearby chair staring at the dog, forgetting he carried pastries in the bag. "I'll bet."

But the scent of food had drifted immediately into Cleo's nose. She turned away from Belle and leaped on Gabe's lap, stretching her curly-haired snout toward the bag. Gabe let out a grunt as the dog's paws rested on his chest. He pushed her not-too-gently off before she got hold of the goodies. Unfazed, Cleo rolled over and trotted toward more friendly environs in front of Belle. While the dog's behavior pissed Gabe off, the sound of Belle's giggles lighted his nerve endings like sparks from a defective electric outlet.

Belle rose and grabbed Cleo's leather collar. "Sorry," she said between laughs. "She's still a puppy and needs a lot of training."

"No kidding." He shook his head. "What made you get a dog?"

"I got her for you." Belle sobered. "You seem bored, restless lately, so I thought you might like more company around here."

Since he wasn't into bestiality, he doubted a dog would ease what ailed him.

"And," Belle continued, the smile back on her face, "I've signed us up for behavior training classes."

Belle looked so pleased with herself Gabe didn't have the heart to stay annoyed. He sighed, wishing he could express his thanks with a brotherly hug, but that was a thing of the past. Those feelings had somehow morphed into deeper, more intimate needs. And he was sure she'd freak out if she knew. So instead he relaxed and nodded. "Sounds like a plan."

Cleo must have sensed his change of attitude because she trotted over. Instead of jumping on him, she sat at his feet and stared up at him with an open, curious look in her soft brown eyes. Something tugged at Gabe's heart and he knew he was hooked.

*   *   *

Months rolled by and Cleo grew taller and heavier. Gabe had to admit to himself that Belle had been right to bring the mutt into their lives. While his sexual tension hadn't decreased, his attention was often focused elsewhere. He thoroughly enjoyed the time he, Belle and Cleo spent together, at the classes and hiking. How had Belle, who'd lived such a solitary life with her parents, developed better social instincts than he? Her mother and father must have been amazing people.

His fingers roboted on the keyboard while his mind strayed. He hadn't thought about his family for a long time. Pushed thoughts of them away whenever they poked at his memories demanding attention. But now he let them sneak in a little. Past the sadness and guilt. Eventually landing on the truth that he'd avoided for so long. They'd just been frustrated worried parents, pushing him to be the best person he could. But he'd seen their demands as limiting his freedom. Not letting him be who he knew himself to be. They'd butted heads for years. He'd been an explosion waiting to happen. Until it finally did.

Cleo's furry face on his thigh brought him back to the present. Big soft eyes gave him that curious look that telegraphed she knew precisely what he was thinking.

Sitting next to Gabe, Belle noticed Cleo and then looked at him. "She knows when something's bothering you."

He shrugged and continued typing.

"She's braver than I am." Belle turned in her seat and watched him.

"What are you talking about? She's just a dog. It's instinct. Bravery has nothing to do with it." He stopped typing and glanced at her. "Besides. You're the bravest person I know. I don't like it when you put yourself down like that."

"I'm not putting myself down. Just telling the truth. Cleo is fearless and I'm afraid of my own shadow."

"Dogs don't have feelings."

"You know, Gabe, for a brilliant man sometimes you are *so* clueless." Belle sounded annoyed.

He frowned for a long moment before resuming his work at the keyboard. "Thanks for the vote of confidence."

Belle let out a frustrated sigh. Got up and walked into her bedroom.

Stormy emotions swirled in his brain. Realizing he'd hurt her feelings, he felt like shit. Belle'd been trying to open up, share something personal, and he'd shut her down. He looked down at Cleo whose head still warmed his thigh.

Patted her. "She's right again. I'm such a jackass. I wish you, oh mighty beast, could talk and tell me what to do to make it up to her."

Cleo whined. Gabe smiled. "You're no help."

He logged off and after gathering his courage, knocked on Belle's door. After a moment she called out and he entered. Her back was to him while she put clean clothes in her dresser drawers. "I'll start supper in a few minutes," Belle said into her laundry basket.

He wasn't very good at this kind of thing. With hands in his pockets, he shifted on his feet, then grabbed at the first words that came to him. "I was thinking how smart you are. Always make the right choice."

Belle looking at him, through curious eyes.

"I was wondering since I was never in foster homes why you turned out better than me."

Belle frowned. "What's wrong with the way you turned out?"

Gabe sat on the bed and studied his boots. "You've got a reason for hiding out here. I have a family I'm afraid to get back in touch with."

"Is that something you want to do?"

"I've been thinking about it lately."

She went over and sat next to him on the bed. "You're my best friend, Gabe," she shrugged, "my only friend. What can I do to help?"

He stared into her soft green eyes filled with concern. Almost a plea. He wanted so much to touch her soft cheek, feel her arms around him. Suck in her strength. Comfort him. But knew she wouldn't like it. So he let the sadness pass. Swallowed. Forced a weak smile.

"Don't worry about me." He straightened. "Just feeling sorry for myself." He stood. "Think I'll take the mutt on a run. Be back before supper." He strode out her bedroom, leashed Cleo and they left the cabin.

After trekking for two miles along a piney trail, Gabe stopped and sat on a large boulder. Cleo, now off-leash, dashed after a mouse she'd chased out of its hiding place beneath a sticker bush. Gabe pulled his phone out of his pocket and stared at it, calling up all the courage he could muster. Maybe there was no cell service. Maybe they'd changed their number. Maybe they wouldn't be home. Maybe they'd hang up as soon as they heard his voice. Maybe. Maybe. Maybe. What a coward.

He shook himself out of his musings and punched in the only phone number he had for his family's home. It rang three times before a soft female voice answered.

"Hello."

Gabe's heart pounded. Even after seven years he recognized his mother's voice. Waves of guilt and shame washed over him. Choking him. He couldn't breathe.

"Hello?"

The phone burned his hand. He wanted to toss it into the woods. Instead he disconnected. He stared at the tall oak on the side of the trail, taking a few minutes to settle. But he knew it would take a lot longer for the litany of self-recrimination that soaked his brain to dissipated.

Coward. He was a fucking coward.

CHAPTER SIX

Only the falling curtain of darkness forced Gabe home. He wanted to stay away longer but hiking in the woods at night was risky. Besides, Cleo kept staring up at him with pleading eyes, reminding him she hadn't eaten yet.

Belle was in the kitchen preparing dinner. She turned when he reached for the dog food. "Just in time. The spaghetti and meatballs will be done in a minute." She bent and took bread from the oven, put it in a plastic basket.

After feeding Cleo, Gabe spread a thick glob of butter on the warm bread and munched, watching Belle move around the tiny space. The hunger he wanted to satisfy wasn't for food. It was getting harder and harder to deny his feelings for his roommate. Gabe had no idea how Belle felt about him. Maybe she was struggling with the possibility of a new relationship between them and the thought of deeper intimacy scared the shit out of her. Maybe her feelings hadn't changed. Maybe...ah, shit. Again with the maybes.

His mind was a jumble. Belle. Parents. He shook his head hoping to clear it. What he needed was a change. In the past he would've run. Well, at least he'd grown up a little. Running was no longer an option. He needed something new to point him in another direction. Until that appeared, he sighed, he'd toughen up.

They chit-chatted about what they'd found on the Dark Web, what they needed from the stores on their next trip into town., how well Cleo was doing with her training. Gabe found their easy-going conversation both warming and frustrating. Cozy yet painful. He was a wad of seaweed tossed around in an angry ocean.

When dinner was done and cleared away, Belle begged off to her room, closing the door behind her. Gabe turned on the goose-neck lamp by his computer. He needed mindless pecking on the keyboard to override his unsettling thoughts. Hacking scumbags and anonymously donating to non-profit organizations was usually a balm to his conflicting thoughts. And boy did he need relief tonight.

After trolling the Dark Web for a while he hit on an ad he hadn't seen before. What was an adoption agency doing there? Nothing legit, that was for sure. So he followed the digital breadcrumbs until he found the source...a website with pictures of smiling children dressed in their finest all hoping for new parents and happy homes. But Gabe's keen insights noticed a shadow of fear behind each child's eyes. A cold chill crawled up his spine. This was a new approach to child porn at the least and child prostitution at the worst.

Musing about the home page, Gabe doubted law enforcement had found this disturbing website yet. Only someone with his or Belle's skills would be able to. And he knew in his gut he couldn't let this one go without advising law enforcement. Since he wasn't sure which alphabet agency handled human trafficking, he decided to send the FBI the tip. He created a complex chain of IP's with a discreet email address and forwarded the info about the website.

When he was done, he sat back, hands held above his keyboard, then rested on his lap. Nervous energy ran through him. Helping law enforcement was definitely a first for him. He used to harass them every chance he got. Now he was assisting them. No. He was only helping the poor kids who got snagged up in the human trafficking net. He wasn't sure how his involvement would play out, but one thing was certain. If Belle knew he might have inadvertently alerted law enforcement to their presence, she'd freak. Really freak.

*   *   *

Each day during the next couple of weeks, Gabe had checked the adoption website. Nothing seemed to have changed. It was still up and running with new pictures of kids constantly added. What was the FBI waiting for? They should've shut down the site by now. He had, however, gotten a few emails on his secure website asking who he was and how he'd discovered the site. He'd ignored them, not wanting to get involved with the Feds. He felt like a creep keeping all this from Belle. He'd never lied to her before and it niggled at him.

Then last night he'd discovered another suspicious website, followed its IP trail and uncovered a potential cyber threat to national security. His heart had raced. He couldn't ignore this one. Now more than children were involved. He'd forwarded the site to the FBI. That morning they attempted to reach him. Gabe figured they couldn't decide if he was a whistleblower or the terrorist who was putting up these before-undiscovered sites. After a few more emails from the feds, Gabe figured he'd better respond.

So now, after Belle had gone to bed, he sat at his computer, cracked his knuckles and stepped into the unknown.

On his encrypted email to the Feds, he typed: *What do you want from me?*

They answered a minute later. *Who are you?*

Gabe: *Just a happy hacker who likes to harass the bad guys.*

FBI: *You're one of the best we've come across. If you're legit, we'd like to use your services.*

Gabe: *Not interested.*

FBI:. *We often work with exceptional hackers who'd gotten caught and choose to work with us rather than jail time.*

Gabe: *Since my work doesn't involve criminal activity I'm not interested in making any deals with the Feds. I'm a freelancer. A Robin Hood having fun fucking over dirtbags.*

FBI: *Our kind of guy. It would be totally anonymous as well as very lucrative. If you're really a patriot we should talk.*

Gabe held back his automatic response. He'd been getting bored with his 'turning-bad-money-into-good' project. Getting involved at a more significant level might be just the distraction he was looking for. A new course. But then there was Belle. This whole deal demanded more thought.

Gabe: *I'll think about it.*

FBI: *Good. In the meantime, thanks for your tips. Keep up the good work.*

That night, sleep alluded Gabe. He couldn't get comfortable. Sweat dripped, dampening the sheets. His head ready to explode. A slide show of confusing pictures. If only his thoughts were as far from reality as most 8mm movie reels. It was nearly dawn before he came to a decision and slowly drifted into an exhausted sleep.

*   *   *

Gabe watched Belle move about the tiny kitchen. Scrambling eggs. Frying bacon. Making toast. The homey aroma settled into him with a heavy sadness. Scenes of the past. Scenes of the present. Worry about the future. Would this be the last breakfast they shared? He pushed down the unsettling questions and surged ahead.

She put the plates filled with food on the table and sat across from him. Began eating. Gabe took mental pictures as if to preserve the moments for the future. His chest rose and fell. Nerves skitted. Ah, fuck.

"We have to talk," he said

She raised her head. Eyes clear and bright. Looked at him and then his untouched eggs. "Not hungry?"

When he didn't answer she frowned and put down her fork. "Spit it out."

His chest heaved when he took a deep breath. "You know I don't lie, right?"

"Yeah." She eyed him suspiciously.

He hesitated. "Well, I haven't really lied."

"Gabe. What are you trying to say?"

"I...uh...found clues deeply hidden in the Web that I figured I better do something about."

"What did you find?"

"Statements. Conversations between two foreign persons. Sounded like terrorist threats."

"And?"

By the look of worry and deep furrows on Belle's brow, Gabe realized he wasn't handling this very well. Forget his fears...he had to spill. "My conscience couldn't let it ride."

Belle stiffened, as though expecting danger. "What did you do?" Her voice was barely a whisper.

"I tipped off the FBI."

Gabe had never seen Belle's face so pale, nor her eyes so fearful. It was as though the air had been sucked out of the room. Silence hung like a dark spirit over them. His chest hurt from trying to breathe. Shit. What had he done?

It was many minutes before Belle recovered enough to break her horrified stare and squint at him. "What else?"

"They kept bugging me. At first I ignored their messages. But then, well, I decided I better find out what they wanted."

Her stare returned, eyes wide with condemnation. "Are you telling me you talked with the Feds?"

Gabe shrugged. "Well, not talked. We IM'd. But don't worry. They'll never trace my encrypted account." Maybe this would reassure her.

Belle sat back in the chair. Folded her arms across her chest. "Tell me."

"They said I was the best they'd ever come across. Wanted me to work for them." He stopped then added. "Anonymously, of course."

"And you agreed?"

"No. I said I'd think about it. That's why I'm telling you." He laid his arms on the counter, reaching for her. "I know how much you value your privacy. Your secrecy. But I swear they'll never be able to trace me." He heard the begging in his voice, but didn't care. He needed to convince her she was safe.

Sans a wall clock, Gabe imagined hearing the minutes tick away before she spoke.

"You do what you have to, Gabe. And I'll do what I have to." She stood, put the dishes in the sink and walked into her bedroom, back ramrod-straight, arms held tightly against her body.

Gabe put his head in his hands. Why had he felt the need to be a hero, protect his country? Let the Feds' comments about his abilities affect him? Was his ego so weak he needed their praise? Had he lost Belle forever? Even if he apologized till he ran out of breath and agreed not to get involved any further with the Feds, would she ever trust him again?

There was no turning back now. One way or the other, he had to make a decision that he knew would change the rest of his life. Again he'd put himself into a lose-lose situation.

He was well and truly fucked.

CHAPTER SEVEN

On the drive back from grocery shopping, Gabe mused over the last two weeks since the BIG ADMIT. That's what he coined his telling Belle about his contact with the FBI. Though they still worked side by side in the garden, strolled the trails with Cleo, worked on their computers and did a hundred other simple activities that meant a lot to him, Gabe didn't know how much more he could take. She had barely said a word. Her silence felt like icicles in his heart. Each night sleep avoided him for hours. When he finally slipped into unconsciousness angry burning dreams woke him panting. The lack of uninterrupted sleep didn't help his daytime mood.

Until that moment he hadn't come to a decision...join the FBI in whatever limited capacity he could or forget the whole thing. He sighed. Probably didn't matter. Belle would never forgive what she felt as his betrayal of her and her privacy. But if he wanted to be true to himself, he had only one direction to go. And the thought of leaving tore him apart.

When he pulled up to the house, he saw her working in the garden. It was exhausting emptying the truck, his arms feeling like thick heavy logs, his legs like tree stumps. He put the groceries away, pulled a cold bottle of iced tea from the fridge and sat at the counter staring at the wall ahead. A condemned man facing his last day on earth. The end of his life.

And wasn't that just the case?

Half an hour later Belle came in, walked to the sink and washed. Gabe watched, the most profound sadness he'd ever felt strangling him. She was so beautiful. Body small, shapely, strong. Mind brilliant, quick, integrous. Spirit kind, generous, committed. He ached at what he'd be throwing away, never to be near again.

"Belle. Please sit down." He hoped to God he would find the right words.

She turned and stared at him with cold eyes. Silent. Then pulled out a chair and sat. Back straight. Hands folded on her lap.

"The past two weeks have been hard on both of us. You're the most important person in my life. Yet I've hurt you." He shook his head in frustration. "Maybe I shouldn't have told you, but I've never lied to you before and didn't want to start now. I'm so sorry."

Silence. Her cold eyes hadn't melted.

Gabe cleared his throat. What could he say that could fix things? Nothing, her unbending demeanor told him. His shoulders drooped. "Something's always nagging me. You named it. Restlessness. I've made some bad choices because of it. Maybe this one is another." Tears stung his eyes. Embarrassed, he shook his head again. "I don't want to leave you, Belle. I...I love you. But I have to do something more meaningful with the brain I was given." He couldn't believe that had slipped out. His church-going mother would've been proud.

He begged Belle with a silent request to say something. Anything. Be angry. Yell. Call him a betrayer. Throw something. Instead, a cold statue sat there. Giving him nothing. At a loss for words, he slumped back and bit his lip.

After a long moment, Belle stood and walked into her bedroom, closing the door quietly behind her. Gabe put his head in his hands. Fuck.

                    *   *   *

It seemed as though he'd just fallen asleep when something woke him. Not a noise. A sense that the air in the room had shifted. A new presence. Groggy, he glanced at the clock on the nightstand. One-forty. Blinking, his vision cleared enough to see the small shadowy figure standing naked next to his bed. He sat up quickly.

"Belle? Is something wrong? Are you alright?"

She rested on the edge of the bed. "You're leaving tomorrow." A statement, not a question. "I've never been with a man before. I want you to be my first. Probably my last."

That jolted his heart. "I don't think that's a good idea."

"You said you loved me. Was that a lie?"

He leaned against the headboard and folded his arms. "No. But making love will only make our parting harder and I've hurt you enough."

She moved closer. "I don't know when my feelings for you changed but they have. After tonight we may never see each other again. I want something I can hold onto in the long dark nights ahead. Something that matters. And you matter, Gabe. You always have." She reached out and brushed her small soft hand along his rough cheek. Slid her thumb along his lips. Her glorious jade eyes sparkled in the dusky light. Curious. Determined.

"Belle," he whispered. "Are you sure?"

She leaned over, placed her hands on his bare chest and kissed him.

After a moment's hesitation, Gabe drew her into his arms. Held her. Content with the feel of her softness so close. The sweet smell of her. Their hearts beating in sync like distant drums.

He slid down. Belle stretched out on him. Still holding onto him as though afraid to let go. Their lips melded. Tongues danced. Hearts pounded. When his hand found her full breast, her nipple, they moaned. He flipped her under him. After endless touching, feeling, they came together. Once. Twice. Until exhaustion took over and they slipped into a deep sleep.

*   *   *

Light filtered through the shades when Gabe awoke. Content for the first time in his life. He knew if anyone had seen the stupid look on his face there'd be no end to the teasing. He reached over and found the bed empty. A profound sadness swept through him. Then he remembered the last words Belle had said before they'd fallen asleep.

"I love you, Gabe," she'd whispered. "But I won't be here when you leave. I can't say goodbye. It's too hard."

Hard didn't come near to what he was feeling. Unbearable. Intolerable. Like his heart had been ripped out of his chest. He stuffed back hot tears.

He gave himself a while to settle before a firm resolve took over. He pulled himself out of bed, dressed in jeans and a tee. Stuffed his meager belongings into his backpack. In the front room, he refused to look around for Belle. Grabbed his laptop. Sucked in the familiar warm scent of the last five years. Their home. Belle. He closed the door behind him. Aware she was no longer a presence, but a deep hole he knew he'd never fill.

He got into his truck and drove away.

CHAPTER EIGHT

Five Years Later

"Been a while, bro." The bartender slid a cold one in front of his customer.

Gabe lifted his chin in greeting. "Been out of town." He took a long pull of his Corona.

"You haven't missed much." The man moved down to take another order.

Gabe's eyes latched onto the myriad shapes and colors of the bottles that rested on shelves across from him. He'd made the bar his first stop before heading to the cabin. Needed to put the past five years in storage. So he used the haunting voice of John Denver wafting out of the old jukebox about country roads taking him home to fill him with peace like a warm and welcoming blanket. God, did he need that. Had to calm the trepidation he felt about the reception he'd find at the cabin.

His attempts to push Belle out of his mind and heart had failed miserably. Not a day had gone by that he hadn't relived every moment of their time together. Wondered what she was doing. Smelled the delicious aroma of her cooking that filled the small cabin. Felt the cool air on his face while they hiked side by side with Cleo. Whoa. He had to put the brakes on his mental meanderings before they landed on his last night with Belle. He couldn't go there. Too wonderful. Too painful.

Enough is enough. Gabe tossed money on the bar, waved to the bartender and left. The crisp night air was a fresh relief from the smoky saloon. He felt drained, having driven the long ride from Tucson straight through. The bed in his room at the cabin drew him like a siren song. He hoped Belle would be asleep. Needed a good rest before he faced her in the morning.

He sensed the absence of life the moment the truck pulled up in front of his former home. An eerie feeling settled over him as he surveyed the cabin and grounds. Weathered boards. Closed curtains. Stone chimney. No change there. But the grounds....No flowers hung in baskets from the porch roof, nor edged the steps leading to the front door. Fallen leaves covered the dead wheat-colored grass they'd worked so hard to cultivate. And Belle's beloved garden lay abandoned, uncared for, taken over by the assault of the seasons.

Surprised his key still worked, he slowly opened the door. A chill swept through him, knowing what he'd find inside.

For the first time he cursed his instincts. The cabin was as empty of life as the yard. No warm smell of recently prepared meals greeted him. Instead, the air was dank and musty. A thick layer of dust covered the tables and furniture. No computers, monitors or printers sat at their usual spots. With each step through the vacant rooms Gabe felt his heart sink. He sat on his bed, memories of the last night they'd spent there refusing to stay away. But the wonder of that night couldn't melt the ice that chilled him to the bone.

Eventually his rational mind took over. Every day for the past five years he'd followed her digital footprints on the web. He'd told himself he just wanted to know she was okay. But the truth was, he needed that connection to her to get through his days. He found nothing new. Nothing to indicate a change of any kind. He'd felt secure that she was fine.

Hurting like he was maybe, but still functioning. This brought him some measure of peace. But now...fear gripped him. Where had she gone? When had she abandoned their home? And most important...why?

He shook himself into action. He had to find her. Make sure she was alright. He wouldn't rest until he was reassured.

*   *   *

The tiny bell above the door tinkled when Gabe pushed it open. The small pet shop smelled clean, fresh. Tanks of various sizes lined one wall, bubbles floating to the surface, plants waving in their wake, little colorful fish darting around in the clear water. Gerbils and mice spun robotically on their wheels in other tanks while small lizards and turtles lay lazily in theirs. On the opposite wall hung collars, leashes, plastic bags with small toys, treats and dog bones. The shelves beneath held ceramic dishes and bowls of varying shapes and sizes. And on the floor sat bags of food for all kinds of pets. A counter running three-quarters of the width of the store blocked what Gabe assumed was the storeroom. Two women browsed the shelves and chatted as they handled several items. Each held the leash of small white dogs who wiggled, pulled and demanded the freedom to investigate the food bags on the floor.

Gabe's attention was yanked away from his assessment of the store and its customers when a very large curly-haired dog scampered out from behind the counter and raced to him, nearly knocking him over when it jumped up and licked his face. Gabe couldn't hold back first a surprised grunt and then a laugh.

"Cleo, you mutt. How've you been?" He pushed her off. "Guess all those behavioral classes we took to you were a waste of time and money." The dog just stared up at him from a sitting position, her soft brown eyes full of love. Gabe ruffled her head.

The women had turned when Cleo jumped on Gabe, shocked at the dog's behavior. When they noticed Gabe wasn't upset, they smiled and returned to their shopping, their pets yapping frantically at Cleo. When Cleo turned and gave a loud, menacing bark at them, they shut up and cowered next to their owners. Gabe had to laugh. Cleo was definitely the alpha controlling her territory.

It was then that he spied Belle coming out from the storeroom, several small boxes in her arms. "Cleo. Quiet," she called out. Spying Gabe she stopped short. Mouth open. Face ashen. Eyes wide and...fearful?

His heart stopped. Her hair, longer now, was pulled back into a ponytail. Wisps of blonde curls hung loosely around her pixie face. The small, trim body he'd last held in his arms hadn't changed. Memories had him sucking in his breath.

The two women, having decided on their purchases, approached the counter. "Morning, Isabelle." The taller of the two smiled and tilted her head toward Gabe. "Guess Cleo's found an old friend."

Belle pulled her gaze off Gabe and gave her customer a weak smile. "Appears so." She put the boxes on the counter, rang up their purchases, placed the items in two bags and handed them to the women along with their credit cards. "Nice to see you again, Jane. You too, Connie." The ladies smiled and dragged their whimpering dogs out of the store.

After staring at each other for a long moment, Gabe was the first to speak. Voice low.

"I went to the cabin. Felt like a haunted house without you there."

She turned from him and busied herself taking bags of treats out of one of the boxes. "What're you doing here?"

She walked to the wall with the treats and added the new ones. "Tired of having the Feds pull your strings?" Behind the counter again, she opened another box.

Gabe realized she wasn't going to make this easy. So he'd take whatever she'd throw at him. It was the least he could do.

"Something like that." He looked around the shop. "Cute place. You buy it like this or set it up yourself?"

After emptying another box and setting cat toys on the appropriate shelf, she turned to him, arms akimbo, angry. "What do you want, Gabe?"

"When I didn't find you at the cabin, I got worried something had happened. Wanted to see for myself you were okay."

She scoffed, walked back behind the counter and glared at him. "Well, thanks for stopping by. Now that you see everything is hunky-dory, you can go, conscience clear, no worries, back to wherever you went. To whatever you've been doing for five years." Blue eyes glared at him like brilliant sapphires. He must've been mistaken about the fear.

Gabe strolled around the shop fingering the merchandise, finally standing in front of the window that faced the main street. "Looks like a nice little town. What's its name again?"

Belle dropped the cans of cat food she'd released from their cardboard prison onto the counter and took a long deep breath. "Harmonee, California, east of Sacramento, nestled in the Sierra Nevada foothills. Established in 1880 by the Harmon family. A farming community of 2500."

Gabe turned and gave her his cute-kid smile. "Thanks, Alexa."

Belle shook her head and resumed re-stocking shelves.

Gabe watched her with more than mild curiosity. "Why the change of venue?"

"Seemed like a good idea at the time."

He shook his head. "Nah. Too flaky. Not your usual M.O."

Belle picked up a 50 lb bag of kibble which proceeded to slip out of her hands. Gabe approached her and lifted the bag. "Where do you want this?"

Lips drawn tight together, Belle motioned to an empty spot on the floor a few yards away. Without a word, she returned to the counter. Cleo followed Gabe's every movement.

The doorbell tinkled and a tall man, maybe early forties, dressed in khakis and a short-sleeved white dress shirt entered. Belle shifted her angry gaze from Gabe to the newcomer. "Morning, Ben. How's the puppy doing?"

The man smiled as he approached the counter. "Suit's getting the hang of the basics but definitely needs to begin the next step in his training. Thought I'd schedule a lesson with you before I start a trial in two weeks."

She ignored Gabe and opened her iPad. "How's Friday at 8:00 a.m.?"

"Perfect. We still on for lunch tomorrow?"

Belle smiled. "Yup."

"Great. Meet you at the Café." The man nodded to Gabe on his way out. The doorbell tinkled.

Gabe stared after him. Didn't the guy have a phone? Did he have to make a personal visit? And the way he looked at Belle...Gabe felt a burning rush of...something...crawl into his stomach. He couldn't hide the edge he heard in his voice when he turned back to Belle. "Good to see you're putting all those dog training classes we took to good use. I'll bet you have a great garden too."

Belle slammed her iPad closed. "I really don't have time for chit-chat, Gabe, so if you don't mind, I'd appreciate it if you'd leave. This foray into the past has been real, but now it's time for you to reset the clock."

He gave her a crooked smile. "I think I'll stick around town. Never know what'll turn up. Maybe I'll decide to put down roots." He put a business card on the counter. "You can reach me here when you have more time for chit-chatting."

She gave the card a quick glance. Raised smoldering eyes. "Don't hold your breath."

Gabe gave Cleo a pat on her head, strolled to the door, then turned. Somber. "By the way, Belle. I'm glad you haven't changed. You're still the beautiful, strong, capable survivor you always were. It's good seeing you." He wondered if she could read the regret and longing in his eyes. He left the shop, the gentle tinkle of the doorbell having lost all pretense of welcoming.

*   *   *

Gabe leaned back in his truck, closing his eyes. It'd been worse than he'd imagined. Apparently she'd fared well with their separation. Better than he. Not that he'd want it any other way. Just proved once again how much more stable and sensible she was. She had a new life. Maybe even a new man. Was using her given name, Isabelle. His questions were answered...she was fine and didn't need him. He should leave and find another place to settle down. Maybe even get up enough courage to reach out to his parents. Yeah. That's what he'd do. But first he'd take a couple days rest. Recover from the drive and the anxiety of searching for Belle.

Pondering his next move, Gabe scanned the layout of the small village. Tall trees, bright flowered bushes and neatly mowed grass made up the large square in the center of town. The two largest buildings were City Hall on one side of the square and the Rialto Café opposite on the other. They were surrounded by small shops, including Belle's Pet

Emporium, the newspaper/real estate office, bank, book store, grocery, pharmacy and not to mention the proverbial old fashioned ice cream parlor. The quiet, slow pace of the town filled Gabe with a sense of peace he hadn't felt since he'd left Belle and their cabin.

He thought about his current role with the FBI. He'd agreed to work with them anonymously and had moved to a new place outside Tucson, physically far away from Belle. The work had initially been very satisfying. Scanning for buzz words on their list of possible threats, tracking them through the maze of IP's that crisscrossed the globe. Advising the Feds when he assessed the risks to be viable enough for them to follow up. A big responsibility that not only tested his skills but validated them. So far he'd been right on. His handlers were impressed.

But after five years his nemesis boredom kicked in. He was tired of living alone. Never really connected with the few people he interacted with on his excursions into town. Had no interest in casual sexual hookups any longer. And God, he missed Belle. It was then the Feds offered him the possibility of working full time in their facility in Langley alongside the other hackers and coders. But he wasn't sure that option would fill the emptiness inside. After much deliberation, he'd decided to return to Belle. Maybe her fear of working with the Feds had softened. After all, Gabe had been safe and secure for five years. He hoped to convince her he could live with her and continue to work anonymously with the FBI.

Ergo, his search for Belle and his trip to Harmonee.

After today he realized he had a long hard road ahead to get back into her good graces, not to mention her bed. But being in her presence, even for such a short time, had reaffirmed his need to have her in his life. He'd do whatever it took to convince her to take him back. But now, sitting in his truck outside her shop, he had no clue how to do this.

CHAPTER NINE

Fate had nothing to do with it. No sir. It was pure planning on Gabe's part that had him sitting at the counter of the Rialto Café the following day. Not having a well-thought-out plan on how to win Belle back, he'd decided to take one day at a time and use whatever clues the Universe offered him. So here he was slowly nibbling at his burger and fries, sipping iced tea, scanning the weekly copy of Harmonee's newspaper, *Chatterbox*. He snorted. It read more like a Lifetime movie than critical news. But as Belle had advised him yesterday...farming community...2500 folks.

So he missed Belle when she entered the Café. She, however, hadn't failed to notice him. He felt her presence the moment she stood next to him.

"What are you doing here?" The glaring anger in her eyes felt like sharp needles pricking his skin.

Gabe grinned and nodded at his lunch. "Sampling the local fare."

"Careful you don't choke."

He let out a short laugh. "Why don't you say what you really feel, sweetheart?"

"Words cannot express what I really feel."

He shrugged. "Well, you're doing a good job."

"And don't call me sweetheart." Her voice rose in anger and frustration.

He was enjoying their little verbal tennis match. Wanted it to continue. But when the figure of a tall man approached Belle his wish vaporized. Gabe groaned and glanced at the man. She must have noticed Gabe's eyes shift because she turned and saw Ben. Her face flushed. Her brief look of confusion and worry surprised Gabe. Something was going on between them.

The man glanced first at Belle and then at Gabe.

Belle sighed heavily, putting a pleasant tone in her voice. "Ben Channing, this is Gabe Carter, my...uh...former roommate."

Ben gave Gabe a long curious stare then reached out his hand. Gabe shook it, noticing the comparison between the man's smooth, unblemished palm and Gabe's calloused one. Lawyer, he remembered.

"Nice to meet you," Ben said.

"You too." The lie sat heavy on his tongue. He glanced at Belle, pale face staring at him as though waiting for some explosion to erupt between him and her new BFF. Well, he wasn't going to give her the satisfaction. He turned away and stuffed the last of his cheeseburger along with the bile that had risen from his twisted stomach into his dry mouth. He reached for his iced tea, ignoring them. "Enjoy your lunch." He drained the glass and called to the waitress. "Check please."

He felt her hesitation, then relief. Out of the corner of his eye he saw them pass and head for a booth in the back. Taking a deep breath, he paid his bill and left the café. What the hell had he expected to achieve by waylaying them? Definitely not what had happened. Belle, clearly upset by seeing him and Ben together. Ben. Friendly. Curious. Protective? Gabe had to find out what was going on with them. But how?

*   *   *

While jogging early the next morning, Gabe decided to approach his task like a mission. He'd been the inside man on many ops with the feds over the years. Surely he could figure out a way to get Belle to talk with him.

Tired and sweaty, he walked into the lobby of the Rialto. Upon arriving in town the other day, he'd rented a room there. The building turned out to be not only a café, but a hotel, bar and dance hall. An authentic country community center straight out of smalltown America.

The pert teenaged receptionist greeted him. "Morning, Mr. Carter." Her smile portrayed the wholesome innocence he rarely saw in city teens. "Out for an early jog?"

"Hey, Olivia. Getting my lay of the land." Gabe took in a few extra deep breaths and finally brought his heart rate back to normal. "Beautiful country around here."

"That's what outsiders always say, but I don't notice since I've never lived anywhere else. It's just home."

He smiled at the thought of a home. "You're a lucky girl."

Her face took on a pensive look. "You don't know the half of it."

Gabe's brief curiosity about her statement was interrupted when a group of little girls entered the lobby. They were herded by two thirty-something women.

"Is Larry here?" The taller of the two women asked Olivia.

"Waiting in the dance hall." Olivia nodded toward the large room on her right.

"Thanks." The woman motioned to the troupe of girls to follow her into the hall. Gabe watched them until they were out of view.

Olivia must have noticed the curious look on his face. "That was Una Merkel. Since school is closed for the summer, she takes the little girls on outings each morning. You know, childcare for working parents. Today they're going to try their hand at Line Dancing. Larry is our local caller." The teen grinned. "If I didn't have to stay behind this desk, I'd be over there watching. Should be a kick."

"How old are those kids?"

Olivia put a finger on her lips. "Let's see. Sophie is four, I think. She's the youngest. The others range up to Amy who's eight."

"Isn't four a little too young to learn to line dance?"

"Not Sophie. She's as smart as a whip. Takes after her mother." She was interrupted when the desk phone rang. "Oh. Hi." Pause. "They just arrived." Pause. "Not sure, but Una didn't think they'd last much longer than an hour." Pause. "Will do." She hung up and smiled at Gabe.

"Anything I can do for you?"

"Nah. Guess I'll hit the shower." Gabe waved as he walked up the stairs to the second floor where the six hotel rooms were. Once inside his, he stripped and stood under the hot water for a long time, planning his next move.

*   *   *

He found her digging in her garden, small hoe in hand, wide-brimmed straw hat keeping the hot sun off her face. The bucolic déjà vu scene filled him with sadness and longing, a reminder of what he'd given up and hoped to reclaim. He watched her in reverent silence until, apparently sensing his presence, she looked up, startled. When a flash of fear sparked her eyes, his reverie was dashed. Why did she always seem so afraid of him?

Belle stood. "Have you added stalking to your repertoire?" She waved the hoe at him. "You can't keep popping up like this, Gabe."

He frowned. "You seem afraid of me."

Her mouth opened to respond but she stopped short. "What...what makes you think I'm afraid? I just want to be left alone. You owe me that much."

"Just talk to me."

"We have nothing to talk about. You left and I found a new life. Period."

"Has it been so easy for you? You'll be glad to know it's been hell for me."

Now she was angry. "Good. You made your choice. Me or the FBI. Now grow up and live with it." She yanked off her straw hat, pushed past him and entered the small cottage surrounded with bright flowers and a few small shade trees.

"Belle, please. If you want me to leave, you have to talk to me." He followed her into the house...and was immediately overwhelmed by the scents that enveloped him. Bacon from the morning's breakfast. Cleo's clean doggy smell. And Belle. The familiar fragrance of shampoo and soap that defined her. He couldn't breathe. Running water in the kitchen eventually calmed him. But he couldn't speak, so he went outside and sat on the front steps, hands folded between spread knees, staring off into the distance, not knowing what to do. Lost.

It could've been ten minutes or ten hours before Gabe felt her standing behind him. Heard her sigh. Felt her warm presence next to him on the step chasing away the chills that ran through him.

"What do you want to know, Gabe?"

He glanced over at her but her face was a blank mask, her eyes looking ahead but he doubted she really saw anything.

"Why did you leave our cabin?"

She seemed to wince at this. Took a deep breath. "I didn't like being alone anymore. I needed some normalcy in my life. Something I'd never had."

Gabe nodded. "I can understand that. I keep wanting to connect with my family but still haven't had the guts." He sighed. "We're a pair, aren't we?"

When he glanced over at her, he was startled to see eyes bright with unshed tears. He changed the subject. "So. Are you and the lawyer a couple?"

"Lawyer? Oh...You mean Ben. No. We're just friends." Pause. "What about you? Anyone special in your life?"

"Nah. I spend too much time wallowing in the past. Wishing. Wanting. Angry. Sad." He paused. "Stupid, huh?"

Silence.

"Belle, I...I've missed you so much...." He shook his head, surprised he'd let that slip out. Didn't want to make her mad again. Spoil the easy conversation they'd been having. He was such an ass.

Just then a silver SUV turned into the driveway. Belle jumped up as though afraid it would crash into the porch. Her body tensed. Hands fisted at her sides. She seemed paralyzed in some kind of emotional trauma. But when the car stopped yards from her, her shoulders sagged, her hands relaxed. A soldier surrendering to the inevitable.

Gabe watched, fascinated by Belle's reactions. And more so when the car door opened and the little girl he'd seen in the Rialto lobby, Sophie he recalled, wiggled out of the car and ran up to Belle who swung her up into her arms.

"Hi Baby. Did you have fun?' Belle asked in a shaky voice.

The child put her tiny arms around Belle's neck, kissed her cheek and then pulled back, a big smile on her face. "Yeah. Ms. Una said I could be a champion line dancer when I grew up."

"Of course. You can be anything you want to be. You hungry?"

"Can I have grilled cheese, Mama? You said I can't have it every day but I had peanut butter and jelly yesterday so grilled cheese is okay for today, right?"

Belle laughed. "For sure. Thanks for reminding me."

It was then the little girl spied Gabe, who by this time was standing, hands in his pockets. "Hi." She gave him a big beaming smile. An innocent who was loved and cared for.

Gabe's mind was reeling. Belle had a child? A four-year-old? With blonde curly hair like her mother's but blue eyes instead of green. "Belle...what the hell?"

Belle put the child down, took her hand and they walked past him and up the stairs.

Sophie whispered, "That man said a bad word, Mama. You should yell at him."

"I'll be sure to do that. Come on. Wash your hands and I'll fix your sandwich."

"Belle..."

She gave him a quick look. "Later." And she and the child disappeared into the house.

He turned and stared after them, hearing childish chatter echo as they moved through the living room into what he assumed was the kitchen. Shock waves bounced off him. Head pounded. His whole body ached.

Stunned beyond belief, he dropped down onto the porch steps. On any other day he would have relished the warm sun on his body. Smiled at the raucous blue jays that chased each other from tree to tree. Heard the hum of the bees and whirling wings of the tiny hummingbirds nearby. But not today.

A good half an hour past before Belle came out and once again sat next to him.

"Where's the kid?" He mumbled.

"Watching one of her favorite videos."

"She why you left the woods for civilization?"

"Yes."

After a long uncomfortable moment, he said, "As usual you made the right decision."

She choked back a sound. "Gabe..."

"You don't have to explain. I understand. If I'd been you, I wouldn't have let me know either."

She got angry. "Damn you, why are you always so willing to let things slide? You should be pissed off. Curse me. For God's sake, Gabe, I kept your daughter away from you."

He continued staring ahead, numb. "Cause you knew I'd make a lousy father. She's better off without me."

Belle Rockyied his arm. "Like you are without your family? I've been riddled with guilt for five years and you sit here like a Stonehenge pillar, so stuck in the past you can't see or feel anything else." She hit him again. This time in his side. "What will it take to wake you up?"

That last punch broke the spell. He looked at her, his chest heaving, eyes burning. Unable to hold back the thunder clouds of emotion that roiled in him, he slouched over, body shaking, put his head on her shoulder and let them let go.

She put her arms around him and held him tight, whispering gentle words he didn't have to understand to feel their meaning. No matter what he'd done, how stupid he was, she cared about him. Maybe even still loved him. The thought was enough to make him shout in relief.

After a while he pulled away and was humbled by the look of love he saw in her beautiful green eyes. Instead of feeling ashamed for his outburst, Gabe felt cleansed. Renewed. Hopeful.

"It was wrong of me not to tell you," Belle said. "I've realized that for some time." She shook her head. "So when I first saw you I was angry. Not only at you for leaving but at myself for keeping Sophie a secret. But now...I'm so glad you're here. Thank you for coming to find me. For not giving up on us." She kissed him softly on his lips.

"Mama?"

Sophie's worried voice torpedoed the moment. Belle turned from Gabe and smiled up at the child who stood at the porch door.

Gabe quickly regained some of his composure. Turned to study the child with the new knowledge that she was his daughter. Sophie definitely favored her mother. She'd probably be small like Belle. But those blue eyes were unquestionably his. And even with his lack of experience with children, Gabe could see the spark of intelligence that shown through them. He was instantly overwhelmed with a burst of pride that filled his hungry spirit.

Belle stood and offered Sophie her hand. "Come here, sweetie. There's someone I want you to meet."

CHAPTER TEN

He stood at the precipice. The wild wind of a tornado screamed around him drawing him nearer the dangerous edge. Enticing him into the unfathomable depth below. Raw nerves spiked through him. His heart raced. This was it. The end of one life. The beginning of another.

Gabe blinked the powerful vision away. Belle drew the child to stand in front of him. He hoped she wouldn't notice the look of fear he was sure showed in his eyes.

"Sophie, this is Gabe."

She tilted her head, gave him a once-over, then smiled. "Hello."

Her soft voice lilted around Gabe like a gentle breeze. Words couldn't pass through his clogged throat. He bit his lip. Then gave her a small almost painful smile. "Nice to meet you, Sophie." He groaned at the stiffness of his words. How do you talk to a kid, anyway?

"You have blue eyes like me," she said.

Gabe cleared his throat. "But yours are prettier."

She giggled. "That's because I'm a girl." She scrutinized him. "You have a nice face."

Gabe frantically searched his mind for something to say. Finally came up with a clue. "I saw you and your friends go in for your Line Dancing."

Sophie pursed her lips. Brightened as though a light had turned on. "You were talking to Olivia."

"That's right."

"Maybe I could teach you how to Line Dance. It's real easy. Anyone can learn."

"I...I guess."

Silence. Belle filled in the lull. "Is the video over?"

Sophie continued eyeing Gabe. "Yes. Can I watch another?"

"How about a nap? You've had a busy day."

Scrunching her nose, the child looked up at her mother. "But I'm not tired."

"Tell you what. I'll check on you in a little while. If you're not asleep you can come down."

Watching his daughter's face, Gabe tried to hide a smile. Her blue eyes narrowed and moved from side to side. Tiny lines slid across her brow. Sophie was giving this a lot of thought. She seemed very smart for a four-year-old. But then, what did he know?

"It's a deal."

Just then Cleo came bounding around the corner and barked when she saw Gabe. She nearly knocked Sophie over to get to him.

Gabe couldn't help but laugh. "Hey. Watch it, mutt." He put both hands on Cleo's face to hold her.

Sophie gaped, mouth open, jaw dropped. She yanked on Cleo's collar and pulled her away from Gabe. She looked at him. "Mama says Cleo has bad manners. Guess she needs more lessons."

"It's okay. Cleo and I go back a long way."

Sophie's eyes widened. "Really?" She looked up at Belle for confirmation.

Belle smiled. "That's right. Gabe and I have been friends for a long time." Belle took a deep breath. "No more stalling. Time for your nap."

The little girl looked at Gabe with renewed interest. "Do you like milk and cookies?"

He was taken aback by her question. "Ah...sure...who doesn't?"

"Good. Cause Mama always gives me some when I finish with my nap. We can share."

Gabe felt his heart drop. "Well, that's up to your Mom."

Sophie glanced at Belle. "Can he stay for milk and cookies?"

"Why not." Belle looked at Gabe.

Sophie grabbed Belle's hand again. "See you later, Gabe."

With a quick glance at him, Belle followed her daughter into the house.

*   *   *

Gabe felt like a tree. Rooted in place unable to move. He couldn't catch his breath, feeling the vacuum created by Belle and Sophia's departure. The tiny face of his daughter filled his vision. A daughter. He couldn't wrap his mind around the concept and all that it implied. He was a father. Panic welled up inside him like a raging tidal wave. He wanted to run from the impending disaster. Pretend he was still in the cabin with Belle. Working side by side on their computers. Sharing cozy evenings together after dinner. Their last night together, wrapped in each other's arms. Whispering words that had sustained him these past five years. He slashed that memory away.

He couldn't tell how long he'd sat on the porch steps, tossed around from past memories to present realities. But when he felt Belle sit beside him he was no longer a boneless observer but a strong capable man who knew he could deal with anything.

Gabe turned and stared into Belle's brilliant jade eyes. "She's amazing," he said.

"She comes from good stock."

He shook his head. "No. You raised her. I don't even know how to talk to her."

"You did fine." She patted his cheek. "Just trust yourself."

He frowned. "Do you know what I wanted to do while I was sitting here? Run. As fast as I could. Leave her in your very capable hands."

"Yet you're still here."

"More the fool," he moaned. His eyes swept past the rolling green hills to the majestic Sierra Nevada mountains in the distance. "How long have you been in Harmonee?"

"A year and a half. I wanted a place where Sophia could grow up like a normal child. Go to school. Have friends. Be comfortable around people and all situations. Everything I never had. I was lucky to find this place."

"And the pet shop?"

"I began emailing the previous owner. She was retiring to live with her daughter in San Diego. We came to an agreement." Belle shrugged. "Here we are."

The silence was comfortable. Warming.

"Are you still working with our fellow hackers in the Robin Hood game you created?"

Belle shook her head. "I'm out of that business. From time to time a legitimate client will request a new ID, passport, a new life for protection. I'm able to weed out those needing to evade the law." She looked at him. "Are you still feeding the Feds?"

Gabe held her gaze. "I stopped about six months ago."

"Why?"

"At first I was content with my work with them. I felt as though I was working off some debt I owed the people in my past who I'd hurt. Atonement or something. Like standing at one side of a seesaw that was slowing leveling off." He shrugged. "I don't know."

"What changed?"

"The balance shifted. I realized the payment was too high. Leaving you. Our home. My need to amend. My world began to crumble." He gave her a shy smile. "I fell off the seesaw."

Belle laughed. "Gabe. When did you become such a poet?"

He grinned. "Like I said...I changed."

Her face grew somber. "You didn't change. You just become more of who you've always been. You grew up."

He studied her clear open face. "Why aren't you mad at me? God, what you must have gone through, having a kid alone, reordering your life. All because I was a selfish bastard who didn't have the good sense to know what he was throwing away." He paused. "And now to find out I didn't know the half of it."

Belle sighed. "Guess I grew up, too."

They were quiet for a while. Gabe stared out into the land beyond the house. He felt Belle's eyes warming his cheeks, her hand resting on his knee, her soft breath floating over his neck as she leaned her head on his shoulder. Maybe this was what heaven would feel like. But better. This was real and he wanted the moment to last.

Finally she spoke. "You staying at the Rialto?"

He nodded.

"I want you to stay here. No strings. Just as long as you like. Get to know your daughter. Find that sense of home you lost. It's here for the taking."

Gabe closed his eyes for a moment. "I'd like that."

*   *   *

So here he was at Belle's kitchen table with Sophie chatting away and Belle placing bowls of steaming meatballs and spaghetti with red sauce in front of them. She took her place at the table and gave him a gentle smile that hinted she knew precisely how he felt. He was so full, he had trouble conjuring up an appetite for food.

Sophie frowned, maybe sensing something was off with him. "Don't you like meatballs and pisgetti?"

Gabe cleared his throat and gave her a small uncomfortable smile. "Who doesn't like pisgetti?"

Belle chuckled. "Gabe is probably full of all those cookies you gave him."

Sophie took on a petulant mask. "Well, he didn't have to eat so many."

"You're right," he laughed. "I made a pig out of myself. But the smell of this food is starting to blow away the taste of chocolate chip cookies." He twirled a big clump of spaghetti dripping with sauce on his fork and forced it into his mouth. He nodded at his daughter. "Hmm. One of my favorites."

Gabe noticed Sophie's eyes shift between him and Cleo who sat adoringly next to him. He couldn't decide if the dog was glad to see him or was hoping he'd sneak her a meatball, shades of mealtimes past.

Sophia must have read his mind. "Cleo really likes you. But don't give her any food. Mama doesn't want her to beg when we're eating."

Gabe reached for his glass of water to escort the pasta down his throat, stumbling for an appropriate response. "That's a good rule. Cleo would be fat as a house if you let her eat everything she sees." Damn. What a stupid thing to say. The kid would think he was a simpleton. It was then he realized how much he wanted his daughter to like him. The idea embarrassed him. He searched for a change of conversation. "Do you go to school?"

"Mama teaches me. But we left the cabin so I could go to a real school." She looked over at Belle. "When can I go, Mama?"

"In September. When the new school year starts."

Sophie put her fork down and counted on her fingers. "June, July, August. Then September." She flashed a big smile. "Only three more months." She sighed. "That's a long time away."

"It'll go fast, honey," Belle said. "You have plenty of time to play with your friends, go on hikes, swim at the lake, line dance, ride your pony."

"Can Gabe meet Snowball?"

"If you'd like."

"Who's Snowball?" Gabe asked.

Sophie was excited. "My pony. Mama bought him for me when we moved here. He lives at the Farm where Olivia lives so they can take care of him when Mama works. I'm too little to wash him and feed him. But I do brush him before my riding lessons. Will you come next time we go?"

Gabe wondered if she invited every stranger to see her pony or did she have some primitive sense that he was somehow important to her? He laughed at himself. Hell. She may be smart but he doubted she was that intuitive. Still, a tiny spark of hope flickered in him.

After dinner, Belle put the *FROZEN* video on for the three of them. Gabe found his eyes resting mostly on Sophie, watching her enjoyment of the animated cartoon. Thrilled by her laughter. The sparkle in her eyes. He felt Belle watching him. When he turned to face her, she smiled and he was lost in what he saw in her eyes.

"Can we watch another one, Mama?" Sophie yawned, rubbing her tired eyes.

"That's enough movies. Time for bed."

Sophie turned to Gabe. "Will you read me a story tonight? Mama always does."

Gabe's breath caught. He looked to Belle for instructions. She grinned as though enjoying his discomfort and gave him a shrug. He nearly groaned. "Ah. Sure."

Belle got up and offered him a brief reprieve. "Bath first," she said, taking Sophie's hand.

The child looked at Gabe. "I'm very little so it won't take long."

"Great." He tried to put some enthusiasm into his words, but knew he'd failed.

"Help yourself to anything in the fridge," Belle called out to him.

Watching them leave the living room and head down the long hall to the bathroom, a bizarre realization hit him in his gut. His family. Or was he jumping to conclusions? Worry lined his forehead. Hadn't Belle offered him that possibility? Or had he imagined it out of some pathetic need on his part? Damn. This was all so new.

He rose and grabbed an iced tea from the fridge. Took a long drink. Leaned back against the cabinet and stared out the window. Only in the clean, clear air of the country could millions of stars be seen brightening the dark sky. No pollution. Just fresh healthy air to breathe and invigorate the soul.

Gabe said a silent prayer, one he barely remembered from childhood, asking for the courage he'd left behind along with his family, the moment he'd climbed out of his bedroom window for the last time and attempted to rob the old bookie. Instead of walking into the forgiving arms of his parents, the rough, judgmental hands of the cops had grabbed him. And his life as a bitter, angry bastard had been born.

Unsure whether God had the patience to hear him anymore, he finished off the iced tea, tossed the empty in the recycle bin and walked back into the living room to await the call from Belle that his new job as storyteller and father of the year would begin.

CHAPTER ELEVEN

He'd moved his things into Belle's small ranch-style home the following day. She gave him the guest bedroom next to hers and he settled in. At first uneasy, little by little he soaked in the new-found peace Belle's life offered. Sophie had insisted he read her a bedtime story each night. But rather than be apprehensive at the thought, now three weeks later, he looked forward to lying on top of the covers with her tucked under them at his side as he recalled the worlds of Dr. Seuss and Beatrix Potter his mother had opened up for him.

There was one problem. The more comfortable he felt being a father, the less content he was about being Belle's friend. The old need to want more from her, with her, was emerging from the deep recesses where he'd banished them. Every moment he spent with her and Sophie together or when they were alone after the child went to sleep, the tension grew until he felt he'd burst with the energy that tore through him.

Belle was sitting on the sofa reading when he emerged from Sophie's room. He watched her from the hall doorway, beautiful, quiet, soft yet strong. His woman. The one he wanted to spend the rest of his life with. He had to take the next step.

She looked up when he entered the living room. "She asleep?"

"Down for the count." He took a seat across from her.

She frowned. "What is it?"

Gabe was always amazed at her ability to read him so well. "These last few weeks have meant a great deal to me."

Was he mistaken, or had he seen a brief flash of fear cross her face? "You opened your home to me and generously shared our daughter. I'll never be able to thank you enough." He cursed himself when he saw the look on her face. The barely noticeable shoulder sag. Dammit. He was making a mess of this.

"You're leaving." Her voice was a whisper.

Gabe jumped out of the chair and knelt at her feet, taking her hands in his. "God no." He kissed her fingers. "Truth is, I don't ever want to leave. I want to be part of what you've built for yourself and Sophie." He knew he looked like a lovesick fool kneeling there pleading his case but he didn't care.

The smile that shone in Belle's eyes could have lited a small city. She cradled his face then drew it closer. She didn't need to speak. Her lips on his told the story. Warm. Welcoming. Promising a future. Gabe pulled her into his arms. Deepened the kiss. A token sealing a bargain.

"It's been so long," Belle whispered between kisses.

"Yeah," he said, "too long." He picked her up and carried her to her bedroom.

*   *   *

They sat on a wooden bench in the backyard watching Sophie play on the swingset he'd built for her. Gabe held Belle's hand. His big, calloused. Hers small, soft.

His body stirred. He brought her hand to his lips and kissed it.

"I love you, Belle."

"I know." And kissed his hand.

They continued watching their daughter. A thousand thoughts, ideas, were scrambling around in his mind needing resolution, but he was afraid to disrupt the amazing harmony they'd reached these past few weeks. But again, Belle must have sensed them.

"Tonight," she said. "We'll tell her tonight."

Gabe's heart dropped. Panic swept through him. How would Sophie react? Would she be happy or sad? Would she run away with tears streaming down her face or would she jump into his arms and call him 'Daddy'? He felt the ridges in his forehead were knife slashes cut deep into his very being. What would be left if she rejected him?

He felt Belle's eyes on him. "It'll be alright, Gabe. You'll see."

He stared horrified at her. "But what if...?"

"Trust me." Pause. "No. Trust yourself. Who you are." Belle gave him a gentle smile. "And trust Sophie."

Gabe swallowed. Trust. Such a huge word reminding him of the many times he'd run away from that cliff's edge. He barely whispered the only word that managed to eek out of the cracks in his fear. "Okay."

*   *   *

They decided to read Sophie's bedtime story together. Gabe mimicked the males' voices, Belle the females'. Sophie laughed each time they spoke. He decided if he died in bed tonight, he'd be okay with everything.

When Sophie asked for a second story, Belle brushed a few blond curls off the child's forehead. "Not tonight, honey. Gabe and I have something to tell you."

Sophie's gaze shifted from Gabe to Belle and back again. She waited patiently, serenely, as though nothing they could say would bother her.

Belle cleared her throat. "Do you like having Gabe live here with us?"

She beamed. "Oh, yes. He's big and strong and Cleo really likes him. And he makes me smile."

Gabe coughed, thinned his lips but remained silent.

"Well, he's going to stay with us. And he's going to stay in my bedroom from now on."

Frowning, Sophie seemed to take a moment to digest this news. Then she nodded as if Belle's statement was a foregone conclusion. "Good. All Mommies and Daddies sleep in the same bed." Then she yawned. "Can I go to sleep now?"

Gabe felt as if a cannon had exploded in his head, turning all worries and concerns to dust. What had just happened? No anger, no fear, no questions. Could it really have been that easy?

Sophie sat up and kissed Belle on the cheek. She turned to him and wrapped her tiny arms around his neck and held onto him as though welcoming home a long lost friend. She kissed his cheek, lay back under the covers, turned on her side and closed her eyes. "'Night," she said in a sleepy voice.

It took a while for Gabe and Belle to stop staring at their daughter before they quietly left the room, turning off the light behind them. In a state of shock, they walked into the living room. Belle sank onto the sofa, a soft smile on her face. Gabe stood in front of her, a huge question mark on his.

"What...? What...?"

Belle laughed. "Of course 'what'. What else should we have expected from a child with our DNA." She patted the cushion next to her. "Sit. You look like you're going to fall down any minute."

It took a while for him the shake the cobwebs out and obey. Belle grabbed his hand. "The lesson to be learned from this is to never make the mistake of thinking we know what's going on in Sophie's head. We were coming from our own fears and trepidations while she had none of those. Just the instinctive knowledge that she was loved by both of us, and who else but her mother and father would love her so much?" Belle sighed. "Oh, to be that innocent again."

Gabe put his arms around her shoulders and hugged her to him. "I want you to know that I'll protect her with my life. Keep her in that safe cocoon. No one will ever hurt her."

Belle kissed him. "Of course, they will. She lives in the world, doesn't she? But we'll be there to support her until she gets to the other side of whatever roadblocks she meets. That's our job."

In the warm glow of the single lamp that lighted the living room, he knew Belle was right. And that he'd keep following her lead, learn how to be a good father, as she'd shown him how to be a good man. He no longer questioned his good fortune the day she'd picked him up in that café. It was meant to be. And wasn't he damn grateful.

*   *   *

The following morning, after Sophie had left on a pre-school trip to the lake with Una Merkel and her cadre of chicks and Belle had gone to open the shop, Gabe sat at the kitchen table finishing off his last cup of coffee, paging through an online copy of the L.A. Times. He'd decided if he wanted to be a good father, he'd have to take steps to make sure that no one doubted the fact that Belle was his wife and Sophie his daughter. So he planned a trip to the mall about twenty miles away in search of the perfect engagement ring for Belle. They'd create the documents of their marriage and Sophie's birth to erase the idea of illegitimacy before it even bubbled up into the minds of mean-spirited people.

An article jumped out at him.

ATTORNEY'S WIFE FOUND SAFE

It recapped the events that had led up to the recent developments of the story. It appeared that several weeks ago a woman had been kidnapped. The body of her abductor had been found in a car that had slid down the embankment of a steep ravine. After an exhausting search, the officials had given up finding the victim either alive or dead. Then suddenly yesterday, a woman who matched the description of the kidnapped woman had been found by some hikers and eventually air-lifted to Santa Monica Hospital. After her ID was confirmed as Mary Logan Carter, her husband, renowned L.A. Attorney Charles Carter was called....

What the fuck. Gabe stopped reading. His heart pumped precariously fast. Sharp pain wrenched his gut. Sweat poured down his face and between his shoulder blades. Couldn't move. Barely breathe.

Finally common sense pushed through the havoc that riddled his body. Shaky hands reached into his wallet and pulled out the piece of paper he'd kept there all these years. He grabbed his cell and dialed the number he'd been avoiding for so long.

PART FOUR
Mary

CHAPTER ONE

Seems like I never use the words 'Gina' and 'no' in the same sentence.

I look around the smoky, noisy bar surveying all the twenty/thirty-somethings who mill about laughing, tossing out cliché come-ons to the opposite sex, and oh, did I forget?...drinking. I shake my head. Once again I followed my best friend Gina to a new bar she'd heard about hoping to find her ticket to the promised land. It hugs a corner in Ozone Park Long Island where the Liberty Avenue elevated train rattles by every once in a while. While I share Gina's long-term goal of marriage and children I hate the bar scene, even though it's the best way to meet guys these days. Most of the men at my job are married. The single ones don't interest me. So here I am. Again.

Gina immediately hooks up with an average looking dark-haired dude, leaving me to fend for myself. I really hate this. Introverted by nature, shackled by a weak heart from birth, I'm definitely not a risk-taker. It's not that I haven't been told many times by my friends that I'm gorgeous, with my glossy brown hair and blue eyes. It's just that I don't believe them. So I stand here sipping my Screwdriver like a lost mongrel in a sea of show dogs.

"Hi."

I pull out of my pity party and look up at the smiling, tall guy in front of me. Is he talking to me? I blink in confusion.

"Name's Andy. I haven't seen you here before."

I clear my throat. "Mary," I manage to get out. "First time."

Creedence Clearwater wales in the background something about a bad moon rising. Andy raises his voice. "Wanna dance?"

Now he had me. Dancing is the one physical activity I say 'the hell with my heart' and indulge in whenever I get the chance. My favorite form of self-expression. Freewheeling body movement. Blood stimulating rhythm. I feel free. Alive. I'm hooked.

We move to the small dance floor away from the crowd around the bar. I allow the music to take over, feeling like a graceful writhing cobra in front of Andy. His movements aren't as smooth as mine, but I don't care. I would've been happy if he was a big lumbering teddy bear as long as I get the chance to dance.

We sing along with the music and slide easily into the next fast song...Bob Seeger and his Hollywood Nights. When a slow tune comes, Andy pulls me into his arms. I hesitate, but only for a minute before I'm sucked into the soft gentle sway of our bodies. He's definitely better at slow dancing. When the song ends, he throws up his palms in surrender.

He smiles. "You wore me out. I'm thirsty." He takes my hand and we shoulder our way through the crowd. At the bar he orders our drinks.

I gaze around the dimly lit place in search of Gina. She's over in a corner, making out with someone. I sigh. Damn. Guess I'm getting home by myself tonight. As usual.

Andy keeps up a 'getting to know you' question and answer volley. He's really not a bad guy. Tall, cute. Thick wavy dark hair that seems to beg for fingers to weave into it. He seems harmless enough. So I answer in short rapid sentences, the noisy bar not allowing any other form of communication. Sometime later, I realize how tired I am.

"I'm beat. Time for me to get home."

"Where's your friend?"

"Busy." I signal to the booth in the back.

"Can I drive you?"

I think hard on this. My instincts tell me he's safe, not out to deflower a virgin or anything. Yet my no risk-taking defenses kick in. Force of habit. Do I want to keep hiding behind them, afraid to break out of the protective mold I've built around myself? After all, I'd purposely delayed going to college so I could meet more mature people in a working environment. Enhance my poor social skills. Maybe it's time to stretch out, as innocuous as this little challenge appears to be.

"Sure." I wave good-bye to Gina on the way out of the pub, walk half a block and get into a ten-year-old white car with an unpainted hood covering the engine.

"I borrowed my friend's car," he says. "Mine's in the shop." He seems embarrassed.

We arrive at my house twenty minutes later. It's moments like these that make me extremely uncomfortable. Does he try to kiss me? Do I want to kiss him? I shudder thinking about refusing, knowing I'll sound like a silly high school girl and not the twenty-year-old I am. But my good little Catholic girl persona along with my own insecurities take over and obscure the tingle of energy that had sparked the moment he introduced himself. Damn. I wish I were more spontaneous like Gina and never had these self-doubting conversations nagging me all the time.

Andy leans over and kisses me. He's gentle, his lips are soft. It's a quick kiss and I'm surprisingly touched by it. But not wanting to progress into a makeout session in front of my house, I smile.

"I had fun tonight. Thanks for the drinks."

"Can I have your phone number? Maybe we can go out sometime."

Not having a full social calendar, particularly in the dating arena, I'm surprised by Andy's request. Guys usually sense my prudish nature and stay away. So it only takes a second for me to grab a pencil and slip of paper out of my pocketbook and write my number down. He takes it and smiles. "Thanks. I'll call you."

I nod and let myself out of the car, climb the five brick stairs to my front door, unlock it, turn and wave to Andy before going inside.

I doubt my parents and older sister will be up at this hour but in case I'm wrong I stand in the foyer of our two-family house and assess the night's events. I didn't get bugged by drunk guys looking for more than I am willing to give. The music was great and the dancing....I'm still reeling with the sense of freedom it gives me. So overall, the night was better than usual. Guess I'll call Gina tomorrow, see how she fared and tell her about Andy. She'll be shocked at what she'll call my audaciousness. That's her way of reminding me what a chicken I am.

I climb the stairs to our second-floor apartment and slowly creep through the dark rooms until I get to my bed. I tumble in and stare at the ceiling for a long time before falling asleep with my clothes on.

*   *   *

I'm a wreck.

But that's nothing new for me. I must've been born with my fingers stuck in an electric outlet. In moments of extreme stress I can feel nervous energy racing through my body. Probably comes from the knowledge that any day my heart might give up the ghost...wrong terminology... and send me to heaven. Scary, huh. Try living with that hanging over your head. And today is a perfect example of a high-stress situation.

I'm getting married.

That's right. I still can't believe it. I've known Andy less than a year and although my virgin body tingles with sexual needs whenever we're together, somewhere in the back of my mind I know this is a bad idea. Over the months I've learned he's a weak man, an adult child of two chronic alcoholics, very insecure, with low employment potential and anger issues that flare up from time to time. I should run out of the church as fast as I can but something holds me. Could be my driving need to prove I'm as good as anyone else and can have a normal life. I see marriage as a way to move forward.

The organ begins the wedding march. I stare at my future husband, waiting for me, at the foot of the altar next to his best friend. Andy's three-years-older than me. Yes, he's tall and very slim, with wavy, brown hair and hazel eyes. But not really handsome. More like a beautiful child than a mature man.

I'm pulled forward, unable to stop. A zombie. A puppet with an unknown master. My body shakes. I take the first steps down the aisle toward my future.

*   *   *

When the church service and reception were finally over, we drive to our new apartment. We'd rented a two-bedroom apartment in Richmond Hill. It's on the second floor of a relatively new house, with a modern kitchen and bath. I had fun decorating it in Early American. We decide to stay here for the night.

I'm in bed waiting anxiously for my new husband to join me. He's standing in front of his dresser fully clothed, takes something out of a drawer and holds the small packet up for me to see.

"What's that?" I asked, my total innocence rearing its ugly head.

"A condom. I don't want to have kids right away. Let's get used to being married first."

Did I tell you that I'm Catholic and Andy is Protestant? Along with years of parochial education and an anchor deep in my belief in God, I am petrified to bend the rules, as though thinking for myself is the fastest way to hell. So...no birth control. No sirree. Not for me. I insist. He surrenders. Something that happens way too often, I later realize. But for now I feel as though I have some control over my life.

Each day we ride the Jamaica Avenue elevated train from Queens to lower Manhattan where we work, Andy as a clerk in a brokerage firm and me as a secretary at U.S.Steel. My first call each night when I get home is to my mother.

"Okay. We're having pork chops. How do I cook them?" No thick recipe books for me. Just Mom and the telephone. It's meat, potatoes and vegetables. Very boring. But nourishing. Barring a few nightmares, like forgetting to defrost the turkey before my first Thanksgiving family dinner party, I eventually become a passable cook.

Then the inevitable happens. My morning commute on the train becomes an embarrassing picture of a woman with bad gag reflexes hiding behind her husband. Thank God I never toss up breakfast. I finally go to the doctor's.

"Mary," my Ob-Gyn says, his face contorted in worry lines. "Because of your weak heart, I'm prescribing full bed rest until the baby is born. With any luck, your child will be full-term and both of you healthy."

In the car, I tell Andy. He's deathly quiet. His reaction definitely doesn't fit the *Father Knows Best* picture I have in my head. Truthfully, he isn't the only one afraid. I'm clued in enough to know that we are immature and ill-prepared for adult responsibilities. Besides there's my heart issue. But I'm a little more positive than Andy is, and well, the deed is done and a baby will be coming in seven months, just two weeks before our first wedding anniversary.

New York State has a law that says a woman can't work beyond her third month of pregnancy. And except for the normal morning sickness I feel fine. And we need my income for as long as possible. Andy and I discussed this, so I put myself and my baby in God's hands and am sitting in front of my supervisor's desk a month later.

"I understand I have to tell you that I'm now two months pregnant." I hate lying to Wilson, my boss. He's a grumpy, crusty middle-aged guy who treats us secretaries with kindness and respect beneath his tough-love approach to managing us.

He looks at me with his usual disgruntled expression but I see regret in his brown eyes. "Well," he says. "I'm not surprised. Getting married usually produces babies." He frowns. "I'll fill out your resignation papers effective a month from today and pass them on to Personnel."

I don't mind breaking the stupid three-month law. I picture a gaggle of old men sitting around a conference table in Washington D.C. coming up with this ridiculous rule, like we woman don't know our own minds and bodies well enough to take care of ourselves and the old goats have to do it for us. Philistines.

"I'm going to miss this place, Wilson. I really love working here." It's true. I've made friends, put some cracks in my anti-social shell and increased my self-respect knowing I'm good at my job. I only hope I'll be as good if not better at being a mother.

*   *   *

One morning in October my water brakes. Andy drops me off at the hospital and goes to work. Fathers aren't allowed in the delivery room. Even though I've spent the last five months shopping with my mother, getting hooked on soap operas like *As the World Turns* and *Dark Shadows,* I'd read a lot of books on what to expect about pregnancy and the birth process. But nothing can compare to reality. The pain's excruciating until the blessed haze of drugs puts me to sleep.

Hours later I awake in the Hospital room, still groggy from all the meds. As my mind clears I call out for a nurse. When she comes in, I stare at her. I'm sure she can see the fear that fills my eyes.

"Is my baby alright? Is it a boy or a girl? Where is it?

The elderly nurse sends me a comforting smile. "You have a son, Mrs. Logan. And he's a big boy. Eight and a half pounds. I'll bring him right in."

My relief is so intense I would've fallen down if I weren't in bed. Thank you, God. I whisper.

The nurse rolls in a crib, with a tiny bundle wrapped in soft blue blankets inside. She picks up the sleeping baby and places him in my arms. "I understand you don't want to nurse, so we fed him an hour ago."

I feel a pang of shame about that. My breasts are so small I'm positive I won't have enough milk for him so I decided to bottle feed from the start.

Unaware of my guilty thoughts, the nurse smiles. "Just ring when you want me to take him back to the nursery." She leaves for parts unknown.

I stare down at the chubby pink cheeks of my son. My son. The fact that I have no brothers and only one sister and have produced a son is mind-blowingly amazing. Then I put him through the usual health checks. Ten tiny fingers. Ten stubby pink toes. All perfect.

Something spiritual slices through me like a magician pretending to saw his female assistant in half. But what I experience is no pretense. I'm no longer one person, but two, myself and my son. As though nothing in the world could ever separate us. He would always be a part of me, my soul, my being.

Tears run down my face as I bend and kiss my son's tiny cheek. So soft. I am moved by the sense of God being in the room with us. Suddenly all fear about the future dissolves and I'm filled with a courage I never knew I had.

I'm still holding my son when Andy rushes into the room and kisses me on the cheek. Then looks down at the bundle I'm holding. His expression is priceless, a combination of fear and awesomeness.

"A boy?" he says.

"Your son." He continues to stare, then whispers the name we'd chosen should the baby be a boy. "Daniel. Daniel Patrick Logan."

CHAPTER TWO

"I love this baby," Andy says one evening while he walks the floor cradling his son in his arms. So much for fear and doubt.

Like most mothers these days, I stay home to raise my son, a happy child with thick hair and dark eyes like his father. And once again, I, Mrs. Holier-Than-Thou, refuse to use condoms. In place of this I suggest we try the Rhythm Method of birth control which is recommended by the Catholic Church for good folks who want to go to heaven when they die. Hah. Andy reluctantly agrees. Sometimes I wonder how my twelve years of Catholic school has turned me off to the church as an organization, yet I still cling rigidly to its doctrines. Thus, for a year and a half I religiously take my temperature each day and when the thermometer shows a rise above the norm, Andy and I abstain from intercourse.

Each day Andy commutes into Manhattan, comes home at night and continually complains about how much he hates his job. But he has no college, no other skills and is stuck there. Money is tight and his resentment builds.

I'm so intent on caring for Daniel, following the rules, taking my temperature, counting the days, that I fail to see the effects all of this has on Andy. He starts smoking again..he'd stopped when we married. On the weekends he drinks a lot of beer. His discontent with work gets worse. The anger I'd sensed at the beginning of our courtship erupts from time to time scaring me. I finally admit that Andy's coping ability is crumbling.

I'm not sure what I did wrong with using Rhythm, if anything, but I find myself pregnant again. Daniel is two when our daughter Eve Marie Logan is born and once again I'm in the Hospital falling in love with a baby swaddled in a pink blanket while I cradle her in my arms. But this time, Andy shows little interest in his child.

I have no one to blame but myself for Andy's slow slide into alcoholism, although clearly the roots had been in his DNA going as far back as his grandparents. The drinking, the abusive behavior, escalates. He loses his job and has a hard time finding work. We're forced to move into a tiny apartment above a store. The building shakes and rattles each time an elevated train whizzes by. Maybe if I hadn't put so much pressure on him...waited to have kids...not spent every extra penny on making a comfortable home for us...I still don't know if things would've been different, and truthfully it's too late to figure it all out.

*   *   *

I hang up the phone, staring at the wall. It's evening and once again Andy's gritty voice rings in my ear.

"I don't have any money." He snickers. "Maybe that God you pray to will send you some. Anyway, I'm just checking in. Still looking for work."

I hear him hiccup and can almost smell the booze laden breath through the phone.

"Maybe God won't send me any money, but He sure has given me the strength to stay with you hoping you'll get your head out of your ass and wake up and take care of your family."

I'm shocked at the vehemence I hear in my voice. A definite first. I've been strong over the past two years since Andy lost his job and left for a few days without a word. Came back. Wallet empty. Left again. Came back. No money. Again and again. Now instead of guilt over my ugly thoughts the tears I've held back for so long run down my face. I put my head in my hands and sob.

I hear the bedroom door open and quickly wipe away the signs of my distress. My darling son walks toward me, a worried look in his eyes, a deep frown on his forehead. And I feel the shame all over again. A five-year-old-boy shouldn't look so sad. Like he had all the burdens of the world inside him. I shake my head. He's growing up too fast.

"What's wrong, Mama?" he says in a shaky voice.

I give him a reassuring smile. Not sure if it will be enough. "Come here, sweetie."

I pull him onto my lap and hug him tight, wishing this small action could protect him from the sad world his father and I have given him.

"I don't like it when you cry," he says.

"I know, Baby. But I'm okay. Just disappointed. Your father hasn't found work yet so we can't have that roast chicken I wanted to cook for you."

He looks up at me with those beautiful soulful eyes so full of love and trust it breaks my heart. "Don't worry. Evie and I love eggs and cereal. And when I get bigger I'm going to make a lot of money so I can take care of you and buy you lots of chicken."

Words clog in my throat for a long moment. Tears threaten to spill. I hug him closer and kiss his soft clean hair. "It's not your job to take care of me. That's your father's and mine. I promise things will get better." I straighten my back.

"Now how about you go back to bed before your sister wakes up. We don't want to worry her, do we?"

He shakes his head then puts his small arms around my neck and kisses me. "I love you, Mama." He pushes off and strolls quietly into the other bedroom.

I can't hold back my tears anymore. Not wanting my son to hear, I lay down on the bed, put the pillow over my face and sob.

*   *   *

I never thought it could get worse. But then I suppose I'm still that naïve immature little girl I was when Andy and I met.

Andy continues coming and going. Sometimes he returns with a few dollars. Usually he's broke. I assume whatever money he's been able to earn goes for liquor. His sober days become fewer. His anger greater. Whether he's angry at himself or me I can't begin to understand. Doesn't matter. I remember the sweet, innocent boy I married and wonder if he's still buried deep inside.

The one and only time he hits me it shocks both of us. It comes after a loud argument that probably sent the kids hiding under their beds. My bad for letting my anger get the better of me. When his drunken rage threatens the kids, I decide Catholic or not, I've had enough.

Daniel is eight and Eve six when I pack our bags and we go to a shelter. There, I get on welfare and find a job as an office assistant. After a few months we move into our new apartment. It's small but clean, with one bedroom which I give to the kids. I sleep on a pullout sofa. But it's in a good school district and close to my office. And it's all mine.

*   *   *

Today is a day full of mixed blessings.

This morning I received copies of my final divorce papers in the mail. I marvel at my many extreme emotions.

Guilt for breaking my marriage vows of 'until death do us part.' I've always prided myself on being a person who keeps her word.

Worry over Andy. Although I'm no longer in love with him, I still care about his wellbeing. I pray each day that he turns his life around before it's too late.

Gratefulness for the new life I've managed to make for myself and my two beautiful children. We're safe. We're comfortable in our apartment. And although we live monetarily on a day-to-day basis, we have all the necessities we need and occasionally a few extras, like McDonald's and birthday and Christmas presents. But I can deal with all the above. Yet I sense a dark cloud hovering over me waiting to dampen my successes.

My premonition appears sooner than I'd expected when I find myself sitting in the principal's office of the local Catholic school.

"I'm sorry to have to call you in like this, Mrs. Logan, but the situation with Daniel is getting worse."

My heart quickens. I clasp my hands on my lap tight enough to stop the circulation.

The principal continues. "At lunchtime he got into another fight in the schoolyard. Bloodied a smaller boy's nose. It took a few moments for the yard monitor to break up the group of children encircling the fighting boys, who I'm sorry to say, were cheering them on."

I could hardly get the words out. "Where's Daniel now?"

"Both boys were treated in the nurse's office. No serious damage. The other boy's parents have already taken him home."

If I drop my head any further it'll brush the floor. I'm so ashamed. Worried. Frustrated. At ten-years-old, Daniel is a head taller than the other children in the sixth grade. Last year his test scores were so far above the other fourth-graders, he was moved into the sixth grade rather than the fifth this year. The thinking by the so-called experts was that his disruptive behavior in class may be the result of boredom, so they advanced him. But apparently this isn't working since rather than decrease, his acting out has escalated to physical fighting.

I look up at the woman behind the desk. "I'm so sorry, Mrs. Mason. I don't know what else to do with him."

The woman looks kindly at me. "What is his behavior like at home?"

I frown. "He's not a problem. Just sullen, moody, hides in his room alone most of the time. I've tried talking to him but he just stares at the wall ignoring me." I feel tears behind my eyelids straining for release but refuse to cry in public.

"I understand there's no father in the home. Could that be an issue for him?"

"Believe me, Mrs. Mason," I shake my head. "It would be a lot worse if his father were here."

The woman nodded as though she understood. "Then my only suggestion is counseling. I can recommend an excellent therapist who's had impressive results working with children with anger issues."

I cringe, wondering where the money for a therapist will come from. But if this is what will help my son, I'll get a second job if I have to.

Mrs. Mason loses her kind expression and becomes the rigid administrator again. "But I must warn you. If Daniel's behavior continues the way it has, we'll have no choice but to expel him."

*   *   *

I take Daniel to the recommended counselor several times. His acting out only seems to get worse. He's big for his age and his dark hair and eyes give him a menacing look when he's angry. For some reason a gang of young local Hispanic hoods lets him hang out with them. Thank God the group is only wannabe gangsters and never gets into any serious criminal activity. But I fear as they get older that won't be the case.

Daniel ditches school more and more, fighting on the streets with his new pals and their rivals. A real-life *Westside Story*. I know about all this because the neighbors are quick to gossip. I talk to my son, beg him to tell me what's wrong, plead with him to stay in school, get an education so he can have a good life, be a good citizen. But he just stares at me with a dark moody expression. When I send him to his room to think about all I've said, he escapes out the window after dark. I pull my hair out in frustration and fear for his future.

Today I get two calls that seem to be answers to my prayers. The first is from Mrs. Mason at the school. She informs me I have to come to her office as soon as possible to sign Daniel's expulsion papers. I turn to stone and stare at the phone after hanging up. I'm paralyzed. I have no idea how long I sit at the kitchen table like this.

The next ringing of the phone breaks the spell I'm floating under. My voice is flat, lifeless when I answer.

"Mary, it's Katherine."

I breathe a deep sigh of relief as soon as I hear my sister's voice. I let all the fear, frustration and worry flow out of me. A waterfall of tears. I can't speak.

"What is it, hon? Are the children okay? Has something happened to them?"

It takes a while for me to get myself under control enough to answer. "It's Daniel. He's been expelled. I don't know what to do to help him."

"Then now's the time for you to make the move I've been begging you to do since you got your divorce. You and the kids have to live with me in Los Angeles. I've got plenty of room. And plenty of money. We'll send the kids to a good private school. Find a counselor for Daniel or anything else he needs. You can go to college. Whatever you want."

I'm touched by the emotion I hear in Katherine's voice. "Just tell me when and I'll make airline reservations for the three of you," she says. "Please, honey, please let me help."

CHAPTER THREE

Maybe it's that mellow haze leftover from the sixties that gives Los Angeles the nickname LaLa Land. Or it could be the yellow-brown smog that hangs over the area.

Don't know. Don't care.

But something is definitely working its magic on Daniel. It's as though the 3,000-mile plane ride across the country morphed him into the sweet, reasonable, loveable boy he'd always been. My sister Katherine has made a name for herself by writing children's books that repeatedly appear on the bestsellers' lists. Her home, nestled in the upscale neighborhood of Santa Monica, is large and airy and both kids are excited about having their own rooms. They take an instant liking to Katherine and the wonderful stories she writes. I enroll them in a nearby Catholic school. Daniel, who's been reading since he was three, spends his after school time either in the pool or in his room reading books I didn't conquer until I was in junior high. Eve, whose calm, friendly personality has never given me a moment of worry, is a beautiful child of eight, with shiny dark hair and light brown eyes. She loves school, gets good reports from her teachers and has play dates with several classmates. In this new environment, the burdens of the past few years slowly fall off my shoulders like a light rain on a blistering sunny day and at least for the time being the future lights up like a surprise birthday cake topped with bright shimmering candles.

With time on my hands and looking for what's next for my family, I take my sister's advice and enroll in U.C.L.A. By the end of my freshman year I decide I want to be a social worker. Something pulls me to help other women who felt stuck in hopeless family situations find the courage to change their lives. It's a lot of work, riding the Santa Monica Boulevard bus to the campus in Westwood, taking a double class load and spending as much time with the kids as I can. But I thrive on the energy I expend to do everything. My self-confidence grows.

But eventually a tiny crack in my world appears. Sometime during my junior year I notice a change in Daniel's behavior. He's no longer content with school. From time to time I get a note from his teachers about him being disruptive in class, not turning in homework. He's contrite and promises to be good and to show me his homework each night. But his slide back to his rebellious ways continues. We settle into the routine of his acting out, feeling guilty, promising to behave, then like an addict he relapses and the cycle continues. It's as though the ghost of his father has taken my son over. My heart hurts for him. I'm at a loss on how to help. But I give it one more try.

Daniel and I are sitting at the kitchen table. Eve's in her room doing homework. "I got another call from Sister Francis. She tells me you've been leaving school before the end of the day."

He drops his head and stares at the tabletop. "She's worried about you. And so am I." Silence. "You have to stay in school and wait for me or Kathrine to pick you up. It's not safe for you to be roaming around by yourself. What do you do when you leave school?"

Daniel shrugs, still unwilling to look at me.

"I thought you liked school?"

He looks up and his sad eyes break my heart. "It's boring."

His answer surprises me. "What do you mean?" I will him to start talking.

"Don't know. Sometimes I have to get away."

I stare at him, unable to understand. Then I remember reading something in a parenting book I read years before. "Daniel, when Sister Francis gives the class a lesson to work on, do you always finish first?"

He nods. "The other kids take so long I hate sitting there with nothing to do."

Tears fill my eyes and I smile at him. "You know, sweetheart, I think I'll talk to Sister Francis about putting you in a different class. Maybe the new work won't be so boring."

I reach over and push a few strands of his thick hair away from his forehead. "Come on," I coax, "how about a game of chess? I know I haven't had a lot of extra time lately, but I promise I'll do better."

His handsome twelve-year-old face brightens. "Okay."

The next day I meet with Sister Francis and the principal. We go over Daniel's scores on the recent IQ and performance tests all the children were given. We come to the conclusion that since his scores are so much higher than the others of his age, he should be moved into the advanced studies class right away. The hope is that he'll be more challenged with the work and enjoy school once again.

Later this year, Eve, now ten, contracts mononucleosis. She spends several weeks at home recovering, but by the time she gets back to school, it's as though she's a different child. No longer the picture of a happy well-adjusted kid, she withdraws into herself. While her school attendance doesn't change, she no longer seems to enjoy going to class and socializing. She's moody, stays in her room each day after class. Hardly talks to anyone. Her teachers are confused by the radical shift in her behavior and suggest I take her to the doctor again. After an extensive physical exam, he remains stymied, except to say that there have been cases of extreme behavior change after a bout of mono. So I resign myself to being there for her, trying to bring her out of her shell.

If it weren't for the self-confidence I'm gaining each day from my education, I'd be lashing myself for being such a bad mother and ruining my children. So I turn to something that has given me strength in the past. My belief in God.

As my marriage had deteriorated, I'd become what they call a lapsed Catholic, no Mass, no sacraments, a little prayer, my excuse now is that I'm too busy. Baloney, of course. I've just become another self-centered human being who thinks she can do it all herself. Too bad my kids have to have problems before I surrender my ego and turn back to God. I insist the kids go along to church, and strangely they don't object too much at first. But after a few weeks, Daniel refuses to go, but Eve hangs in there with me. I find these mornings together with my daughter very peaceful and I sense the bond between us strengthen. While she doesn't return to her earlier self, she does seem to be more at peace, though she still prefers her solitude.

*   *   *

I've been looking forward to taking the Family Law course. The scuttlebutt in the Social Work department is that the instructor is a 'hunk', I believe the young women call him, and that he 'really knows his stuff', so sayeth the young men. The instructor's name is Charles Carter. In my mind the fact that he isn't an academic but rather a successful attorney with a thriving firm and tons of experience working with families is what draws me to his class. Naturally I Google him.

Charles Carter is forty-three, divorced with no children, a graduate of USC Law School with over twenty-years experience defending victims of crimes against children. He started out as a county prosecutor then switched to private practice. Carter takes on the most complicated cases and his win/loss ratio is extraordinary. He has the respect of both sides of the law, Prosecution and Defense.

So today, iPad in hand, I sit among a couple of hundred eager students in one of the large auditorium classrooms anxiously awaiting Professor Carter's entrance. The low chatter of voices halts as soon as the side door opens and a very tall man enters, followed by most likely his teaching assistant. Those giddy young women were right. Carter is very handsome, with thick sandy brown hair and blue eyes. He appears at ease, his lean body exudes a presence that demands attention. As he scans the crowded auditorium, I get the feeling he's looking at each of us, which of course is ridiculous, but nonetheless effective. I'm drawn to his commanding presence as he smiles. Not a fake 'look at me, I'm going to impress the hell out of you' smile, but one that attempts to enroll each student in an exploration of family law with him. A partnership.

It's my final year and I'm completing a counseling internship with the Southern California Counseling Center, when the L.A. County Department of Children and Family Services comes around recruiting new social workers to investigate child abuse and neglect. The thought of knocking on doors and talking to strangers about child abuse petrifies me, but the county offers an excellent starting salary with great benefits that are hard to pass up. So I take the plunge, interview for a job and get hired. I'm all set. I graduate in June and have a job that begins in September.

*   *   *

It doesn't take me long to realize how much I love my job.

I work in the Emergency Response section. As ER workers, it's our job to respond to child abuse referrals, investigate the allegations and determine if they are Founded, Unsubstantiated or totally Unfounded. Our recourses, depending on our findings, are to close the referral, keep the family under supervision for eighteen months or remove the children from the caretakers if it's determined the kids aren't safe. The idea of being responsible for making such critical decisions for a family is very overwhelming. But after a few months of one-on-one training with an experienced social worker I learn the ropes. This helps relieve some of my anxiety.

On rare occasions I have to detain the children and place them either in foster care or in a relative placement. When this happens, the family must appear before a judge in the Edelman Children's Court in Monterrey Park. After reading the court report I write, the judge determines if the child stays in placement or is released to the parents. It is then that I have to go to court to be interviewed by the county and the clients' attorneys. My investigative skills, experience dealing with police, attorneys, doctors, nurses and teachers, relatives and children have given me a strong self-confidence. I've also learned that my instincts are right on.

I've been working for a year when I get a subpoena to appear in L.A. County Superior Court on one of my old cases. Surprised by this very unusual request, I retrieve my files from storage and immediately recall the details. After several abuse referrals made by the mother against her ex-husband and exhausting investigations with each referral, I decided that the mother was the abusive parent and gave full custody to the father. Now, apparently realizing that she's burned all her bridges with Children's Court, she's turned to punishing her ex in Family Court. The woman definitely has issues.

So here I am in the L.A. County Superior Court building in Downtown waiting to be called as a witness for the father. The Prosecution had already put on their case and I was to be the first witness for the Defense. When the summons comes from the bailiff, I enter the courtroom, approach the witness chair, take the oath and sit. Imagine my surprise when I stare into the blue eyes of my former professor as he stands at the podium to question me.

While I'm in shock, it's clear Charles Carter, who's representing the father in the nasty custody case, doesn't recognize me. Understandable since I was one in two hundred students in his class that year. I calm my rapidly beating heart and speak clearly and concisely into the microphone.

"Good morning, Mrs. Logan. Could you please tell the court how you came to be involved with the Arnold family."

I give a clear, concise, brief explanation of my justification for giving custody of the two children, ages five and three at the time, to the father. Carter watches me closely and nods his understanding from time to time.

"How did the children behave while with their mother?"

"Steven, the five-year-old, was sullen and at times angry. He never sat on his mother's lap or showed any signs of affection for her. Stephanie, the three-year-old was also very distant with her mother."

"Did you ever have a chance to observe the children with Mr. Arnold in his home?"

"Yes. I visited Mr. Arnold when the children were with him along with Detective Martinez of the L.A.P.D. Abused Child Unit."

"And what was your conclusion at that time?"

"Both children appeared happy, calm and loving with their father. I found no evidence that they were at risk with him."

"Did you advise the mother of the results of the visits with the father?"

"Yes. I explained I would be closing the referral as Unfounded."

Carter shuffled some papers on the podium. "Did the child abuse referrals from Mrs. Arnold stop at this point?"

"No. Two more came in. After visiting the children in the father's home each time, I again told Mrs. Arnold that the allegations of abuse were Unfounded."

"Did that satisfy Mrs. Arnold?"

"Apparently not. She called in another report and after investigating this one, I suggested to Mr. Arnold that he employ an independent monitor to be present when the children were at his home. I gave him a list of monitors we use."

"Did the monitor give you a report of her findings?"

"Yes. She concurred with me that the children are very well cared for by the father as exhibited by their playful, loving behavior."

"Was that the end of the referrals from Mrs. Arnold?"

"No. When another one came in I immediately called for the police to assist me in detaining the children into the father's custody. My court report stated that the father was given full custody based on a Founded allegation of severe emotional abuse by the mother, confirmed by statements from police and counselors who'd interviewed the children."

Carter looked at his notes, then smiled at me. "Thank you for your testimony, Mrs. Logan."

Instead of rushing back to my cases, I decide to observe the rest of the Defense's case. I admit it isn't because I'm unclear about the outcome of the proceedings. Even with my limited knowledge of law I'm certain the father will retain custody. No. My ulterior motive for staying in the courtroom is purely personal. I can't keep my eyes off Charles Carter. He calls only two other witnesses, Detective Martinez and the counselor who'd spoken with the children. I find his closing arguments mesmerizing, the way he gives the judge a brief, concise summary of his case and his passionate belief that the children are better in the custody of their father. By the end of the day, the judge rules in favor of the father and grants him full custody.

I stay in my seat and watch everyone shuffle out of the courtroom quietly murmuring to each other, some pleased with the decision, others not so much. When quiet fills the room, I realize that only myself and Charles Carter remain. His head down, stuffing papers into his briefcase, it's a few minutes before he realizes that everyone has left. Except me, of course. When he looks up we lock eyes. A deep heat rushes through me. What is it about this man that affects me so much? Embarrassed by my reaction, I turn away from his penetrating stare, rise and leave the courtroom on shaky legs.

CHAPTER FOUR

Talk about life-changing moments.

My heart jumps the second I recognize the strong, deep voice on the other end of my work phone.

"Mrs. Logan? This is Charles Carter. I hope I'm not disturbing you at work."

My mouth is so dry I don't think I can speak. But after swallowing several times I manage to get a few coherent words out and hopefully sound relatively calm and mature. "Not a problem. How can I help you?"

"I was wondering if we could meet for drinks later. I have a proposition to offer you."

Besides surprised by his directness, I'm confused as to what kind of proposition he's referring to. I find the thought that he might be nothing more than a sleazy woman-chaser very disappointing. I'm sure he can hear my brittle voice when I speak.

"Tell me, Mr. Carter. Since I don't know who you are outside of a courtroom, what makes you think I'd be interested in any proposition you have for me?"

Instead of being insulted, which I would've expected, Carter chuckled. "Sorry. I guess proposition isn't the correct word. I certainly didn't mean to insult you. I, uh, I'm not very good at this. Been a long time since I was interested enough in a woman to ask her out on a date."

Thank God for the gravity that holds me in my seat or I would have found myself flat on my face hugging the cold linoleum floor.

"I, I don't understand." Now I'm the one stuttering.

"Damn. I've really messed this up, haven't I?" I hear him take a long deep breath. "Let me start over. I was very impressed with the way you presented yourself in court. Professional, unflappable. Confident. I also noticed instead of leaving the courtroom you stayed to the end until the case was settled." Another breath. "The truth is, I'm interested in getting to know you better. Ergo, this botched phone call."

My surprise and anger melt away at the almost boyish admission I hear in his voice. Apparently I'm not the only adult who reacts like a teenager when he or she faces the rejection of having someone refuse the request for a date. A little smile warms me. "A date, huh. It's been a while for me also."

"How about we start with drinks and take it from there. I know a quiet spot where we can hear ourselves think and talk."

"Tonight?"

"If you're free."

It only took a minute for me to embrace the courage I've found over the past few years and once again charge ahead into unknown territory.

"Alright. Where can I meet you?"

"Nonsense. I'll pick you up. How's seven?"

*   *   *

So here I am, in a small cozy dimly lit café on Santa Monica Boulevard sitting at a corner table across from the amazing man I'd drooled over in the courtroom last week. Apparently we've both decided to dress casually in jeans and cotton tops. My date...those two unfamiliar words slip awkwardly into my mind...is dressed in navy slacks and a sky blue long sleeve shirt opened at the neck. I sip iced tea and nosh on the nacho platter heaped with spicy ground beef and cheese that Charles ordered. He nurses a beer for which I'm eternally grateful. Since divorcing Andy, I'm hypersensitive to anyone who seems to like any form of alcohol in excess.

I look around the quiet café. "You're right. This place is a perfect venue to get to know someone."

Charles offers a slight smile. "In that vein, do you mind if I ask you a few questions?"

"You may ask whatever you like but I might not answer if I'm not comfortable with the question." I'm thrilled by his directness, since I also have never been fond of ambiguous conversations. I smile to myself. I would've been great with speed dating if I'd ever been so inclined to go that route.

"I wouldn't expect you to." He put a nacho laden with goodies in his mouth. After swallowing, he continued. "Are you married?"

"If I were I wouldn't have agreed to this date."

He nodded. "Any children?"

"Two. Daniel is ten and Eve is eight. What about you?"

"To my deepest regret I don't have any. But since my marriage ended in a nasty divorce eight-years-ago it's probably for the best." His brow furrowed. "I was surprised when I noticed you stayed to the end of the Arnold case. Usually witnesses leave as soon as their testimony finishes."

Just how open is a person usually on a first date? I decide I'll go with one of my most strongly held principles...there must be trust in any relationship and trust is built and maintained by always being truthful. So I grit my teeth and forge ahead. "I didn't stay just to hear the verdict. I knew the judge would find for your client. I enjoyed watching you work. How you treated the witnesses and the opposing counsel with respect. The assertive yet professional way you interacted with the judge." My face flushes. "Basically your humanity. In my short time in this field I've come across few attorneys who prefer that trait to dominating people."

Carter is quiet for a long moment, just looking deeply into my eyes. Oops. Too much truth? This time I blush profusely.

He clears his throat. "Thank you," he says in a husky voice.

The tension between us sparks like a 4th of July firecracker. Thank God the waiter comes and refills our drinks. Carter smiles and the air lightens. "I'm glad you agreed to meet with me. I have a feeling the future holds good things for us."

And so the evening goes. Open honest sharing between two people definitely interested in one another. The hours go by and he drives me home. At the front door, we set another date for a few days later. He bends and kisses me lightly then drives away, leaving me standing there watching him disappear around the corner. With a frown, I look up at the clear sky wondering where that bolt of lightning I'd felt the moment his lips touched mine had come from.

*   *   *

I'm apprehensive about telling the kids about Charles. For some reason I'm embarrassed at the thought that they'll consider me in a sexual context. It was different when they were little and had no idea what happened between a husband and wife other than what they saw. Now they understand about sex and what my dating implies. Also, since they remember the bad times with Andy, I'm not sure how they'll react to having another man in their lives. But I can no longer avoid the "talk" with them.

"Guys, I want to talk with you both."

Daniel shoots me his usual angry glare. Eve, calm and non-confrontational, just watches me.

I clear my throat. "You know I've been seeing a lot of Charles Carter the past month. I really like being with him. We get along very well and he treats me with care and respect. He's coming over later and I want you to meet him."

Daniel stands up ready to escape to his room. Eve remains in her seat.

"Sit down, Daniel," I demand.

Pinching his lips together, he stares at me for a long moment. When he sits, I continue.

"I'm not asking you to like him. Just be courteous and respectful." I shift my eyes from Daniel to Eve and back again. "You don't have to stay and entertain him. Just greet him when he comes. Then we're going to a movie. Can I count on you to be polite?"

"Whatever," Daniel growls. "May I go to my room now?"

I nod.

"I finished my homework, Mom, so I'll help you with the dishes so you'll be ready to leave."

I smile at my sweet Eve. "I'd appreciate that, honey. Thanks."

An hour later the doorbell rings. I stand in the doorway between the kitchen and living room when Eve opens the front door. "You must be Mr. Carter. I'm Eve."

Charles's hand reaches out and Eve takes it. "Nice to meet you, Eve," he says with a kind smile on his face. She steps aside and he enters the house.

Wonders will never cease. Daniel walks into the living room at that moment. "Charles, this is my son, Daniel."

Charles walks over and attempts to shake hands with Daniel, but he stuffs his hands in the pockets of his jeans. Charles takes no offense, but smiles. "Hi, Daniel."

With a tight expression on his face, Daniel nods. I sigh. I can tell my son is trying, holding back the snippy remarks he usually spews when addressed. That's the best I can expect for the moment.

The doorbell rings. I open it to my sister Katherine who eagerly agreed to babysit. I introduce her to Charles. I look at Charles. "Do we have time for a snack before we go?"

Charles glances at his watch. "Better not push it. The theatre is usually crowded on Friday nights."

"Okay. I'll grab my purse."

Once we're settled in his Audi A6, I relax. "I'm sorry, Charles. That must have been really awkward for you."

"I wouldn't expect anything else. It's hard for kids to imagine their mother with another man. Give them time. They'll come around." He leans over and takes my hand that rests on my lap and smiles.

My eyes fill with tears. I can't believe how important this man has become to me in such a short time. Knowing he's in my life touches me in so many places, releases me further from my past. I hope and pray my kids will accept him in our lives because I would never want to have to choose between them.

CHAPTER FIVE

The last time I did this I was petrified. Now I'm ecstatically happy.

After a relatively short but intense courtship, I'm standing in the vestibule of the church anxiously waiting to join my soon-to-be husband at the altar. No worries. No fears. Only a deep sense of contentment knowing how right my relationship with Charles Carter is. As with our first date, every time we met, the more we found out about each other, our connection only grew. For me it was like being with a mirror image of myself, but only better. Not only do I see the part I show to the world, but I've come to accept and appreciate the half I've denied my whole life. I'm like the Tree of Life anchored in the soil, reaching into the sky owning the world around it.

The loud strident sound of organ pipes returns me to the present. With my son Daniel on my arm I step into the church. While still rebellious, I know he's touched that I asked him to walk me down the aisle, showing the world how very proud of him I am. I have reassured him time and again over the past months that no matter what, he will always be my first love. I only hope he truly believes this and lets go of some of the anger he still holds from his childhood.

Eve had beamed when I asked her to be part of the wedding party along with two of my closest friends from work. My sister Katherine is my Maid of Honor. The church is full of Charles's and my friends, who smile at me as I walk forward. At the altar Daniel hands me over to Charles, and we stand before the priest. I'm so aware of Charles next to me, his calm strength, that I barely hear the words the priest says. It's like I'm outside my body standing there watching me go through our vows, the I do's, the rings. It's only when my husband kisses me that I fully integrate and join the present. I say my own silent prayer of thanks to God for bringing this man into my life. The following morning we drop the kids off at Katherine's and Charles and I fly to Paris for our two-week honeymoon.

*   *   *

The next few months whiz by. Charles and I decide to purchase a new home in Beverly Hills where the four of us can start our new family in a fresh environment we can truly make our own. I've enrolled the kids into a local Catholic school a short drive away from home. It's a lot for them to adjust to...a stepfather, new home and school. Perhaps as a buttress against all the changes Daniel and Eve seem to have grown closer. I'm grateful they have each other. While Eve seems to tolerate Charles and his attempts to get to know her, Daniel, still brooding and at times hostile, ignores Charles. On my part, at least now I have someone I can share my worry and frustration with about my son.

It is on our six-month anniversary and I find out I'm pregnant. Although I'm a little apprehensive about another change for the kids to adjust to, Charles is ecstatic. Unused to being loved and cared for by a man, I finally relax and enjoy the pampering he bestows on me, the housekeeper, chauffeur and gourmet cook he hires to make my life easier, the fresh flowers he orders sent every week to the house. I'm cocooned in the safety net he has given me and the children.

Once again, I'm in the Hospital cradling another son in my arms. But this time his father is at my side. I stare into the bright blue eyes of the eight-pound baby who seems so alert and content watching me. I take the risk and decide to nurse him. Then regret I hadn't done this with Daniel and Eve. I can't begin to explain the bonding I experience as his tiny mouth tugs at my breasts. Staring down at him I'm determined to do better for him than I had with Daniel and Eve. Give him a stable home filled with love and peace. A place where he can grow into a self-confident, moral, sensitive man.

We name him Gabriel Charles Carter.

*   *   *

After six months it's clear my worst fears have been confirmed. Daniel and Eve do not adjust well to their new brother. I'd hoped that an adorable infant in the house would bring out Eve's sweet nature. That she'd fall in love with him. Find the happiness that she seems to hide from the world. But she avoids Gabriel, never asks to hold him, feed him or show any interest whatsoever in the baby. Instead she seems to get more involved with outside the home activities at school and friends. And she clings to her relationship with Daniel like a lifeline.

"What's the matter, sweetheart?"

I shouldn't be surprised with Charles's ability to see through my 'everything-is-great' cloak, but once again he does. He puts his arm around my shoulders, pulling me close, as I stare down at the peaceful baby in his crib. The fact that Charles doesn't let me get away with pretense very long touches my heart. Tears fill my eyes. I slouch against him.

"I had such hope that Gabriel's presence in our lives would help Daniel and Eve be happier. More content. But I'm afraid they've only grown further away from me."

Charles kisses my cheek. "Give them time. They'll come around."

I shake my head, my sadness negating all possibilities. "Their father and I failed them so completely I'm afraid their wounds will never heal."

"Don't let me hear you demean yourself like that. You did the best you could, Mary. And you got out of that rotten situation as soon as possible. Give the kids time to heal themselves. It might take longer than you'd like, but trust in the foundation of love and support you give them."

I sniff back tears. Maybe Charles is right. All I can do is continue to be there for Daniel and Eve and pray God will keep them safe.

*   *   *

It's the night of Gabriels's first birthday. He's his happy chubby self, sitting in his highchair clapping his tiny hands after we sing Happy Birthday to him. Well, honestly, only Charles, my sister Katherine and I sing. Eve barely mumbles the words and Daniel totally ignores us. Instead of getting upset I smile at them and cut the dessert I'd baked that morning. Yellowcake with fudge icing. Daniel's favorite. Eve accepts a slice but Daniel refuses and asks to be excused. I try to hide my disappointment behind an understanding smile while he heads for his room. The rest of the...I'm embarrassed to call it a party...ends a short time later when Katherine leaves for her house. I put Gabriel into his crib with a kiss on his forehead and a silent prayer for him. I look in on Daniel and Eve who are asleep in their rooms and Charles and I shower. Once in bed, I sigh deeply and snuggle into my husband's arms. I refuse to give in to the tension I felt during the little family get-together. It is what it is, I remind myself, and eventually fall into a dreamless sleep.

*   *   *

Two years later another horrendous disaster strikes our home. Daniel, now fourteen, has escalated his acting out to cutting class, staying out till all hours of the night...I can only imagine what kind of trouble he's been getting into. He refuses to talk to either Charles or me. Each night I fall asleep with prayers and kiss him up to God for protection.

Tonight I'm suddenly awakened by the sound of feet running down the hallway. Curious, I drag my sleep-deprived body out of bed and check on the kids, first to three-year-old Gabriel who sleeps the sleep of the innocent, curled up on his side. It's then I see Eve standing like a statue in the doorway of Daniel's room. A sense of foreboding chills me.

"Are you alright?" I ask.

I follow her stare into his dark room. My body tenses as though it knows something is wrong. I step into his room, find the light switch and flick it on. Daniel isn't there. His bed hasn't been slept in. Several of his open dresser drawers are empty. The closet claims half of its usual accouterments. I sink farther and farther down the rabbit hole of despair until I come to grips with the fact that the only remnants of him are his school books that lay strewn on the floor. I can't breathe. I'm so dizzy I drop down on the bed before I hit the floor. A silent scream blasts my head like the piercing whistle of a racing train. I can't speak or cry or move.

Eve comes over and sits down beside me. Grabs my hand. I turn to look at her. Tears run down her face. Her beautiful light brown eyes have a haunted look that stops my heart. I'm reminded how close the two of them have been and my fear for both my children accelerates. We stare at each other for a long moment, sunk in our own personal hells. Finally she manages a few words.

"Where's my brother, Mom? Where's Danny?"

*   *   *

It's been a month since Daniel ran away. The police were called. Newspaper ads placed. Radio and television announcements made. Charles has spared no expense in our effort to find Daniel. The few leads that come in are quickly found to be useless. A private investigator is hired. All this is for naught. No word from my son.

During this time my mind is imagining the worst. He was in an accident and has amnesia. He's in a drugged-out state existing in a dreamworld unable to call and ask for help. And the absolute worst...he was abducted by a sexual predator and murdered, his body buried in some forest where it was devoured by animals, never to be found. I can't sleep. Lose about ten pounds. A constant migraine holds me hostage while I try to get through the days at work. If it weren't for Charles I'd go out of my mind.

And Eve. She retreats more and more into herself. Loses interest in school and friends. Hardly talks to us. Wanders around the house in a daze when she's not hiding out in her room. I don't seem to be able to reach her. I'm drowning in questions, confusion, guilt.

From time to time I sense Daniel is out there watching me. I know it's just wishful thinking, but somehow I find it comforting. I tell myself he's safe, unharmed, just needs space to come to grips with all the anger he's been carrying for so long. I talk myself into believing this because if I didn't I'd empty that bottle of sleeping pills that sits on my nightstand.

Six months. A year. No word. Nothing. Eventually I realize that time does seem to put a bandaid on pain. Dulls it. Makes it more tolerable. Easier to get through the long days and nights. But it never goes away. Somewhere inside

I still cling to the belief that one day the bell will ring and Daniel will walk into the house and all will be forgiven. In the meantime....

CHAPTER SIX

I sit in the front pew of St. Monica's church, comforted by the solemnity and the warm wafting scent of lighted votive candles. Instead of staring up at the crucifix, I close my eyes and allow them to see the events that filled the thirteen years since Daniel left us. A trip down the proverbial memory lane, so to speak. Not sure why this seems important at the moment, but I go with my gut.

That's right. It's been fourteen years and it's as though I never carried that child inside my body, never cuddled my beautiful son in my arms. Never held his tiny hands while he took his first hesitant steps. Never escorted him into school his first day, tears in my eyes as I watched him walk proudly into his classroom. No. He'd just disappeared, leaving behind questions that he'd ever existed at all. But one thing was certain...the pain still in my chest was real. Had never left.

Eve never recovered from the loss of her brother. She withdrew from me...our relationship strained as though she blamed me for her brother's departure. Well, I guess she had to blame someone. After high school she decided to go to Berkeley. While I was disappointed she'd passed on a more local school, I'd hoped she'd finally find some peace for herself. It did please me when she took a nursing degree program. With a Master's in hand, she returned to L.A., got her own apartment and a position with the Home Health Care program affiliated with Santa Monica Hospital. I rarely see her, but I'm okay with knowing she's near.

As Gabriel grew it was apparent he would be tall and muscular like his father, with brilliant blue eyes but darker brown hair. Charles and I work very hard to instill moral values and a good work ethic in him. He excels in math and science, yet often seems bored with school. As his restlessness increases, so do our efforts to keep him on the straight and narrow. Warning bells occasionally sound in my mind, wondering if we're pushing him too hard. But I'm continually haunted by the fact that I've already lost one son and refuse to have Gabriel follow in his brother's footsteps.

I open my eyes and focus on the crucifix. With nimble fingers I *Hail Mary* and *Our Father* my way along my rosary beads until I come full circle. Like my previous mental meanderings. When I finish, I rise, genuflect in the aisle and leave the church, fully at peace and ready to take on another day in the life.

*   *   *

I wish I'd taken those warning bells about Gabriel more seriously.

The phone rings, jarring me out of a sound sleep. I roll over and pick it up. Still under the haze of sleep I answer in a gravelly voice. "Hello?"

"Is this Mrs. Carter?"

"Yes."

"Good evening, ma'am. Sorry to call so late. This is Sargeant Nogales at the Beverly Hills police station."

I'm totally confused. "Police? Why are you calling me?" I tense. A picture of Daniel flashes in my mind, a wisp of smoke from a long-ago burned-out fire.

Probably sensing the urgency in my voice Charles stirs and turns on his side to face me.

"We need your presence at the station. How soon can you get here?"

Now I'm really freaking, knowing that nothing good comes of late-night calls from the police. "What is it?"

"I can't go into the details on the phone, but it's about your son Gabriel. The detective will explain when you and your husband get here." The sergeant hangs up before I can say anything else.

I sit on the edge of the bed and look at Charles. "That was the police. They want us down at the station. Something about Gabriel." My chest tightens. "I'm scared, Charles."

He sits and draws me into his arms for a quick hug of support. "Whatever it is, we'll deal with it together."

We hurry and dress and arrive at the Beverly Hills police station in Mario Andrade time. Charles and I check in at the front desk and the sergeant makes a telephone call. In a few minutes we're introduced to Detective Johnson who ushers us into a small conference room off the main lobby. Johnson is middle-aged probably near retirement.

"Sorry to meet you on such an occasion." He shakes our hands. "I'm familiar with your work with Family Court, Mr. Carter."

"What's this all about, Detective?" Charles says.

Johnson clears his throat. "Are you aware that your son Gabriel has been running errands for a local bookie operation for the past six months?"

"What?" My mouth has opened wide enough to fit a baseball. "That's impossible."

"I'm afraid not." Johnson opens a file and reads silently for a moment. Then he looks at me. "We've been aware of the activities of this particular bookie joint for a while and have documented your son coming and going in the evening on many occasions." He slides over pictures taken at night of a man leaving what appears to be a laundromat. Charles leans over and examines the photos with me. My heart stops as I recognize our son.

Johnson continues. "Tonight our surveillance paid off. Patrol picked up Gabriel leaving the scene a few hours ago. He carried over $10,000 in his backpack. When we ran the license plate of the old truck he was about to drive away in we found it was stolen earlier in the day. He's being charged with felony burglary and grand theft auto. Lucky for him he had no weapons on him or the charges would've been more severe."

I grab Charles's hand. I can hardly breathe. "I need to speak to my son. He'll explain everything to me."

"That isn't possible at this time. He's being processed. We asked you to come down here only as a courtesy." Johnson turned to Charles. "Will you be representing him?"

Charles, his face pale beneath his tan complexion, shakes his head. "I'll retain a colleague for him. I don't want my presence as his father to hinder him from being open and honest with his attorney."

I stare at my husband. "But Charles..."

"It's better this way, Mary. Trust me."

I give him a weak smile then look at Detective Johnson. "When can we see him?"

Johnson's face softens as though he knows how his response will hurt. "Gabriel has refused to see anyone."

This is more than I can stand. It's as though a sharp knife has sliced me in two, severing my mind from my body. I'm beyond words. Yet I feel tears trickle down my face.

I barely comprehend Charles when he speaks. "I'll have my son's attorney here within the hour."

Detective Johnson gathers his files. "I'm truly sorry. I've seen this time and time again. It's always the family who gets hurt the worst." He sighed. "You may stay here as long as you want." He stands and leaves the room.

Charles immediately grabs his phone. In a matter of moments his voice echoes across my brain but comprehension of the words eludes me. He puts the phone back in his pocket, turns and pulls me into his arms, his lips a gentle press on my forehead. "It'll be alright, sweetheart. We'll get through this. All of us. I promise."

His words of attempted comfort pass through me, leaving me unconsoled. I only have thoughts of Gabriel, the sweet little boy I once held in my arms, not the sixteen-year-old angry young man who now sits alone in a jail cell awaiting his future. What happened along the road of his life that has brought him to this juncture? With all the degrees and experience working with children and families Charles and I have, why haven't we realized what was going on with our son and done something to prevent this?

I don't know how much time passes before there's a knock on the door and a man enters. Looking up at him I recognize Charles' friend Peter Waterston. Charles stands and they shake hands.

"Thanks for coming down here on such short notice." Charles indicates the chair Detective Johnson has recently vacated.

"You'd do the same for me." Waterston said. "Fill me in."

While Charles does this, I force myself to get a grip. Realizing I won't do Gabriel any good in my present emotional condition, I sit taller, take Charles' hand and listen to the men discuss the legal implications of Gabriel's case. I manage to get in a few pertinent questions and the three of us brain-storm. But deep inside the new hole that has ripped open my heart I know there's nothing much we could do to get the charges dropped and bring our son home.

After a while we all stand. "I'll see Gabriel now," Waterston said. "Why don't you go home. I'll call you as soon as I'm finished here."

Charles nods. We shake hands and Waterston leaves. Charles turns to me. His face is lined. Worry swims in his usually calm eyes. He pushes a lock of my hair behind my ear. "He's right, honey. There's nothing else we can do here. Let's go home."

With my hand tucked firmly in his we make our way through the corridors of the station. As we pass cops strolling by I can't help but wonder where inside this cold impersonal building Gabriel is. What's he thinking? When will I get a chance to see him? Talk to him? With each step toward the lobby of the police station I draw farther and farther away from my son, leaving pieces of my heart and soul in my wake.

The following day Charles and I are in the courtroom waiting to see our son at his arraignment hearing. Gabriel still refuses to talk to us. I can't decide if he's angry or just ashamed to face us. Waterston told us that he was lucky to get Gabriel tried as a juvenile rather than an adult. What I don't understand is why he's pled guilty to all charges? Why doesn't he fight? Explain why he got involved. Let a jury see that he's really a good kid who deserves a second chance.

Gabriel walks into the courtroom dressed in an orange jumpsuit, hands cuffed in front of him, accompanied by a deputy. Completely ignoring us he stands before the judge and listens to the charges being read, as well as his guilty plea. In a stern voice the judge announces Gabriel's sentence...two years in the juvenile detention facility in Sylmar, to be released when he turns eighteen.

I take a sharp intake of breath and grab Charles' hand. Two years. Away from us, living among gang members and career criminals. My head's spinning. I sink against my husband.

Gabriel exits the courtroom without a look or word for either of us. As the door closes behind him, I shudder as though it hits me square in the face.

The next two years were the longest in my life. Even though Gabriel was hardly ever home and hid out in his room when he was here, the house has been so empty without him. It's been like an ever-present ghost is no longer among us, leaving a void nothing has been able to fill. Charles and I go about our business, he in court, me supervising child abuse investigators. Eve draws farther away from us, Gabriel's absence a stark reminder of the brother who'd vanish years ago. I refuse to wallow in the painful truth that all of my children seem to have deserted me. Have I really been such a bad mother? Charles, in his constant ability to read me, offers whatever consolation he can, but my pain is too deep for words to heal.

Two days after Gabriel's eighteenth birthday, Charles and I wait outside the juvenile detention center in Sylmar. When Gabriel finally emerges from the long single-storied brick building, I'm shocked at his appearance. Sure, we'd gone to visit him weekly, but not once did he agree to meet with us. So now the young man who walks toward us, seems a stranger. Older beyond his years. Bigger. Stronger. Dark brown hair tied back in a short ponytail. Brilliant blue eyes dull from memories I can only begin to imagine. My chest tightens until I can barely breathe. Words fail me.

"Welcome back, son," Charles says. I feel the tension he holds inside denying its presence in an attempt to make Gabriel comfortable.

My son merely nods. No expression. As though we're strangers.

I want so much to pull Gabriel into my arms, telling him it's over. Things will be better from now on. But the cold stony look he gives me crushes these words down my throat before I can get them out. I can only touch his arm.

We walk to the car and silently drive home to an empty house.

Now even with Gabriel home, the place feels more like an empty tomb. We don't communicate. He comes and goes at will. I think he has a menial job somewhere because he always seems to have money. Charles has tried to encourage him to do something together with him, whatever Gabriel would like, but Gabriel just shrugs him off. I feel the tension in the house building, afraid of the explosion that I know in my heart will come.

Sure enough, Gabriel is home less than six months when we get the call from the police station. This time it's from his court-appointed attorney advising us that he has been arrested for violating his probation and fighting, sending a fellow bar patron to the Hospital. He'll be in court tomorrow for final disposition of his case.

The myriad of feelings I have is so confusing. Relief that the expected eruption has happened. Sadness about my son's future. Is there no hope for him? And then there is that good old Catholic guilt that kicks in a thousandfold.

Charles and I sit in the courtroom once again and watch Gabriel enter handcuffed in the familiar orange jumpsuit. Stoic. Refusing to look at us. The judge sifts through his papers.

"I see Mr. Carter that you haven't learned your lesson from the two years you spent in the Hall." He shakes his head. Then looks at Gabriel directly. "I've been persuaded by your lawyer, probation officer and parents to give you one more chance to turn your life around. So I'm offering you a choice...jail or the Army. And trust me when I say you'll find the Army a lot better than four years in Wayside Correctional. What will it be?"

Gabriel doesn't hesitate. "Army."

The judge nods. "Good choice." His attention shifts to Gabriel's attorney. "See the court clerk for the necessary papers." He bangs the gavel. "Next case."

Once again my son walks out of a courtroom without a glance in our direction. Again he refuses to see us. I'm left with a hole in my heart the size of a dead volcano. Will I ever see him again? Or will he disappear into the ether just like Daniel?

CHAPTER SEVEN

I lie in the Hospital bed and stare into a small handheld mirror the nurse was kind enough to bring me. Since my dark brown hair now shows streaks of white I no longer have to frost it to brighten my face. Sure, my hazel eyes have a few crow's feet at the edges but all in all, not bad for a sixty-two-year-old woman retired now for the last two years. My heart...well... given the deficit I've learned to live with and the sorrow life has sent me, it's a blessing I'm still here on the planet. Now if only my creaky joints would cooperate.

I check out the time. I hate to call Eve so late at night, but I don't want her to worry should she stop in tomorrow before I get home. I never know when she'll do that. I grab my phone and click on her number. Her voice is groggy when she answers.

"Oh, Eve, dear, I'm sorry to call so late but I wanted you to know that I'm not sure what time I'll be home in the morning."

"What? Why won't you be home? Where are you?"

"Well," I try to make light of my accident. "I tripped going into the bathroom tonight and my hip went out again. So I called the EMT's and I'm here at Santa Monica Hospital."

"The EMTs? Where's Charles?"

"He's out of town again. But don't worry. I'll call my driver in the morning and he'll pick me up."

"The hell he will," she says. "I'll come and get you. Just call me when you're ready to leave."

"No. No. Eve. I don't want to bother you."

"Don't you dare call your driver. I'm picking you up."

"Okay, dear. If it isn't too much trouble. I'll call when I'm discharged."

"You better." Why does my daughter always sound so angry and annoyed when she talks to me? I sigh and put the phone down, closing my eyes. I sometimes forget that Charles and I aren't the only ones who have suffered the loss of our sons. It's been hard on Eve, losing both her brothers at so young an age. But I shake my head before I get sucked up into the past again.

The medication the doctor gave me starts to kick in. I draw the sheet up to my chin and snuggle down, looking forward to a peaceful, pain-free sleep.

*   *   *

Thank goodness I recover quickly. I barely have to lean on the cane the Hospital gave me. With Eve by my side I feel very safe. As we amble into the house, the scent of warm pasta leftover from last night welcomes me home. We walk into the recently updated kitchen where granite and stainless steel catch the sun rays through the many large windows. Since I've retired, I spend a lot of time here cooking, baking, planting herbs in colorful pots that sit on window sills. I love the enticing aromas the plants give.

A little more winded than I would've liked, I sit at the counter. "I don't know about you but I'm hungry. Why don't you get the pasta out of the fridge and heat it up in the mircrowave? It's been a long time since we sat and talked."

Eve seemed about to brush me off but then relented. While the food heated, she went through the cabinets and got out bowls and utensils. When the microwave beeped, she dished out the pasta and sat down across from me.

Eve is such a beautiful woman with long shiny dark hair and maple syrup eyes. She's in her late thirties now and beginning to show signs of stress. She continues with her home health care duties, although whenever we meet, which is only once a month or so, she always seems to carry heavy burdens on her broad shoulders. I'm usually the one to initiate a conversation with her.

"How's that little girl you told me about? Is she getting better?"

A dark cloud passes over her face. "She died a few weeks ago."

"Oh, Eve. I'm so sorry. No wonder you look a bit down. Do you want to talk about it?" I know she hates it when I try to play therapist with her, but I can't help but want to bring some peace to my daughter.

"No."

"Okay. So...any new interesting patients?"

A light flickers in Eve's eyes but she ignores me. "When is Charles getting home?"

"I spoke with him just before I fell. He said he'd be back in two days."

"And I'll bet you didn't call him back and tell him you were in the hospital."

"Of course not. There's no need to worry him. I'm fine."

Eve rolls her eyes and shakes her head and we finish our meal in silence. She then cleans up the counter, putting the plates in the dishwasher. "I have to get going. Do you need any meds before I leave?"

"No. I don't like taking them. They make me groggy. I'll just lie down and rest for a few hours." I rise and make an attempt to head into the guest bedroom on the first floor. I doubt I'm ready to tackle the stairs right now. Eve comes beside me and takes my arm. We walk silently into the room. She watches as I get into bed, then retrieves a glass of water from the bathroom and puts it on the nightstand.

I give her a grateful smile. "Thanks, honey. You go along now. And thanks for picking me up."

Eve bends down and gives me a quick kiss on my forehead. "You better call me if you need anything or I'll be mad at you."

I laugh. "Yes, Eve. I promise I'll be a good girl. Now scoot."

As I hear the front door close behind her, sadness rolls over me as it does every time Eve leaves. I'm left with wondering if things will ever get better between us.

*   *   *

A week later I'm surprised to see Eve storm into the house. I'm at the stove preparing a hearty stew, when I turn and get a good look at her face. Now I'm even more concerned. "What is it? You look upset."

Eve's chest is heaving apparently from rushing. "I...I need to talk to you."

I blink a few times, confused. "Of course. Let me turn off the pot. Would you like something to drink?"

Eve steps back and sits at the granite-topped island. "No thanks."

I join her, folding my hands on the island, my brow lowered in concern. "Are you alright? Is something wrong?"

"Is Charles home?" Scanning the room Eve's eyes lands back on me.

"He's in New York on a case."

"I, uh, I'm worried about you being home alone so much."

I scoff. "I've been alone many times when your stepfather travels. Don't worry. I'm fine." I study my daughter's face. "We may not have been close over the years, but I know you, Eve, and you look like the world is about to end."

"No, Mary, you really don't know me."

"Then let me in." My eyes fill. "There's nothing you can say that would make me love you less."

Eve rises and paces around the kitchen, hugging herself. As though coming to a decision, her shoulders slump. She turns and faces me. "I'm in trouble. Someone is blackmailing me and threatening to hurt you if I don't come up with the money."

I feel the color drain from my face but I hold Eve's gaze steadily. "Who's blackmailing you?"

Eve takes a deep breath. "My ex-husband."

"Do you mean Jerry? Why would he do that?"

Eve shook her head. "Not Jerry." When she notices the confusion on my face she explains. "I, uh, got married again to a loser named Tony Parma. It only lasted a couple years. When I found out he was running scams on seniors, I turned him in to the cops and he went to prison. Now he's out looking for revenge

I'm shocked that my daughter had married years ago and not told me. Would the hurts never stop? "I don't understand why he'd want to hurt me?"

"I know it's hard for someone like you to understand. But trust me, this guy's an asshole. I want you to get some kind of protection."

A defensive shield rises. "What do you mean people like me?"

Eve swallows. "You're a good person, Mary. You see the half-full glass in everyone. But that's not me. I've known a lot of assholes in my life and Tony Parma is the worst."

Her remarks strike a blow to my ego. Does my daughter still see me as the weak woman from her childhood who'd allowed her father to rampage through our home and not the strong, educated, capable woman I've become?

Apparently, Eve realizes how her words have hurt me. A look of regret fills her face. In a very unprecedented gesture, she reaches out and puts her hand on top of mine. "I just want you safe until Tony's locked up for good. Why don't you move into a hotel room temporarily? I"ll let you know...."

But I pull my hand away, determined to disabuse her of any leftover opinions of my vulnerability. I sit taller, my eyes piercing my daughter's. "I won't be threatened by some lowlife. Never again will I let a man treat me like a doormat." I take a deep breath. "How much does your ex want?"

"More than I have. But my friend Vin is working on a plan. I'll check with him and keep you informed. I'm...I'm sorry, Mary. I haven't been a very good daughter and now..."

My heart aches for the sadness I see in her beautiful eyes. I come around the island and embrace her, wet tears on my checks. "I've known for years you've been unhappy, and I'm sorry for the childhood your father and I put you through. I hope you can forgive me."

Eve releases a long sharp breath. Slowly her arms go around me.

"We'll get through, this Eve. Don't worry. The only thing that matters is we love each other. You do what you have to and make this go away but this is my home and I won't run scared anymore."

Eve pulls away, unable to look me in the eye. She clears her throat. "I'll call you. Be careful," she says in an emotionally charged hoarse voice. She turns and leaves the house. As I watch her, I realize how shaken I am. Not with fear for myself, but with a mother's worry over her child.

*   *   *

I'm curled up on the sofa watching the latest Masterpiece Theatre Mystery when I hear a noise in the kitchen. Like something dropping to the floor. Or a foot banging into a cabinet. I stiffen and grab my cell phone. Hopefully I'm years away from needing medic alert jewelry, so instead Charles reminds me whenever he travels I should have the phone on my person at all times in case I have to call 911. I rise and slowly walk toward the kitchen. I know this is stupid but my curiosity gets the better of me. Before I reach the doorway, a man jumps out in front of me, grabs the phone out of my hand and pushes me back into the living room, his hands on my shoulders. A wave of fear washes over me. My weak heart pounds and I'm worried about the possibility of cardiac arrest. I try to calm myself but I only seem to get more frighten. Could this man be Eve's ex-husband? His next words confirm my greatest fears.

"So you're the bitch who birthed my ex-wife. Did she tell you about me? What she did to me? What I plan to do to you if she doesn't come up with the money?"

Struggling to take deep breaths I'm unable to push words out of my mouth and just stare into dark angry eyes. He turns me, grabs my arms behind my back, and I feel thin ties tightly wrap around my wrists binding them together.

"No? Well, no matter. You'll find out about the real me soon enough." He shoves me down onto the sofa then binds my ankles together. "There. All wrapped up like a Christmas goose."

His mouth twists into an evil smirk which doesn't help to calm my pounding heart. I can feel the angry beats scream out in protest. "What do you think you're doing?" I manage to spit out between breaths. "Eve has told the police about you. You won't get away with this. If you were smart, you'd stop now and run as far away as you can."

He bends over and slaps my face so hard my ears ring and tears fill my eyes. "Shut up!" he shouts. He stares at the wall, his eyes shifting from side to side as though moving things around in his brain. Finally an ugly smile twists his mouth. "Thanks for the tip. Change of plans." He picks me up off the sofa and slings me over his shoulder, fireman style. Ceramic floor titles sweep past my vision as we leave through the back door. I bounce on his shoulder and after a few long strides I see the tires of a truck. He struggles to open a back door and tosses me onto the bench seat. "I'll be right back," he says.

I wiggle to sit up and watch as he runs back into the house. It feels like hours before he stumbles out and runs toward the truck. At that moment a small explosion shatters the back of the kitchen and flames erupt in the house. I stare in horror as the fire seems to spread quickly from room to room. An emotional memory overwhelms me as I recall when Charles and I bought the lovely home years ago. Moments of the happy and sad times we shared there soon disappear in a cloud of smoke. Like my sons. It's more than I can bear. As the truck pulls away from my home I slide onto the seat and feel myself slipping into the cavernous hole of depression. Daniel. Gabriel. My home. I sink into unconsciousness.

CHAPTER EIGHT

Charles Carter sat on the vinyl chair next to the Hospital bed staring at his sleeping wife, life-giving nutrients dripping into her arms, a tube jutting out of her mouth, machines tracking her vitals. It had been two days since the police had called and advised him that Mary had been found and was now at Santa Monica Hospital. Two long days with impassive doctors giving no clues as to what was going on with his wife, except to say that physically she was getting stronger but they have no idea why she hadn't regained consciousness. He reached over, took her hand and kissed it. "Please come back to me, Mary my love. I don't want to go into old age without you," he whispered and closed his eyes.

The last week had been the worst one of his life. Finding out Mary had been kidnapped. Their home burned to the ground. The kidnapper's truck found in a deep ravine in the San Bernadino mountains, his body slung over the steering wheel, neck broken. But no sign of Mary. Finally the police had called him with the wonderful news that Mary had been found unconscious by hikers. The detective explained that apparently she had been physically able to walk away from the wreck and had walked miles before passing out, the results of a severe head wound.

Charles's stepdaughter, Eve entered the room, a steaming cup of coffee in her hand. She offered it to him and he took it without a word, his eyes beseeching his wife to wake up.

"Sure you don't want a sandwich or something?" Eve asked him.

He shook his head.

"You have to take care of yourself, Charles. Mom will need you when she wakes."

"Thank you, Eve, but I'm fine. You go home. Get some rest. I'll see you in the morning."

His eyes never left Mary's face. His mind barely registered the door closing, leaving him alone once again with his wife. He vowed never to leave her side, Mary who'd been abandoned by so many people she loved.

*　　*　　*

Eve stepped into the hallway straight into the arms of her best friend and lover.

"Is your Mom any better?" Vin Ramone wrapped comforting arms around her.

She shook her head against his chest. "No. And I'm worried about Charles. He hasn't left her side since the ambulance brought her in." She let out a heavy sob. "I feel so helpless, Vin. This is all my fault. If I hadn't had Tony Parma in my life Mom would be home now in her beautiful kitchen preparing dinner which she loves." Eve hiccuped. "Now her home is gone and God knows if and when she'll wake up."

Vin's arms tightened around her. "You need to drop the guilt trip and hold onto the hope that she'll be fine. She loves you and Charles too much to stay away." Vin kissed her forehead. "Come on, sweetheart, let's go home. Your stepfather isn't the only one who needs to take care of themselves."

*　　*　　*

Daniel shifted nervously in his first-class seat. Even the steady hum of the tremendous plane engines failed to lessen his anxiety. He was battered by flashes of thoughts and feelings that rifled his body. Home. That thought alone scared the shit out of him. And the feelings? Well, he'd only just begun to find the courage to allow feelings to filter through his cracking stone walls. Thank God for Julia. He reached over and took her hand. She glanced up at him and gave him a reassuring smile. It's been...how long? Twenty-five years since he'd been back in L.A. Right now he'd rather face a ruthless competitor than the woman who lay asleep in the Hospital bed.

He recalled his sister's words on the phone last night. Their mother had been kidnapped...*kidnapped* for God's sake...survived a truck crash and more than nearly a week alone in the dense forests of San Bernadino county. She now lay in the hospital in a coma. Eve was right. Mary did need her family around her now. But would his return help her recover or send her deeper into unconsciousness?

The pilot announced they'd be landing at LAX within the hour. Daniel closed his eyes and squeezed Julia's warm hand, praying he was doing the right thing for his mother by showing up after all these years.

*   *   *

Gabe stood at his kitchen window trying to get his mind around the conversation he'd just had with his sister. After reading the article in the paper, he'd finally pushed through his guilt, dialed information for Santa Monica Hospital and gotten through to Eve. Their mother lay unconscious after a harrowing experience that had lasted for days. Eve and his father Charles were worried she'd never awaken. So Eve had taken upon herself to call his brother Daniel and beg him to come home. She was certain that knowing her sons were there would help Mary choose to live rather than remain in her current vegetative state. Gabe thought of all the pain both he and Daniel had caused her and seriously doubted their presence would help. But he couldn't deny Eve's plea. So he'd roused himself out of his malaise, stuffed his backpack with essentials for an extended stay in L.A., drove to the Pet Shop and explained to Belle why he had to go. Trooper that she was, she'd understood immediately and with a hearty kiss and hug, sent him on his way with instructions to call when he had news of his mother's condition.

So now as the miles of asphalt flew by under his truck's wheels he had time to process everything. From time to time he felt drawn to sink into the all-too-familiar guilt and shame that had run his life these past fifteen years. But thanks to Belle and her love and support Gabe found his courage. Shaky nerves aside, he looked forward to reuniting with his family. His only hope was that his mother would recover quickly so he can beg for her forgiveness and explain that he'd never stopped loving both his parents.

$$* \quad * \quad *$$

With a cup of hot coffee in hand, Eve stepped out of the elevator and immediately her eyes rested on the tall form of a man who waited for assistance at the nurses' station. She stopped short and stared, wondering who he was until she recognized the deep timbre of her older brother's voice.

"Can you tell me which room Mary Carter is in?" he asked the nurse.

She smiled up at him. "Mrs. Carter is in the ICU and only family members may visit."

"I'm her son."

"Danny?" Eve called out.

He turned and frowned at the interruption. Dark brown eyes gave her an intense stare for a long moment before he spoke. "Eve?"

A nervous laugh threatened to escape her lips as her hand covered her mouth. But she regained her composure quickly and stepped up to him, unsure how to respond. He was her big brother, the one who'd always protected her from the ranting abuse of their father. She couldn't stop shaking. She wished Vin were here right now. She needed his strength and support, but she'd left him in the cafeteria finishing breakfast. She'd rushed down her bagel with cream cheese, grabbed her coffee, anxious to be at her mother's side.

Brother and sister stood staring at each other in a long awkward silence. Then he gave her a small smile. "You grew up good."

Commenting on the difference between their heights, she said, "And you definitely grew up." Looking at him, thousands of questions begging for answers ran across her mind but she pushed them away. Time for catching up later. "I'm so glad you're here," was all she could muster before overwhelming emotion nearly crippled her.

"How's...Mom?" The word seemed to falter on his tongue as though he was uncomfortable with the intimacy of the label.

"No change. But the doctors say it's important that we talk to her. That she somehow knows who we are and needs us to help her come back." With a deep breath to hold back all the emotion that was flooding her, Eve sucked in a heavy sob. "Come. I'll show you to her room."

*   *   *

Waning afternoon light filtered into Mary Logan Carter's Hospital room through thin drapes that covered a large window when Eve left Daniel at the doorway. His head still throbbed from all the brain matter he'd burned during the long six-hour flight from New York thinking, wondering, planning what he'd say to his mother after so long. And seeing Eve...well, those thoughts and feelings had to wait. But standing there now he found renewed energy, like the adrenaline rush a runner gets at the end of a long marathon.

Two people occupied the room. The woman in the bed attached to tubes and monitors and the gray-haired man who sat in a chair hunched over her, elbows resting on clean linen. Daniel couldn't understand the litany of words the man whispered but he didn't need to. His imagination took over.

Daniel's heart quickened, remembering the last time he'd seen his family. It had been at dinner a few hours before he'd climbed out his second-storied window and made his escape. It seemed impossible that so many years had passed, so much life led.

As he approached the bed, Charles must have sensed his presence because he turned slowly and stared up at him. Curiosity then recognition lit Charles's face. Frowning, he gave Daniel a long thoughtful look from head to toe. The tension in Daniel that had momentarily disappeared returned tenfold with Charles's intense scrutiny. Daniel sucked in a protective deep breath as he waited for the condemnation, rejection and anger to spew out of his stepfather's mouth. But instead the older man walked over to him. They stood face to face, giving Daniel a moment to assess his stepfather. Nearly seventy, Charles had aged well. Still tall and lean with a straight back, his gray hair the only visible sign of age. He gripped Daniel's shoulders tightly as though afraid his stepson would leave. "Thank you for coming, son." And he pulled Daniel into his arms.

Taken aback by Charles's response, Daniel was frozen in place. Apparently aware of his stepson's stiffness,

Charles dropped his arms and stepped back. The two men stared awkwardly at each other. Then Charles spoke in a husky voice. "Sorry." He gave Daniel a contrite smile. "The last few weeks have been very emotional."

Daniel cleared his throat. From somewhere in the pit of his clenched stomach he found some words. "No problem," he mumbled.

"You're looking well, son. The years have been good to you."

Needing to take the heat off of himself, Daniel said, "How's Mary?" He winced inwardly at the formal use of his mother's name. Damn, if he didn't feel like a scared kid on his first day at school.

Charles sighed. "I'm told that physically she's fine. It's her mental state that worries us. She doesn't seem to have the will to come out of it." He shook his head looking like a lost puppy.

"What can I do?"

"Just sit by her, talk to her. The doctors say she can probably hear you. I'll leave you alone." He patted Daniel's arm and walked out of the room.

With the closing of the door Daniel felt as though he was locked inside a heavy vault blocking out the rest of the world. He walked over to the bed and stared down at his mother. Though hard to reconcile his last sight of his mother with the woman who lay eyes closed, pale and hooked up to monitors, he saw that she was still a beautiful woman. He struggled to fight off the shameful memories of how he'd abandoned her so many years ago leaving her to fight off the brutality of his father, Andrew, alone. His weak legs nearly send him to the floor before he dropped down in Charles's recently vacated chair.

"Hi, Mom." He pushed husky words out. "You probably don't recognize my voice, but it's Daniel. Eve called and told me what happened. I don't fully understand all of it but I'll find out later. You...uh..." He stopped and cleared his throat. "I...uh...don't know what to say. I'm sorry seems so empty after all this time. When you wake up we can talk more. And you have to wake up, Mom. Charles needs you." A catch in his throat cut off his words for a moment. "I...I need you," he whispered.

After another long hesitation, he began to speak. Haltingly. Sharing an overview of the last twenty-five years. His education. His work. Julia. Mostly Julia. He was unaware when the sun dropped slowly into the horizon and the Hospital room darkened. As he droned on and on about this and that he felt the heavy burdens of the past slowly lift.

And wondered why it had taken him so long to come home.

CHAPTER NINE

With two glasses of iced tea in hand, Eve stepped out onto the small patio of Vin's house overlooking the Venice canal. What she wouldn't give for a shot of bourbon to calm her nerves. It had been wonderful as well as shattering to see Danny at the Hospital. Taller, more muscular, his thick dark hair showing a few strands of gray, he now exuded the strength and power of the wealthy businessman he'd become. Yet beneath it all she still saw the angry, sullen little boy who'd been her rock in those scary early years. Tears begged to spill out, but she held them at bay. God, she'd missed him.

Now as she approached the woman leaning over the wooden railing Eve found herself a little jealous of Julia Tyler's relationship with her brother. But when Julia turned and smiled at her, Eve felt her petty fears disappear. She handed Julia a glass of tea and stood beside her.

"This is such a beautiful, peaceful spot," Julia said. "Have you lived here long?"

"Actually, this is Vin's house. I'll move in once Mom is back on her feet." They both grinned at the clanging of pots emanating from the kitchen. "My place is too small for company and Vin's a better cook. Good 'ole Italian genes, you know."

Julia smiled "I was raised to run a business so I'm afraid cooking wasn't something that my father thought to teach me."

"A businesswoman, huh. Is that how you met my brother?"

"Yes, but we had a very rocky beginning."

"How so?"

"He tried to take over my company."

"Really. I'm surprised you survived. Even now Danny seems like the kind of man who doesn't take no for an answer."

Julia laughed. "That is so true. But I've managed to whittle him down to a more congenial level." She dropped her smile. "Actually, he's really a very loving, caring man."

Feeling the sense of loss of the relationship with that part of her brother Eve was overwhelmed with sadness. Maybe now...

She was about to speak when Vin, red and white striped apron hugging his tall body, came to the patio door. "Since Danny told us not to hold dinner for him," he bowed, "Cucina Ramone is open for dinner, my ladies. Tonight I recommend the veal parmigiana with angel hair pasta."

Eve's sadness disappeared the moment she saw him. Instead she grinned. "Sounds wonderful." She turned to Julia. "Shall we?"

*   *   *

It was late morning the following day when Gabe stared at the home of his youth. He'd decided to come here first before his meeting with his family. Now a blackened skeleton of the once-proud mini-manse, the structure stood like a stark reminder of what he'd tossed so carelessly aside fifteen years ago. Home and family. His thoughts shifted easily to Belle and Sophie and a smile warmed him. They were his ticket to ride into the future but first he must confront the past. With a deep sigh, he got back into his truck and headed for Santa Monica Hospital, anxiety rising with each mile.

*   *   *

The following morning after a quick visit with her mother Eve approached the hospital waiting room and stopped short at the doorway. The room was empty except for a man who leaned against the wall, arms crossed. Instinctively recognizing her younger brother, her eyes latched onto Gabe's. She'd lost all hope of finding him as she'd had no phone number, email or snail mail addresses. Yet there he was, watching her, apprehension steaming off him, as though waiting for the recriminations to start. Seeing him now, a grown man, tall and strong, her heart was so full she was sure it would explode.

"I tried to find you...how did you know?" Her voice was low.

Gabe pulled away from the wall. "Newspaper." He paused. "You look good, sis."

Eve shook her head. "I can't believe you're here. All grown up." She took a few steps closer. "Where are you living?"

"Northern California. A small town called Harmonee. With my daughter and her mother."

Eve smiled. "A daughter. Wow. Mom will be so happy to hear she's a grandmother." She sobered. "Have you seen Mom yet?"

"No."

"Why don't you go now? I'll wait here for the others."

"The others?"

"Your father is here, of course, as is Danny and his fiance', Julia. And my boyfriend, Vin." She took a deep breath. "When you see Mom, talk to her. Tell her all the good things that have happened in your life. Especially about your daughter. What's her name?"

"Sophie. Her mother's name is Belle. Isabelle. We've known each other for nearly ten years."

Eve smiled. "We all have a lot of catching up to do." Her eyes filled. "I'm so happy to see you. I've missed you so much, Gabe." Unable to stop, she stepped forward and put her arms around her brother. Slowly, his arms surrounded her in a light hug. When the awkwardness disappeared their arms tighten. After a long moment, she pulled away, a small teary smile on her face. "Go see Mom." She kissed him on the cheek. "We'll talk later."

Gabe nodded and was about to turn and leave when he was startled by several people entering the room. He stopped and scanned their faces, his eyes initially landing on a woman and a man he didn't recognize, then slid off them to rest on his father. At first Gabe thought he saw anger flash across Charles's face, but it passed so quickly he doubted himself. For what hit him square in the gut was the love that filled his father's eyes.

Charles approached and held out his arms. All the strength Gabe had called upon after reading the article in the newspaper, during the long drive south to L.A. and his meeting with Eve vanished. As Charles's arms surrounded him, Gabe's knees buckled. His breath released a cleansing sob. He grasped his father for support.

"Dad...Dad...I'm so sorry. So sorry. I..."

"It's okay, son. It's okay. I'm just so grateful you're here."

"But Mom..."

"Don't worry about your mother. Now that all her children are here, I know she'll want to come back to us. She's never given up on any of you. All she'll want to do is hold you, embarrass you with a million kisses and tell you how much she loves you." Charles pulled back and looked into his son's teary eyes. "There are no saints here in this room. We all have regrets. But in families, there is always a place for forgiveness."

*   *   *

Julia Tyler blinked tears from her eyes. She clutched Daniel's hand harder and looked at the others. Eve was slouched within the protective arms of Vin Ramone, tears streaming down her cheeks. A knowing smile lighted Vin's face. Julia looked up at Daniel who stared at his stepfather and halfbrother and saw a crack in his usual austere expression. She smiled to herself and rested her head on his chest. A deep warmth settled in her. So many years. So much pain. But she could see the healing beginning. For all of them. Guess the heartthrobs had it right. It was never too late.

*   *   *

An emotional basketcase, Gabe stood over his mother lying peacefully in her hospital bed. He couldn't help but wonder how much peace her life had brought her, what with a rotten first husband and then he and Daniel abandoning her. Gabe was so choked up he could barely breathe never mind talk. His chest hurt as he sucked in extra oxygen. He felt like the rebellious teen he'd been last time he'd seen his parents in the courtroom. So much anger. Unwilling to talk to them about what was bothering him. Now that he had a child of his own he put himself in the role of his own parents and imagined what his rejection must have felt to them. What it would've felt like if Sophie had rejected him when they'd first met. He had so much to atone for.

Eventually he managed to string a few thoughts and feelings together and choked out what was in his heart. "Hey, Mom. It's me. Gabriel. I came as fast as I could. I've wanted to call you for so long, but I...I was ashamed. I'm only sorry you had to get hurt for me to get past my shit and come back." Damn. He sounded like an idiot. Still the bratty spoiled kid he'd been. Suddenly sick of his own cowardness, he dove down into his heart like a deepwater drill and suddenly felt an explosion rip him apart. He blinked to protect his eyes from the imaginary flash of light that seemed to erupt from his gut to his chest. His lungs seized. Heart pounded. Next came an unfamiliar lightness of body and spirit, one of those ah-ha moments when the cloud lifts and sunlight beams. Gabe realized that before he could accept his mother's forgiveness he had to forgive himself.

Tears wet his face as he lowered his head, rested it against his mother's arm and released deep grunting sobs. So immersed was he in his swirling emotions that he barely felt the hand that gently, hesitantly stroked his head. When he finally realized what was happening, he looked up at his mother, who now stared at him through tearful loving eyes.

For a long moment, Gabe doubted what he saw. But when he felt her hand gently touch his cheek he knew. "Mom. You're awake. Thank you. Thank you for coming back to us. We're all here. Even Daniel."

The tube in Mary's mouth blocked her voice but all those tears running down her cheeks were silent words that told the story. "Let me get the doctor. Maybe he can take that tube out." Gabe squeezed her hand. "I'll be right back." He bent and kissed her cheek.

He rushed to the door, opened it and called out "Nurse. Get the doctor. My mother's awake." The hospital staff hurried in. While they worked on Mary, Gabe trotted down the hall to the waiting room.

"She's awake. Mom's awake."

The quiet conversation halted. Charles turned to Gabe, a look of complete joy on his face. "Is the doctor with her?"

"Yeah."

Charles gave Gabe's arm a light squeeze and they hurried toward Mary's room.

*   *   *

They stood in the doorway watching several nurses and a doctor hovering over Mary. "What's happening?" Charles called out.

The doctor turned, then joined them in the hallway. "Your wife's vitals are good. Her minor physical injuries have healed nicely. I've removed the breathing tube. A basic neurological exam shows no deficiency in cognitive functioning, but I've scheduled an MRI to make sure. Unless the test shows otherwise, I believe she's on her way to a complete recovery."

Charles's body sagged briefly but then straighten. "Thank you doctor. When can I see her?"

The doctor smiled. "I'd prefer to wait for visitors until after the MRI, but your wife's insisting she wants to see you and her boys, she calls them." They stepped aside for the rest of the staff to leave the room. "Just the three of you for now. Then we'll take her upstairs."

Charles shook his hand. "Thank you so much."

The doctor nodded and left them standing in the hall. They were silent for a moment. Then Charles said, "Give me a few minutes alone with your mother then go get your brother."

Gabe nodded and returned to the waiting room with the news.

Charles slowly approached the bed and took Mary's hand. Her eyes sought his immediately, a desperate question seemed to liken her stare to a drowning victim seeking air.

"Charles," she whispered, her throat probably hoarse from the breathing tube. He bent down to hear her. "Is it true? Are my boys really here? Did I hear them or was that just a dream?" More tears.

Charles smiled. "Yes, Mary my love. Daniel and Gabriel are here. They came as soon as they heard about your troubles. How are you feeling?"

She gave him a weak smile. "I couldn't be better."

"We're all so glad you're back. I don't know what I would've done if you left me for good."

She squeezed his hand. "It's all such a haze. I guess it will get clearer with time."

"I'm so sorry I wasn't there for you. I'll never forgive myself for leaving you at the mercy of that monster."

Mary slowly moved her head from side to side. "Nonsense. You didn't know Eve was in trouble. If anyone is to blame it's me. But no more guilt for either of us. That's all in the past. It's the future I want to embrace." She took a deep breath. "I want to see my sons."

*   *   *

After Gabe gave his family the news about Mary, he stepped aside and watched the joy on their faces, heard the relief in their voices. He stiffened when Daniel walked toward him. Gabe had been three-years-old when his brother had run away, yet it seemed to Gabe that Daniel had never left. His parents had constantly reminded him of their failure with Daniel and put so much pressure on Gabe that he had no alternative but to strike out and assume his own persona, albeit a negative one. So he'd blamed his parents. But now as his brother approached, he realized everyone had done the best they could to survive.

"You look a lot like your father," Daniel said, reaching out his hand.

After a short time, Gabe took it. "You're not as big as I remember."

Daniel laughed. "That's because you were just a runt when I left." He sobered. "Sorry I wasn't there for you. I...ah...let you all down. Have a lot to make up for. Hope you'll give me a chance."

Gabe shook his head. "I don't blame anyone anymore. We all did the best we could at the time. I'm just grateful we get a chance to get to know each other again."

Daniel seemed to be holding back a lot of emotion, but then he grasped his brother in a strong hug for a long time. As he put his arms around Daniel, Gabe's gaze fell upon Eve who watched her brothers with a smile on her lips and tears in her eyes.

In a moment, Charles came into the waiting room. "Mary is awake and seems her old self." He glanced at his sons, who now stood apart. "But before they do another MRI, she wants to see you boys. You'll only have a few minutes. She's tiring easily."

Gabe and Daniel nodded to their father and left the room side-by-side. Gabe wondered if his brother felt as nervous as he.

EPILOGUE

I've been home for a week now, the most glorious week of my life. Charles has rented a house while a new home is being built on the skeletal remains of our old one. Rather fitting, I think, since a new home represents the next chapter in the book of my life. Although my body tires easily, my spirit is buoyed with the presence of my family. They're all here now with the arrival last night of Gabriel's family Isabelle and Sophie. A granddaughter. I'm still reeling from the fact that I have a granddaughter, a beautiful child of four who looks so much like Gabriel did as a child. My heart swells when I think about it.

I glance around the dining room table, needing no words to express how I feel. I'm sure my joy shines in my face like a child who awakes early Christmas morning to the brilliant sparkling lights of the holiday tree.

I glance at Daniel, my firstborn. He is quiet, subdued and seems to be struggling with letting go of the past. But when he looks at Julia I can tell how much he loves her. I know I can count on her to help him piece together the parts of himself that had been lost. It may take a while but I know he'll come to forgive himself eventually. He's lucky to have found such a wonderful, supportive woman in Julia.

And Eve. Who never physically left me, but stayed out on the perimeter of my life for so many years, has now blossomed. While she's never explained what her life was like during the past twenty years, perhaps someday she'll feel comfortable enough to unburden herself, but I don't have to know. I'm only glad she seems more content. I give thanks to her man Vincent for helping her through whatever transition she had to experience to get where she is today. I smile to myself every time she calls me 'Mom' instead of Mary.

And my baby...Gabriel. No longer the rebel but a steady family man who's some kind of computer genius they tell me, the meaning of which is so far beyond my ability to comprehend I don't even try to figure out what the others are saying. His Isabelle, so bright, so grounded. A perfect ying to his yang. I simply cling to the knowledge that he's turned his life around and appears to be very relaxed and happy.

And Charles. My rock. The glue that has held me together all these years. I glance at him and smile. He returns an understanding smile and takes my hand in his under the table. Large. Warm. Strong. Tears fill my eyes as I stare into the future which includes him and my family who sit around the table talking as though the past twenty-five years have never happened and tonight is just the continuation of our unbroken family ties.

My mind shifts to the last time I sat in the pew of St. Monica's church giving the care of my children up to God for his safekeeping. Looking around the table once again I thank Him for answering my prayers.

THE END

Dear Readers:

For those of you who've read any of my previous books, you'll notice a change in the style and formatting of THE JOURNEY HOME. I hope you find this book a worthy read.

I would be most appreciative if after reading you put a review on Amazon.

Thank you for your continued support of my work.

Eileen

APR – 2 2023

Made in the USA
Lexington, KY
08 November 2019